Other books by Tess Marset

With My Little Eye
(Book One of The Mia Series)

On Frogs and Princes

The X-Mas Tree

Like Us, The Polar Bears

What readers are saying about

With My Little Eye: Book One of the Mia Series

"Haunting and creepy in all the right ways! Tess Marset is a master of paranormal suspense. Book 2 was so good I don't want to have to wait for the next installment."
~ SHELLY SHARP MACER (*BookSharp Book Reviews*)

"*With My Little Eye* was an engrossing story. I couldn't put it down. I read it within 24 hours. The characters, the setting, the pace was terrific."
~ AURA M.B. (Hempstead, N.Y.)

"I thought I would wear out the page turner on my Kindle; also had a hard time putting my device down. I would highly recommend this; it was unusual for a psychological thriller and it is a gripping story from start to finish. The storyline made me think about sanity versus insanity. I really appreciated a minimum of characters so you weren't always trying to keep track of who's who. Very well written; the entire book is suspenseful and keeps you guessing until the end."
~ CLAUDE MORGAN (Chicago, IL)

"The characters in *With My Little Eye* were very believable and were like people you might know, or meet on the street. This gave more of a realistic sense to the story, which in turn made it more frightening."
~ GEN HEYER (Wichita, KS)

"*With My Little Eye* kept me coming back for more and wondering about the storyline when I wasn't reading. It is a suspenseful and engaging novel that will draw you back in. I can't wait for the sequel to be released so I can continue on the journey with Mia and Dan!"
~ AUBREY V.P. (Phoenix, AZ)

"I couldn't put *With My Little Eye* down. It was so exciting, and intriguing and scary all at the same time. I truly enjoyed it. I am so looking forward to the sequel."
~ SELMA RIVERA (Orlando, FL)

"*With My Little Eye* is an intriguing book that will keep you thinking long after you close the cover."
~ VICTORIA HAZELL (Hutchinson, KS)

LEST WE FALL

BOOK TWO of the MIA SERIES

by

TESS MARSET

1 Lone Crow Media

Cover photography: © 2014, 2019 Zachary Martzke

Book & Cover Design: Vladimir Verano, Vertvolta Design

PUBLISHED BY

1 Lone Crow Media

www.1LoneCrowMedia.com

ISBN: 978-1-7333609-1-3

For my Readers

In memory of our Madrina, the real Aunt Lydia

PROLOGUE

Talbot looked around the room. Every last detail was in place—the dresser where she would put her clothes, a clean set of towels in the bathroom, fresh flowers on the coffee table, what they would eat for their first dinner together. The house was almost complete. He wanted to make sure she would be settled in comfortably before he had to take one last business trip before the year's end. He was relieved to have accepted a new position as a program coordinator at the for-profit medical institute he worked for that required no more travel, even if it meant a cut in income. Nonetheless, it was worth it to make her happy.

Although his home had every conceivable comfort, it echoed as empty as a tomb. Without companionship he knew it always would. Thus the thought of another relationship excited him, filling his days with possibilities of a new life with a new someone. He knew it was ridiculous how he felt—he was nearing forty-seven already. But the dinners, the romance, and the way that special female could make him feel had him acting as nervous as a schoolboy. At night, he found it hard to sleep from the anticipation.

In reflection, he realized his first relationship with Chloe was an utter and complete mess. After all, she did not have to get upset with him. Next there were the tears and wanting to go home to her family after all he had done in trying to make her happy. It didn't have to end the way that it did. To say the very least, it was a clean break. She hadn't given him much of a fight. He resolved that this time though, he would try even harder. It wouldn't end.

Scanning through his well-stocked pantry and cupboards one last time, Talbot finalized his shopping list. Candles might be a nice touch. *And maybe a stuffed bear—girls usually went nuts over that stuff,* he thought as he noted the items on the list after the steaks and wine. The wine was for him. He wasn't sure if Leanne would even touch the stuff but if she did, he made up his mind that he would be all right with that.

This last item worried him. *What if she didn't like the food?* It didn't seem like what he had was adequate enough, although he had pored over his staples and stores. *Everything was there. Except...* Surveying his stocks once more, he decided that maybe he should get some gummi bears. She seemed to really enjoy them. It was adorable to watch how she chose the red ones first, next the orange, then the white, saving the green ones for last.

Concentrating on finishing his tasks at hand, he sent off a quick email to Mike Rhines in financial aid with the number of enrollees for the upcoming summer quarter. He fired off another email to the dean of the institute regarding his new position, paid up the taxes for the year on his out-of-state childhood home his parents had left him, and checked his schedule on his smartphone. There was so much to catch up on after these cursed business trips, even if they were only as far as the neighboring state.

Savoring the best for last as a treat for getting his dull tasks out of the way, he checked his message board just in case she had posted something this morning. That usually made his day. He was still getting used to the idea of forging a relationship entirely through social media. Of course he had fibbed a little. He had even submitted a photograph of a good-looking young 'dude' in his profile instead of his own image. How else was he going to get someone like Leanne to ever notice him? Now that they had met online, been emailing and texting, and got along fabulously, he knew she would overlook this minor indiscretion. After all, everybody did it. And in all fairness, she had fibbed a bit too about her age. So they were even. Scanning the message board for today, all that was posted was a ☺. It was enough to make him feel a little heady in anticipation.

The phone rang. 'Cheryl Becker,' the caller ID read. *I wonder what she wants?* With a degree of annoyance, he sighed and waited for the answering machine to pick up, unwilling to answer it.

"Tal? This is Cheryl. I was able to get two tickets to the theater next Saturday. I was wondering if you'd care to join me? We could grab a bite to eat after the show. I know what you're thinking, but it's all perfectly innocent. What I mean is we can just go out as friends, okay? Give me a call and let me know. And don't stand me up this time."

He shook his head and wondered when was she ever going to get it that he just wasn't into her? She never had the ability to make him feel the way he was feeling right now.

After one last check to make sure that everything was set, he scooped up his keys, stepped outside, closed the lock and deadbolt, and made his way to his garage. Inside he slipped in behind the wheel of a brand new performance sedan. It was nothing like the old green ragtop clunker he used to drive. This one smacked of dominance. Talbot thought it peculiar how power disguised itself in so many different ways. Some seemingly benign people could wield such great power and not even be aware of it, yet some objects, such as this impressive machine, implied power just by its form and size. He savored the smell of the leather seats and the feel of the hand-stitched padded steering wheel. Leanne was going to love it.

Anticipating the low purr of a finely tuned engine, he turned the key. To his chagrin, the car wouldn't start. He retried the ignition. The engine turned a few times, and finally caught, only to idle roughly. This vexed him greatly. Apparently those idiots at the service department still did not get it right. The recall was ludicrous. The car was no more than two months old and was already facing issues with its fuel injectors. *Seems as if everything was junk these days. Planned obsolescence was more like it.* He knew he should bring the car in but that would cut sharply into his plans. *No, it would just have to wait until next week.* He had so much on his plate already with preparing for Leanne to move in. He wasn't going to waste precious time sitting in some service garage for hours, waiting for some incompetent grease monkey in coveralls to tell him that they had fixed the problem again when he knew darn right well they hadn't.

The garage door lifted and the sedan rolled out. He turned out of his driveway and headed toward the long road lined with winter naked trees sprouting buds in the early spring air. Talbot's mind couldn't help but wander back to that other huge mistake last month. He was surprised that he still felt put out by it, especially since it was so short in duration. But what did he expect? She was too young for him. *Way too young.* He knew that's where he went wrong. They just weren't compatible. *Nothing in common at all.* Talbot knew he had rushed the relationship. *Probably a rebound thing from the first go-around with Chloe.* He had acted too hastily. More tears. More angry words.

Just what exactly is it that they want? he wondered with renewed frustration. It seemed that no matter how hard he tried, he couldn't please them. He kept making mistakes—stupid mistakes. When was he going to learn that they always had all the options, held all the cards?

He reminded himself to calm down. *Now there was going to be a new person in my life and she was moving in to stay.* Careful contemplation revealed where he had gone wrong with the last encounter as he continued to sort and turn events over in his head. For one thing, starting something with someone while on the road was a very bad idea. He knew that was the first part of the mistake. So this time he decided to search for someone in his own neck of the woods and it worked. Next, he made sure that Leanne was more mature. He also checked that they were more compatible—they both loved action CG films, pizza, and shopping malls. If he tried really hard to make this relationship work and she was happy, there should be absolutely no reason for it to end. No reason at all.

It was raining and the rear tires breaking loose at the change of the traffic light signaled that he should be on the lookout for standing water on the roadways. The grey day made it feel cold. Spring was three weeks under way yet it was crazy how the chilly weather continued to persist.

A few miles later, a small red import that had been lowered pulled up alongside of him in the left lane at the stoplight. It was one of those… *what did the kids call them?* He suddenly recalled, *Oh yes—rice burners* with the fat tailpipes spewing noise and the pulsing loud stereos vibrating everything within the car's proximity. Talbot tried not to look but impulse took over him as he stole a glance at the driver beside him.

Oh. One of those nimrods who think they own the world, he mused as he permitted himself a longer look at this young competitor. He studied the designer sunglasses, the gold chains thick around the rear view mirror, the baseball cap slanted sideways on the cocky head. Talbot hated these pompous self-centered punks. He wished there were laws that kept them off the streets. Or better yet, he wished he could introduce them to his revolver to make sure they'd stay off the streets for good.

Sensing his glare, the driver in the import turned his head and returned the scrutiny. Talbot's eyes immediately snapped forward and he stared straight ahead. He hated dealing with these sorts. There was no telling what they were capable of doing or worse yet, what personal connections they had with criminal element.

The light dropped to green. The red import easily pulled out and then sliced in front of him in a sudden deft move. Talbot hit his brakes, his blood pressure rising. *Figures—so typical.* He downshifted, getting ready to show off a few moves of his own. When he gave it the gas, his big and bold performance sedan shuddered and stalled. The import driver gunned it and tore off. A loud horn blast from the car behind confirmed that he was officially now a roadblock. The insistent sound shook Talbot as he tried his car again. A smell of raw gas indicated that the engine was flooded from the faulty injectors. Another long and steady blast from the horn behind rattled him. As his armpits oozed nervous perspiration, Talbot half waved an apology and then tried the ignition again. It caught. Revving the engine, he put the car in gear and slowly eased it back up to speed, hazard lights still blinking.

Underway once more, he checked the next lane where two teens stared back, laughing to each other as they passed, he surmised most likely over his car's antics. A simmer of resentment ignited in Talbot. He pulled up alongside of the insolent teens. Carefully, without making any eye contact and his foot mashing down on the accelerator, he overtook them. Looking at them growing small in his rear view mirror he laughed out loud. *Now who were the fools?*

Still riding out his anger, Talbot laced into the car, wanting to punish it for its bad behavior and his subsequent humiliation. He maneuvered from lane to lane, swerving haphazardly around other cars. Feeling the rush of righteous revenge he continued inching up in speed. He was forced to a stop by a changing yellow light to solid red. He set the gear in neutral and kept his foot on the gas pedal not wanting to take a chance for the engine to stall again while readying himself for another go when the light turned green. Just then, he spied the red import that had cut him off earlier exiting from a convenience store parking lot just ahead of the intersection. This would be his chance to show the punk ass with the sideways hat a thing or two.

Without waiting for the light to change, Talbot shifted the car into first, checked to see if there was any oncoming traffic, and floored it across the intersection. He easily blew past the import and raced up the hill ahead of it. The road serpentined and a sign warned of more turns ahead. The small low import held the road nimbly as it started to gain on the big sedan. Talbot took this as a challenge as his anger rekindled. He stomped down on the accelerator. Trees lining the road whipped by in an endless frenzy. The two cars crested the top of the hill and started down the other side.

In a large shady spot, the road curved sharply to the left. The sedan moved into the turn but suddenly seemed to take on a mind of its own. Talbot pulled hard on the steering wheel to make it respond but the car continued its forward motion. It was then he realized he was hydroplaning. He immediately hit the brakes only to find that they had faded while the car fishtailed fiercely in its determined path. The red import zoomed by, its traction control holding the squat car to the drier side of the road, the loud drone from its tailpipe growing faint as it put distance between them.

Talbot wrestled the wheel hard one way and then the other trying to make his car obey, but it wouldn't respond to brake or wheel. As the road veered left, Talbot and the sedan went straight. He could see the guardrail approaching rapidly. He had only a split second to raise his arms to shield his face.

The heavy car smashed through the guardrail, deploying its airbags. The panel covering the airbag compartment jettisoned off with a mini-explosion from the propellants and became a projectile that slammed Talbot square on the forehead and into unconsciousness. He was unaware of his car plunging nose first through the air toward a thick stand of evergreen trees. He did not see his car spear itself into a net of tangled branches a hundred yards down from where it had smashed through the guardrail. He could not perceive that his car dangled precariously, thirty feet off the ground, caught in the boughs of the treetops on the steep hillside choked with heavy undergrowth that obscured visibility from below.

He remained unconscious and unseen and unnoticed.

Chapter 1

"I'm Mia. And who are you? It's okay. Please don't be frightened," she said to the image of the child appearing in her living room mirror as her own heart pounded in fear.

It was happening again.

It was mid-afternoon and she had just sat down on the sofa with a basket of clean laundry to fold. The baby was finally down for a nap and her husband Dan tinkered in the garage. Dan's parents were at the RV show downtown, so she still had a few hours to catch up on her neglected chores. The sun streamed through the window and except for the sounds of kids playing outside on the block, all was serene.

Until now.

She thought it was over, all behind her. It had been a little over a year already. Seth's appearance was supposed to have been an isolated event, an anomaly. For whatever reason, their fates had crossed and she had helped him on his way. However, with this unexpected visitor in the mirror staring back at her, it now looked like The Occurrence wasn't a chance encounter after all. Mia's short reprieve wasn't meant to be. The young child with frightened eyes confirmed that these appearances from wayward visitors from the Afterlife were going to continue.

She was caught unprepared for this unusual encounter that was reminiscent of that much darker time. Life was normal again. Her battered marriage was recovering. She had a family to take care of. Fear and dread clutched their icy claws around her heart as she thought, *Must I go through this again?*

The phantom's shift from one foot to the other made Mia refocus. The little girl's chin quivered as she struggled to put on a brave face. Her long blonde hair was a bit disheveled and her clothing was dirty. Aside from that, she looked no more mussed up than if she had been playing in her own backyard. Mia estimated her age to be around eight years old. Summoning her own courage and inhaling a deep breath of resolve, she decided to go forward. At the very least, she could find out what it was the child wanted.

From an initial once over, she looked thin but healthy, intact and vibrant, definitely a far cry from how the tortured teen had appeared not so long ago. The girl's physical condition made Mia wonder immediately how she came to be in this horrific predicament. It frightened her to guess what fate befell the child that had brought an end to her young life.

"Why are you visiting me?" she asked. "It's okay. You can tell me."

The specter offered only a twitch of a shrug to her small shoulders.

Hoping to disarm her and put her at ease while trying to quell her own anxiety, Mia tried, "Why, those are pretty rain boots. I bet you like them a lot."

The girl looked down at her brightly colored boots splashed with large yellow sunflowers and then back at Mia, her light blue eyes fixed steadily upon her. She nodded.

Mia knew she had made contact. Deciding to try a method she had used countless times to communicate with Seth, she opened a drawer in a side table and withdrew a notebook and pen. For a moment, she held her breath. How often had she repeated these exact motions before? And what did it lead to last time? More importantly—what would it lead to this time? A part of her told her to put down the notebook immediately, ignore the mirror and the implications it held, and get on with her folding and her life. However, another part of her stubbornly resisted as her heart reached out to this lost child and her family who must be stricken with grief.

Resolutely, she flipped through the written pages filled with that spidery scrawl from the previous encounter, opened up to a clean page, and folded back the notebook. She then held it and the pen up to the mirror.

"I have a notebook and pen here. Now, judging by the size of you, I'm guessing that you have absolutely no problem in printing your letters, am I correct?"

The girl nodded once more.

"And I am going to guess that you probably received a very good grade in penmanship right? Maybe a 'Good Job' or even 'Excellent'?"

The slightest tug at the corner of the child's mouth hinted at a smile.

"So, how about we try something here? I knew a boy once, he was older than you, and he used to visit me through the mirror just like you are now. The way we used to talk to each other was that I would place this pen and notebook down. Like right about here." She pointed to the sofa table that stood next to the mirror. "And then whenever he wanted to tell me something, he would write it down and hold the notebook up to the mirror so I could read his message, like this. Does this sound like something you'd like to try?"

The girl nodded again, her somber face slowly brightening with expectation.

"Okay, what would you like to tell me?"

Her shoulder twitched again.

"How about we start with your name. Can tell me what it is, please?"

The child reached for the notebook and pen and then carefully wrote out each letter. She held the notebook up to the glass.

ahtnamaS

As before, Mia stared at the backward letters, her mind so familiar with the reverse perspective that she immediately translated it.

"Samantha? Is that your name?"

With a nod, she indicated yes.

"What a pretty name! And I guessed right. Your letters are *very* good."

For the first time, the child smiled. A missing front tooth revealed a charming gap.

Mia couldn't help but smile back. The little girl was darling.

"And how old are you, Samantha?"

7 1/2

"Seven and a half! My goodness, you look more like eight!"

Samantha's face bloomed with pride and she stood a little straighter, lifting her chin.

"Are you willing to tell me some more, Samantha?"

Like what?

"Well, like your last name. And where do you live?"

Her open expression clouded into a determined scowl. With a shake of her head, she put down the notebook and crossed her arms in front of her.

"Oh, I'm sorry. Is there a reason why you don't want to share?"

She picked up the notebook once again and jotted down:

Mommy will get verry mad. Strangr dangr.

Mia pondered the child's predicament. "That's okay. Your mommy is absolutely right. And you are doing the right thing. But do you think it'll be all right to tell me where you are now?"

Shrug.

"Do you live there?"

The bright blue eyes opened wide. Samantha shook her head with a definitive NO. Then as if she couldn't contain herself, she wrote:

I am in a dark place. I can't get out. I am all alon. I miss Mommy and Daddy and Buddy. I want to go home.

Mia's skin crawled. *Not again. Oh please not again.* Where could she be? She thought of Seth's desperate plight trapped in the hellacious mine pit. Had this little girl suffered a similar fate? Her chest tightened and she swallowed hard to fight back feelings of alarm and pity. She needed to keep her wits about her.

"Samantha, I want you to think carefully. How did you get there?"

The child hung her head. Her mouth turned down at the corners.

Can I go home now?

A cry erupted from the nursery down the hall. Nathan had woken from his nap. Mia paused for a moment, listening to see if Dan would hear their infant son from the garage. She was reluctant to interrupt this session she was having with Samantha. It was so tenuous—there was no telling whether the child would disappear if she left the room, and if she would choose to return or not. From her experience with Seth, Mia knew she had no control of these visitors' comings and goings. She wasn't even sure if Samantha could follow her about in reflective surfaces like Seth used to when she had to move about the house

"Listen sweetie, I may have to go to the other room for a moment to get my son. He's getting up from a nap."

Pleeze cuold you help me find Mommy and Daddy?

Nathan's cry grew fiercer. An ear toward the direction of the garage told Mia that Dan was working with his power sander on a hobbyhorse he was determined to make for Nathan and couldn't hear anything. It appeared that she would have to retrieve their son.

"I want to talk more with you and I am going to help you. But you are going to have to stay right there for just a minute while I go get my son. He's only a baby and he's crying right now. Okay?"

Samantha looked doubtful.

"Can you do this for me, Samantha? Please stay right there? I'll be right back…" Mia held out her hand, motioning her to remain while she rose to her feet. When she reached the hallway, she could hear Nathan bellowing now. With one last look at the child in the mirror, she said, "Stay there."

Just as she turned down the hall, she could hear a young voice answer. "Okay."

Mia froze in her tracks, stunned by what she had just heard. Was she imagining it? Despite the baby's wail, she bolted back to the living room. Looking at the mirror, Samantha was gone.

‡ ‡ ‡

"Probably I would say the most interesting thing we saw in Nebraska was an old house that was genuinely haunted," Sherry Labont said as she doled out a portion of salad and then passed the bowl. The conversation at the dinner table had been centered on their most recent road trip in their motor home. "If you ask me, I'm thoroughly convinced it was."

Unintentionally, Dan's head snapped up in attention and he looked directly at his mother, the serving spoon for the scalloped potatoes still clutched mid-air in his hand. His mother was a calm, practical woman, not known for possessing a wild imagination, let alone a belief in the supernatural.

Sherry smiled and scrunched her nose affectionately at her son's surprised expression. "Why, what's the matter, Danny—don't tell me you believe in that stuff?"

"I didn't think *you* did," he managed.

"Oh not really. It's just kind of fun to wonder what if."

"What if what?"

"Ghosts and spirits and all of that existed. Don't you think so, Mia?"

Mia paused and then nodded, "Sure, Mom." She directed her gaze down, concentrated on cutting her ham slice, and hoped the conversation would move onto another topic.

She and Dan had decided never to discuss the Occurrence with the senior Labonts. They knew all too well how realistically grounded Dan's parents were and how they would have a hard time conceiving the incredible circumstances that took place in those long, arduous months. Dan, having had his own sense of reality tested after Seth appeared, found it difficult to believe it had happened himself.

"They sure liked to play it up," Dick Labont joined in. Until this point he had been busy delighting in how his infant grandson seated beside him handled a spoon. The generations appeared to share a mutual fascination with each other. "The owners made sure the place was complete with old furniture, creaking boards, and lots of mirrors so you think you catch something moving in the shadows or out of the corner of your eye only to find out that it was just you or someone else in the tour group. As usual, it wasn't a state of the art, well-lit modern home. It was clear it was all a gimmick."

"But Dad, I thought the point was that nobody would live in a house or even consider buying it if it were haunted," Jenna observed. "Of course it hardly ever is up-to-date and modern. Besides it wouldn't be as 'spooky' anyway if it was just your normal average home."

"And when did you get so smart, missy? Must be because you're going to college." Dick beamed at his youngest child. "But I was reading something the other day on the Internet that talked about how they can tweak different frequencies to create all sorts of weird phenomena. Isn't that right, Dan?"

"You got on the Internet? *That* in itself is truly a weird phenomenon," his son answered, sharing a laugh with Jenna.

"Har har. Very funny. Your old man is known to get on the Internet nowadays. Even your mother will look up a recipe or two every now and then."

"Whoa, Mom! Way to go!" Jenna teased.

Sherry shrugged, "What? Your mother is hip."

This sparked another round of snickering from the siblings.

Dick continued, "But seriously Dan, since this is right up your alley, have you heard anything about using frequencies in that capacity?"

"Well, from what I understand although certain frequencies may be too low or high for our ears to hear, they can affect lots of things—from rattling shelves and objects, to creating a feeling of unease, to even making people sick.

"There was one case I read in which employees constantly felt ill at the business where they worked. When the building was thoroughly inspected, it turned out a piece of metal in an air conditioning unit was vibrating at a frequency that no one could hear yet it had an actual physical affect on the workers there. Some felt tired; others had headaches. A few were even dizzy and nauseous.

"So yeah, I can see where frequencies could potentially be used to create haunting effects. All they would need are large speakers hidden in various spots and an amplifier to drive them. No one would be the wiser."

"Oh my goodness. How fascinating. But then again, it kind of takes the fun out of the house being haunted and all, doesn't it?" Sherry said.

"Yeah, right. All the fun…" Dan replied and looked at Mia.

Although she raised an eyebrow at him in agreement, she seemed unusually quiet. If he wasn't mistaken, she looked sad. He attributed it to exhaustion knowing that she had been putting in long days keeping up with Nathan and her job. The Labonts being in town on a stop from their RV travels about the country and Jenna in from college resulted in a weeklong visit from the family. While they were not a problem and he and Mia enjoyed their company, Dan knew there was a certain amount of effort that was exerted whenever they stayed over. Perhaps Mia wasn't quite ready for it, despite her insistence that it was fine. Nathan's birth surely changed their routine but not as much as the Occurrence had.

Things had just been getting back to normal.

‡　‡　‡

"So how's your mother these days, Mia? If I recall correctly, the last time I saw her was when she was visiting you and I believe she was preparing to go to the Holy Land. I always thought that was so adventurous! I can't get Dick to travel outside of the Lower Forty-Eight, let alone to another continent," Sherry said with a sigh as she accepted another soapy pan from Mia to rinse while they washed the dinner dishes. The sleeves on her cardigan were pushed all the way up to her elbows.

"Mom made it to the Holy Land and spent three months there. She returned home for about a month, but now she's off again, this time to Herzegovina."

"My word! What is she doing there?"

"She's on a pilgrimage to Medjugorje because of the reported miracle appearances by the Virgin Mary. She's been wanting to go for the last thirty years since the appearances began, so she made up her mind to finally go."

Mia stared ahead through the steamy window over the sink. She always felt uncomfortable talking to her in-laws about her mother's fervent devotion. As for herself, she had left behind her religious upbringing, much to her mother's disapproval. The senior Labonts were far from being atheists, but they weren't churchgoers either. When it came to religious matters, they were as middle of the road as it got, finding themselves in a church only for weddings, funerals, tours, or the gothic architecture that Dick liked to study.

"That sounds so interesting! I'm envious. Has she seen anything so far?" Sherry stopped to brush back a lock that had escaped from her neatly coiffed hair.

"Uh, no. Not that I know of. I'm not sure if it's necessarily a 'seeing' type of experience as much as just living the experience itself."

"Well, does she believe in all of that? You know, saints, miracles, visions…?"

Mia picked up another pot and started to scrub. "As a matter of fact, she does. She has for years."

"Oh, so you were raised like that. Then do you believe in what is going on over there with the appearances and everything too?" Sherry pressed.

Mia couldn't help but wonder why her mother-in-law was so particularly tenacious with this subject tonight. In the five years that she had known her, she had never seen her inquire so thoroughly before. Sherry Labont typically kept conversations light. Mia made a mental note to ask Dan later if he had any idea of what she was after.

Before she could answer, she caught a familiar glimpse of something reflected on the chrome side of the pot she was working on. She paused for a moment to study the surface. Her pulse quickened as it had once before when this had happened. All of a sudden, Samantha's face came into view. Mia smiled with relief. The little girl had returned.

Sherry caught her smile and said, "A–ha. So you *do* believe it."

"I believe the three children were definitely seeing *something* at the time, and it may very well have been the Virgin Mary. In fact, I saw a news report just last week that showed the children, as adults, still receiving messages and claiming that Mary appears to this day. That is why the pilgrimages to Medjugorje continue."

"Isn't that simply amazing?" Sherry asked. "With all the things going on in the world today—famine, war, disease—don't you ever question why this is happening? I know I do."

"My question is not necessarily whether or not these things happen—I think life is full of strange occurrences. What I want to know is why do they seem to happen only to certain people? Take miracles for example—why do they manifest for select individuals and not others? There are countless people out there praying for the sick or injured or for loved ones with incurable diseases, yet so very few miracles ever occur. Who are these people that experience them and why are they chosen?"

As Mia picked up the next pot, Samantha showed up on it as well. She looked about in all directions, apparently investigating this new mode of appearing in different locations.

"Why, that's a good question. I don't know… Maybe God has chosen some people to see things and others not to," Sherry responded thoughtfully. "Maybe some are more sensitive than others in these matters…In fact, there's something I'd like to share with you."

By the serious tone of her voice, Mia knew this was something of importance to Sherry. It was uncharacteristic for the usually cheery woman to be so somber. She stopped washing to give her undivided attention.

As if she were about to share something of great magnitude, Sherry leaned in closer and lowered her voice. "I would never tell Dick this, or even Dan for that matter—neither of them go for this kind of stuff, men are so pragmatic. And I think Jenna would only tease me. But just between us girls, I think I might be sensitive to, to… what is it that they call it again? The phrase is right at the tip of my tongue… Para…para…something or other. You know, when you can see or sense things out of the ordinary."

"Paranormal activity?"

"Yes! That's it. I think I may be sensitive to paranormal activity." Her secret was out. She settled back with a satisfied look on her face.

"You are? How so?"

"Like I said, I haven't mentioned this to Dick or anybody else. In fact you're the first person I am telling this to, but when we were in that haunted house in Nebraska and we were standing in the hallway upstairs, I felt someone touch my hair! And when I turned around, there was no one anywhere near. Dick was about five feet away looking at an old photograph hanging on the wall. And the others in the group had moved further down the hall. Right after that, I felt a cold draft on my face, like something had passed right in front of me. I've never experienced anything like that before. When I looked around, it didn't seem like anyone else in the group was experiencing it. I asked Dick if he felt anything and he said no.

"Dan's explanation of frequencies may explain some of the more obvious things like creaky boards or noises, but it doesn't explain the sensation of having someone touch my hair or feeling a cold draft come up out of nowhere. So yes. I believe that I am 'gifted' in that respect. What do they call it? A 'Sixth Sense' or something like that."

"Is that right?" Mia tried her best to summon enthusiasm as she handed the pot displaying Samantha's face to her.

Sherry dosed the pot under the running stream of water, rinsed it thoroughly and placed it in the dish rack to dry. Samantha by this time was making goofy expressions by sticking out her tongue and waggling it, as any active seven-year old would do to get attention, while giggling, "Nanny-nanny boo-boo!"

"It's such a relief to be able to share this with you. I hope you don't think I'm being silly," Sherry continued.

"No, Mom. I don't think you are," Mia reassured her. "If you believe you felt something, then you felt something. And who knows? Maybe you are one of those chosen individuals." She glanced at the pot in the drying rack. Samantha smiled and waved back.

"Yes, Mia. I believe I most certainly am," Sherry responded resolvedly with a sigh, as if the weight of such a gift was a considerable one to bear.

‡ ‡ ‡

After settling a sleeping Nathan in his crib, Mia wearily climbed into bed and snuggled under the puffy comforter. It felt good to finally get off her feet. The in-laws had retired to their motor home and Jenna was watching TV in their guest bedroom. The house was quiet. Even Samantha had taken off after the dishes were done and Mia did not see her for the rest of the evening. She figured the child had grown bored with the fact that she would not engage with her while her mother-in-law was present. She waited for Dan to finish his shower while she enjoyed the peace and quiet.

Upon his nightly ritual of checking the locks on the front and back doors, making sure the lights in the house were off, and taking one last peek at their son, Dan walked into the bedroom. Her eyes wandering over him, Mia felt a deep affection for her husband. He had endured so much already with all the past events, his stalwart belief in how the world was and should be, thoroughly shaken. Only lately was he able to relax as their marriage healed and strengthened once more. She almost hated the thought of opening up yet another chapter into this bizarre role they had both been unwillingly thrust into.

He approached her with a smile and a kiss. "Did you pay the mortgage, babe? It completely slipped my mind and I just remembered it today when I saw the date."

"Already taken care of. Oh and there's been a change in our medical deductible. But we can go over it when Mom and Dad leave."

"Sounds good to me," he said. Then he plopped down on the bed beside her and laid out flat on his back, stretching his toes and curving his arms up behind his head.

"Ahhh. I never thought I would ever make it to bed tonight. I'm beat. Don't get me wrong—I love having the folks over but it sure makes for some long days."

"Yeah, I guess it does. But they sure are having a blast with Nathan," Mia said as they both stared at the ceiling.

"They really are. The feeling is mutual. And did you see that little monkey? The way he was jabbering away and tossing his toys off his tray tonight? If he wasn't just turning six months old, I'd swear he was showing off." Dan tried his best to sound put out but Mia recognized the pride in his voice.

"I think he was, to tell you the truth. Your dad was getting the biggest kick out of it all. I know my dad would have loved that."

"Pop? Oh yeah? Why?" He turned to face her.

"He used to tell me all the time how I used to do the same exact thing at that age. Except instead of jabbering he said I would sing at the top of my lungs. It was probably more like screeching."

"How come I don't find that so hard to believe?" Dan teased as he tapped his wife on the tip of her nose and smiled. He turned wistful. "God, I miss Pop. I know he would have been crazy about our little guy."

A familiar twinge tugged at Mia. "Yes, he would have. They are a lot alike. I can already see some of his mannerisms. Something in his grin. And the way he is so happy all of the time."

Dan rolled onto his side to face her, propping his head up with his hand. "Can I ask you something, Murph?"

"Okay."

"This is going to sound kind of strange but have you ever, you know, seen your dad *after*? I mean in the way you used to see Seth. I can understand if you don't want to share that with me. But I couldn't help but wonder if you had. You two were so close and it's become obvious that you have that ability."

A heavy sigh escaped her.

"Hey, I'm sorry. I shouldn't have asked you that. I am a jerk. I thought it had gotten easier for you. You're looking down. I noticed it tonight at dinner."

"No. It's all right. It has gotten a little better for me. Something else was on my mind at dinner, that's all. And I know you cared for my dad as much as I did… So to answer your question, it's no. I haven't seen Dad. At first, when Seth used to appear to me, I thought it was unfair that I could communicate with a total stranger in that way but not with my own father. I miss talking with Dad so much! However, once I realized where Seth was and why he was held there, I knew then that if I wasn't able to see and talk with my dad, perhaps it was a *good* thing. He must be in a better place where he didn't need any help to find his way. Eventually, when my own time comes I feel I will see him again. For now, he continues to live on in our memories and in Nat-a-tat already."

Dan lightly stroked her cheek and then kissed her. "You're beautiful, you know that?" he said softy. "So what's on your mind, then? Everything okay?"

Mia knew the time had come. She regretted having to bring this up now but reasoned it would be better for him to find out sooner rather than later by surprise, especially while his family was visiting.

"Murph, there's something I have to show you. It can't wait any longer," she said.

"Huh? What is it?"

She sat up, plucked the notebook off of the nightstand and opened up to the page for him to see. "It seems there is someone else that I am going to have to help out next."

At first, he took the notebook from her with a puzzled look on his face. Then, after reading a few words, his eyes widened and his mouth opened. He bolted straight up and shook his head slowly.

"No… don't tell me. What the—? Aww. You can't mean that it's… oh no," he barely managed. He studied it again and then looked at her with alarm. "Is this Seth? Is he back?" he asked.

"No. This time it's a little girl. Her name is Samantha and she's only seven years old. I just saw her for the first time in the mirror this afternoon while you were out in the garage. And then I saw her again while I was washing dishes with your mom tonight. She appeared on the side of a pot."

"What? Why didn't you tell me?"

"I was going to, but she didn't stick around very long. I went to get Nathan from his nap and when I came back, she was gone. Then your parents arrived, and then Jenna, and well, I couldn't find a good time to tell you with everyone here."

"Oh," was all Dan could reply. He rubbed the back of his neck and stared at the page as if he were trying to glean a deeper meaning from it. The memory of the blood and handwriting mystically appearing on the page before him was enough to send chills through him despite the fact that he was still warm from his shower. He looked up suddenly and asked, "Wait a minute—am I going to see her too? Like I did with Seth in the end?"

"I'm not sure, Murph. Only time will tell."

The two of them fell silent in thought for a few moments, trying to sort through the implications of what lie in store for them. Each held their own fears, anxieties and questions in check that were too overwhelming to share. Neither wanting to frighten the other with their concerns.

"So did Mom notice anything, you know—with the pot?" Dan asked distractedly.

Mia recalled her conversation with her mother-in-law and shook her head. "No. At least she didn't seem to indicate that she knew Samantha was there."

"Wha—?" He looked up at her with an eyebrow cocked.

"Long story. I'll have to tell you later. Oh, and one other thing—I can hear her."

"Come again?"

"Sam talking. I can actually hear her voice."

"You can *hear* her? No way… Like the way we heard Seth? Seriously? How did you find that out?"

"I had no idea that I could. She wouldn't say anything and only shook her head to answer. So I took out the notebook and showed her what Seth and I used to do, and she started writing. Nathan was waking from his nap, so I told her to stay put so we could talk more when I returned. By the time I reached the hallway, I could hear her say out loud, 'okay.' I haven't figured why it is I can hear her, yet."

"Are you sure you heard it correctly? Wasn't the baby crying?"

"It was very clear. It was her."

"Did she talk to you in the kitchen from the reflection in the pot too?"

"No, she was just saying the 'Nanny nanny boo boo' kind of thing—you know how kids do. It seemed like she was more preoccupied with trying out how to appear in different locations than necessarily speak with me. After that, she seemed content to just make faces."

"Make faces? Why?"

"Because she's a seven-year-old, I'm guessing."

"Seven years old? Geez, what the hell—I mean, heck, do you think she is doing there?" Dan had become more aware of his swearing since Nathan had been born and was making a serious effort to keep it in check. It was one of the many things Mia found endearing in his new role of fatherhood.

"That's what I'm wondering. I can't figure out exactly what her circumstances are. She looks very pale and thin. Other than being a little dirty, she looks relatively healthy. But for her to be there, I'm thinking she must be in real trouble—enough for her to reach out, just like Seth did. Maybe there is no one else for her to contact, except for me. And don't ask why it has to be me! But check this out… she wrote that she missed her mother, father, and 'Buddy.' It broke my heart when she wrote that."

"But what does this mean for us, Murph? And what about the baby?"

The question was out, naked before them. There was no avoiding it now.

"I don't know yet," Mia answered quietly.

"Are you ready to start into all of this again? I mean, we just finished settling down and putting that whole other thing behind us. Things are back to normal, and—"

"I really don't feel I have a choice. It's not that I want to do this. But, just like before, this is a soul—someone who needs my help. Remember what we did for Seth? What if this is another situation like that? I don't know if I could forgive myself if I turned my back on her. And she's so young, Dan. She's only a little girl and all alone in there. I know she is frightened out of her wits."

Dan didn't reply. Instead, he contemplated the wall as silent moments ticked by. Mia wasn't sure if he was angry, annoyed, frightened, or all three. There was no doubt that this situation she was facing would most likely be difficult. Her intuition told her that it would be. And there was no way of telling where it would take them or for how long. Worst yet, neither was sure how much more their relationship could endure. Just when she was about to apologize to him once more, he inhaled deeply, let out a long sigh, and patted her leg.

"You're right. You're absolutely right. What do you need *me* to do? How can I help you this time?" He looked at her in earnest.

"Really?"

"Yes, really."

She breathed her own inward sigh of relief. This was so remarkably different than before when she had to experience the first half of the Occurrence alone before he believed it was even happening.

"Well, if she comes back, and I think she will, I need some time to talk with her to try to figure out what is happening and why she is appearing to me. It might be a situation where she is trying to find her way out, or needs to get a message to someone, or… or, well, I don't know. But I'm guessing that this time might be a little easier than with Seth because we'll be able to talk directly to each other instead of having to write things down. What's more is she looks really good—alert, like you and me. You never saw how tortured Seth was physically. At least she doesn't outwardly appear like she's suffering from any kind of physical pain."

"Hmm, well I have some production work, but I think I can do some of it here at home so I can take care of Nathan. Maybe I can get Ho to cover for me in the afternoon. After I tell him about this, he'll probably—"

"Wait a minute. You're going to tell Hoason about this?"

"He can't get enough of this stuff. I must have had to retell him about the Occurrence at least five times already."

"Wait—he *knows* about the Occurrence? I didn't realize you had told him about it." Typically, she and her husband shared everything with only each other. She didn't think that Dan would ever disclose that harrowing event to anyone else.

"Let's face it, he knew all about the writing in the notebook. He was the one who helped me figure out what I was looking at. And you know how Ho loves to eavesdrop—he must've heard every conversation I had with Gerry when I was at work. So there was no way he was going to let this all go without hearing every last detail. I swear, he nagged me every day for about two months until finally I cracked."

"So… what did he think about all of it?" she asked tentatively.

"Ho? He thinks it's the most awesome thing he has ever heard."

Mia rolled her eyes, "Oh brother."

"Yeah, but at least he doesn't think we're nuts."

"True."

"So, if he'll cover for me, maybe I can take Nathan and the fam out for a ride or go tour something. We'll just tell them you have some editing work and a deadline. That ought to give you at least a few hours. And then the day after tomorrow is their last day here before they take off to New Brunswick and Jenna goes on her ecotour with her class."

"I think *you're* beautiful," she said giving him a kiss back.

"Really? I was kinda hoping you would say sexy. But hey—beautiful is good too," Dan quipped with a shrug and a grin.

"You're that too," Mia answered, giving him another kiss. "Thanks Murph, for helping me with all of this."

"Well, we already know what to do—sort of. So I'm just thinking that we might as well get this over with as soon as possible, so it doesn't cause too much disruption in our lives again."

"Agreed."

‡ ‡ ‡

Aunt Lydia woke up screaming. She stared wide-eyed into the darkness of her room panting and moaning, and then screamed once again, her old voice cracking. Only when she finally recognized the soft light coming through her window from the street light outside did she realize that she was in the same room she had been waking up in for the last forty years.

She clapped her hands, turning on the bedside light. In the orange glow of the 25-watt incandescent, she could see everything was in its place: her and Benny's wedding picture on the dresser; her small ivory jewelry box that held her mother's amulet; Vespers, the large orange and white striped cat curled up at the foot of the bed. He ventured only a slit of an eye to view what all the fuss was about and then broke into a purr as he went back to sleep.

Feeling shaky, Lydia looked about the nightstand for her glass of water and pulled the cool liquid to her lips with trembling hands. As she regained her composure, she scanned her memory, but could not recall at all what the dream was about. This troubled her. The images that flooded her sleep at night often were her best messengers. She relied on them to sort out the important stuff and critical matters and never took any of them lightly. However these particular dreams, although terrifying, were usually the signal that something big was going to happen. She just had to figure out if it meant something grand, horrifying, or tragic. Deep within her bosom, she felt sure that nothing grand was going to come out of this one.

In an effort to probe deeper, she took up the pen and paper she kept by her bedside just for these moments of obscurity.

What was it? What was it…?

Jotting down the first thing that came to mind, she wrote:

Murky

With that prompt, the images came faster, her hand struggling to write them down as fast as they came to mind:

Invalid

Apple

Night

Organ

She paused and reviewed the list thoughtfully. Nothing else came to mind. It was complete. However, turning it over in her head, it made no sense at all. Next, she decided to take only the first letter of each of the words and assembled them in order:

M I A N O

Sounding it out, she tried, "Miano… Mi-ano…Mian-o…"

This was going nowhere. Maybe she had written down the wrong images? She'd have to try something else. Suddenly, Lydia stopped short, the pen dropping from her outstretched hand while the other covered a gasp escaping her mouth as her mind solved the acrostic.

"Mia…No."

The old woman clutched at her heart beneath her nightgown and moaned low, frightened by the cryptic message spelled out before her. She had always thought of her niece with great affection, sometimes more so than her own daughter and son. This was a source of guilt for her. There was an inner beauty and grace about Mia that was undeniable, and once Lydia found out that she was gifted in the realm of the paranormal, she grew even closer to her feeling a kindred spirit with one who shared her unusual calling.

There was just no taking a chance with this message. Mia had been institutionalized the last time something like this had happened because she hadn't intervened like she should have then. And now the message was stronger than before. Lydia couldn't bear the thought of anything happening to her niece, let alone her husband or their precious baby boy.

But how to warn her? She certainly didn't want to alarm them by calling in the middle of the night. Lydia didn't think Dan would care for that at all. He made it all too clear in the past that he wasn't a believer in these sorts of things. Although he had witnessed firsthand the teenager Seth who had relied on Mia for help, she sensed he still had trouble accepting all that had happened. She herself would have given her eyeteeth to be there for that moment. Yet it was wasted on a non-believer instead. Some things in life were never fair.

Lydia looked at the small brass clock on her nightstand. *3:15am.* Taking into consideration that she was on the east coast and they were on the west, she would have to wait for at least another five more hours before she dared call them. Wide-awake now, she put on a kettle of water for some herbal tea and retrieved her dream dictionary and numerology book from the shelf. She studied the wedding portrait of Mia and Dan hanging among other family photos on the living room wall across from the kitchen. Dan wore his Navy dress uniform while Mia was lovely in antique lace with a wreath of flowers crowning her long dark hair. *Ah, if they could've only remained so happy and life were more simple*, Lydia thought sadly. With a heavy heart, she lit a few candles and shuffled through her deck of tarot cards determined to get to the source of this ominous communication she had received.

Cutting the deck and then shuffling it one last time, she coaxed out a card from the stack in her hand and turned it over. The image of the Lovers adorned its face. *Relationships and choices.* Aunt Lydia's eyebrow rose. She placed the card square on the table and studied the entwined coupled pictured before her.

The kettle started to whistle and she got up to turn it off, but before she left the table she plucked out another card and laid it face up next to the first. This time, the image of the Moon made her brow furrow with concern as she clucked her tongue and shook her head. *Uncertainty, dreams, nightmares…*

Distractedly, she poured the steaming water into her cup, took down a saucer from the cupboard and returned back to her chair. As she proceeded to pick up the deck to resume her reading, a card slipped from her grasp and drifted to the floor. Reaching for the sugar bowl, she spied the fallen card. Upon seeing the image of the castle turret face up on the floor, the old woman shrieked with alarm and lost her grip on the bowl. It crashed down, spilling sugar and shards of pottery across the card's face.

The Tower.

Chaos, ruin, catastrophe.

Mrs. Anita Lopez stepped out into her backyard, pursed her lips, and proceeded to make loud kissing noises. She knew he was lurking most likely behind a bush watching her at that very moment.

"¡Díablo! ¡Díablo! ¡Venga aquí!"

The plump woman walked to the edge of the patio and surveyed the yard. He was nowhere in sight. She approached the fence that bordered her young neighbors, the Labonts, and stepped up on a crate she had placed there that allowed her to peer over on the occasion she got to converse with them. Looking about their yard where he frequented, she could not see Díablo anywhere.

She glanced at their house and wondered how the couple was doing. They were such nice kids. Everything seemed to have quieted down since that dark time, almost a year and a half ago. At least she hoped so. Young people should not have to deal with such evil in their lives. Remembering her nightmarish experience in their living room sparked instant goose bumps up and down her arms. Her blood ran cold. What she saw that day would remain permanently etched in her memory.

Rubbing her arms to erase the chill and comfort herself, she focused on the fact that there was a new life in the house. Babies, with their fresh souls direct from heaven, usually corrected such matters. What's more, she noticed the big motor home that was parked in their driveway. Dan had told her that his mother and father were coming for a visit, along with his sister who was on break from college. It was good. A warm and loving familia was another strong force that helped to drive the darkness out.

Mrs. Lopez felt a soft bump against her leg. A large black cat had jumped onto the crate beside her. With his tail flicking, he peered up at her with his flaming yellow eyes. His demand for dinner came in the form of a throaty meow.

"Oh Díablo! There you are. Where were you hiding? Anyway, I hope you are not pestering Mia and Dan or killing their little birds," she cooed as she scooped up the cat and patted him. *They've had to deal with enough death too much already,* she thought to herself.

‡　　‡　　‡

Mia decided to try it. Sherry and Dick were out grocery shopping to stock up on supplies for their upcoming road trip. A proud Aunt Jenna had taken her nephew for a walk in his stroller. Aunt Lydia had left some kind of cryptic message on the voicemail and Mia knew she should call her, but that would mean losing a valuable opportunity in making a connection with Samantha. This might be the only time in the next couple of days that she could experiment while the little girl was still around.

That was *if* she would reappear.

"Murph? This would be a good time. Would you please come over here?" she called from the living room.

Dan was reviewing production schedules on his laptop in the bedroom when he heard her. He rolled his eyes and took a deep breath, knowing what his wife had in store for him. Recalling all the times he complained about her simple "Honey-Do" tasks regarding repairs and maintenance, compared to what she wanted him to do now, he regretted thinking the list was ever difficult. He would gladly pay to go back to those innocent times. Straightening up and squaring his shoulders, he entered the living room.

"Did you know that your aunt left you a message sometime this morning?" he said. "It was early—I dunno—around six-thirty or seven? I was shaving and you must've been really out if you didn't hear the phone ring. Anyway, I don't know what she was going on about. I couldn't really understand it— something about a tower? A moon? Who knows. But she sounded pretty excited."

"Thanks. I plan on calling her back later. But I think I'm going to try this now while everyone is out and we have the house to ourselves. Are you ready?"

"To be perfectly honest, Murph, I don't think I'll ever be ready for any of this. But go ahead. We could try." He stood stock straight and faced the mirror with his arms crossed and his feet firmly planted beneath him. His demeanor was nothing less than formidable. It was clear he was bracing himself for this event.

"Honey, do you think you could—I don't know—lighten up a bit? I don't want you to scare her," Mia asked, gesturing to his stance. "She's only a child."

"What? I sure as hell—I mean heck, hope that she doesn't scare *me*."

He uncrossed and shook out his arms while stretching his neck muscles and swiveling his head, looking more like a prizefighter getting ready to step into the ring. Finally he settled on an at-ease posture from his Navy days.

Mia sighed, knowing it was the best he could do given the circumstances. This was certainly a leap of faith on his part. She turned toward the mirror.

"Samantha? Are you there, sweetie? Please come out so we can talk some more."

Searching the mirror for any movement, she instead caught the grim expression on Dan's face. She wished he wouldn't look so intimidating.

"Samantha? Please. It's okay. This is my husband, Dan. He wants to help us find your mommy and daddy."

Before her eyes, Samantha slowly took shape in the reflection of the mirror. She stood as before, large blue eyes, a mop of disheveled blonde hair, and those cheery rain boots.

"Why, hello again Samantha. It's so good to see you," Mia said brightly. Then she tossed over her shoulder, "Do you see her, Dan?"

"See what? Where? Is she there already?" His eyes searched the mirror from edge to edge, top to bottom. Seeing nothing more than the reflection of his wife and himself, he threw his hands up in defeat, shook his head, and returned to at-ease.

"Would you like to talk some more today?" Mia continued to the reflection.

"Uh huh," the child answered.

Mia beamed. She hadn't imagined hearing her after all. "Did you hear her Dan?"

"What? No." Then he muttered skeptically, "I didn't think this was going to work."

Ignoring him, Mia asked, "So what would you like to talk about today, Samantha?"

"Can we write in the notebook again?" Her voice was clear and high with a little girl's lilt to it.

"No, sweetie. There's no need to now that I know I can hear you."

"Oh…" she said. "Can I ask you a question?"

"Sure."

"Why am I here? And why can't I go home?"

"There are a lot of things we have to figure out first. But for us to do so, you are going to have to trust me and tell me everything you can, okay?" Mia answered, having decided it might not be constructive to inform Samantha that she wouldn't be returning home from where she was. *First things first,* she reminded herself before pity's tug on her heart grew too strong. "I know your mommy told you not to talk to strangers, but if you need help and there is no one else around to help you like mommy or daddy or the police, I think she'll say it's all right to talk to me because I am trying to help you."

The child looked doubtful. Then she pointed at Dan. "Is he going to help too?"

Mia smiled. "Who Dan? Yes, Dan is a big help in times like these. But he can't see or hear you like I can."

"No kidding," he muttered again. "And I don't think it's gonna happen anytime soon."

"But he looks angry. Maybe he doesn't like me here," the child said.

"That's not true, Sam. Dan doesn't mind you coming to visit us at all." Mia turned quickly around to her husband. She narrowed her eyes and placed her hand on her hip. "Could you at least try?" she whispered to him.

Catching her glare, he broke at ease, looked directly at the mirror and waved, pasting on an exaggerated grin that widened his face.

"Hi Samantha! I'm Dan. I want to help you too. I just don't know how yet, since I can't even see you or hear you… but I will. Oh yeah, and I want you to keep visiting us. Come over any time you like." Then he leaned close to Mia and whispered back, "I'll just let you two work things out. Holler if you need me." Then one last time to the mirror, he grinned again and annunciated, "Bye Samantha! I'm going now. Talk to you later. Heeeere's Mia." He sidestepped and with two hands, gestured toward his wife.

"He's funny," Samantha giggled.

"Yeah, Dan is hilarious," Mia said sarcastically as she watched her husband exit. She had really hoped that he would have seen the child. It would have made this predicament she was in so much easier. Once he understood what she was dealing with, he wouldn't be so resistant. She turned back to her small visitor. "So Samantha, do you feel you can trust me?"

The girl paused for a moment and then nodded. "Okay."

"Wonderful! I'm so glad we are going to work together. How about we start with where you are…"

‡   ‡   ‡

It all came back like a bad déjà vu: Mia exhibiting bizarre behavior by talking to a mirror, and him not being able to see one damn thing in that mirror, no matter how hard he concentrated. Dan shut the bedroom door. He could still hear her in the living room carrying on the strange monologue. Getting caught up in this situation with so few choices and little to no control was bad enough, but perhaps the worst thing was the nagging doubt that had returned bringing nothing but worry and second guessing. *Could this really be happening - again?*

Last night, he tried to be as accepting and agreeable as possible. However, he had to admit, to any normal person this would be insane. *Conversing with the Dead? Heck—no, hell—even Mia would have thought this was over the top a couple of years ago.* That aside, the difficulty in following through with believing at all was it opened up a whole other can of worms. When a dead teen appeared in their living room in effort to communicate, he had chalked it up to a once in a lifetime experience. Some people call that sort of stuff miracles. But no one expects miracles to keep repeating themselves to the same people, do they? If so, when do they cease to be miracles? Now that Samantha showed up, it proved that there was potential for even more of these occurrences. Not only would they have to deal with them, he had to convince himself that this was somehow becoming their new reality—quite possibly for the rest of their lives.

Dan recalled watching cable shows about psychics, real and fictional. Sure, as a viewer, it was suspenseful and entertaining as the plotlines unfolded and mysteries were solved, but those were strangers in the altered reality world of TV. This was not that world and it was happening to *them*—he and Mia. They were now the actors in a twisted, dangerous, real-world drama.

He certainly did not want to end up like the people in those shows. He felt that if they did, it would mark the end of the home life they knew and all of their dreams. And how was it going to affect their child? How would they explain to Nathan what was going on when he became old enough to start noticing and asking questions? If this scenario of visiting entities persisted, he wasn't sure what he could do to protect Nathan and ensure that he would have a stable home and as normal of a life as possible.

In addition, there was the question of any future siblings. He and Mia discussed having two children. If this went on, would they ever have that chance? If they decided to accept these occurrences in their lives, he would be crazy to submit yet another child to the chaos and turmoil that would most likely ensue.

And if that wasn't enough, there was the talk around the break room at Pryus Productions, about Greenlee running the small company in the red and the possibility of either a buyout or bankruptcy. Either way, it looked like a huge shake up was on the horizon regarding his employment including the fact that he could very well be out of job within the next year or so. Dan chose to keep this news from his wife, so as not to worry her until there were definite details, but it was yet another problem adding to the home mix that was already brewing with trouble.

Mia, being in the middle of it, was too close to the situation to see all of the ramifications. She only saw that there was yet another soul to save and she was obligated to do it whether it destroyed her home or not. Dan knew that his wife wasn't being selfish. In fact, it was her very selflessness that blinded her making this predicament that they were in even more precarious. Nonetheless, it left him carrying the brunt of immediate issues.

As Dan changed out of his sweatpants and tee shirt, he tried to quell the rampant thoughts swirling in his head. He hadn't gotten much sleep last night and by morning, all of his questions had resurfaced once more. He worked at clearing his mind as he rounded up things for Nathan's outing. His folks would be returning from the store soon and he was about to take them sightseeing to allow Mia more time to figure things out with Samantha.

It was best to keep these concerns from his family as they were astute at noticing when he was upset, particularly Jenna. As siblings who were close, they were sensitive to each other's moods. This meant he had to be sure that whatever nagging fears and doubts he had about the perilous journey Mia and he were embarking on once again didn't reflect on his face. He wouldn't be able to answer his family's subsequent questions. More so, he knew they weren't ready for the answers if he gave them.

Miracles were difficult enough for practical, logical, realistically grounded minds to comprehend. A curse, like this one, would be impossible.

‡ ‡ ‡

The crowding clouds darkened the sky so that by three in the afternoon, it looked like evening. The wind picked up and what had started as a mild sea breeze, now howled through the foothills in powerful gusts that rattled tree limbs and rumbled about houses. As the marine system moved in off the coast, a light rain began to fall that steadily increased over the hour until it became a downpour. This wouldn't have been a problem in a normal year, but springtime in Washington had already been the wettest on record with an accumulation of over seven inches of precipitation. The earth was saturated.

Within a few hours, the rivers were swollen, ambitious towards cresting their banks. Trees shuddered on steep hillsides, and the soil that bound their roots transformed into gooey mud, foundations washing out from beneath them. One large alder wood tree toppled, followed by another, blown down by roaring winds that heralded the weather system. The soggy bank that once held the alder woods gave way to a mudflow that started down the hillside in a sudden, blinding rush. Its course barreled straight toward the houses and outbuildings below.

‡ ‡ ‡

"A deadly roadside bomb claimed the lives of three more U.S. soldiers outside of Kabul today, bringing this month's death toll up to thirty-two… Riots spread through London, killing at least five people in unrelated incidents. Parliament remains baffled by the motives… In local news, an elderly Bellevue woman was robbed and stabbed several times in the parking lot of a book store by a man allegedly high on meth… Two more mudslides from the record rainfall that is falling in parts of Western Washington covered slopes and outlying buildings in the town of Orting."

The evening news droned on Dan's tablet perched on the kitchen counter as Mia stirred the bubbling chicken stew in the Dutch oven and set the table. She paused only for a moment to look out the kitchen window at the rain that continued to fall steadily. Everyone would be hungry when they got home. Dan had taken the entire family downtown to the aquarium hours ago. Feeling the damp that seeped inside the house during the drenching rain, she worried that they all would be soaked and Nathan might get chilled.

Mia missed her little boy. Since his birth, mother and son hardly spent much time apart. There had only been a couple of hours here and there when Dan could convince her to go out on a quick dinner date; she was never entirely comfortable leaving the baby with anyone. It had been a tenuous and anxious wait throughout her pregnancy, wondering if she might spontaneously abort like she had her first. Her obstetrician had declared her pregnancy high-risk since it followed an unsuccessful one. This led her to immediately quit work, stay home, and take it very easy for the nine months she carried her child, not wanting to take any chances. She and Dan remained on high alert until they crossed over the twenty-fourth week milestone when the baby was considered viable. And with each passing week thereafter, their anxiety gradually subsided.

Once Nathan Stephanos Labont entered their lives, they couldn't get enough of him. They didn't know how they had ever managed before without him. Whereas their world used to center around each other and didn't feel like it could possibly fit another, now Nathan was their world. His bright eyes, eager personality, and ready smile filled their hearts as nothing had ever before. And every moment they spent with him, made him that much more precious.

Mia resumed part time work by writing freelance articles and editing online so she could be sure to be home with their son. It didn't make a lot of money, but at least it supplemented Dan's salary permitting them to get by. They both had agreed that one of them needed to stay home to raise Nathan and although Mia was the more logical choice, they knew that it wouldn't be any other way.

Now worrying over the weather and hearing the constant misery reported on the news, her anxiety mounted. Although Dan was an attentive and doting dad and Sherry was an excellent caregiver, she still couldn't quell the bit of an ache in her heart for her baby.

While she held dinner for them, Mia tried to distract herself by reviewing the notes she had gathered from her talk with Samantha. Now a mother herself, she couldn't imagine the agony the little girl's parents would be suffering over the fate of their child. It made her that much more determined to resolve this as quickly as possible despite the outcome, although she shuddered to think that it may entail those parents having yet to learn of their child's death.

Mia squeezed her eyes shut, pushing the thought from her head. She had to believe that this was happening for a reason and given her unusual ability to communicate with them, it was her duty to ease the suffering of any souls who appeared to her. It was the only way she would be able to cope with this burden. She found it odd how, instead of affirming and strengthening her religious faith, the last occurrence with Seth instead shook her faith, causing her to question more than ever. *And now another innocent child…* Bearing witness to the suffering that took place in the world through the evildoings of others raised doubt in her mind, causing years of forced devotion by her mother's hand to unravel.

She directed her attention to the print before her. In the two and a half hours they were able to talk, she and Samantha had covered much ground. Once the girl relaxed, she had disclosed details in depth. She was captive in a tiny shed where the only window was boarded up tight and little light found its way through the hairline cracks in its walls. Samantha had tried the door, but it was locked. Sheets of plastic were packed in around its edges. The rock hard ground deterred her from digging her way out. The shed was just wide enough for her to stretch out on an old blanket that was thrown on the floor. She used a bucket in the corner to do her business and it was more than half full and getting smelly.

Nighttime was the most frightening. It was cold and pitch black to the point where she couldn't see anything at all. Sometimes animals came rustling and snuffling close outside and she thought she heard ghosts calling "whoooo whoooo" through the night. The wind flapped and tore at the plastic and whenever it rained, water seeped in through the cracks and puddled on the floor, soaking the thin blanket she kept wrapped tightly about herself in an effort to stay warm.

Her abductor left her little food—a few slices of bread, a half jar of peanut butter, a box of crackers, and a travel mug of milk. But it was all gone now. She had grown thirsty enough to drink from the dirty puddle when she had to. Mia urged her to estimate how long she had been there, but Samantha wasn't sure. She couldn't tell whether it had been days or weeks.

The only thing she wouldn't talk about was who had put her there. She was stubborn about this. When she was pressed for details, Mia detected fear in the twitching arch of her eyebrows and the way she wrung her hands. At that point, the child would only say was that she was hungry and wanted to go home.

When asked about how she came to find her way to Mia's home, Samantha told her that one day one of cracks between the wooden boards in the wall grew a little brighter than the others, until it was extremely bright. She approached it and when she peeked through the crack, she could see Mia's living room. Then she knew anytime she was lonely and wanted someone to talk to, all she had to do was look through that crack.

Their conversation had ended abruptly when Samantha paused mid-sentence and cocked her head as if she had heard something. Mia asked if something was wrong, but she wouldn't answer. Then Samantha simply vanished from view and didn't reappear for the rest of the afternoon.

Nathan's bright eyes fixed intently on his mother's face as he reached his finger up to touch her chin. He had the eye color of his grandfather Stephanos, a warm walnut brown. Mia cooed and talked tenderly to him, kissing him on his forehead as he nursed. It felt so good to have him back in her arms. He was getting close to being weaned within a few weeks and these precious times they shared were growing few. She enjoyed their quiet moment while the rest of the family was setting dinner out on the table. They had all returned safe and sound, a bit cold and plenty hungry.

Sherry's high voice carried down the hall to the nursery as she spoke with her daughter Jenna.

"Did you see the news? What a shame that another child is missing! Her parents must be going out of their minds," Sherry said. "Oh and look at that… she's a pretty little thing with all that long blonde hair."

Mia's heart skipped upon hearing this. *Could it be?* She tried calling to her mother-in-law, but Sherry didn't respond.

"Did you need something, Murph? How's our little guy?" Dan apparently had heard her calls and appeared in the doorway to investigate. "You should have seen him at the aquarium. He was going nuts over the jellyfish exhibit. I got some pics of him on my phone I got to show you."

"What is Mom talking about? There's a missing child?"

"She was just watching the news. Why?"

"I was wondering if the child might be Samantha."

"Seriously? How so?" He tilted his head in question.

"The timing would be right. And if it is her, we just might get this over with sooner."

"Good point. I'll go check."

Dan disappeared and then returned moments later. "She's eleven years old, and she's from the Chicago. Mom wasn't quite sure of the name. She hadn't caught it—Crystal or Christina, something like that."

"Oh," Mia said, looking crestfallen.

"What's up?"

"I thought we got lucky there for a moment. I don't know what I was thinking. I guess that except for the age, she fits the description."

"Yeah, but at the risk of sounding callous, there are a lot of little girls out there that fit that description."

‡ ‡ ‡

The rain pelted against storm windows muting the brilliant stain glass panels beneath them. The ancient church yawned cavernous in the descending twilight, the alabaster Stations of the Cross offering the only relief in intervals against stained mahogany walls. After surveying the imposing surroundings, a young Mia ventured a look past her mother and observed the few others in attendance on that late Wednesday afternoon in winter. A middle-aged woman prayed fervently, lips twitching, eyes squeezed shut, a black loop of rosary beads escaping the confinement of her tightly clasped hands. On the other side of the aisle, a grizzled old man sat solemnly staring ahead and lost in thought. A young priest, dressed in street clothes save for his collar, walked through, stopped to genuflect briefly before the altar, and then continued his brisk pace to the sacristy. Apart from the faint echoes of rustling and voices in hidden rooms beyond the pulpit, the church was silent.

Perched upon on a kneeler at a side altar, Mia's child legs were too short to allow her toes to touch the floor as she knelt. Two brisk taps on her shoulder from her mother kneeling beside her reminded her that she was to stop daydreaming and pay attention. She obediently fixed her eyes straight ahead and arched her hands in prayer, lifting her elbows in effort to rest them upon the rail, to mimic her mother's.

She began to pray the timeless words that had been taught to her over her seven years, but within a few moments her attention was drawn once again first to the sorrowful looking Virgin Mary towering above them, and next to the candle station made of wrought iron in front of them. The station was the only bright spot in the dim church on that gloomy afternoon and she was glad they were near it. At least it felt warmer here. She studied the metal collection box and the container holding the long matchsticks, as the mingling scents of incense and wick smoke filled her nose. The child remembered her mother telling her that each lit candle was in prayer for a person to be healed, saved, or remembered. There were rows and rows of lit candles before her. So many prayers!

Her eyes drifted across the cylinders of yellow beeswax, mesmerized by the flickering flames that opposed the dark in a lively dance. She stopped at one where there was nothing left but a clear puddle of melted wax at the bottom of the glass votive. The short blackened wick was bent over as if in grief, its tip gradually burning white, then yellow, then orange, until it completely extinguished itself, a thin wisp of smoke signaling its end. Mia wondered if that meant the prayer had been answered for the intended person or worse yet—the prayer had stopped working. Her pulse quickened.

Curiosity overcoming her, she tugged at her mother's sleeve.

"Mommy, that candle there—"

"Shush, child. Be still and go back to your prayers."

"But Mommy—"

"Mia…" Her mother glowered at her.

The little girl quieted and compliantly squeezed her eyes shut. But soon, she opened one and then the other. She stared at the spent candle and others like it that were interspersed throughout the glowing grid. Were her deceased brothers' and sister's candles still lit or had they burned out? Could she and her mother light more for them or was there only one candle per person forever? She would have to remember to ask Daddy when she got home. He always answered her questions and never shushed her, no matter what.

In the darkness of her bedroom, Mia stared up at the ceiling, replaying the old childhood memory in her head. It had been years since she thought about St. Jerome's where she and her mother had attended every Wednesday afternoon and Sunday morning without fail until they moved to the West Coast. *Whatever brought up that old place?*

Unable to sleep, she slipped out of bed, checked on Nathan, and then continued to the quiet living room, feeling compelled to go there for some inexplicable reason. Not wanting to wake Dan who was exhausted and sleeping peacefully, she left the lights off. In the hallway, she halted in her tracks as her ears picked up a barely perceptible disturbance somewhere in the house coming to her first in whispers, then a mewling. It stopped for a moment, and then resumed once more. Listening carefully, the sound of sniffling echoed back to her. Moving through the house, it was then she recognized the plaintive sound of a child weeping. In a whisper she called out, hoping the little girl would appear. The weeping continued, its sound flooding the living room.

Mia searched the reflective surfaces about the room but could not locate her. "Samantha? Where are you hiding? Please come out, honey," Mia entreated. Within the next moment, Samantha finally came into view. Her slight face was fraught with sadness and her cheeks were wet from tears. She rubbed her swollen eyes.

"Oh sweetie, there you are. Where have you been? I've been so worried about you," Mia spoke in a reassuring voice. She wanted to ask her why she had disappeared so quickly when they had last talked, but decided against it. There would be time tomorrow. Instead she asked, "What's the matter? Can't sleep?"

"I'm scared."

"Do you need some company?"

The child nodded.

"Want to come back to my room?"

Another nod.

"All right. I have a small mirror in my drawer. When I take it out, you meet me there, okay?"

Samantha nodded one last time and then disappeared.

Back in the bedroom, Mia quietly slid her nightstand drawer open and withdrew the hand mirror she had used with Seth. Feeling its familiar weight in her hands gave her pause. It wasn't that long ago when she held it last. The memory of his face, bits of their conversations, and their last moment together tumbled through her mind's eye. She remembered his vivid blue-green eyes staring back at her when this mirror was perched on her nightstand. Searching the glass illuminated only by the light from her alarm clock, she could see that Samantha had reappeared. Lying down and turning on her side, Mia propped the mirror against her pillow so she could see the child's face. In return, Samantha gave her a small smile of satisfaction and consolation. Within minutes, she fell fast asleep.

Mia contemplated the sleeping child with the tearstained cheeks. In the moment, she felt so utterly powerless to save her. Was there anyone grieving over and missing little Samantha at this very minute? Were there candles lit somewhere in her name or had they already burned out?

‡   ‡   ‡

"And you are sure Taylor is meeting you at the airport?" Dan questioned his sister. He watched as she double-checked pockets in the backpack she had borrowed from him as she readied herself for a class trip to Costa Rica on an eco-tour. Her visit with them was culminating with her leaving directly from Seattle.

"Yes. For the third time already, I'm telling you he is. But did I tell you that we get to go zip-lining through the jungle canopy? I'm so glad I transferred to SDSU. They didn't offer trips abroad like this back in Vermont," Jenna said excitedly. Then she rolled her eyes in thought. "Toothpaste. I better not forget my toothpaste and a clear baggie. Do you remember what size baggie I need to pass airport security?" she said determinedly as she rose and left the room once again.

The minute she left the room, Dan quickly checked the contents in the pack, just to be sure. Jenna was new to both traveling and her independence, and she was making the most of it. However, if it was up to her over protective big brother, he would have her housebound and babysat alongside her young nephew.

"And Justin and Bonnie are going too?"

Jenna returned and threw down a travel-size tube of toothpaste, the baggie, and a small hand towel. "*Yes*, and Marcus and Frank and Yukio are meeting us in San José. Just like I told you before. We've been planning this in class for weeks and Professors Nwachuka and Engles will be with us. They've led this program for the last five years. Now will you please quit worrying about me already?"

Dan couldn't help but worry. His once pudgy kid sister had blossomed into an athletic, shapely young woman. He tried to advise his parents about the hazards of contemporary relationships, but they were confident that she could take care of herself. Whereas before, he used to worry when boys weren't looking at her, now he worried that they may be looking at her too much. Mia wasn't much help either, insisting that Jenna was a smart girl who made good choices and had good common sense.

"Did you pack the solar phone charger I got you? Make sure you call if you need anything at all. I've been to Costa Rica and I still know my way around."

"Dan, we'll be fine! And here it is, right here, okay?" she said as she undid the Velcro on a side pocket to show him the charger. Before he could start in on something else, Jenna decided to steer him to another subject. "So, do you and Mia have anything planned? With Mom and Dad on the road and me leaving, it'll be good for all of us to finally get out of your hair. Besides, I'll be back to bug you when I get back. But for now, I'm sure you two can use a breather to spend time with Mr. Nat-a-tat. He's so cute and smart too, that little monkey—I just want to eat him up! Did I get to tell you what I saw him do the other morning? It was hilarious."

"No. What did he do?" Dan knelt down beside her and started to cinch up her sleeping bag snug against the pack for her. His mind was still grinding on the list of things he felt she really should pack for her trip.

"We were sitting on the floor and he was playing with all of his chew toys, babbling away. Then he crawled over to the mirror and started to pat it with his hand. The next thing, he lets out a big squeal and laughed. Then he gave kisses to the mirror and patted it some more. I asked him if he loved the baby in the mirror and he kissed it again. Then he sat back down on his little bottom and waved bye-byes to it. Just like I taught him. It was so darn cute. I wish I had my phone." Jenna delighted in talking about her nephew.

Dan looked up suddenly. "The mirror? How did he reach the mirror?"

"Oh. It was down on the ground against the wall for some reason. Mia must've taken it down. Anyway, he was safe. I made sure it wasn't going to fall over on him or anything."

"Right. Well, thanks for doing that," he muttered, looking perturbed.

"Sure." Jenna could see the dark change in her brother's expression. "Danny? Is something the matter? All of a sudden you look, I dunno, kinda put out or something."

"No… It's nothing. I just remembered something I have to talk to Mia about."

"About what? If you don't mind me saying so, it seems lately that you guys are out of sorts or a little bummed. I'm not sure which yet. I noticed it when Mom and Dad were here. But I just thought it was 'cause you had a houseful of guests. Come on, you guys are like, the best couple ever. It's pretty obvious when something is going on with you two."

For a moment, Dan contemplated whether he should just lay everything out for his sister. It would be so easy to tell her all about the Occurrence, the appearances, and now this new situation with the little girl showing up. At the very least it would be a relief not to keep things covert anymore. There was a time, throughout their childhood, when the siblings would share their troubles, victories, and challenges with each other. But that seemed long ago. So much had changed since then. Jenna looked at him expectantly. He studied her inquisitive face and knew she was bright and usually acceptant of most things, unconditionally.

However, he reconsidered. His almost boringly normal upbringing acted as a certain stabilizer in his life when things spun too crazily out of control for him. If Jenna ever found out about the Occurrence and what was going on now with Samantha, she may very well accept and believe it readily. He decided therefore it was best for her not to know. She and subsequently his parents getting involved in all of this proved just too much for him to deal with. He simply wasn't ready for them to believe in it. It would usurp everything he knew to be normal and sane in life.

"Nah. Everything's good. Just tired from work and chasing Nathan with everyone visiting and all. Stop worrying," he said with a final cinch to the strap.

CHAPTER 3

On the twelfth row, amidst the fifty-eight photos arranged in three columns cascading down the Washington State Patrol's website for missing children, a familiar sanguine face smiled back at her. Mia gave a start. It was only a hunch—she never expected to actually find Samantha there. The child that had been showing up in her mirror was indeed seven and half years old. The location where she was last seen was the town of Puyallup. She had been missing for three weeks already. Her last name was Oswego. Mia carefully turned over each detail in her mind as if she could glean some hidden message that would reveal the truth about what had happened to her.

She also hoped that if, indeed, she should find her on this website, her photo would be among the ones stamped with the bright red word "recovered" across it. With sadness, she could plainly see that Samantha's was still an open case. The trouble was, the child's fate had already been determined. It was eerie to think that all of the faces she scrolled across were children currently missing with lives precariously unbalanced and on hold.

"Samantha," she said, making herself concentrate on the one who was presently her visitor, "I know that you didn't get where you are all by yourself. Someone had to bring you there and then lock the door. There's no use in trying to keep it a secret. It is not helping us get you back to your family and I think it might help in locating you. So listen, it's okay to say who it was. You will not get in trouble. Do you understand?"

The girl nodded.

Three more days had passed since the last disclosure. The child was wasting away before Mia's eyes. Her movements were labored and her face bore a mix of exhaustion and worry. Dark circles had formed under her eyes and a bluish tinge ringed her mouth. They had to make some kind of breakthrough very soon or Mia was afraid she might lose her. The thought of the evil shadow that had enveloped Seth taking over this little girl was too much for Mia to bear. As much as she hated to do it, she had to get firm with her.

Additionally, she found it took more coordination of her time to converse with Samantha than it had with Seth. Whenever Seth appeared, she could drop everything and easily spend hours deciphering his many lines of writing, all the while piecing together the clues of the mystery around him. But now she had to tend to Nathan and all the extra tasks a baby in a household generated while trying to keep up with her freelance contracts. As it was, she had already resigned from two projects. She didn't want to rush Samantha, but she did not have the luxury of time. Looking at the clock, it was already late afternoon and she would have to start preparing dinner soon.

"So please, do you remember if it was a man or a woman who brought you there? Think carefully."

"A man," she answered slowly.

The child's voice was growing more faint each time she appeared. It now rasped scarcely above a whisper and Mia had to listen carefully to hear her.

"Thank you, Sam. Now we're on the right track," Mia said gratefully. "Do you remember anything—anything *at all* about your trip there? Did you see anything different or special along the way?"

"No. We drove and drove a long way. It was kinda like when we go camping. Lots of trees and not so many houses."

"That's good! Anything else?"

"I think there was a train track… Oh, and we passed by one of those big tall round things next to a barn." In giving the description, the child attempted to space her skinny arms apart, but it was apparent she was growing too weak to hold them up.

"A silo?"

"Yes. That's what my teacher calls them too. A silo. It was purple."

"Okay, a purple silo. Any road signs?"

"Road signs? Ummm. I think so."

"There were? That's great! Now honey, you've got to think very hard. Can you remember what was written on the signs? Any of them. Even one sign would be good. I know you can do it."

Samantha scrunched her nose and furrowed her forehead in concentration. Her eyes rolled up to the left and then shifted right as she thought. In a few seconds they opened wide in recall.

"I know! I remember one that was green and white and had a one and a six in it. But I can't remember the others," she said apologetically.

"Excellent! I knew you could do it."

Samantha managed a small smile and looked relieved.

"Okay, sweetie. Let's talk about the man who brought you there."

Samantha's brow creased again. Her smiled melted to a frown.

"Can you tell me what he looks like?"

The little girl shook her head in an emphatic NO.

"Are you sure? It would really be a big help."

She remained silent. Mia knew that they were very close. If only the child would open up fully she might be able to derive some vital clues as to where she could be found.

"Okay. How about this—have you ever heard of 'bad touches' and 'good touches?'"

"Uh huh. Mrs. Yakumura came to our class and talked to us about them."

"Mrs. Yakamura? Who is she?"

"Our school nurse."

"And what did she say? Do you remember?"

"Mrs. Yakumura said a good touch is like a hug or when we shake hands. It makes us feel good right here." She placed her hand over her heart. Then she continued, "And a bad touch was anything that makes us feel bad or scared. And sometimes it makes us feel like we are doing something we are not supposed to."

"That's exactly right. Now, did the man ever do any good touches with you?"

"No. He didn't…" She trailed off.

Mia held her breath, not wanting to ask the next question, but it was inevitable.

"Did he do any bad touches with you?"

Samantha's small hands clenched into fists as her expression darkened.

"It's okay to tell me. It seems like something is troubling you," Mia softly urged.

Suddenly, the child blurted out, "When he told me that he wanted to sleep in my bed, I told him that we wouldn't fit. It was too little for the both of us! And then he kept saying we would fit if we cuddled really close together and then he gave me a hug. But it didn't feel like a good touch like Mrs. Yakumura said. My tummy felt bad, right here." She rubbed a circle around her navel. "So I told him no. He kept saying 'please please please' and my tummy got worser.

"I got scared so I started crying and told him I wanted to go home and I wanted to be with my mommy. When he told me not to cry, I couldn't stop. Then he hugged me really hard and made me lay down on the bed with him. I hit him and pushed him and he told me to stop squirming. By accident I kicked him really really hard in his private place. He scrunched over and said a bad word. Then he got really really mad and hit me." Samantha stopped for a moment and rubbed her cheek.

She continued, "I wanted my mommy and daddy, so I started to scream and scream. He got mad again and yelled at me and said if I screamed one more time, he would hit me again and harder. And he did. Then he put me in the car and told me he was taking me to a place where all the bad girls go. He said I needed to go there to think about my behavior. We drove and it got dark. And then I fell asleep. I woke up when the car stopped. And then he put me in this little room. I told him not to, but he told me I was very very bad and he didn't want to see me any more. And I wouldn't see mommy or daddy ever again because of my behavior.

"He came back one more time after one—no, two days, and gave me some food. He asked me again to come back with him and that he would sleep in his own bed. But when he came near me, I started to scream again. So he told me that he doesn't love me because I was wicked and no one loves me anymore, not even God. And he hasn't come back. And now… and now I won't be able to see my mommy and daddy ever again. I was very bad. Mommy told me never ever to get into a stranger's car."

By now, Samantha was sobbing. Her words had rushed out in a torrent until she couldn't say any more.

"Aw, sweetheart. It's okay. It's okay," Mia consoled gently. Her own heart was breaking over the anguish the child was feeling. "You are *not* bad or wicked, do you understand me? You are a brave girl—a very brave girl and your mommy and daddy will be very proud of you on just how brave you are. They love you so much. And I want to help them find you. So, please, maybe we can talk just a little bit more so we can help your mommy and daddy find you?"

Samantha's sobs were reduced to pitiful weeping.

"Can you tell me where this man picked you up in his car?"

"I'm tired."

The child wiped at her eyes, her dirty hands leaving smudges across her face. Mia wanted only to hold and comfort her. But she knew for Samantha's sake, she must press on.

"Come on, Sam. Please, we only have just a little more to go. If you could only tell me how or where this man found you it will be a big, big help."

Samantha only shook her head and repeated, "I'm tired, Mia."

The girl was spent. What little energy she had, had been tapped by her outburst. It was no use in forcing her anymore.

"Come here, honey. Let's sit down, okay?" Mia crossed her legs and sat on the floor next to the dressing mirror in her bedroom. She had placed it there so she could be close to where Nathan was playing. Samantha did the same and then scooted as close as she could to the glass and leaned her head against the pane. Nathan, busy chewing on his teething ring nearby, saw her, dropped his toy and crawled over to the mirror as well. He reached up his hand and patted it, making baby gurgles. Samantha saw him and woefully put her hand against his.

Mia touched where Samantha's head was. "I so wish I could hug you right now."

"Mia, will you sing to me?" Samantha asked.

"Will it make you feel better?"

"Uh huh. My mommy sings to me."

"Okay, big girl. I will."

Mother scooped up her son and held him in her arms as she leaned her head against Samantha's, separated only by the hard glass. She sang one lullaby followed by others that she sang to Nathan at night. Soon, the trio was snuggled down. The late afternoon sun was golden as it illuminated the bedroom and bathed them in warm light. Peace settled over the room. At that moment, it felt as if nothing could disturb them. Having breastfed, even Nathan started to nod off. Eventually, Samantha slid away from the mirror and curled up on the floor, her thumb going to her mouth and her eyes closing.

Mia continued singing softly when a thought suddenly occurred to her. When she was institutionalized at Meadowbrook, she remembered being able to connect with Seth through a dream that allowed her to step into his world and witness things first hand. Could she possibly do it again? Looking at the thin child resting so peacefully, she knew she had better attempt it. Although Samantha had been through so much already, her nightmare wasn't over yet. The child wouldn't last much longer. Worse yet, the shadow could come to claim her and take her to some dark place full of eternal misery, pain, and suffering.

Mia knew they were out of options.

‡　‡　‡

The bell sounded and for a brief moment more, the courtyard was silent. Five seconds later, the doors opened, flooding the outside with excited talk, laughter, and the sound of hundreds of feet finding their way to the schoolyard. It was recess time, a precious fifty-minute reprieve after lunch, away from books, whiteboards, desks, and the confines of walls.

The afternoon was unusually warm for early spring with clear blue skies. The primary grade students did not seem to take notice of the weather, but their bodies were energized by the bright sun and their lungs filled with fresh air as they stretched their legs and ran as fast and as far as they could, away from the three teachers who stood playground duty. The large playing field came alive with children spreading out like oversized ants across its grass and migrating to the furthest boundaries hemmed in by chain link fence.

Samantha heard the recess bell in the nurse's office. Her eyes beseeched Mrs. Yakamura as she squirmed in her seat. In return, the nurse smiled kindly with understanding at her young charge. It was so hard to get these little ones to remember their medication schedules.

"I'll let you go to recess as soon as you take your methylin, okay Samantha? And next time remember that you are supposed to come here *before* you go to lunch, not *after*. I don't want to have to come find you again like I did today, understood?" she said patiently, but firmly.

Samantha continued squirming to be free but nodded and took the paper cup containing the pill handed to her. Then she popped the chewable tablet into her mouth and chomped it while baring her teeth to show the nurse that the deed was, in fact, done. She took a sip of water offered to her and next she was out the door.

"Bye Mrs. Yakamura! See you tomorrow," she called over her shoulder as she trotted down the hall.

"Good-bye Samantha. And walk please."

Heading out into the clear day, the child paused for a moment to locate where her friends were congregated out on the playing field. Close by, the teachers on playground duty, Mrs. Farrow, Mrs. Badesha, and Ms. Ramirez stood in the shade. She could hear them talking as they faced each other, concern dulling their voices into low, angry tones. Impending cutbacks and RIFs announced in the before-school staff meeting that morning were still on their minds and they were eager to share their thoughts with one another.

"I don't know what my family is going to do if I get laid off. Achir is still on medical leave after hurting his back at work. His doctor is not sure how much he is going to recover or how long it is going to take," Mrs. Badesha said, her face worn with worry.

"Well it's been bad enough with no pay increases for three years already. And now they expect us to just take this one lying down?" griped Mrs. Farrow.

"You two are covered. At least you have more than five years with the district. I only have three, plus I transferred from my old district. If there are lay-offs, I'll probably be the first one to go," Ms. Ramirez lamented. "I knew it was a mistake to leave Highline."

"Do you really think so?" asked Mrs. Farrow.

"I know so," Ms. Ramirez answered. "Didn't you hear what Stan said? He was at the district office last Wednesday and it looks like they'll be narrowing the RIF down to those teachers with less than five consecutive years in the district."

"There's something terribly wrong with the system," Mrs. Badesha offered. "Terribly wrong. So many children to teach. We just can't take on any more. How do they expect us to do that? I already have thirty-eight in my classroom and there might be another one coming in by next week."

Mrs. Farrow pressed, "The teachers in Tacoma are striking for more pay and continuing contracts. We really should start getting our act together here and start organizing…"

The three women went on, intent in their conversation as the children mixed and mingled throughout the schoolyard. In the far corner away from the watchful eyes of the teachers, a group of second grade girls were having their own intent discussion. Samantha's eyes settled on them. She ran over to where they were sprawled out on the fresh grass, relieved to be away from the boring grown-up talk of the teachers.

There, she plunked herself down between her two best friends.

"Where were you Samantha?" Moira asked.

"I had to take my meds in the nurse's office."

"Oh."

"Why did you wear those? It's not even raining today," Pippa asked pointing to Samantha's footwear.

Moira giggled, "She's been wearing them *every* day. She's crazy."

"I like them. They are my most favorite, favorite shoes. I would sleep with them on, but my mom won't let me."

Moira giggled again, "But they're not even shoes. They're rain boots!"

"But why are they your favorite?" Pippa couldn't contain her curiosity.

"'Cause they are my Wallies. I like the flowers on them. My mom says they are sunflowers." She stretched out her legs before her and admired her boots while tapping the toes together.

"Samantha, you're crazy," Moira grinned and opened her eyes wide, touching her forehead against her friend's, then sat back.

Samantha brushed back the long hair away from her face as she lifted her chin with pride. "My Wallies make me a fast runner too. And I can kick hard with them."

Just then, a collective cry of despair interrupted their talk. The girls looked over at the group of first grade boys who had been playing a rowdy game of 'keep- away' with one of the gym balls. Apparently the ball was now over the fence and the boys huddled together trying to figure out how to get it back.

"Uh oh. Looks like they lost the ball again. My brother always throws it way too high," Pippa studied her younger brother in the group.

"Pippa! Come here!" One called to her from the huddle.

"No, Tyson! It's too bad," she answered.

"Aww. C'mon Pippa… Samantha! Samantha! Will you come here?" he called next.

"Don't go. Just because he likes you doesn't mean you have to go," Pippa said to her friend.

Instead, the gang of boys came running over to where the girls sat in the grass. They were perspiring from their active game with wet hair clinging to their ruddy foreheads. The girls wrinkled their noses in disdain as they squinted up at them, shielding their eyes from the sun.

"I told you not to throw the ball so hard," Pippa scolded her brother in her best know-it-all voice.

"I know that, Smarty Pants, so shut up," Tyson snapped. "You're not my mother."

"You know what Mrs. Farrow said to everybody about losing another ball. She said that this would be the third time this week and we won't get another one."

"I *know!*" Tyson countered as he glared at her and set his jaw.

Samantha sat up straight. "I can go get it for you."

"You can?" Tyson and the other boys were encouraged.

"Samantha, you'll get in trouble if the teachers see you," Moira said.

Samantha glanced at the teachers who were still engrossed in their discussion. They probably wouldn't even notice that she was gone.

"I'll be really quick. You keep an eye out and let me know if the teachers are coming," she said.

She rose and when she did the others gathered around her in a loose escort to the fence, throwing glances over their shoulders to see if any of the teachers were alerted. The children all knew that Samantha shouldn't be doing what she was doing, but they were thrilled by the danger of it all. When she got to the field entrance in the fence, she slipped out. Some members of the party gasped at how boldly she had entered such perilous territory. If she were caught, she would surely wind up in the principal's office and her parents would be called. She might even be expelled. The word passed through the group like a small wildfire.

Samantha scanned the blacktop before her. The ball was nowhere in sight. She looked back at the others. Some of the children were clinging to the chain link and calling for her return in loud anxious whispers, others were pointing toward a large old car that was parked across the street. Taking a deep breath, she decided to continue. She was so close to getting the ball and getting back unseen. Her heart was pounding, yet she felt emboldened and proud by her daring mission.

A minivan turned the corner down the block and was coming toward her. She scampered to the sidewalk and ducked behind the old car out of sight. The minivan passed by. Her classmates cheered quietly. Others begged her to come back, looking like prisoners gripping the chain link. The girl got down on her knees and peered under the car to spy the gym ball that rested against the curb. Fishing it out, she grasped it and stood up.

"Samantha? Is that you?"

Samantha turned toward the sound of the voice. A petite child, she was barely tall enough to see into the vehicle. It startled her to see that its windows were rolled down. Why hadn't she noticed that before? A man was seated in the front seat and he knew her name. Was he going to tell her teachers?

"Samantha, that *is* you. My, you have grown so much! When I last saw you, you were only about this high," the man said in a friendly way while hovering his hand about a foot off the seat.

The car looked vaguely familiar to the child although she didn't know why. The man speaking to her, she had never seen before. At least she couldn't recall if she had. He was wearing a baseball cap and dark glasses and had a beard. But he was talking the same way some of her aunts and uncles who only saw her at Thanksgiving did and he looked old like them too. So maybe he was a relative?

"Come closer. Don't you recognize your Uncle T.J.? I'm your daddy's long lost brother and I've been away on a trip, but I've come back. In fact, your daddy asked me to come to your school and pick you up today. We are all going out for some pizza and ice cream and he thought it would be a nice surprise if I picked you up since I haven't seen you since you were a baby. Do you like ice cream?"

Samantha nodded. But her feet remained glued to the sidewalk. A stirring started deep in the pit of her stomach and her breath quickened.

"It's okay. I got a note right here from your dad. It's for the office to tell your teachers that I'm here to pick you up." He unfolded a piece of paper he had lifted off the seat and she could see it was written in long hand. She couldn't read long hand like the big kids in fourth grade, but she knew her mom and dad could read and write like that too and always sent notes to her teacher written that way.

"So climb on in and we'll go around to the front office to sign you out, okay? That way you won't get in trouble if your teachers see you returning back through the fence. In fact, I think one is coming out right now, so hop in." Uncle T.J. smiled congenially. "Hurry. You don't want to get caught," he chuckled as he leaned over and opened the door.

Samantha took one last look at the playground. Mrs. Farrow was on her way toward the cluster of kids at the fence looking out. Despite the churning in her stomach, she quickly hopped in.

"You don't have a booster seat. Mommy says I always have to be in my booster seat before we drive," she observed.

"We're just going around to the front of the school, pumpkin. It'll be fine. I have one in the trunk and I'll take it out when we get there."

"But I'm supposed to be in—"

"Uh oh! Here comes your teacher. Quick, duck down, so she won't see you or else you'll get into big trouble."

Out of fear of being caught, Samantha did as she was told. Uncle T.J. started the car, put it in gear, and drove away.

Samantha felt the weight of his heavy hand rest upon her head. His palm was moist and smelled funny. She felt a little afraid to move with it pinning her down against the vinyl seat. She stared at the dashboard in front of her and noticed that the radio's knobs were broken. The man said nothing more as he turned the corner, pulled over, and stopped. He lifted his hand off her head, then reached down past her and retrieved something from under the seat.

"Are we there yet?" she asked.

Just as she sat up, he quickly held a cloth tight against her nose and mouth. Instinctively, she panicked and pushed and screamed, but her cries were muffled. She choked on the sweet smelling fumes coming from the cloth, but he held her firm. In a few moments more, her cries lessened as her limbs grew weak. The radio with the cracked knobs grew fuzzy and out of focus and slowly faded to black.

‡　‡　‡

Mrs. Farrow approached the group of children clinging to the fence. They had made such a commotion that she was forced to leave her discussion with the others to come and investigate. It was one of the reasons she hated playground duty—never a chance catch up on her grading or with her colleagues. She looked beyond them and glanced at the car driving off down the street. She wasn't cognizant that it was the same one that had been returning everyday for the past three days to park across the street from the schoolyard at recess time. It had also escaped the notice of the three playground teachers that the bearded man in the driver seat sat with the windows rolled down, his eyes fixed on the young moving bodies that romped lithely around the field. Watching, as if he were waiting for something, or possibly someone.

"What are all of you doing hanging around the fence?"

The children turned to face her and started talking all at once.

"Wait a minute! Wait a minute. One at a time. Tyson, lower your voice and stop yelling. Moira, why are you crying? And why were all of you calling Samantha? I heard you calling her name over and over again… Wait, where *is* Samantha??" Mrs. Farrow asked with alarm. The children's voices crescendoed in frenzied excitement. More of them started to cry. Suddenly, pieces of the fractured scenario all came together to form a horrifying realization. Her eyes flew back to the street where the car once was.

"Oh dear God."

‡   ‡   ‡

Here was the one she was looking for. Holding up the faded, magenta colored snapshot, Aunt Lydia was pleased. Sitting cross-legged on the floor, she was sorting through a stack of photographs she kept stored in an old leather suitcase that had belonged to her late husband. The one she selected featured her at forty-years-old and cuddling an infant on her lap. The child had dark hair and pretty yet soulful eyes in spite of the fact that she was smiling.

"Ah, here's my Little Potatoes. She was such a darling little girl," Aunt Lydia cooed out loud.

A persistent feeling nagged her to locate the photo and as always, she validated such feelings by following through with what they wanted of her. She wasn't quite sure what it all meant yet. There were *a lot* of nagging thoughts gnawing in her head lately and they seemed to be centered on her niece. Having access to her kind of insight was a responsibility along with an obligation to do right by it. It troubled her that Mia had never returned her phone message from a few days ago. Lydia considered calling again until she reached her, but she didn't want to pester the busy couple. Besides, it had been in the middle of the night when she received that dubious yet ominous warning. *I probably just worked myself up*, she thought in retrospect.

The old psychic knew she shouldn't rush hither and thither into these scenarios. Many misinterpretations and unforgiveable mistakes were made that way. And if this particular summons should become critical in the near future and her niece needed to rely on her, she wanted to make sure they trusted her as a credible source. She felt that Dan was only being polite by not considering her a certifiable crackpot and that didn't make matters any easier.

Stretching up to reach from her position on the floor, Lydia placed the photo on her nightstand. With sentiment warming her heart as it always did whenever she looked through her photos, she continued to rummage. The pile of photographs in the suitcase were layers of time and, like an archaeologist excavating through sediment of images, she peeled back the years. Through her fingers she sifted past recent pictures of Nathan and his birth announcement. Beneath them were snapshots taken at Mia and Dan's wedding, more various shots of the couple, and next, Mia's graduation portrait. Digging deeper, she uncovered her own son's wedding photos, shots of her grown daughter with her partner, and captured moments of them both as children at numerous occasions. She had always hoped for pictures of grandbabies to be added to the collection some day, but her son and daughter had decided against raising families to pursue careers instead. *Some things are what they are,* Lydia concluded sadly.

Soon, she unearthed pictures of a short stocky man with a wide grin and laughing eyes. *Ah, my Benny.* Affection tinged with regret mingled in her heart over her late husband. *Such a sweetheart of a man.* He was funny, simple, and affable. What's more, he put up with whatever she wanted to do, never questioning her 'psychic' forays or spiritualistic aspirations. And he loved her. Oh how he loved her. She recalled the unexpected bouquets of flowers, the patient ear, and the ready shoulder to cry on. *I should've been better to him,* Lydia thought as she nodded and readjusted her reading glasses.

However, a greater regret filled her as she extracted Margaret's wedding photos, revealing the reason why she couldn't give her heart totally to Benny. A sigh escaped her lips as she studied the image of a young handsome Stephanos by her sister's side. In all her sixty-nine years, Lydia never confessed to anyone and hardly admitted to herself that she secretly was in love with her brother-in-law. He had lit up the room the way he laughed and made her feel. Stephanos was so sensitive and honest, intelligent and kind. And all of it had been wasted on Margaret.

She could not figure out what he saw in her sister. It must have just been his big heart getting in the way. Lydia was well aware that Margaret never cared for Stephanos. She had only married him for little more than convenience, giving him nothing except years of misery, frigidness, and religious fanaticism. She also knew that he was never privy to her sister's wild ways prior to their marriage.

Lydia was confident that if, instead of her sister, she had won his heart, she would have made him happy for the rest of his life. They had always found so many things to talk about and were completely at ease in each other's company. *But he married Margaret.* Just about that time, Benny came along and Lydia married him, heartbroken and knowing that Stephanos could never be hers.

Now Stephanos was gone. Lingering on his features and the soulful eyes that his daughter now bore, she sighed once again as she tenderly stroked the photo and then placed it upon the others in the suitcase and shut the lid. Anger's old burn flared up within her whenever she thought of how Margaret withheld the news of his sudden death from her. She had to find out about it inadvertently through a phone call with Mia, long after the fact. She hadn't even the opportunity to pay her last respects. Lydia always wondered if her sister secretly knew of her desire for him. *It would be just like Margaret. To squander all that she had and yet still be selfish to the very end.*

She slid the suitcase back under her bed, and rose with effort to her feet, using her bed to steady herself until the feeling came back into her knees. Trying to dispel the melancholy induced by Stephanos' image that had crowded out her nostalgia, she plucked the lone photograph she had selected off her nightstand and concentrated on her initial mission. Lydia dialed Mia's number. The answering machine came on, so she hung up. She only needed to hear her niece's voice to be comforted. At least for the time being, it would have to do.

‡　‡　‡

Dan attempted a few disinterested pecks on his keyboard, trying to enter data into a video log. Greenlee had been riding his and Hoason's asses about keeping it updated. But the technical producer's mind was elsewhere at the moment. *What would be the best way to break this to her?* he wondered. He couldn't say that she was putting Nathan in harm's way. That would be unjustified. Dan knew his wife would never endanger their son in any way. He hated to question her about what was best for the baby as she had been an exceptional mother from the very start.

Nonetheless, dread and uncertainty pervaded his thoughts. The fact that his seven-month old child was interacting with spirits, lost souls, or who knows what they were in the reflections Mia was seeing made him uncomfortable. *He* did not grow up with such chaos in his life and there was absolutely no clear reason why his son should.

Rising from his workstation, he grabbed up a few pages he needed to copy. He figured if he couldn't focus on data entry, he might as well be productive in some other way. There was always work to be done and they always seemed to be behind. Passing through the doorway, his thoughts were jarred as his shoulder inadvertently clipped the doorframe hard.

Ouch. How did that get there?

Rubbing the sore spot, he pondered how a person could perform the same task over and over again, a thousand or even a million times, his or her body going through the exact same motions. But then one day, for no good reason, they are off a hair—a fraction of an inch too low, too high, too far out. That was what got them into trouble. That was when they missed figures on a balance sheet, got into car accidents, lost their footing or… clipped their shoulders. It was an unavoidable statistical reality.

Suddenly it illuminated exactly what he had been unable to put a finger on. No matter how many times he was destined to go through these scenarios with Mia, probability would dictate that ultimately there would be those times when he would miscalculate, misjudge, or be just slightly off, resulting in some kind of predicament or worse—someone getting hurt. Last time it was his wife. This time he didn't want that someone to be their child. It was a dangerous game of roulette they were playing with these 'visits' and what frustrated him the most, there was absolutely nothing he could do about it.

Although it was an incredible moment when Seth had stood before and spoke to them in their own living room, it still was not normal. It should have been merely a fluke. *Or a freak of nature.* He certainly was not ready to accept it or the current situation with Samantha as common occurrences. By all rights and what was real, he shouldn't have to. If he did, what else would start to unravel in the fabric of his beliefs?

An hour and a half later, he arrived home after work to a quiet house. Usually, it was the highlight of his day to be greeted by his little family. Often he'd find them in the kitchen where was Mia preparing dinner and Nathan was playing nearby on the floor or in his high chair or playpen. However, there were no sign of either one of them. *Maybe they're visiting Mrs. Lopez or out for a walk,* he guessed, fighting off disappointment. Mia's car parked in the driveway suggested they couldn't be very far. *They should be back soon.* He took off his jacket, put down his messenger bag, and headed to the bedroom to change out of his work clothes.

In the dimming light of early evening, he came upon Mia and Nathan asleep on the floor next to the dressing mirror in the bedroom, his wife resting against the wall and their son sprawled out comfortably in her lap. *There they are.* His spirits brightened. Dan took a moment to take in the peaceful scene before him and had to smile. *Looks like Mr. Nat-a-tat wore them both out.*

He knelt down and studied his wife's features. She hadn't changed much since the day they met. *How did I ever get to be so damned lucky?* he pondered as he surveyed her fine nose, high cheekbones, and full lips. A few fine locks of hair had escaped from the French braids she wore to keep her hair away from the baby. To him, she was and always had been, beautiful. He felt good that his desire for her was still so strong. So many couples they knew hadn't made it past their first five years of marriage, let alone having a child. He certainly couldn't imagine any of them sticking together after what he and Mia had to endure with the Occurrence or what was in store for them next…

Dan pushed the thought aside and refocused on his wife. The top three buttons of her blouse were undone, he surmised most likely from feeding their son. He hated to wake her, but she would have to get up now if she ever wanted to sleep tonight. *Or maybe they wouldn't necessarily have to go to sleep right away,* he thought lustfully as he admired the soft curves of her breasts revealed by her open blouse. He let his finger gently caress the side of her cheek. She murmured and moved. His finger retraced its path.

Mia's eyes opened wide. She inhaled sharply and stared past him, unseeing. He had seen that look on her face before and pulled back instinctively.

"Murph, it's me. Wake up. You're okay," he quickly informed her. He dared not touch her again in any way. The last time she had awoken so startled, she wound up swinging at him.

This time, she viewed him with fleeting panic. Her expression was drawn. Visibly shaken, she looked down in her lap at their sleeping child, lightly touched his head and then returned her gaze to her husband. She held out her hand for him to come closer and when he did, she grabbed him in a fierce hug.

"Murph? What's wrong? Did something happen?" Dan asked gently as she clung to him.

She released him, but her hand remained planted on his shoulder, as if she were afraid he would disappear.

"I, I was there. I saw Samantha get abducted! He was there… in a car, just waiting for her to leave the playground. Like he had been stalking her all along! And he was so prepared—a note, chloroform—"

"What? Wait, wait. Are you sure? Couldn't it just be a dream that you were having? Something that your mind put together from everything else that is going on?" he said, trying to calm her down.

"No, Dan. I *was* there. Like I was with Seth when he thought he had killed his stepfather. And just like then, I could see everything that was going on. I felt the wind and the sun on my skin, smelled odors, and heard sounds and conversations so clearly, as if I was standing there right next to her. It's something I found out that I can do if I concentrate and if they are willing." Her eyes searched his. "I'm somehow tapping into their memory. The first time it happened was when I was at Meadowbrook. And now it just happened again."

Dan sighed inwardly. This was going in the wrong direction. Things were chaotic and surreal enough before with her just seeing these spooks in mirrors and other reflective surfaces. Now she could visit them onsite and in person? He scanned his own memory and vaguely recalled her talking about seeing Seth in the Arizona desert, but realized in his mind he had grouped the conversation and shelved it away with all the rest of the events that had transpired during her stay at the mental hospital.

Suddenly he realized that perhaps he should revisit more of those memories to make sure he wasn't overlooking something. His hand went to his shoulder where her hand was and he could still feel the bruise from where he had clipped it this afternoon. *Just a fraction of an inch off…*

Although certain that he was unconvincing, with effort he tried to be encouraging. "Okay, babe. I believe you. If you say that you were there, then you were. So, did you find out anything useful from the dream? A license plate number? A description of the car? How about the perp's name? Or even a good look at his face?"

"No. He was wearing a cap and sunglasses and he had a beard so it was hard to see his features. He was Anglo though, possibly around his late thirties? Maybe forties? I don't know. It all happened so fast. The car was old and I did not see the plates. Oh, and he referred to himself as 'Uncle T.J.' I only wish I could have seen where he took her. Damn it." Mia swore as she rubbed her temple. She looked perplexed and disorientated.

"So when you 'were there' with Seth in his dream, basically you witnessed the events in how he came to be, well, you know—I don't know any other way to put this, but… dead?"

"Well, at least leading up to his entrapment. I didn't actually see him *die*. Thank goodness for that. I don't know what I would have done if I had. The rest was bad enough. But wait, what are you getting at?"

Dan stared at the floor as if the words he was searching for were hidden within the contours of the carpet. Struggling to pose it as sensitively as possible, he faced her and asked, "What I'm getting at is, if you were able to visit there with Samantha in person like you did with Seth, does this mean that she is, too?"

Mia replied solemnly, "Yes. I believe so."

Nathan stirred in her lap and let out a small cry, as if he were troubled in his sleep as well. Within the next moment, he stirred again and woke.

"Hey there, little man. How's it going?" Dan said as he reached for their son, cuddled him, and then placed him against his shoulder. "Why don't I take care of Mr. Nat while you get yourself together. And don't worry about dinner. I was thinking that maybe we can go out tonight if you're up for it. Save you some cooking." He stood up with Nathan, then offered his hand to Mia to help her to her feet. "We can talk more about your dream and what it could mean at the restaurant. In the meantime, don't get too worked up over it. Remember, this is all new territory for you," he said reassuringly. "You still are learning what information is useful and what is not."

Over dinner, Mia carefully recounted each detail of the dream while Dan listened intently. There weren't many clues to go on or a clear direction to take. It was going to take hours or possibly days of research to make sense of where to start. The fact that his wife most likely could do it, he didn't doubt. He knew that her tenacious nature would emerge and she wouldn't let it drop until she figured it out. However, this in part, was precisely what had been troubling him all afternoon. After they tossed around a few last conclusions and speculations regarding her dream, Dan summoned courage to broach his subject with as much tact as he could muster.

"So, are you seeing Samantha now?" he glanced around at the reflective surfaces of the dining area in the Chinese restaurant.

They had been watching the baby grasp fried noodles they held out to him and maneuver them to his mouth between the spoonfuls of rice and shredded chicken Mia fed him. An old couple seated at the next table over was laughing and commenting on how cute he was.

"No, I've been checking," she held up a hand mirror she slipped out from her pocket, "but I haven't seen her since the dream this afternoon. She'll most likely be back tomorrow or before I go to bed tonight. Either way, I hope it's soon. I'm worried about her. She's probably frightened after sharing that dream with me. I know Seth was. It was like he had relived every minute of it all over again. It really took it out of him."

"And Nathan was there when you last talked with her?" Dan moved his food around with his fork.

"Yes. He usually is."

"So, what do you think he makes of all of this? I mean do you think he is cognizant of what is going on?" he asked pointedly.

Mia looked quizzically at him and wondered where his questions were headed. "I'm not sure. I don't think so. Why do you ask?"

"I don't know. He sees you talking into the mirrors all the time and interacting with your reflection. Don't you think that in his brain somewhere, he's logging it away and probably trying to figure out what Mommy is doing?"

Mia glanced at the old couple and then lowered her voice. "I don't think he can really differentiate yet between what's a reflection and what is face to face at his age. He probably just thinks that I am talking to another person like I always do—like to Jenna or Mrs. Lopez. Besides, he's seen Samantha already."

"He has?" Dan leaned forward. This was what he was afraid of. "How can you be sure?"

"It's pretty definite. He crawls up to the mirror right where she is, pats the glass and babbles to her."

"Oh." Another young family with a toddler and an infant was seated across the way from them. They appeared to be enjoying their dinner and conversation with each other. *I can bet dollars to donuts that they won't ever have to discuss <u>this</u> problem about their kids,* Dan thought as he observed them. At that moment, he envied the family.

"He thinks the world of her. You should see him carry on when she comes around. He loves giving her kisses through the glass. And Samantha is really fond of him too. It's so sweet to watch how they interact with each other. She says she had always wanted a baby brother."

"But do you think that's a good idea? You know, to let him meet, well, *these* people?"

"Oh, Samantha's just a little girl. She looks as normal as any other child he would see. I'm sure to him she's another friendly face. And don't worry—I wouldn't ever expose him to anything grisly or horrible. I mean at first, believe me, I was hesitant to involve him in any way. She just happened to show up when I was holding him. I couldn't tell if he could even see her or not. But his eyes went immediately to her and then he started holding out his hand and squirming to get closer. I thought, as long as she appears completely normal, it shouldn't make any difference. If by some remote chance he has a latent memory of her, it probably would be as if he had met her in person."

"Are you sure he isn't just seeing and interacting with his own reflection? I've seen babies do that before."

"No. I'm sure he sees her. The way he reacts to his own reflection is entirely different to the way he reacts to her."

"But why do you suppose he can see her when I and everyone else can't?"

"I'm not sure. Maybe it's because babies are such open books at this age, absorbing everything they experience. Maybe certain filters aren't in place yet. Or it could be somewhat instinctual, like the way animals can sense certain things that we cannot simply because as rational, thinking adults, we aren't letting our natural receptors do their jobs. Or maybe it's just genetics, something that he got from me. Who knows? Perhaps we should have a couple more babies and test this last theory?" she queried lightheartedly in effort to soften his darkening mood.

"Uh huh. Funny, but no." There was no hint of amusement on his face.

"I didn't think so."

They fell silent for the next few moments. On the pot shelf behind Mia stood a large ceramic cat sitting and holding one paw up in the air. It was the maneki-neko that symbolized good luck. Dan recalled seeing them when his ship made a stop in Okinawa. Peering at her from over his cup of tea, Dan pressed on, "So you think he's taken after you and will be cursed by being able to see or sense these things too, unsolicited?"

"First of all, I wouldn't necessarily consider it as being 'cursed.' I think there are far worse things that could happen in life. But I think it's impossible to tell right now if he will keep it or not. We'll just have to wait and see. Maybe he'll outgrow it as he gets older."

"Yes, but if he is constantly exposed to it will he ever outgrow it? Don't you think it is kind of like nurturing the ability or at the very least perpetuating it by encouraging it to happen?"

"Hmmm… Well all I can say is that it was never 'nurtured' or 'encouraged' with me and look where I am now."

Dan conceded and sighed. "Good point." He looked at his son, who jabbered and held out a fried noodle in his chubby fist for him to take.

"Oh look, I got a double fortune this time," Mia said upon cracking open the cookie she chose from the plate of three that had been placed on the table with the bill. "Let's see—the first one reads, 'Make serious decisions in the last few days of the month.' I wonder what that means?"

"Oh yeah? What about the second one?"

"It says, 'Make it a rule of life never to regret and never to look back.' Let's see what Nathan's says…"

She held out the plate to Dan to choose a cookie, then cracked open the remaining one.

"Hey, listen to this—'You will meet an interesting person this month.' Well guess what? I think he already has. It's strange how they hit the mark," Mia said.

"Nah. They're so general. They're written that way to apply to just about anyone at any given time," he answered skeptically. He was weary enough from having to navigate through the realm of shadow and fantasy as it was already.

"What does yours say?"

Dan opened his and held up the small slip of paper. He silently read, *May your faith always exceed your fears—no price is too great to go through life afraid.*

"C'mon. What does it say?" Mia asked again.

Dan studied the fortune one last time and then crumpled it.

"What a bunch of bull," he answered.

CHAPTER 4

Yakamura…Yakamura…

Mia's fingers flew over the keyboard, fueled by a notion of where to start fitting this puzzle together. The idea had formulated the night before while she was in the shower. It was there under the warm stream of water that many revelations and solutions to problems often came to her. This idea though, took some effort to bring to fruition the next day. Her initial search for a state highway containing the numbers 'one' and 'six' in it yielded at least fourteen different possibilities. Next, she combed through twenty-one elementary schools in the Puyallup School District. Each school had their own homepage, and many of them showed staff lists, contact pages, calendars, and photographs of smiling happy students. Mia kept hoping, in the off chance, to spot Samantha's face in the images. It was a long shot, she knew.

On the other hand, what if Dan's assertions were true? This was all new to her. It was only her second such encounter with an apparition in reflections and she was making a huge assumption in thinking that what had worked for Seth was going to work for Samantha. Who was to say whom or exactly *what* it was that she was seeing? As it was, another day had passed since the dream and when she last saw the child. Samantha had not made herself present in any way and Mia was beginning to worry. She called to her and placed out all the mirrors, keeping her eye trained on every reflective surface she passed. Still there was no sign of the seven-year-old. The last time she saw her, Samantha appeared to be very weak. Could it be that she had succumb to something and was lost? *Or perhaps… she never was?*

Focus.

The district webpage had a slideshow featuring its schools. For some inexplicable reason, one slide caught Mia's eye just as it faded to the image of the next school. Impatiently, she waited until the show looped around again. When the image filled the frame once more, she studied it—Francis L. Wainwright Elementary. Something about the school intrigued her. Clicking on the school's link opened up to its home page featuring the same photo.

Looking over the building carefully, it suddenly occurred to her that the roof shape was similar to the school in her dream with Samantha. She had only seen the back of the school from the view afforded by the schoolyard but if she recalled correctly, the brick color was the same as well. *Maybe, just maybe...*

Taking a chance, Mia clicked on the staff list. No Mrs. Yakamura was listed. She sighed, questioning her hunch. But then she noticed on the side menu a tab labeled "Nurse's Notes." Selecting it opened up to a general statement of the school nurse's care and treatment for students. Scrolling down, the content continued with the role of the school nurse, health tips for children, reminders for vaccinations, and a short blog post talking about a recent measles outbreak in the district. Just as the cursor neared the bottom, Mia's heart leapt as she read, "~ Kristi Yakamura, School Nurse, Wainwright Elementary."

Almost too excited to type, Mia continued her research by choosing the satellite feature on the online map app on her computer. The street side view offered little more than the school's front drive. However, expanding out and to the side street that bordered the back of the school, she gasped out loud as the view swung into focus. This was the school in her dream. Panning slowly across, the sight of the schoolyard, the buildings, and the fence where the children had gathered when they begged Samantha to return gave her a sick feeling.

Oh my god. This is the exact perspective the abductor in the car must have had.

Now that she had positively identified the school, Mia wracked her brain over some of the clues Samantha had told her. She returned to traffic view and zoomed out, scouring the map until she found the nearest train track. Close by was state route 162. *A sign that had a one and a six in it...* Quickly, the pieces were falling into place now and her finger danced and tapped on the track pad, eager to uncover more. Following the road northwest a few miles lead into a residential suburb and next into commerce and a higher density housing area. It obviously was not a rural setting of fields and outbuildings. *Dead end.*

Switching and going in the opposite direction while tracing the route southeast yielded more of what she was looking for. About seven miles down from where she had started, the map opened up to large undeveloped tracts of acreage where the roadways were fewer and farther between. Satellite view showed stands of trees and scattered houses. Although her hope was rising, it still was like looking for the proverbial needle in a haystack. How would she ever be able to search for what she guessed was nothing more than a tiny outbuilding in all of that below?

Mia grabbed the notebook off of the kitchen desk where it lay. Turning back the pages, she scanned her notes to reread the lines where Samantha had described the rain coming in as well as the details of her own reactions, observations, and speculations of their discussion. In one corner of a page filled with her brainstorming scribbles, she locked onto one notation her subconscious had been actively churning away on: *Samantha's sudden departure—noise, darkness?* Rechecking the dates on the calendar and recalling the recent rainy weather, suddenly it all clicked—heavy torrential rains, flooding, and… *mudslides! Now where did I just hear about mudslides?*

A sharp pop over the speaker from the baby monitor followed by a scuffling sound indicated that Nathan was starting to stir. Somewhat reluctant to leave her search she pressed on, speeding up in scrolling to find information. Another sound of movement and then Nathan letting out a burble told her she would have to retrieve him before he started to fuss. Just as she was passing through the living room on the way to the nursery, she glanced at the mirror more out of habit now instead of conscious effort. There stood Samantha. Her face was ashen and her eyes hollowed. She waved her thin arm beckoning Mia to come closer.

"Oh, honey! There you are. I've been so worried about you. What is the matter?" Mia asked as rushed to the mirror.

The little girl's lips barely moved. She was breathing in rapid pants.

"Please Sam, tell me what is wrong?"

Tears rolled down the girl's dirty cheeks as she reached out both hands to Mia, her fingers pawing the glass in desperation. Suddenly, she faded from view once more, leaving Mia with her mouth agape and palming the mirror before her, hoping to draw her back. After minutes had passed and she didn't reappear, Mia knew exactly what she had to do. She quickly packed the diaper bag, dressed Nathan, grabbed up the car keys, and left.

‡   ‡   ‡

J.J. Vanberger knew it was going to be one of those nights. She could feel it already although she was still a mile out from work. It stood to reason —the atomic clock in her kitchen displayed a full moon on its status bar and full moons usually brought out all the weirdoes. Besides, she was under enough stress from this job already. The seemingly endless suicides, failures-to-resuscitates, domestic violence calls, and assaults were really starting to get to her. There just didn't seem like much good was going on anywhere. What's more, according to her women's magazine, the swing shift hours were causing disruptions with her circadian rhythm. It was no wonder she was having trouble sleeping and her nerves were shot.

Now a full moon. Just what she needed.

Pulling into the parking lot of the 911 call center, she stared at the low concrete building nestled under the radio towers and sighed as she switched off her car. With growing dread she gathered her jacket, lunch bag, purse, and a Lexan water container that had been lovingly inscribed by her husband in encouragement to get her through these tough nights.

J.J. sighed again as she pulled open the door and entered the control room. It was like entering into a beehive of sights, sounds, and movement. Three big screen TVs on the wall featured CNN, the Weather Channel, and local news, keeping staff apprised of breaking events. Operators waited, idly at their stations lined with brightly lit consoles reading or chatting with each other, while others were intently talking into their headsets and guiding panicky callers through precise instructions. It was like walking into a warzone. At any moment's notice, it could be hours of nothing or all hell could break loose.

Four o'clock pm roll call. Most of the night shift operators wolfed down their dinners while their supervisor briefed the new shift of the day's events. A prowler had been reported in the 200 block of Amherst Avenue of Sumner and had not been apprehended. Station 51's squad had been t-boned this morning, and another new Amber Alert had been added to the current alert that was still in effect after three and a half weeks time.

It looks like it's going to be a wild one. J.J. rubbed her temples hard. The aura of an oncoming migraine flashed before her eyes and for a moment, her hearing dimmed. After quickly downing a coke from the vending machine and four tension headache aspirins, she reported to her console that had just been vacated by Marty from day shift, slumped down into the warmed armchair, donned her headset and started checking work emails. Within a half a minute, her line lit up. With one last sigh, she braced herself, pushed the button, and answered the call. *Here we go.*

"Pierce County, 911, what city is your emergency?"

"This is, umm, going to sound kind of strange but please bear with me. I'm calling in on a missing child. I think I might know where she is."

"Your name, ma'am?"

"I prefer to remain anonymous."

"Okay, I need the address of the emergency."

"I do not know the address."

"Cross streets?"

"Uh, no. I don't have that either."

"Okay. I need the city then."

"I'm not sure. It's possibly in Orting or maybe Buckley."

"Okay. I see you are calling from a Quick 'n Ready convenience store located at Webb and 211th Avenue Northwest?"

"I'm calling from a pay phone. Hold on… Yes. That's where I am."

"All right. Is the abductor still on the premises?"

"I'm not sure. I don't think so."

"All right. Anybody injured?"

"I'm not sure, but possibly."

"Are there any weapons involved?"

"I don't know. This is regarding the seven-year-old girl, Samantha Oswego, that is on the Missing Child Network."

J.J. sat up straight at the news. "Can you please hold a moment, ma'am?"

"Hold? But she needs to be located immediately!"

"Yes, I understand, but hold on the line. Do not hang up. Do you understand me? Do not hang up."

The operator hit the mute button and immediately turned to dispatch a police unit, giving them the pay phone's location and the nature of the call. She returned to the woman on the line.

"Ma'am? Are you still there?"

"Yes. Please. You need to hurry."

"Are there other children involved?"

"No. I don't think so. All I know is that Samantha is slipping away. She doesn't have much time and she's not going to hang in there much longer."

"Slipping away? Is she on some sort of ledge? Please clarify."

"No. I don't know if she... if she is alive, is what I'm saying."

"How do you know this, ma'am? Have seen the child?"

"Uh... yes. Well kind of. In a way."

"Can you be more clear, ma'am? In what way have you seen the child?"

"I, I... No, you wouldn't understand. Please listen to me. She's being held in some sort of outbuilding on a property. I believe that building has been covered by the mudslide that happened the day before last in the vicinity of Orting. There were two mudslides shown on the news. Have the police search the ones that covered some sort of outbuilding or gardening shack. Something small. They should use tracking dogs."

"Exactly what is the location of the building?"

"I said, I don't know. But I think it is completely covered with mud."

"Can you give me any road names?"

"No. I don't know what road it is on. All she knows is that a sign she saw along the way was green and white and has the numbers one and six. I think she might be somewhere close to SR 162."

"How about landmarks?"

"She said she passed by a railroad track. And there is a purple silo close by. Just have them check where the mudslides occurred."

"She told you this? Are you in contact with the child now, ma'am?"

"No."

"When did you last see the child?"

"Right before I called you."

"You saw her inside the building that was covered with mud?"

"Yes. I did see her. But not inside the building."

J.J. hit the mute button—a relief tactic the operators used to ease stress and keep calm during trying calls. "This crazy woman is making absolutely no sense!" she exclaimed out loud in frustration to no one in particular. Some of the dispatchers chuckled. Others shook their heads in empathy. She took a deep breath, hit the button again and resumed the call.

"Ma'am, you are going to have to be more specific. Did you see the child through a window or a doorway?"

"No. The building that she is in has a window that is boarded up and the door is lined with plastic around its edges and is locked from the outside. That is why she couldn't get out."

"Excuse me, ma'am, but how *exactly* did you see the child?"

There was a hesitation on the line.

"Ma'am? Are you still there?" J.J. rubbed her forehead hard. The migraine muscled its way forward past the caffeine and painkillers. It felt as if her head was being squeezed to the point in which it would explode.

"Yes, I'm here. This is going to sound unbelievable, but I am kind of a… a psychic of sorts. Samantha has been appearing to me through reflections. She tells me what she can about where she is and what is going on, but she is only a child and can't elaborate. I know it sounds crazy and I wouldn't blame you if you thought I was crazy, but what is important here is that Samantha Oswego is under a mudslide by either Orting or Buckley and you need to send the police out to search for her immediately. Please, this is *not* a crank phone call."

"Yes, ma'am. I understand. But I need to make it clear that there are criminal penalties of fines and or jail time if we find out this is a false call. Do you understand?"

"Yes, yes, I understand. And I am telling you the truth—this is not a false call. Just send someone out im—"

Silence.

"Ma'am? Ma'am? Are you still on the line?"

For the next half a minute, J.J. continued calling out over the line, hoping to resume the call, but the woman on the other side remained unresponsive. Eventually she heard a car drive up, its brakes squealing to a stop.

Next, a heavy male voice spoke up, "This is Deputy Paul Warrens, badge number 9728."

"Deputy Warrens, this is Dispatcher 333. Is the caller still there? Female, possibly in her twenties or thirties?"

"No. Was it a false call?"

"I'm not sure. She was calling in on the Missing Child Notice for Samantha Oswego. Claims she is a psychic and the girl spoke to her somehow through reflections or something like that. I already dispatched another unit to investigate the location she gave me. There wasn't much information to go on."

"I'm guessing she must be psychic all right."

"Why do you say that?"

"'Cause she seem to know that I was coming and split," Deputy Warrens chuckled. "Just left the phone sitting on the top of the counter. So Dispatcher 333, do you have a name?"

"J.J. Vanberger."

"Well J.J., it's been good talking with you. Can I help you with anything else?"

"No sir, I've done what I can do. Hope you can catch her."

"We might just do that. Have a good one. I'll be hearing you over the waves."

"Right. Be careful out there. In case you haven't noticed, it's a full moon tonight."

‡   ‡   ‡

The petite brunette picked her way carefully through the fan of mud as she clenched the microphone and stared into the camera. Looking directly at the tiny red LED that indicated that she was live and her perceived audience was watching, she reported, "Today's reunion was a joyful one as police and firefighters rescued seven-year-old Samantha Oswego from an outbuilding near Orting where she had been trapped under mud for two days from a mudslide that buried and collapsed the building.

"Samantha has been missing since April 17th when she was abducted from her schoolyard by an unknown perpetrator. The abduction triggered a massive search for the girl along with an active Amber Alert that extended over three states. The search has been ongoing—until now. The Amber Alert that has been in affect for Samantha for the last three and a half weeks since her abduction has been canceled.

"A woman who claimed to be a psychic called in an anonymous tip concerning the girl's whereabouts. The woman told the 911 operator that she had 'seen' and spoken to little Samantha through what she called 'some kind of reflection,' although she admitted to allegedly having no idea where the child was being held. Police followed clues the psychic reported the child had given her, and used tracking dogs to narrow down the location.

"The seven-year-old is dehydrated, malnourished, and suffering from mild hypothermia, but otherwise does not appear to be hurt. She has been sent to Vanguard Hospital for a more complete examination. It appears that little Samantha escaped being crushed by tons of mud and asphyxiation when a plastic bucket inside the outbuilding supported the collapsed wall and created a pocket of air where she was trapped.

"The mud is a result of the record rains the area received earlier this week, triggering mudslides here in Orting as well as in Buckley. After an hour and a half of digging in and around the collapsed building, rescuers first spied Samantha by her brightly colored rain boots."

"I saw a bright piece of sunshine in all of that muck and just reached in for it. And there she was. It's a miracle she hung in there for as long as she did," said paramedic Agustin Robles.

"Samantha's mother, Dawn Oswego, said that the boots are Samantha's favorites, and she hardly is ever without them," the reporter continued. "The suspect in Samantha's abduction is still at large and his whereabouts are unknown at this time. Police have no leads in the case and are investigating the property owners of the land where the outbuilding is located. Police are also looking for the woman who phoned in the 911 call for questioning.

Reporting live from Orting, this is Mindy Yang, Channel 2 News."

His eyebrow arched, Dan turned from the screen and looked directly at his wife. His mouth slightly open, the words he was grappling for crowded the exit to the point that none escaped.

Mia returned his gape, still feeling at a loss to explain all of this. And then the reality of what she had just accomplished struck her with a surge of amazement.

"She's *alive*? Oh my god! She's alive! I can't believe it!" she exclaimed, grasping her head.

When she had spied the police squad car approaching the phone booth outside of the convenience store, she bolted and headed straight home. All the while she was driving, she kept checking her rearview to make sure that she wasn't being followed. She had no idea of what would become of her anonymous phone call. Not wanting to be identified through her cell phone, she had mistakenly thought the call would be virtually untraceable if she used a pay phone. Once she realized this wasn't true, the remainder of the afternoon passed in fear that the authorities could track her with some kind of high tech surveillance device. Thinking of a way to explain to Dan what had transpired hadn't crossed her mind in all the excitement.

In addition, it was never her intention to be viewed as a psychic and she wondered how he would take it. She hadn't anticipated the 911 dispatcher to recount verbatim what she had said, let alone it being televised on the evening news. When it came down to it, she had never been completely certain that Samantha was even a reality, and if she were, that she would ever be found.

She's alive! The thought sunk in and ignited her. *They were able to reach her in time.* "Oh my god, Dan," was all she managed to say again, as her trembling hand went up to her mouth.

Her husband looked at the TV searching for confirmation, but all that was playing at the moment was a fast food commercial. He turned back to her while pointing to the screen.

"Okay, so *this* was Samantha? This is the one you've been seeing recently?"

"Yes! I was just talking to her this morning."

"So, she is real? And she's alive?" he asked incredulously.

Mia clasped her hands together, elated. "Yes, she is Murph! Yes she is."

"And you did that—you called 911 to report it?" Dan's expression was one in which he did not understand the punch line and was still trying to get the joke.

"I had to. Oh, you should have seen her! I was going to lose her at any moment. She was so thin and weak and I couldn't bear to let that shadow thing take her. I couldn't think of what else to do."

"Holy shi-ee-ikes!" Dan caught himself from swearing just in time, casting a furtive glance at their young son playing in his playpen nearby. "You did it Murph! You actually did it!" He laughed while he rose to embrace her. "You're unbelievable, you know that? You saved that little girl's life!"

Mia opened her arms to gladly welcome his hug and praise.

"How in heck did you even know where to look? Did she finally tell you where she was?" he asked excitedly.

"No, she couldn't really comprehend where she was. It was dark by the time they had reached the shed. I don't think she was able to think straight between being frightened out of her wits and starved for days. But she was able to tell me enough information to start piecing things together. For example, she remembered her school nurse's name. I was able to track that down to a local school here in the state. And then with this rain and the mudslides and what she was describing, I had to follow my intuition and some deductive reasoning."

"And 911 believed you?"

"Not exactly. I think the operator thought I was some kind of nut job. But I'm glad she followed through with sending out officers with tracking dogs to check the locations I gave her, including sending a cruiser out to the payphone where I was at."

"Seriously? So did you have to tell the officer how you knew where she was being held?"

Mia looked sheepish. "I didn't stick around. I totally chickened out and got out of there the minute I saw his car driving up. I didn't want to get nicked for making what they thought was a crank call. As it was, the 911 operator had advised me that if they thought this was a false call, I'd be facing fines and possible jail time. I mean what if Samantha wasn't in the location where I suggested? Or what if she wasn't real at all?"

Dan laughed and held his wife close. "Yeah, I guess it would've been hard to explain to Mr. Nat-a-tat how his mom was sent up to the Big House."

She looked into his eyes and grew serious. "I was also worried because I wasn't sure how I was going to explain this to *you*. I was taking a big gamble that this would even play out the way that it did, if at all. I had no idea that Samantha was alive. There was always something different about her, though, and I had to rely on my gut instincts this time."

"Hey, I can't argue with gut instincts. I'm sure you made one little girl and her family very happy today. Just think—Samantha is getting her chance to grow up because of you. That's really something. I'm proud of you, Murph," he said and then kissed her. "Although I have to say that you are persistent. But I guess if you weren't so stubborn, you might have given up altogether."

"So you don't mind the 'psychic' thing? It was the only way I could describe it to the operator."

"No. In this instance, you did what you had to do."

‡ ‡ ‡

Under the incandescent glow from the lamp on her nightstand, Mia clung to her blanket and stared at the ceiling, her eyes refusing to shut. She had to report to pre-op by 7:30am, so she knew she had better get some sleep, but anxiety kept her thoughts rampant. A congenital defect in her heart valve had gone undetected for the sixteen years she had been alive. *Regurgitation through the aorta, or something weird like that* was how she described it to her friends. She didn't exactly understand the doctor's explanation but she was certain it wouldn't have made her feel any better if she had.

Her condition would have been overlooked entirely had she not tried out for her high school volleyball team. She never considered herself athletic but her two best friends persuaded her to try out so they could all be on the team together. To play any school sport required a complete physical exam. So here she was.

Mia remembered how ashen her father's face was after their conference with her pediatrician. *How could it be? How could he and Margaret have overlooked this? She had always been a healthy child, never sick. Rarely ever had to see the doctor. It was what the others, her unborn brothers and sister, had died from in utero—heart defects. Why had the obstetrician declared her healthy at birth? And why hadn't anyone caught this until now?* She recalled the way her father was seated forward on the edge of his chair and the rapid-fire way he questioned the doctor. It was so uncharacteristic of the soft-spoken airplane mechanic who typically accepted everything as it came. Her mother in the meanwhile was the total opposite, pushed back in her seat with arms and legs firmly crossed in front of her. Her jaw squared rigid and unyielding, she refused to look at the doctor. For once, she was silent.

The doctor tried to reassure Stephanos that it was a fairly common condition, every nine out of a thousand births, and often an individual can go through life without it ever being discovered or becoming a problem. However for right now, from what they could tell after reviewing her MRI and ECG reports, the best course of action was to repair it while she was still young and growing. Best to err on the side of safety than have it develop into possible complications in her adulthood.

A slight rap on her bedroom door broke her concentration. Her father poked his head in. Assessing the worried expression on his daughter's face and the blanket white-knuckled in her grip, Stephanos smiled tenderly at her.

"How are you holding up, honey? I noticed your light was still on. You've got an early day tomorrow," he said.

Mia tried to manage a smile in return but her face crumpled into tears when she heard the concern in his voice. She shook her head and sniffed. When Stephanos sat at the edge of her bed, she hugged him tightly and buried her face in his sweatshirt, letting her tears flow freely.

"Is it the operation? Aww, my beautiful girl, it will be all right," he said as he held her close. "The pediatrician reassured your mom and me that this is a routine procedure and done very quickly nowadays. You'll be up and running again in no time."

"But Daddy... I'm scared."

He pulled away and looked at her, his hand cupping her chin. Looking into her large eyes, he could see her fright and fought hard to keep his own tears from coming on. It took all of his will power to cloak his own concerns so she wouldn't see them.

"Shhh, it'll be all right. I'll admit this is not something that happens every day. It's natural to be afraid and it is the unknown that scares us the most. With you being so healthy all your life, how could you—we—ever prepare for this? Tell me, what scares you the most?"

"I don't know."

"Okay, what if I tell you what scares *me* the most with this situation?"

She blew her nose in the tissue he handed her and nodded.

"What frightens the wits out of me is that this is happening to you, my precious girl. I would gladly take this all on and spare you, if only I could. I feel so helpless and yet I have to stand back and let the doctors take care of it all. And after that, the rest is up to you to heal and get better. There is nothing I can do, but watch." He held her hands. "Okay, now it's your turn. Tell me what's worrying you."

"I guess I'm scared from what Becky and Candace were saying about what happens to people when they are under anesthesia. They weren't trying to be mean—they're my best friends. But they were scared because Candace said her great aunt never woke up after surgery. And Becky said she had also heard of that happening. Someone—her friend's dad's uncle—died on the table. What if I don't wake up?" Fresh tears welled up in her eyes. "I know Mom says that if we are god-fearing, we will go to heaven. But to tell you the truth, I never really did pray in earnest when she made me. I mostly said the words so I wouldn't get into trouble. So if I don't wake up tomorrow from the anesthesia, where will I end up? Mom has also told me a lot about Hell too."

Stephanos paused for a moment, suddenly mindful of what his wife's strict dogma had done to his child over the years. He regretted that he hadn't stepped in to temper it.

"Yes, honey, there are certain risks to any surgery. However, your pediatrician and surgeon both feel that you are young and strong and should get through this with flying colors. I'm not saying that it can't ever happen to a younger person but it sounds like in those two cases, the people were older individuals. And who knows what existing conditions they had and how strong or weak their bodies were? There are so many factors to consider.

"As for Heaven, Hell, and all that might be in between, no one really knows. I'm not sure if there is anyone who can say what is there for certain. I wish I could be clearer than that, but I can't. Your mother and others like her profess those places are real. And maybe for those individuals, they are because they believe they are. But for others who don't believe… Listen, all I'm saying is no one really knows for sure. How can they?

"But I do know this—when you start feeling afraid, I want you think of love, kind of like a big warm blanket. And think of yourself wrapped up in it. There are so many people who love you and are concerned about you, including your friends, Becky and Candace. You can hold this blanket of love close and let it comfort and protect you and give you strength during times in which you feel the most afraid. Maybe this will help you to calm down enough to think clearly. All right? I hope that helps, at least a little bit?"

Mia nodded. A smile found its way past her tears. There wasn't anything that she couldn't tell her father. He always found a way to make everything better. When she hugged him, he engulfed her in a growling bear hug until giggles finally erupted.

"Steve? Does Mia need something?" Mia's mother called from the master bedroom down the hall.

"No, she's fine. Sixteen years old and she still needed some tucking in, that's all. Just a little worried about tomorrow. And whaddya know? She's not too old to be tucked in after all," he called back with a laugh in his voice.

"Tell her to stop it with all the nonsense already and get to sleep immediately. I've already said three rosaries on her behalf and the Rosary Circle will be saying more tomorrow. She's got to get up early and be rested. Lights out right now."

Father and daughter looked at each other in mock sheepishness while shaking the finger of blame at the other until they fought to keep from giggling again. Stephanos made her lie back down, pulled her blanket up to her chin, and kissed her forehead.

"Goodnight, sweetheart. I love you so don't you forget it. And your mother loves you, although it's a little harder for her to say it sometimes. I think even the ladies in the Rosary Circle are fond of you."

"I love you, Daddy, and Mom too. But I'm sorry, I can't really say the same about the ladies in the Rosary Circle. The jury is still out on that one."

"Why, you ungrateful girl," he played along and laughed again.

"Right now!" Margaret called again.

Mia looked one last time at her father and with eyes full of sincerity, whispered, "Thanks, Dad."

Stephanos winked at her and shut off the light. Within a couple of minutes, sleep caught up with her.

That time in her memory felt like ages ago as she picked up the mirrors, pages of notes, and a few of Nathan's things while tidying up the house. *How much has changed since those simple teenage years,* she thought. A mother now with a child of her own, she missed her father more than ever these days. There was so much she wished she could have shared with him.

She wondered what he would have thought of this new journey she had unwillingly been led upon. Her mother had always been very quick to squelch the numerous episodes she had experienced as a child, demanding that she pray instead. If Mia wasn't mistaken, she remembered spying her father shake his head sadly in being powerless to curb his wife's religious zeal. Now, she glanced up at the big mirror in the living room still feeling the glow of pride and satisfaction in what she had accomplished with this unnatural gift. *One soul and one life: saved. Dad would have liked that.*

Feeling vitalized, she considered everything involved in this new phase of her life so far. Success in solving the separate mysteries surrounding Seth and Samantha made her come to the conclusion that maybe she was cut out for this psychic stuff after all. Once she got used to it, it really wasn't too difficult. Weighing all the events carefully, she decided that she wouldn't mind helping some more lost souls if they should appear to her. Of course it was going to take practice and she had to admit, it initially put a strain on her marriage and personal life. But now that she had proven what she could do, Dan was even more on board with it than ever before.

In fact, she noticed that he even started to watch a popular TV show on the paranormal that featured expert ghost hunters. Before, he was entirely skeptical to the point in which he wouldn't watch anything about the genre. Now, catching up on past episodes on the Internet, he was becoming a fan and totally engrossed in the shows. So engrossed that he started to critique the team that was exploring whatever alleged haunted house they were investigating by comparing them to her and his own experiences.

"It never does that where it gets cold in only a certain section of a room. What are they talking about? It's probably just poor insulation. They don't know the difference between a draft and a visit. We never had that happen here," he criticized. Or another time he admonished, "What's with these people?" as he watched the show's hosts fiddle with gadgets, meters, and instruments to detect paranormal activity. "You don't need all of that night vision paraphernalia to see anything, Murph. You see spooks in broad daylight. Heck, I didn't even need it that time Seth made himself visible and I'm not good at this stuff like you are. I can't believe these phonies call themselves 'experts.' I mean, where did they get those titles anyway? You can run circles around them."

While Dan focused on the shows, Mia checked out books from the library on the subject. Within the pages she discovered a smorgasbord of spiritualism, voodoo, the occult, and ESP. It seemed clairvoyance was considered part esoteric and part superstition. Still another part appeared to be mainstream culture and widely accepted. Every region in the world had individuals who claimed to have extra sensory perception, throughout the history of mankind.

As she read through the various sources, her mind kept returning to the one person she knew who could make sense of all of this. Finally, while Dan was busy changing the oil in her car and Nathan was taking a nap, she had a chance to give her aunt a call.

"H-Hullo?" the old voice on the line shook a bit.

"Aunt Lydia! Hi, it's Mia. How are you?"

"Oh, I'm fine, dear. Just fine… Everything all right by you? Dan and the baby are all right?"

She sounded distracted and Mia detected a note of sadness in her aunt's normally bright voice. She wondered what was troubling her. It was typically the opposite problem where Lydia tended to talk too much.

"Yes, we're all fine. I'm sorry I didn't get to return your call. There's been a lot going on here that I'll tell you about in a moment. But how are things over there?"

"Quiet. Normal. Nothing else going on."

"Oh. Well, that's good, right?" Mia said.

No answer.

She decided to cut to the chase. Maybe Aunt Lydia would perk up with her news. "Auntie, something amazing has happened. Remember how I had helped that visiting soul, Seth? Well, it happened again—last month. This time, it was a little girl. Did you see the Amber Alerts for Samantha Oswego on the news? She's the seven-year-old that was missing for three and a half weeks?"

"Who?... Oh, no. I haven't."

"I thought all of this was over, but she started to appear to me in the mirror just like Seth had. What I didn't know was that she had been abducted from her schoolyard and then imprisoned in a garden shed. The unusual thing was I was actually able to talk with her directly just like I'm talking to you. I didn't have to use the notebook. I could hear her voice, although I still haven't been able to figure out why."

"Hmm… interesting. Yes."

"Well, Samantha gave me clues as to her whereabouts and I was able to connect with her through a dream. I didn't know it then, but the shed she was being held in was buried in a mudslide. All I felt was that I had to act fast, so I ended up calling 911 taking a chance that they could find her. And they did!"

"Oh, that's wonderful, Mia."

"But the best part was I found out that she is alive! The entire time I thought I was talking to someone in the Afterlife. I never knew I could connect like that with a living person." Mia thought that the mention of this clincher would bring her aunt around. She waited for an enthusiastic response.

However, Lydia simply replied flatly, "That's probably why you could hear her. The Living always have more energy than the Departed."

"Really? Okay, wow! Thanks, I was wondering about that. Your explanation makes perfect sense."

There was no response on the line.

"Aunt Lydia?"

"Huh? Oh, yes, I'm here, darling. Well, I better get going now. It was nice talking with you. Give my love to Dan and Nathan."

"Okay. Auntie, are you sure everything's all right?"

"What? Oh… yes. Everything is fine. Love you, bye."

She hung up the phone. Mia hit the end call button and stared at the phone's screen for a moment, a little dumbfounded and disappointed. *What was that all about?* There were so many things she wanted to ask. Typically, Lydia would have been ecstatic to discuss what had transpired with Samantha and they most likely would have spent hours on the subject. Instead, she acted as if her niece had called merely to tell her about a recipe. Mia pondered her underwhelmed reaction. *Maybe she was put out because I didn't return her call sooner?* But she knew her aunt didn't tend to be a sensitive sort.

It was possible Lydia was in one of her harmonic convergence phases again. Snippets of family discussions when Mia was younger came to mind. She recalled relatives speaking about the time Lydia dropped everything and took off to Sedona back in August of 1987 to take part in a large gathering of other convergence believers. From time to time, it was occasionally whispered about and referred to with sidelong glances and raised eyebrows at family get-togethers throughout the years.

Since the gathering, Aunt Lydia took the liberty of interpreting her own convergent phases whenever the sun, the moon, and correct planets aligned to create what she called "shifts in positive or negative energies" but with a much more personal conviction than that August event. Her phases usually required her to go into a meditative state that lasted for days. Most people, including Dan, always thought that she was just whacked out when she was in one of these moods. Mia knew differently. Lydia wasn't merely being crazy or spacey. The old spiritualist was simply doing her thing and her belief was strong.

"Hey, you gotta see this. You're not going to believe what I found." Dan interrupted her thoughts as he entered the kitchen clutching his tablet.

"I just had the strangest conversation with Aunt Lydia on the phone right now. She didn't sound herself today."

"Why doesn't that surprise me?"

"Be nice. I thought you were changing the oil in my car?"

"I finished already. It doesn't take that long. But look at this. Guess who I came across?" He zoomed up the screen and held it out to her for inspection.

It was an ad for sport therapy for children. The webpage laid bold claims to improving a young athlete's confidence, raising performance, and helping one win not only in the desired sport, but in life as well. For a brief moment, Mia recalled Seth dressed in his baseball varsity jacket. She didn't understand what Dan was getting at until she scrolled down. Instead, a photo of Gerry Monroe, her former therapist filled the screen.

"What? I don't believe it! Gerry? A *sport* therapist? You've got to be kidding me. I wonder how many kids' heads he has screwed with so far?" she exclaimed in wonderment as she studied the counselor's face. The smug smile and wide eyes were enough to make her uneasy. The last time she had seen that face was when he successfully had her committed to a mental institution.

Dan said, "Well, hopefully he doesn't feel the need to psychoanalyze any of them. I'm sure there's a parent who will lay him out with a baseball bat if he crosses that line."

"He got rid of his grey hair and he looks so different without his beard. Wow, he looks ten years younger. Unless that's an earlier photo of him."

"Probably wants to appear younger so he doesn't scare off the kids by looking like some creeper crack pot. I wonder if he still wears those god-awful ties?"

"I bet he does," she said. She scrolled down a bit more to reveal the rest of the photograph and a garish tie displaying a collage of footballs, soccer balls and baseballs. "Bingo."

"Hideous as always. The man always had incredibly bad taste," Dan remarked as he took back the tablet. He opened up another page on the Internet. "But this is what I really wanted to show you." He proudly handed her back the device.

This time the page before her featured a follow up piece on Samantha. According to the article in the online newspaper, the child and her family were happily reunited and healing while piecing their life back together after their ordeal. A photo showed her with her parents and dog in their backyard. The caption read, "Abductee Samantha Oswego is adjusting to life again with the help of parents Dawn and Peter, and best friend, Buddy."

As Mia read through it, her eyes glistened as she blinked back tears and smiled. "Look at her! I'm so happy for them. Thank you for showing this to me."

"Come here, hero," Dan said as he hugged her.

Mia looked at the article again. "Aww. It says here that she refuses to wear her rain boots anymore. She associates them with the abduction. Poor little thing. She really loved those boots."

"I got to show this to Ho. He's gonna flip," Dan said.

"Hoason? Murph, I hope you're not going around telling everyone about this?"

"What? Is there something wrong about me being proud that my wife saved someone's life? I wish I could tell the whole world about it but unfortunately I can't for obvious reasons. No. For now, it's just Ho."

"Okay," she kissed him. "That's good, because I'm not sure if I'm ready to present myself to the world as a full-fledged psychic just yet."

"Me neither."

‡   ‡   ‡

Sometime in the early morning hours, she landed upon the floor with a soft 'thunk,' her fall mitigated by the tucked in bed sheet tangled around her middle and holding her like a sling. Tossing and turning so much in her sleep resulted in her falling out of her bed. Exasperated, she clapped her hands and instantly the sound activated switch turned her nightstand lamp on, causing her to squint in the sudden light. As her eyes adjusted to the glare, she and young Mia drifted down off the nightstand as the photo she had found earlier landed on the floor beside her.

It was undeniably a sign.

Lydia determined there and then that she must go to them. There was just no taking a chance with this one. The past couple of nights had been spent in fitful sleep since her niece's phone call. Mia sounded so innocent and enthusiastic about her growing psychic abilities and Lydia was extremely proud of her and the fact that she was embracing her talent. However, she couldn't possibly share her joy remembering the ominous message the tarots spoke of. If she didn't go to guide her, there was no telling what Mia might stumble into and provoke.

As she piled clothes into a suitcase that had been dragged off a closet shelf and now lie open on her unmade bed, Lydia made a mental list of all she had to do in preparation for this trip. Jacqueline, her apprentice, would have to be contacted to feed the dozen or so cats that roamed in and around the house, water the herbs, and fill any orders coming in. She also had to cancel her appointments for three herbal remedies, the séance with Mrs. Sills, and the two purifications she was scheduled to perform later this week.

And she would have to drive, not wanting to risk any more blood clots in her legs from the long flight cross country. She consulted her twenty-three year old road atlas for mileage and drive time to chart her route. Her '63 Chevy Impala had a full tank of gas and good tires. It was hard to decide exactly what she thought she would need in the way of equipment. Unable to choose amongst her implements, she scooped them all into her satchel and hung her mother's amulet around her neck. In a food hamper, she packed a half loaf of bread alongside some homemade peanut butter, four apples, a bag of potato chips, a small wedge of cheese, and at the last moment, included a bottle of Merlot.

Forty-five minutes later, after waking Jacqueline, posting a note on her front door telling her neighbor she would be out of town, putting a key under the mat, and setting her answering machine, she hugged each of her thirteen cats. Last she lit a stick of sandalwood and sage to purify her car and to mitigate any negative forces.

Aunt Lydia was ready to go.

CHAPTER 5

Perusing the webpage, she was disappointed to see there were no worthwhile assignments posted on the freelancer's site. Nor were there any emails containing project offers waiting in her inbox or responses to her article proposals. Mia sighed. It looked like the household budget was going to be tighter at least for this week and possibly for the entire month. She could never tell how it would play out.

In reality, solving the clues that led to Samantha's rescue also took away valuable editing and project hunting time that she had so little to afford after Nathan's needs were met. Dan's promotion to technical producer gave them just enough extra income to allow her to stay home. Doing any more than just getting by would take her bringing in additional income. As Nathan grew older, they knew their expenses would rise once he was school age.

And they were also hoping to have a little brother or sister for him within a year…

She sighed once more and shook her head. After her miscarriage, they were encouraged once she found out she could carry a baby to full term. How would they ever be able to afford to have another now? Mia glanced at Nathan gnawing contently on his teething ring. He dropped it to nibble on his bear next. The baby was built like Dan and sturdy as he sat upright on a blanket on the floor, his back straight, and his baby belly rounding out above his outstretched legs.

It occurred to Mia that while he was engaged, she should sneak out for a quick bathroom break. Nowadays, she had to take the opportunity when it was granted her. Surveying the room, everything was safely out of reach from him and the front door was locked. Mia placed a few more of his favorite toys closer to him in arm's reach and then sprinted down the hall calling over her shoulder, "Mommy will be back in just a minute!"

When she returned, she could hear Nathan laughing hearty chuckles followed by squeals of delight. She was eager to see what he found so amusing. Upon entering the room, she spied a black fluid shape curve its way around Nathan's side and out of sight. Her heart froze. A shock coursed through her body as her memory flashed to that evil presence that had tried to claim Seth, its inky, liquid motion permanently etched in her mind. Mia gasped, flew to the infant's side, and clutched him protectively.

Just then, Diablo showed himself as he sauntered out from behind Nathan and meowed. His narrow yellow eyes in his flat face were hard upon her.

"Diablo, what—? How did you get in here? Who let you in?" Mia stammered in puzzlement. Bewildered, she picked up Nathan and held him close, looking about the room. She could have sworn the door was closed and locked before she had left.

The large cat circled her legs and let out another plaintive yowl. With the baby in her arms, Mia first checked the back door and next the garage door. Finding them closed, she systematically went through each room searching for the cat's access. Finally, she found an open nursery window. She recalled cracking it to air out the room after emptying the diaper pail for the service this morning. Diablo must have found the open window and squeezed in through the gap. Although there was no reasonable explanation, the seemingly innocent incident bothered her, making her feel paranoid. She shut the window and latched it tight, feeling unsettled. Her notion of Nathan's safety had been compromised.

Returning to the living room, she placed Nathan back on his blanket, scooped up the complaining cat, opened the front door, and placed him outside. Closing the door and turning toward her son she said, "Okay Mr. Nat, Kitty went bye-bye."

The little boy raised his baby hand to grasp the air in a gesture of waving good-bye. The sweet sight was enough to disarm her and chase away her anxiety.

"That's right! Are you waving bye-bye? Yes, Old Diablo had to go home." She sat down beside him and gazed lovingly at him as she stroked his fine dark hair and then kissed the top of his head. "And what do you have here, honey-pot?" In his other hand, Nathan was holding a soft cloth book full of various textures. He crumpled the book and started gumming it. "Oh, you love your present from Auntie Jenna? Let's read it and then it will be time for some lunch."

Folding herself around her son, she opened the book and pointing to the cover began, "Baby's Book of What Do I See?.... I turn the page and what do I see? I see two fuzzy squirrels sitting in the tree."

Nathan grew intent on the colorful images in the book and the lilt to his mother's voice. He patted the soft texture on the squirrels as she continued to read.

"I turn the page, and what do I see? I see a shiny lock and a golden key… I turn the page and what do I see? I see a yellow duckling, soft as can be… I turn the page and what do I see…?" She opened the book to the last page to reveal a reflective square. "I see a baby, looking back at me."

Just as Nathan grabbed the book and took it to his mouth to give kisses to his reflection, Mia gasped and pulled it away from her son, for on the shiny square a strange man's face stared back at them. Within the next second, the face was gone. She studied the square to see her own distorted image in the soft plastic. Mia closed and reopened the book as if somehow there was something wrong with the book itself.

When she rose to her feet, she verified that the image she saw was real. A man was present in the mirror in her living room.

His brooding appearance was startling, generating an instant chill within her. She had grown accustomed to seeing the teenager Seth or little Samantha, but never expected to see a mature adult. And an ordinary looking one at that. With a serious expression on his face, he viewed her blankly as if trying to comprehend not only who she was but also how he got there. Mia instinctively picked up Nathan and placed him in his playpen away from the mirror, her paranoia returning in full force.

The visitor had light brown hair that was combed over in an unassuming way, a hawk-like prominent nose, and square chin with a crooked cleft. He was lanky in build, and stood over six feet tall. Mia placed his age somewhere in his late thirties. His most striking feature was his large elliptic grey eyes that stared unabashedly at her, accentuated by the dark rings that outlined them against his pale complexion. He did not look visibly frightened or in distress or horrible. Instead he said nothing, while viewing her with the same interest he would a piece of merchandise in a store window. What was even more unusual was that his clothes appeared to be wet. If she wasn't mistaken, there were a few tree needles scattered through his hair and on his jacket.

"Hello?" she queried, feeling as if she were questioning a person on her television, since he made no move to communicate.

He didn't respond, but instead his eyes inspected her from head to toe, then the baby, and then the room. When he turned his head, she noticed a strange discoloration below and behind his left ear.

"Can I help you with something?" she asked, not knowing what else to say. "My name is Mia."

The specter in the reflection studied her one last time and then vanished, leaving Mia feeling even more disconcerted than before. Her involvement with these unwelcomed apparitions had suddenly taken a strange twist. The possibility of dealing with an adult had never occurred to her. One thing was helping a scared child in distress. Another was an ominous looking man showing up unexpectedly. That uneasy feeling reminiscent of long ago seeped in once again making her feel jumpy at all reflections. Her living room he had just surveyed suddenly felt intruded upon, as if she had stumbled upon a prowler in her home, her privacy violated. She began to immediately question her earlier thought of becoming a psychic.

Maybe she wasn't cut out for this after all.

‡   ‡   ‡

"That is just friggin' awesome! She's got the chops, Dan. Real skills," Hoason said, admiring the article that had just been shown him. "How does she do it? She's two for two so far."

The friends were eating a late lunch in the break room at Pryus Productions after a morning-long video conference with their clients. Unless either was out, they hadn't missed a lunch together since they started work at Pryus on the same day five years ago. Since no one else was around, Dan decided it was safe enough to bring the article out.

"I don't know Ho, I wish I could tell you. I think she's pretty amazing myself," Dan said proudly.

"What's weird is that this is all new, right? I don't remember you ever mentioning her doing this before."

"Nah uh. All new, since Seth showed up."

"So is there anything special that she does? Like go into a trance? Or does she need candles or an Ouija board or things like that to summon them?"

"Nope. They just appear to her out of nowhere. Mia didn't even need the notebook with Sam to communicate this time. She could hear her speaking outright. It was trippin'." Dan said as he unwrapped his sandwich and peeked between the slices of French bread. He noted the roast beef piled high, Monterey jack, a dollop of mayo, lettuce, and a dab of pesto. Mia had prepared it just the way he liked it. He didn't like to recall that troubling time almost two years ago when she could barely get herself out of bed in the morning or remember to buy groceries. Things had continually improved since then. *Maybe she does have a handle on this psychic stuff now*, he thought with a degree of reassurance.

"Whoa! So none of that freaky backward writing like last time?" Ho poked around his anemic microwave meal of stuffed green pepper with his fork. He paused for a moment to covet Dan's hearty sandwich, a hungry look on his face.

"Nope."

"Now that's tight. That's *real* psychic ability. Anymore, you have all these posers out there saying that they're *feeling* this and they're *sensing* that. And here's Mia—the spirits come right out and talk to her direct. My granny would've gone ape shit invoking the Ancestors every two minutes if she had those skills."

"Yeah, it's something else. I'm still getting used to it myself," Dan answered between bites.

"So is she going to bank on this?"

"What? No. I don't think so. So far this is only the second time it's happened. Who knows if it's going to continue? And if it did, I don't see how she could make a living off of doing this."

"Are you serious?" Ho asked, astounded at his friend's lack of vision. His eyebrow was cocked and his fork halted mid-air en route to his mouth. "There are millions of people who would pay her beaucoup to talk to their dead relatives. Or how about cops that need help with cases? Or both? She could work as one of those police psychics by day and moonlight in channeling people's relatives during her off hours. She could be raking it in. What's even better is she could mentally link with them while they're still alive, like she just did with that little girl. Imagine what emergency services could do with something like that? Earthquake victims, kids falling down wells, people who are lost. That kid she helped last, Seth? He sure could've used some help while he was still alive." Making his point, he popped a piece of soggy pepper into his mouth and chewed smugly.

"You know, I never considered it," Dan admitted.

"You should. Not only that, you could film the events as they happen just like they do in all of those shows and maybe a cable channel will pick it up.

Or you could get some monster hits on the Net and start your own series that would lead to advertising royalties. It would be better than any of those other psychic shows because it's the real deal. She could become famous and you could run your own production company. You should give it some serious thought and talk it over with Mia. Speaking of which, would you mind if I come over to check it all out?"

"Check what out? I've seen what happens and let me tell you, there's not much to see. Mia talks to the mirror and that's about it. There's nothing there but any ordinary reflection you would typically see. It's not like the kid appears or jumps out or anything. Then she talks some more to the mirror and waits. And it's not just mirrors. She claims they show up on whatever shiny thing they want—spoons, pots—stuff like that. But you still can't see them. Only she can, so it's just like listening to a one-sided conversation like you'd hear from someone talking on the phone. That's about it," he said with a shrug and took another bite from his sandwich.

"Yeah, but I still think it would be awesome to see."

"Seriously? Why?"

"'Cause the kid she is talking to is right there, *in the room*. Just because we can't see anything doesn't mean that he, she, or it isn't there. And obviously he, she, or it is."

"Huh. I never thought of it that way. I guess you're right," Dan answered. "But there isn't anyone in the mirror right now. Samantha is home with her parents."

"Ah, you say *right now*. But who knows by tomorrow, right?"

Although Dan wasn't all together comfortable with Mia's increasing involvement into the 'netherworld,' Ho made him think of possibilities he had never imagined. If she could make a go of this professionally, they might be able to get their finances stabilized—pay off the car, credit cards, and afford a second child. If it really took off, they could possibly pay off the house and stick some money away in a college fund for the kids. *Why not?* Maybe if he would just embrace this thing, it could open a whole new world for them. And she didn't seem to mind doing it.

But before Ho could continue, Dan decided to change the subject. He needed time to digest the possibilities without his friend barraging him with even more questions and considerations. If he knew Ho at all, he would never give it up. "Hey, getting back to the real world, did you get that email from Mark? We need to review the timecodes again for that last segment of the documentary. Something is off with the audio. Not by much, but enough. And the director wants to make even more changes and Greenlee's approved it. That's going to push back post production another three more weeks if we're not on top of it."

"You're shitting me." Ho kept his eye on the tangerine he was peeling for dessert. "What does Bloomberg want now? First of all, it's a documentary on irrigation practices. No matter how we edit it, it's still BORING. But that doc is damned near perfect and he wants to screw with it some more? I can't figure it out—first he wants one thing and when he finally gets it, then he wants to scrap it all and go back to the way it was? Sounds like some people are never satisfied."

"Nope, my friend. I suppose some people are not," Dan answered.

‡ ‡ ‡

It was all very shocking. Of all places, she had never expected to see him here in her hospital, let alone on her floor. Nothing short of a bizarre twist, one of the very many people she had encountered in life was suddenly lying before her, out of context, time, and place. It took almost a full minute for recognition to sink in. As his unconscious face registered in her cognition, she realized it *was* him—Mr. Talbot Bradford, her career counselor from the Croft Institute of Professional Medicine where she had received her Certified Nursing Assistant degree. He was one of the few men she knew who had actually changed her life for the better.

"Oh my goodness. What are you doing here, Talbot?" she asked him quietly, her voice clouded with concern. It was a rhetorical question that had escaped her thoughts past her lips. She had seen his name on the patient roster under the new admits when she started her shift. Of course she couldn't be sure then it was *her* Talbot Bradford, necessarily, and had prayed that it wasn't. Hospitals, especially big hospitals, had their fair share of duplicate names, no matter how unique the name was. But as she examined the features on his swollen face, she knew there was no mistake—it was, indeed, him. What troubled her more was his diagnosis: brain trauma.

Bailey Hague paused for a moment to make sure no one was about to enter the room before she pulled up his blankets and gently tucked them about him. As she went through her routine of checking vitals, noting the fluid level on his IV, and emptying his urine drainage bag, she worked at keeping her mounting fear in check. In her experience in the ICU, head injuries were some of the worse.

It really was terrible what had happened to him. *Car accident. Unconsciousness. Prognosis of a persistent coma state.* There were already notes of a feeding tube being inserted within the next few days.

She knew she had to leave to give Mrs. Hastings in 342 a sponge bath next, and she was running behind schedule as it was. Jerome had called in sick again, so she had to help cover his shift. The nurses were keeping a sharp eye out for any mistakes by the certified nursing staff. Seems the whole floor got pegged because of Jerome's goof up with the charts. No wonder he called in sick.

Still, Bailey lingered on, studying the man before her. She recalled the many times she had sat across his desk from him at the career counseling center at the institute. He was always so patient and genuinely interested not only in her progress and achievements, but in her problems at home being a single mother as well.

She remembered how she felt when they had first met. In contrast to the men she dealt with, Talbot was polite and kind, always saying please and thank you. He never forgot who she was and always greeted her by name. Bailey wasn't memorable to most people with her dowdy figure, plain features, and mousy demeanor. The majority of her life was spent in being overlooked or forgotten. Yet every time she had entered the career center, he made it a point to ask her how her day was going. He remembered the small details about her. And before she left, he would ask her about her two daughters and son, and if she was having any problems getting her financial aid.

She liked men refined like that. Not like her exes who were loud, ill mannered, with a tendency to hit. Nope, Bailey Hague was not going to make that mistake again. She had put up with that mess for the past twelve years combined—seven years with the first husband and then five years with the second. Neither she nor her kids needed that again in their lives.

There was also something uncomplicated about Talbot Bradford. He seemed to not only know exactly what to ask, but when, and he never complained or demanded. He was very precise in everything he did. She remembered the hours he spent with her in filling out financial aid paperwork, explaining program requirements, and enrolling her in classes. Even after she was fully settled into her program, he would always find time to talk with her about her progress when she would pop in to say hello. He assisted her through all the career portals on the computers and helped her in deciding between being a dental hygienist or a nursing assistant. Heck, she barely knew how to use a computer, let alone choose a career. *Bailey,* she remembered him saying, *you have too much compassion not to share it with others.* Under the warmth of his approval, she realized she was cut out for nursing work.

Mostly, his directed guidance enabled her to find her freedom, away from abusive marriages into steady employment where she could finally make it on her own. Although money was tight especially with the large student loan she took out for schooling at the for-profit institute, she was extremely proud to be independent.

Bailey hoped that he would awake to notice how tidy she made his room or the smiley faces she drew on the status whiteboard next to her name when she was on shift. It was hard to pull off any additional pleasantries without drawing the attention—and ire—of the RNs. Bailey certainly didn't want them to think she was playing favorites among the patients.

By the end of the week, Talbot continued to lay there unmoving. Bailey thought it unusual that with such a grim prognosis, no family or friends came in to see him. He was such a sweet man; there must be tons of people worried sick about him. She wondered if any next of kin had been located and notified and made a mental note to ask the others if they had seen anyone visit. In the meantime, she smoothed back his hair and softly clucked her tongue in pity, trying to ward off the overwhelming sadness she felt for him.

‡　‡　‡

A breeze from nowhere swept through, rippling the endless prairie grass. As far as Lydia could see in any direction, it was at least a hundred miles of brilliant blue upon sun washed green. A perfect balance of sky upon earth, with only the thin line of horizon squeezed between. If she squinted against the noonday sun she could make out a lonely co-op way out yonder, its towering cylinders reduced to looking like miniature organ pipes at this distance. The co-ops were ubiquitous; there always seemed to be at least one teetering on the horizon in this state and usually planted close to a sizeable town. But which co-op was which?

Lydia climbed back into her car and rolled down the windows to catch the breeze. She knew she had pushed the old car too hard. And from the headache that pounded her skull from within, she had pushed herself too hard as well. She remembered the days when she and Benny would go on round-the-clock road trips, stopping only for gas and bathroom breaks. As long as he had his coffee and she, her herbal tea, they would switch off and drive for hours soaking up the country that rolled past their windows. With a sigh, she realized just how long ago that was.

She started out the trip feeling confident that she could make Washington state within forty-eight hours. She had traveled through Pennsylvania with ease, stopping to stay the night in Columbus. However, by yesterday, she made it only as far as St. Louis before having to call it quits for the day, her legs feeling crampy and her tailbone aching. This morning, she rallied after breakfast, ready to cover more miles but somewhere past Topeka, she was filled with the imminent need to detour around a negative energy force she sensed without a doubt was up ahead. As a result she inadvertently found herself off the Interstate on a stretch of state highway that gave a good impression of a lonely farm road.

Just when she thought she had successfully dodged impending doom, the acrid smell of something burning flooded her car, followed by a heavy clunking sound and shimmy when the car moved through its gears. When she put the pedal to the floor the engine revved, but the old classic wouldn't engage. She barely managed to coast it to the side of the road. Although the engine hummed, the car refused to move, much like a worn out lame horse awaiting a bullet to put it out of its misery. It was now obvious what the negative energy force was that she had sensed. Unfortunately, she could never pinpoint exactly when, where, and how they would occur.

So she sat. A car sped by but was going too fast for her to flag it down. Twenty-five minutes later, a pickup truck drove past going in the opposite direction with the same results. It was apparent that nobody was curious enough about a single woman sitting on the side of the road in an old car.

"Isn't anybody in this state concerned about karma?" she muttered out loud. She suddenly remembered to try her cell phone but there was no signal.

With nothing else to do but wait, Lydia resorted to daydreaming as her eyes fell upon the photo of Mia and her that she had propped up within the contours of the car's massive dashboard. Her mind wandered back to the conversation that had precipitated right before that moment was captured. They were in her sister's kitchen, almost thirty years ago to the day next week.

"I've tried to understand it, Lydia, but I can't. I just can't. It doesn't make any sense."

"Stop trying to make sense of it. It is what it is."

"I don't like being frightened all the time. I never know where and when it will happen again. I just know this is a result of my days of sinning."

"Oh, it's not that. You're being ridiculous. We both know that you more than likely took after Mother."

"But what is the point of having this if it does me no good at all? I can't use it to see my babies. And I can't use it to know if… if…"

"If what? Randall is here? With you right now? I know that's what you are getting at."

"It's unnatural. It's a curse—"

"A curse? Don't be a fool. It's only a curse because you chose it to be. Why do you continue to seek out Randall? Let him rest in peace, already. You have Stephanos. He's with you. And your baby—this darling, beautiful little girl right here, right now. I don't know how you can turn a blind eye to every blessing bestowed to you, Margaret. That's the real sin."

Margaret looked doubtful and opened her mouth to argue, but her ear caught the sound of her husband opening the front door in the foyer. "I hear Steve. Not a word of this to him, Lydia. Promise me. I've never told him about this or Randall and I don't intend to."

Just then, Stephanos Pappas walked into the room carrying a box and looking excited. Lydia perked up and smiled prettily.

"There are my girls. Hello everyone!"

Stopping to kiss Margaret in greeting, she only offered him her cheek. His spirits undeterred by the gesture, he turned instead to his sister-in-law who was holding his baby daughter on her lap. "Lydia! So good to see you again. How are you doing? And how's my little one?" He embraced them both in a warm hug and then kissed the top of Mia's head.

"It's good to see you too," Lydia beamed.

"I just saw Bobby and Evelyn talking with the kids next door. I can't believe how much they have grown! Bobby's almost as tall as I am. And Evelyn is turning out to be a real head-turner."

"Why thank you, Stephanos. In no time, little Mia here is going to catch up with her cousins. She has gotten so big since the last time I saw her."

"And how's Benny? Is he here?"

"Benny's doing well, thanks. He's in Atlanta for a convention this week, but I'll let him know you asked about him. My, you look excited about something."

"I just got this new camera. Benny would love it. Here, let me load it and I'll try it out on you three."

Margaret eyed it skeptically and said, "Seems like a waste of money. Our old camera works just fine."

"Yes, but this one works better. And I want to be able to capture our little girl before she is all grown up. Here, let me get you with your Auntie." He tapped Mia on her chin to get her to look up and then stepped back, centering up the shot. Lydia straightened up and smiled, holding up one of Mia's hands in greeting. The flash went off.

Now by the roadside, Lydia looked at the photo and rested her hand upon her throat. She was a bit surprised to feel her heart still beating fast at the memory of how near Stephanos was to her that day. She closed her eyes and recalled the smell of his aftershave and the warmth of his cheek.

Yes. Margaret was a fool indeed.

Just then a toot from a truck horn followed by a squeal and *psh!* from air brakes startled her back into the present. The semi-truck cab came to stop a few feet behind her bumper, settling down with the rattle of an idling diesel engine. Lydia peered up first in her rearview and then out her window. A short, burly man climbed down out of the rig and approached.

"Is everything all right here, ma'am?" the driver asked, tipping the bill of his cap.

"Oh, thank you so much for stopping. My car has broken down and I can't get it to go."

"Well, that can't be good now can it? You're not going to get very far like that. I can take a look at it if you want. But if I can't fix it, would you like a lift into town?"

"That would be wonderful," Lydia answered. "I'm so glad you stopped. Out of all the people who passed by, you have been the only one. I've been broken down here for close to an hour already and was beginning to wonder if anyone believed in compassion or karma anymore."

The truck driver paused for a moment, puzzled by her statement. "Oh… right. Well, I know a world more about compression than any compassion, and if you'll just pop your hood, we'll see if there's a problem with your, eh, 'car-ma,'" he chuckled good-naturedly.

"You're looking too close," she said.

"Huh? What?" Ho glanced up. His nose was almost touching the glass.

"You don't need to be that close to see him, if you are going to see him."

Dan was changing Nathan's diaper in the nursery and Mia had just entered the living room carrying drinks and dessert to find their guest scrutinizing the mirror. Embarrassed at being caught, Hoason grinned sheepishly. He thought he'd try scrying after dinner, having read up on the ancient practice before he came. Knowing that spirits actually frequented this house, he figured he stood a pretty good chance of seeing one for himself.

"What happens in this case is not the same as mirror gazing, just in case you want to know."

He nodded. "Yeah… Wait—I was just wondering that—you must've read my mind. Wow, you're good."

"No," she laughed, "I don't know what Dan's been telling you, but I'm really not."

"Sure you are! Seriously, you're the real deal, not some phony. There are millions of people, including myself, who would be all over this like ants on candy. I would love to be able to do what you do. I have read tons on the subject and tried a few times, but so far, zip. In fact, I'm working on something myself and was wondering if you could possibly help me out?"

"Really? What is it?" Mia was surprised at Ho's admission. She had no idea of his interest in clairvoyance, let alone that he was currently practicing. This was a different side to his usual cocky nature.

"It's some kind of sequence that's been running through my head, like it's calling me to act upon something and quickly, too. I know if I can just make it out, it will lead to all sorts of change. Big change, as a matter of fact."

"Really? What kind of seq—"

"Wait, just hear me out. Now, you and I have always been square with each other ever since Dan and I started at Pryus, right? I mean, I like to think that I really have your back and you really have mine?"

Mia looked at him quizzically. This sounded serious. "Yes, of course. So will you tell me what's up already?"

"Okay, six numbers that have been stuck in my head are 15, 22, 6, 12, 32, and 24. Now if I were to ask you, what are the first six numbers that come to YOUR mind, what would you say?"

"Six numbers? Hmmm… 17, 2… 28, 31, 5, and… 4. Why?"

"Uh huh. Okay, that's good. Actually they're quite important," he answered as he wrote them down. Then he folded the paper and carefully tucked it into his shirt pocket. "Thanks a million, Mia. Well, let's hope one hundred twenty-five million to be exact."

"What? What are you talking about?" she asked, thoroughly confused.

"I'll be seeing you later," he said as he grabbed his jacket. "I have to go buy a lottery ticket!" He flashed an impish grin and then burst out laughing, unable to contain the joke any longer.

Mia gasped and her eyes opened wide. "What? Oooh, I should've known." Laughing, she grabbed up a throw pillow and swatted him with it, launching a fit of giggles between them. "You planned that all along, didn't you? And I played right into your hands."

"They've got to be winners since I got them from a psychic, right? It's time for some *big change* all right! Oh yeah!" He clapped his hands together and rubbed them briskly.

Dan entered the room with Nathan in his arms just in time to catch their antics. It was like the good old days when Ho used to visit on a regular basis before all of their troubles had started.

"Let me guess—he asked you for lottery numbers? He's been busting at the seams all day waiting to pull that one on you," he joined in. "Next he'll be asking you to forecast his love life."

"Hey, if I hit the jackpot, I won't have to worry about any forecast. The ladies will be throwing themselves at me." Ho's eyes danced with mirth.

"Yeah, more like the faster ones will be throwing the slower ones in your path to block your advance!" Dan howled.

As he and Hoason continued to laugh and joke, Mia suddenly felt odd. Her spine crawled and a feeling of dread pervaded her thoughts. There was a faint scent in the room that was unfamiliar to her. When she glanced at the mirror, her laughter faded to silence and her smile quickly disappeared.

"He's here, guys," she said in a low voice.

Her husband and friend instantly quieted when they realized what her gaze was fixed upon.

"Seriously?" Ho asked amazed. He glanced all around the room as if he expected someone to materialize in person. Then he looked back at the mirror and squinted hard, forcing his eyes to scan for minute details in the reflection before him. "Holy shit."

"Hey, watch your mouth, will you?" Dan said, shooting him a dirty look as he tried to cover Nathan's ears by cradling the baby's head to his chest.

"Hello again. I'm Mia, and this is my husband Dan, our son Nathan, and our friend, Hoason," Mia said to her reflection.

Ho looked at Dan. Dan shrugged in reply and then returned his attention to Mia as he jiggled the baby in nervous anticipation. Mia had forewarned him that it was a grown man that was appearing now.

"What? O-Okay. Yes..." Mia nodded.

Dan remembered the notebook and scooped it up to give to her. She waved it away. "Thanks, hon. I won't need it. I can hear him too," she said quietly, her eyes never leaving the mirror. Dan felt that something was up by her solemn expression. He couldn't help but worry if this really was a good direction to be going in.

"No. I don't know how this is happening… Excuse me…? Yes, this is my living room we're in."

Hoason followed the one-sided conversation like a tennis match, his eyes toggling between the woman and the mirror.

"No, I don't know why it's so dark… Can you tell me where you are… What? The day? It's Friday, April 11th. No, wait—" Mia held up her hand. After another second, she lowered it. Then she turned to Dan and Ho. "He's gone."

Ho plunked himself down on the floor and stared straight ahead. "Whoa. That was intense," he said.

"Are you okay?" Dan asked Mia, coming to her side.

"I could hear him but his voice is so strange, kind of garbled-like. The pitch is all over the place. And he seemed out of it. Not as bad as Seth was at first, but still out of it."

"That was friggin' awesome. It was like a movie or something," Ho continued to comment to no one in particular.

"Is he going to return?" Dan asked.

"I think so—more than likely," Mia replied. Her fingers massaged her forehead as she felt a headache coming on. "And he has this really weird mark, I don't know. I guess more of a discoloration, right here, under his ear. Like a really deep bruise." She touched the side of her neck.

"When is he coming back?"

"I'm not sure. He didn't say. But probably very soon. This is the second time that he's reached out and this time he talked."

"Oh," was all Dan could respond. He grew pensive and continued to jiggle Nathan who was starting to nod off.

"Wow, Mia. That was tight. Damn, when I think about it, we should have been recording. You're very fortunate to have the ability to do this. I know I would feel lucky if I could," Ho said, the playful voice now replaced by one of respect.

"Yes, I guess I am," was all she could answer. But she was the one in most need of convincing.

"Do you know why I'm here?"

"Not exactly. I hardly understand how it works myself. All I can tell you is that you are not the first person to show up to me this way. How do you feel?"

"Okay, I guess, given the fact that I have no idea where I am. What time is it?"

It was the next morning and the stranger stood before her in the living room mirror. He appeared as he had the last two times before—his face set and expressionless, his demeanor abrupt. Mia had barely seen Dan off to work when he materialized. She hadn't expected him to start showing up so early.

"It's half past seven."

"Well, do you know how long I am going to be here? And what is that noise?"

"Noise?" Mia listened for a moment. Her house was quiet at this time of the morning and most of the neighbors had already left for work.

"That constant beeping sound. It's maddening."

"I'm not sure what you are hearing. Unfortunately, I don't know how long you are going to be there."

"So who are you anyway? And can you get me out of here?" he asked.

The man in the reflection studied his surroundings. If she wasn't mistaken, he was starting to look agitated. She proceeded with caution.

"I told you last night that my name is Mia. And for some reason I am not entirely sure of, I've been chosen to help individuals who are 'lost' to find their way. I don't know why I've been chosen or who or what chose me. But it seems that whenever someone is on the side of the reflection you are on, they cannot find their way out on their own. That much I have determined. And as far as getting you out of there, I can't make any promises that I will be able to do it, but I will definitely try my best. It's going to take some time to get down to the bottom of why you are there."

"Great," he answered sullenly. "My father always used that expression, 'Get down to the bottom' of things. Basically it meant that he had no clue of what to do."

"Well, how about we start with your name?"

"I don't remember it," the apparition replied. "It's ludicrous. I can remember a dog I had when I was five, but I can't remember my own name. What in blazes is that noise?"

"Okay, so what should I call you until you remember it?" Mia flipped open the notebook to a clean page. She waited, pen poised to start taking notes.

"How about John? You know, like in John Doe. That should be good enough."

"All right, John. Can you describe where you are? Are you in any kind of room?"

"I don't have the slightest clue where I am. It's pitch black all around me except for where I can see out to your room. That's the only light I have. Now and then an extremely bright light appears for a second or so, and then it goes away."

"But when you are not appearing here, where do you go?"

"There's no where to go. And my limbs feel funny. I can move them, but they don't feel right. Sluggish. I don't know...." He flexed his arm while clenching and releasing his fist.

"What I mean is when you are not appearing to me, what is happening on that side?"

"Nothing. The light fades away and I am in the dark again. I don't know. It's like I'm being held here."

"Being held by someone or something?"

"No. Not necessarily. I just can't get out. There are no walls or doors or anything. Just blackness. It's like being, what was it—'lost'? As you put it."

Mia took notes, trying to be as systematic as possible. "Can you control when you appear or not?"

"Sometimes I can. When I think about it, I guess." His eyes followed her writing.

"Do you know your address or where you live?"

"Of course I know where I live. I just don't remember it at the moment. And while we're at it, I can save you some time—I can't recall my phone number, or my birth date, or social security number, or if I am married, or any other obvious identifiers. Don't you think I would've told you already if I had? What I do remember is fishing by a waterhole, hot, sunny, must be July of '85."

"Excuse me?" Mia said, confused by this change in his discourse.

"That's what I remember."

"All right then, can you recall what the last thing you were doing before you got there?"

John simply stared at her, as if he couldn't believe the question.

Mia caught his look. She redirected, "How about small things? Anything at all. Sometimes the smallest unrelated clues help. That is how I helped the others. They told me whatever they could remember and eventually we figured things out."

"You really want to know? I remember a large tree in a yard somewhere. I remember my mother's Singer sewing machine. I remember a pocketknife with a pearl handle that I got for my twelfth birthday. I remember our '73 Ford Fairlane, green with a black top. I remember a dead cat that I found floating down a creek. Is any of this helping? Why is it so warm in here?" John tugged at his collar.

"Well there's not much more I can do except to keep asking questions. There's bound to be something that we come upon that will help eventually."

She tried hard to summon pity for him over his plight, but she couldn't. There was something endearing about both Seth and Samantha that made Mia's heart reach out to them. Helping them to be free of their imprisonment proved to be incredible experiences and quite rewarding for her. Ten minutes into this conversation was enough to determine that for some inexplicable reason, it wasn't going to be the same with John.

In fact, Mia's strongest instinct told her to distance herself from him immediately. He would be a person she probably would avoid if they ever met on the street, although she didn't understand why. However, she knew that it wouldn't be right to forsake him. He seemed to be harmless enough, and although he was impatient, it wasn't intolerable. She, on this side, had the power to help him and felt a sense of obligation to stick it out.

Just then she heard Nathan stirring. "That's my son. I've got to go get him. I'll be back in a minute."

"But wait, don't you want to go another round of Twenty Questions? I'm just warming up."

"Hold on."

"No really, I'm getting quite good at it."

When she came back a few minutes later, the stranger was gone. Although she knew she shouldn't feel that way, she found his absence was a relief.

‡ ‡ ‡

Spanky's was bustling as regulars stopped in for the lunchtime break. A steady buzz of conversation mingled in concert with the sizzling grill, ringing counter bell, and orders called back to the kitchen. When Lydia entered, however, she noted an obvious three-second silence on her behalf. The citizens of Beauford, Kansas seated at the lunch counter were not used to many visitors passing through their small town of four hundred twenty-three souls. A new face was a novelty and it usually generated at least a few seconds of contemplation and sizing up.

Lydia took note of the dilapidated hostess sign missing a few letters and standing crookedly by the entrance that read 'Pl ase S at Yourse f.' She accepted this as an invitation to find a booth by the window. Her appetite was stirring but she sought out the diner more so because there wasn't much else to do in the town that was comprised of only one main street. At the garage, a mechanic named Stoney told her that if he was lucky, it would take the rest of the afternoon to drop the transmission out of her car. From there, it would most likely take another couple of days to track down an old transmission that fit it, then another few days to ship it and install. If all went well, she might be back on the road by the middle of next week. In the meantime, she checked in at the Coombs Family Bed and Breakfast, which she found was little more than a ramshackle farmhouse with an empty bedroom for rent.

A husky waitress with a faded uniform and hair swept up in a French twist approached her table. Her open expression and under-bite smile set in a square jaw appeared friendly.

"Good afternoon! My name is Deb and I'll be your server. What can I get for you, hon?" she said politely. "Our special today is a Monte Cristo sandwich with fries and a pickle for $5.50."

Aunt Lydia was reading the yellowed menu trapped under the pane of glass covering the tabletop. With her reading glasses perched at the end of her nose, she looked up to view the waitress. "Thank you but I think I'll just take the chicken sandwich. Oh and a cup of coffee please, with a little cream and sugar."

"Coming right up," said Deb.

Within minutes a young woman came in from the parking lot and glanced around the eatery until she spied Lydia. As she approached, Lydia observed that she appeared to be a younger version of the waitress—the same square features and heavyset body.

"Uh, excuse me, ma'am. I'm sorry to bother you but Stoney told me that you might be here."

"Yes? Is there something wrong with my car?"

"No ma'am. He's working on it right now. Stoney's my neighbor's cousin and I hope you don't mind but he told me that you were a real psychic."

"I prefer to be called a spiritual guide but some people consider me a psychic."

"Well, I was wondering if you could... if you would tell my future for me? I would so appreciate it." She was a little breathless and her expression was bright with excitement as if she was attempting something daring.

A few heads raised in their direction at her request along with some eyebrows. It was apparent their conversation had suddenly become the focal point of interest in the diner.

Lydia let out a soft easy laugh. "I can try. Please, have a seat."

Upon the invitation, the young woman eagerly slid into the booth. "Really? Oh this is so exciting. I've never had my future told to me before. And there is so much I want to know. I've never even met an actual psychic before either," she gushed.

"Well, how about we start with your name? I'm Lydia Castaneda," Lydia said, extending her hand.

The woman shook it happily. "Pleased to meet you, Ms. Castaneda. My name is Krystal Mudd. But people just call me Krys. Krys with a 'y'."

"It's a pleasure to meet you, Krys. Before we begin, I want you to know that I can't tell your *exact* future with specific dates or names, but I can instead give you some clues as to what it holds for you. Do you understand?"

"Huh? Yes. That's perfectly okay with me. How much do you charge? And will you take a check?" Krys asked, digging about in her purse.

"No charge. I am not doing anything right now anyway. I guess you can say that technically I am on vacation. So Krys, how can I help you?"

"Why, that is so sweet of you to do this for me, Ms. Castaneda. Anything would be wonderful. Anything at all."

"Well, what would you like to know? Let me get out my tarot cards—"

Krys thrust out her hands, extending her stocky fingers. "Can you read palms? I've always wanted my palms read."

"Uh, all right. Sure, I can read your palms. It's just that my tarot cards—"

"Are you talking about those playing cards that have all the strange pictures on them instead of numbers and suits? My friend Angie has some of those. She tried to read our fortunes back in high school except she wasn't a professional psychic like you. Now I don't want to offend or anything but the pictures on those cards gave me the willies. And none of the fortunes Angie told came true. Except for Jared winning the Lotto. The cards said he would find wealth in his future but he only won twenty dollars.

"No, I'd rather put my trust in something I understand and know, like my own hands. And I can look at them any time I want and remember what you said."

Lydia studied her for a moment. There was something friendly and honest about the enthusiastic young woman and the spiritualist liked her. She adjusted her reading glasses.

"Okay, let me see your palms," she said, reaching out.

Krys giggled with delight and offered her hands. Lydia grasped one and then the other and examined them closely. Her finger tracing the crooked lines arching through the valleys of the girl's meaty hands, she murmured soft 'uh huhs' and 'ahs' at its discoveries.

"What do you see? Anything good? I can't believe I am doing this."

"Umm… huh. Very interesting… Yes." Lydia continued her analysis.

"What is it? Oh lookit—I'm getting chicken bumps already," Krys exclaimed holding out her free arm for inspection.

"Okay, see this line here right in the middle? It's called the Line of Head and it tells me that you are an imaginative person. Am I right?"

"Ohh, yes. I've been told that by my teachers and my mother."

"All right, and I also see that you are someone with a strong will."

"You can tell *that*?"

"Yes, right here—by the length of your will to the length of your logic on your thumbs." Lydia pointed to the young woman's thumbs that were sectioned by the dividing line of the joint. "This section represents your will," she said tapping a thumb pad. "And this section represents logic." She indicated the base of the thumb. "Whichever is the longer section is the most dominant."

"Well, I'll be…" Krys blushed lightly and smiled. "I guess I've been told that too. Especially by a certain someone I know."

"And may I ask, are you well off now?"

"What do you mean?"

"This," Lydia pointed to the crease running center in the woman's palm. "Your Line of Fate is very defined. Do you have money or were you born into money?"

Krys snorted, "Us Mudds with money? That's like a hen with teeth. No, ma'am, never."

"Well then, it indicates that you will come into money or a career somewhere in your life. Also, according to your Line of Marriage, it seems that you are or will be deeply in love and will have a long happy marriage as well. That is, if you are not already."

"No, I'm not. At least not yet." She closed her hands and withdrew from Lydia's hold. "But that's all I need to know!"

"Are you sure? There's still a lot more there."

Krys grinned and then pumped Lydia's hand. "I'm good. In fact, I'm more than good. Thank you so much, Ms. Castaneda. I've got to go now. There's a phone call I've got to make."

"All right then. It was very nice talking with you, Krys," Lydia said.

"Likewise—oh you'll never know how likewise," Krys laughed as she stood up. Without another word, she left.

Lydia's eyes followed her out to the front of the diner where she watched her dial her cell phone. Krys talked intently for a few minutes. Then suddenly she let out a booming "YES!! Oh yes!" The patrons in the diner turned and stood to stare at her unusual outburst.

The young woman then faced the big glass windows of Spanky's and laughing, shook two enthusiastic thumbs up in the air. Looking back at her, Deb responded with whoop of joy and clasping her hands together above her head, shook them in triumph.

She turned to Lydia. "You just made my sister a very, *very* happy woman. You've seen that big tractor dealership up on SR4? Her fiancé owns that and is the second wealthiest man in Wabaunsee County. And by the looks of it, he just asked her to marry him."

Lydia opened her mouth wide with surprise. "How lovely! But I didn't have anything to do with that. I just read her palm, that's all."

"Well, she wouldn't have called him to ask him to make up his mind unless she felt absolutely positive that it was going to turn out right. Her fiancé, Ed Shaughnessy, is not the easiest guy to pin down. And Krys' been fretting this for months now."

Lydia laughed, cocked her head, and softly said, "Is that so? Well what do you know…" Then she pointed to an item on the menu. "I'm so happy for your sister. Say, do you have any peach cobbler? I feel like celebrating. I think I'll have some while I'm waiting on my order."

"One peach cobbler coming right up. And after what you did, it's on the house," Deb said happily.

At the start of her journey west, the older woman couldn't suppress the nagging feeling that she wasn't going to be much help to her niece once she got there, despite her being summoned to aid by the powers in place. But as she spooned the sweet and tangy peaches into her mouth, a sense of satisfaction washed over her. She now felt confident that she could actually contribute and quite possibly guide Mia through the inevitable ordeal that lay ahead. She caught the patrons in the diner pointing at her and nodding their heads in approval.

Yep, this old psychic's still got it, Lydia thought with a sly smile.

‡ ‡ ‡

Dan knew the business card for the audio engineer was hiding somewhere in his wallet. His boss, Mr. Greenlee, wanted a top of the line sound guy for a big project coming up in August, and Dan had just the person in mind. Ravi Duvvoori was not only a personal friend and Navy mate who served with him for six years of his eight, but also a genius in audio.

He rummaged around in the wallet's folds and unable to locate the card, decided to empty it of its contents. Amidst receipts, discount cards, and credit cards, he came across a photo that he carried of Mia and Nathan. It was taken at the hospital when their son was only an hour old. Mia was cradling him in her arms, and although she was exhausted from the delivery, she looked absolutely radiant with happiness. Dan took a moment to savor the image. The woman before him could be absent-minded, impetuous, and downright stubborn at times causing him worry and frustration. However, she was also sweet, smart, loving and kind, and he adored her. And now, Nathan—he never imagined his life could be so full. Looking at the two he held most dear brought to mind just how quickly things could change in such a short period of time.

His thoughts went back to that Sunday afternoon when she gave him the first clue signaling the impending shift in their life together. It was one of those wild weather days that hosted rain, fast moving clouds, and sun breaks alternating with showers. The day dawned soggy and grey applauded by claps of thunder. For a brief interval, the sun broke through although it continued to pour. The result was a dazzling display of light and water.

He and Mia stepped out onto the porch to witness the magical moment of the sun shower, warmed by the light and each other's company. Recently there had been bleak periods when he feared she would never surface from her intense depression brought on by her father's death followed by a devastating miscarriage. In addition, the harrowing events they had just been through with Seth's visitations had been brutal on her and he often worried if they had taken their toll.

Now his wife's smile was as bright as the raindrops that shimmered through the air illuminated by the sun's rays. Mia always found beauty in the simplest of events and she was so delighted at the spectacle that Dan had the overwhelming desire to hold her close. It was good to see her enjoy life once more.

She turned and encircling her arms around his neck, gazed lovingly at him. He found himself lost in her dark eyes that never failed to captivate.

"Hey there," she said and then kissed him.

"Have I ever told you just how happy you make me?" he asked her.

"I believe you have but I never grow tired of hearing it."

"And how I am still so very much in love with you?"

"Mmmm, that's nice too," she said dreamily.

"And have I ever told you how complete you have made my life?" he continued.

"Yes, Murph. Yes you have. But are you sure that it's complete?"

"I think so. We have our house, our health, our jobs, each other, this moment. I can't think of a single thing that could make it any more perfect."

"Oh, I can think of something."

"Oh yeah? What?"

She had been waiting for that exact opening. Then she simply said, "Hello, Daddy," and smiled.

It took a few seconds for her meaning to register. When it did, his eyes opened wide. "Daddy?" he asked in amazement.

She nodded and grinned.

He threw his head back and laughed out loud with joy. "YES!" he exclaimed. Then he hugged his wife tight and swung her around. She laughed with him, the sound of her voice as bright as the sunlit raindrops that fell around them. Their lives had never been the same since, only better.

Dan took one last look at the photograph then carefully tucked it back into his wallet. He and Mia had worked so hard past the setbacks, grief, and terror to regain their equilibrium. He recalled his days serving in the Gulf when a single belief got him through the worst times. He promised himself then that if he made it back home, he was going to find the girl of his dreams and they would start a family. Now that his promise was realized, he wasn't about to let anything or anyone jeopardize that.

‡ ‡ ‡

It had followed her most of the morning. The feeling persisted through breakfast and while dropping the kids off at school. It occupied her during her commute and as she worked her daily rotation in and out of patients' rooms.

She couldn't stop thinking about his calm demeanor, his voice, and the tilt to his head when he was pleased. Bailey sighed. Try as she might, she could not get Talbot to leave her thoughts. Her mind filled with memories of every occasion they had spent time together. If only she hadn't been married to Neville at the time, she might have pursued a relationship with the silent man who lay before her. So for now, she made every attempt to make sure he was the first patient she tended to on shift and the last one she saw before she left.

He should have been getting better. At least that's what his initial prognosis had predicted. Instead he was getting worse. Day after day he slept on, unmoving and unresponsive for almost two and a half weeks. She held his hand and talked quietly to him while stroking his hair or arm in hopes that something was getting through. She had heard of many cases that supported the fact that comatose patients could hear and notice when someone was in the room. She was also aware of recent research suggesting that patients fared better if they knew someone was around who truly cared for them.

Ultimately, Bailey envisioned him awakening to recognize she was the one who had hung in there attentively caring for him all along. When he was alone with not one person to visit or worry over him, she was concerned and vigilant. And when he finally regained consciousness and heard her speak, somewhere in his subconscious he would seek her reassuring voice that kept him company during these long hours when the others only centered on grim outcomes, failing test results, and despair.

Then maybe, just maybe, he would really look at her not as a student or a nursing assistant, but as a person… who loved him.

It was a dangerous thought and Bailey tried to evict it from her head. She knew exactly what her mother would say if she ever found out—that she was crazy and always putting herself out like a doormat for everyone to walk all over. That she had three children to look after and she should not be wasting her time on ineffectual men. Worse yet, she could only imagine what a ruckus her mother would raise if she ever found out that her daughter had fallen in love with a man—*while he was in a coma*. She would never hear the end of it with all the ribbing, criticism, judgments, and insults.

Maybe it was crazy but she knew what she felt. He was worth it. He was different than anyone she had ever known and if she only had another chance with him under normal circumstances, she knew she would be proven right. It had taken this accident to make her realize what she never thought was possible before. Analyzing her reactions, Bailey knew now that she had had feelings for him back when she was attending class. He always seemed so unobtainable then to a nobody like her. This coma, while unfortunate, had acted as a leveler in a sense, giving her the ability to assist *him*. Now that the tables were turned, she finally could permit herself to love him. In the meantime, she prayed over him and wished with all her might that he would recover. Not only to rouse from his deep sleep, but also to consider her a person who was loving and worthy of his love in return.

Chapter 7

"There's something I'm just not getting here. Who exactly were the 'others,' and how did you help them?" John asked Mia the next day. When he appeared in her bathroom mirror, he found her clad only in her bra and panties and scrambling to put her clothes on. It was a mistake on her part—clearly it was time to take the glass down or cover it up again. Yet somehow, she couldn't help but feel his timing was suspect. With a bit of embarrassment mixed with annoyance, she left for the living room, forcing him to follow her there.

"So, as I was saying—" he started when he caught up with her.

"The first was a teenager named Seth," Mia answered, cutting him off before he repeated the question. It appeared that this predicament was boiling down to a control issue and she didn't like him being able to demand whatever he wanted at will. "He lost his life in a mineshaft, but his soul couldn't rest until the murder of his stepfather was resolved. Seth mistakenly thought he had killed him, when he hadn't. He suffered from some amnesia, much like you. I helped him by figuring out who he was and what had happened."

"I see." John raised an eyebrow. "So you're saying that he was some kind of ghost? Some specter rattling his chains in unrest and all of that?" he asked skeptically.

"Well, not exactly, but he wasn't alive anymore. It's kinda hard to explain."

"And specifically, in what way did you assist him by merely identifying him? I'm still unclear about that," John persisted.

"By sorting out all the events leading up to his death, his soul was released from… well, um, his soul was allowed to continue on its journey and not be left in a state of uncertainty." Mia shifted uncomfortably in her chair. The miraculous events that had occurred in aiding Seth suddenly sounded odd and unbelievable as she retold them.

"So obviously you believe in Heaven, Hell, Purgatory, and Limbo," John said.

"I was taught them. I can't say exactly where Seth was headed, but I knew it wasn't good." She felt she had to be very careful to hedge her answers.

"And you believe you were granted this power to save souls from eternal damnation?"

"I didn't say that. I can only tell you about my experience. It's not for me to determine what is damnation or not," she replied matter-of-factly.

John's eyes narrowed. "Then how do you know that you actually 'helped' him? Perhaps he descended into Hell just the same despite your assistance."

"All I can say is that he appeared to me to be a lot better off after our experience together."

"'Wherefore let him that thinketh he standeth take heed lest he fall.'"

"Excuse me?" Mia asked perplexed by his statement.

"1 Corinthians 10:12. Surely you should know this if you learned about Heaven and Hell."

Mia could only blink in silence at this strange man. Why did she feel the need to defend her position to him? She wished that he would stop interrogating her and treating her as if she were an adversary.

"And what about the second individual? What was your role in 'helping' that one?"

"Well, that was an entirely different situation. Samantha is a seven-year-old that had been abducted and locked in an outbuilding, left to die. She was alive when we made contact, but she was in a very desperate situation."

"Alive and abducted? How unusual. And what did you do for her?" He looked up with interest.

"She gave me enough clues that eventually I was able to pinpoint her general location and send the police to search for her. I'm satisfied to say that she was rescued and reunited with her family. The other day my husband shared an article on her that he found regarding her recovery."

John fell silent for a few moments as if he were contemplating something. It was extremely hard for Mia to get a read on him.

She continued, "It was a very rewarding experience for me to be able to help her like that."

He snapped to, his eyes riveting back on her. "Oh, I'm sure it was." Then he asked, "Could Seth tell whether he was alive or not?"

"I don't know. It wasn't discussed and I didn't ask him directly. Why?"

"I can't tell whether I am or not. However, if I'm stuck here with no way to get out, I'm as good as dead now, aren't I?"

"That's why I'm trying to help you in whatever way I can."

If she weren't mistaken, John's face bore an eerie smirk. "Well, we'll just have to see about that, won't we?" In the next instant, he vanished.

Mia inhaled sharply, the rush of air into her lungs bringing a fresh relief. It was then that she realized she had been holding back her breath.

‡　‡　‡

The darkness of the surroundings was so complete and total it enveloped the senses as if a velvet shroud had been placed over the world. The only things that pierced through the black were the sharp call of an occasional night bird or the lonely horn of the train echoing in the distance. Adding to the solitude was an icy penetrating to the bone cold that froze everything in the midnight air.

A lone figure emerged from the modest house, silhouetted against a burning bright rectangle of doorway illuminated from within. Although the figure was odd-shaped, appearing to be plagued with some sort of hunchback, he moved with graceful ease and his frame stood erect. Within a few moments, one could make out that the figure did not have a hunchback at all, but instead was carrying a bundle on his shoulder. Puffs of exhaled air streamed from his nostrils like an ancient beast.

There was no moon and he carried no flashlight. He had no need for one, as he was comfortable and confident in the darkness, his feet familiar with the path having traversed it throughout a lifetime. He knew exactly how many footsteps it would take to get to where he was headed. The fabric of the sky was studded with white stars that shone brilliantly in the crisp air. It was a lovely night.

He paused to pick up a shovel that was propped against a tree between a garden rake, a leaf rake and a snow shovel. He knew the tool simply by the feel of its well-worn wooden handle and hoped that it and the other tools wouldn't get ruined being stored temporarily out in the weather. Whistling a tune that billowed out in small clouds past his lips, he continued through the rambling yard with the bundle and shovel, past the garage and the tiny garden shed. He was headed towards the area he liked to call "The Lower Forty" at the edge of the twenty-acre property.

When the solitary figure arrived at a stand of the trees no longer within view of the house, he veered off the path. He let his feet lead him to a place where the ground was soft and the undergrowth had been recently dug up before. When he arrived at what felt was the right spot, he laid the bundle down and rummaged around in his barn jacket for the penlight he stowed in its deep pockets. A lot of light would disturb the endless perfection of the darkness. He needed just enough to make sure he didn't forget anything.

He put his boot to the shovel's shoulder and sunk the blade deep into the loamy earth. Exposed and vulnerable, a few night crawlers the length of a ruler wriggled about in the newly made hole. The man whistled slowly in admiration as he gently picked them up one by one, examining their length and girth. He slipped them into his jacket pocket, knowing they would make irresistible bait for hunting birds.

With patience and care not to break taproots and damage stems, and with intention to return them to their places when he was done, he removed every plant and shrub within a tidy three by five foot rectangle. Next, he really put his foot to the shovel and dug hard. Within an hour or so he was up to his chest. He paused to wipe his brow and let his breath escape into the frigid night air. Taking the penlight and shining it about his handiwork, he settled, knowing it was good enough.

After placing the light down carefully at the edge of the hole so it wouldn't fall in, he stretched toward the bundle that was within his grasp. Catching a couple of fingertips on the coarse material, he inched it toward himself until he got a fistful. Then he gave it a forceful tug.

The end of the bundle came undone. As he gave another tug he became aware that the fabric was caught on something. He pulled again but it would not give way. Muttering under his breath, he shone the penlight once more along either side of the bundle to see what was the hold up.

The thin beam of light crept across the folds in the burlap sack until it spotlighted a smooth long object just barely out of view. He sighed with impatience then clamping the light in his teeth, hoisted himself out of the hole. Light in hand again, he examined the bundle once more. He quickly saw what was holding everything up.

Clucking his tongue softly, he removed the sack from around the base of the fern where it had gotten snagged on a knobby tree root. He let the penlight play across the ground to double check that all was intact. The light cast a dim circle on a small upturned hand with chipped pink and yellow polish showing gaily on chewed fingernails. The light searched beyond until he spied what he knew was missing. He located the fuzzy teddy bear, a few inches from where it had escaped its owner's grasp, its beaded eyes staring blankly into the ground. The figure snatched up the toy and returned it to its place in the hand. Then he cinched the sack up tight and double knotted it to make certain it wouldn't come undone again.

On his feet, he easily lifted the bundle one last time and with casual release, dropped it into the hole. He paused for only a few moments more before he took up the shovel and returned the dirt back to where it had come. After another twenty minutes or so, he worked at returning the uprooted plants to their places. Within no time, the area looked virtually undisturbed. If it rained, as predicted for the next few days in the weather forecast, it should erase all traces of activity in this spot. His work done, he set off toward the house, shovel on his shoulder, and continuing to whistle his tune through the night.

Seeing something next to her in the dark, Mia fought to stifle her alarm. Within a few seconds she made out the shape of her husband. Her clock told her that they had only been asleep for a couple of hours. She struggled to quiet her agitation and erase the fear that had set within her.

A nightmare.

What could have caused such a vivid parade of sinister images? *The hole dug out in the forest late at night. The child's hand falling out of the sack.* The figure—she wished she could have seen his face—but it was too dark. It wasn't long ago that bad dreams had plagued her, leaving her anxious and terrorized. She had to learn to take them for what they were and nothing more. She had certainly seen much worse in her conscious state, although she doubted that she would ever get used any of it.

Her mind systematically reviewed the day's events. Nothing shocking there—pretty much their normal routine. She and Dan hadn't even watched TV before bed, both more interested in playing with Nathan and catching up on each other's day instead. She recalled something she had read about dreams being nothing more than a recombination of a person's perceptions and associations assembled, catalogued, and played through the brain while sleeping. However, that held little comfort when she recounted the grisly scene etched in her memory.

A nightmare... Or was it?

The vividness of this terrifying dream was reminiscent of when she witnessed firsthand the events surrounding Seth's and Samantha's predicaments. *Sights, sounds, temperature...* It was all there, before her once again, which led her to wonder—was she really dreaming or was she connecting somehow with her newest visitor? *But that isn't possible,* she concluded. *Or is it?*

She reached for the hand mirror on her nightstand. Not wanting to disturb Dan, she used the light of her cell phone to look into the mirror. John was not present. *A bad dream. That's all it was...* Given the nightmare's murderous context and horrifying implications, she surely hoped so. While John was unpleasant to work with, she hardly believed he could possibly be responsible for the death of a child, let alone the methodical and callous concealment of a body in a dark forest on a moonless night.

Just then a thought struck her—*perhaps he is the victim of a similar tragedy?* Maybe it was the connection she was seeking and the dream could shed some light on his imprisonment. She would have to ponder the details in depth tomorrow. *That is, if it is something more than my own imagination....*

As Mia lay there letting her terror subside, the rustlings of Nathan in his crib across the hallway redirected her attention, followed by a whimper and then slowly crescendoed to a cry. He was hungry. Dan stirred beside her. Robotically without saying anything, he fumbled in the dark to pull back the blanket and in response to the baby's cry, started to rise half asleep.

"I got him, Murph. It's okay. Go back to sleep," Mia patted him.

"Huh?... Are you sure?" he murmured drowsily.

She kissed his cheek. "Yes, I'm sure. Now go back to sleep."

Dan settled back down with a mumbled, "All right." Within seconds he was still and breathing heavily into his pillow.

Mia pulled on her robe and went to the nursery. She preferred to leave off lights that would wake both herself and the baby up fully. The effort was wasted on Nathan, however. When she reached his crib, she could see his bright eyes staring up at her. His crib mobile pivoted slowly about with her entrance.

"Come here, my love," Mia said softly as she picked him up and cuddled him to quiet his cries.

After changing his diaper, she sat down in the glider chair, unbuttoned her nightgown, and put him to her breast. Nestling down into a quiet coziness, he fed as she slowly rocked. All was still in the house. The only sounds were the soft friction rhythms of the glider and the mingling of mother and infant's breaths. Mia was starting to doze, when an overwhelming sense of protectiveness overcame her and woke her fully. For some inexplicable reason, she could not bear to leave her child alone in the darkness of his room.

During her pregnancy an ongoing discussion between Dan and her was whether or not to share a family bed. They agreed finally that it was in Nathan's and their best interest not to have one. But scenes from the nightmare resurfaced raw in her mind and she felt the need for the baby to be close tonight. She returned to bed and snuggled him between them, making sure the blankets were warmly in place. Only then could Mia settle in to finally nod off.

As they slept, mother, father, and infant couldn't know they were being watched in the night.

‡ ‡ ‡

Within the next instant, his eyes opened wide. Bailey Hague gasped. The suddenness of it all coursed through her like a jolt, almost making her jerk his feeding tube she had been checking. Collecting herself, she knew it was not uncommon for comatose patients to awaken to a vegetative unresponsive state. She also knew the charge nurse should be contacted immediately. Yet after logging the time of this recent development on his chart, she couldn't help but draw near to her mentor to study him instead.

"Talbot? Can you hear me? Please, if you can, blink. Or move your finger... anything. Just please let me know that you are hearing me," she tried. She scanned him over, desperately searching for the slightest indication that he was receiving input.

"Come on sweetheart. Please try," Bailey said, as she stroked his cheek. "I know you can do it."

His stare registered nothing, with a look not dissimilar to the dead.

In her readings on different techniques for dealing with comatose patients, she had come upon a blog that discussed untraditional methods that generated responses. They varied from using pet therapy animals, to playing music, to even one that employed a psychic medium to communicate with coma victims and Alzheimer patients. Feeling frustrated, Bailey wished there was some way or someone who could connect with him, to know what he was thinking and most importantly, to encourage him to return.

Checking his upcoming tests, she winced with sympathy and worry to find that Dr. Chen had scheduled a battery of pain stimuli applications for the next day. Bailey hoped that she would not have to be present for it. It would break her heart knowing that he was suffering and there was nothing she could do to make the doctor stop. In the meantime, her mind searched for alternatives to reach him within her own means.

At this point, Bailey was willing to try anything.

‡ ‡ ‡

It was time for a change. Dan knew he had better get to it right away before it became a problem. Nathan, on the other hand, was oblivious to the fact that he was wearing a loaded diaper. His mother was at the market on a much-needed reprieve, unencumbered by a diaper bag, stroller, and their squirmy young son. Dan knew how much she had looked forward to this small break even if it was just for a routine errand. However, this meant that he was on watch, entailing everything from feeding to cleaning—things he felt he was still a novice at. He noted that Nathan's timing was impeccable, saving the worst for their morning together.

Before the infant could crawl off, Dan scooped him up midstride. The baby squealed with delight as he felt his father's strong hands around his middle.

"Gotcha! This is not the time to go AWOL in this man's service, son," Dan said as he took a moment to nuzzle Nathan's chubby neck. The baby gurgled and chuckled a deep belly laugh at the feel of his father's unshaven face. Dan treasured these moments. Putting in long hours at work did not give him as much time as he wanted to spend with his son. However, an undeniable stench emanated from the diaper, causing Dan to pull away and hold his son at arm's length. "Wow. For such a little dude, you sure give off a powerful defense! Time to make some adjustments," he said as he hustled him off to the nursery.

Just when Dan felt he had things reasonably under control at the changing table, the doorbell rang. Looking at his half-dressed son clutching a toy and babbling away while patiently waiting to be diapered, he knew he should finish up before any accidents occurred. Pressure mounting, he fumbled with plucking out a clean cloth diaper from the folded stack on the shelf. For these types of occasions, he wished Mia had gone with disposable diapers instead.

The doorbell rang again.

Feeling flustered, he called out in a loud voice, "Just a minute!!" hoping it would carry to the front door.

At that moment, Nathan let loose with a fresh stream, a mini fountain shooting forth with little accuracy. It hit his father in the shoulder. Surprised, Dan recoiled instinctively but managed to toss the clean diaper on the child before he could soak any more targets.

"Awww shoot, Nat-a-Tat! Couldn't you have waited until I got the diaper on you first, bud?" he said with exasperation, glancing down at his shirt and then feeling about the changing table for any wetness.

The doorbell rang three more times in rapid succession.

"I said hold on a frickin' minute!! Now who in hell—oops—heck is so ding dang persistent?" the harried father said out loud.

Doing what he could to re-clean Nathan and fit him quickly with a new diaper before any other mishaps could occur, Dan finally commenced with the fifteen minute long diaper change that usually took five. He dashed to wash his hands, grabbed up his son, and went to the door.

The doorbell rang one more time, followed by insistent knocking.

Irritated, Dan flipped open the locks and swung open the door. "Now what the heck is going on…?" Before him stood a smallish woman with short silvery hair and a wide smile, dressed in rumpled clothes. In one hand, she held a suitcase. In the other, a food hamper. She was the last person he would have expected to see standing on his doorstep.

"*Lydia?*"

"Hello darling! It's so good to see you, Dan!" she said with a flourish as she walked in with arms open wide to hug him. "And this must be my grandnephew," Lydia took the infant out of Dan's arms and immediately cuddled him. "Oh Dan, he's absolutely beautiful! Hi there, handsome. I'm your Great Auntie Lydia." She grinned at the baby and hugged him again. Nathan contemplated her calmly, pleased by all the attention from this strange woman.

Dan looked at her with consternation. *Now where did she come from?* As he brought in her bags, he glanced outside before shutting the door to see her big blue Impala resting in the driveway like a moored cruise liner.

"Uhh, Lydia. Yeah, we weren't expecting you… What a *surprise*," Dan stammered. "Were you in the neighborhood?" He eyed her suitcase warily.

"I thought I'd drop in to see you kids and how you're doing and finally meet this darling boy." She pressed her wrinkled cheek against the baby's soft rounded one. In return, Nathan grabbed at the large orange beads on her long necklace.

"I see you drove here? That's quite a haul. Mia's at the market right now. She should be back any minute. So, are you staying somewhere in town or passing through?"

"Why I thought I'd stay with you guys," she said, pleasantly.

He blinked. "You are? I'm sorry, Mia never mentioned anything…"

"Mia doesn't know. I decided it would be fun to just pop in and say hello."

"Fun? Right, uh, okay," was all Dan could manage with a weak smile. He had never been good with surprises, especially when they involved visits from eccentric relatives.

"I would've been here sooner—last week in fact—but my transmission went out in Kansas."

"Wow. In Kansas?"

"It was the damndest thing. But I should've known by the negative vortex I was feeling just about then that something was bound to happen. It was as big as a billboard. I shouldn't have missed it," Lydia spoke with serious conviction.

"Negative vortices… right. Yeah, totally unpredictable," Dan fumbled.

He had no idea what she was talking about and sincerely hoped that his wife would walk in at any moment. He had met Lydia only once before while vacationing back East; they had had dinner with her. Other than that, their relationship was comprised of brief chats on the phone whenever he happened to be the one who answered. With the Occurrence, when all hell was breaking loose, he knew he had been less than courteous to the old lady when they had last spoken and he wasn't sure if she ever forgave him for that.

"Uh oh. Looks like you were targeted." Lydia pointed a scarlet-red fingernail at the wet spot on his shirt. "Baby boys are fine shots, aren't they? Why don't I hold Nathan while you change? He and I will get along just fine. Won't we, sweetheart?" she cooed, as the baby gummed her necklace.

Dan looked down to where she had indicated. With all the excitement, he had forgotten about the spot on his shirt. *Now how did she know what that was?* he wondered. He excused himself and retreated to the bedroom, thoughts tumbling through his mind. *Negative vortex? She's really a weird old bird. Just how long is she going to stay? Mia better get back soon…*

The sound of his wife's car pulling into the driveway interrupted the swirl in his head. Now that she was here, she would know how to handle Lydia. He sighed with relief, knowing that he could just go into courteous autopilot mode. The less he had to talk about that psychic stuff, the better.

In the meantime, Lydia observed the extreme effort her nephew-in-law was exerting in being polite. In a way she found that confounded look on his face endearing. To her, it was proof that her niece had married a decent, albeit obtuse man.

There wasn't any possible way she could reveal the real reason she had showed up on their doorstep, at least not with him. He was a Non-Believer and probably would always be no matter what he witnessed. More importantly, this was a matter of great urgency and no time for lay-people to get in the way or intervene, as what had happened last time. This situation could not be taken lightly, at least not according to what the Universe was trying to tell her.

All of that aside, it was exciting to finally be here where all the action was taking place. Lydia had to admit there was a strong feeling of foreboding present in the house and this one was not going to be an easy sort to deal with. She studied the large mirror in its tile mosaic frame that hung on the living room wall and got butterflies, knowing it was Mia's main vehicle for communication with the Netherworld. She was looking forward to her niece divulging all the details on what's been going on up until now and hoped to witness some of the extraordinary events firsthand. While it was fresh on her mind, she decided to put in a request to the Universe that she, too, would be able to see the apparitions with her own eyes.

In fact, she wished this with all her might.

‡ ‡ ‡

He stared back at her from the driver's side window of her car as she unlocked the door, startling her. Mia had hoped he would never figure out how to reach her in remote locations away from home. It was now apparent that he had.

She was enjoying a quiet morning to herself to do a few mundane things that everyone else took for granted like a trip to the market and mailing packages at the post office. Something routine, almost boring. A break from the bizarre world of lost souls interrupting her life with death, purgatory, and mayhem; of the constant presence lurking about during private or most intimate moments; of worry over how all of this would ultimately affect the baby and Dan.

But John's appearance in that cool pane of glass affirmed the cruel realization that her life would never be hers alone again. There was no more normal.

With dread, Mia climbed in the car and adjusted the rearview to view the back seat where she expected to see him next. He wasn't there. Reflexively, she turned around to scan the area, then turned back feeling a bit embarrassed. As she readjusted the rearview for driving, the corner of it caught something. Angling the mirror found John instead in the front passenger seat, right beside her. The discovery unsettled her. Seth had always seated himself in the back seat for whatever reason unknown to her. Aware that John's sullen presence was less than a foot away from her boiled queasiness in the pit of her stomach.

"Good morning," she tried in as steady of a voice as possible, hoping that he didn't detect the slight tremble that coursed through her.

He looked rumpled and unshaven—a departure from the well-groomed man she had first encountered. He had lost weight and his skin was growing dull and pale, emphasizing the dark rings under his eyes and discoloration beneath his ear. She turned the mirror back for driving and started the car. Not having to look at him eye-to-eye helped somewhat.

"How are you today?" Mia was almost afraid to ask.

"Like total hell. I have a splitting headache from the constant noise and commotion. Can't get any rest. My throat is killing me and I feel nauseated. Is that what you want to know?"

"Oh… I'm sorry to hear that," she answered although she wasn't entirely honest.

In fact, she was having her own troubles. Had she unintentionally encouraged John to show up? Why did these spirits continue to seek her out? And why was she the one responsible for helping them find their way? Was she sending off some kind of signal or vibe that beckoned them? No matter which way her mind sorted through the possibilities, nothing made sense. She was no detective. Never having done this type of work before, she was fooling no one. Just because she was able to assist in locating Samantha didn't mean she was cut out for this, especially when the child just about described the exact location for her.

"You know, there's one thing I can't figure out. Of all the people in the world—scientists, doctors, metaphysical specialists, clergy, and police psychics—why *you*? Why is it you who sees me? Bad draw is all I can think," John said, speculatively. It was obvious that he had been doing his own thinking.

Mia wanted to answer, "I agree," but held her tongue.

"So how *do* you plan to 'help' me today? Drive me to a soccer game?" he asked.

"I had to pick up a few things at the market this morning, but we can get started as soon as we get back to the house."

"Oh goodie, I can't wait," he said sarcastically. "This should be rich."

Mia tried to shrug off the remark and instead concentrated more on his voice. It had changed again, sounding even more garbled than the last time they had spoken. He barely spoke above a hoarse whisper now.

"Must you turn up the heat everywhere you are?" John complained.

"The heat is not on."

"It must be."

Mia drove on, trying to formulate the right words to avoid an angry backlash on his part. She wanted so very badly not to have to deal with him especially with the nasty temperament he was developing. With most people, she had always been very empathetic. Attempting it now, she tried to imagine herself in his predicament and guessed that she wouldn't be in the best of moods either if she were there.

Mustering up determination she said, "Listen—I know you want to get out of there as soon as possible. I completely agree with you. But I can only help you if you are willing to help me. Have you thought of any possibilities of where you are or anything else that has happened in your previous life? Anything that immediately comes to mind?"

"Previous life? So you've finally determined that I've popped off? How did you ascertain that? Through incantations or séances or any of that other mumbo-jumbo? Oh no wait—don't tell me—you're into reincarnation. That would make perfect sense. Well, let's give it a try… I am in a lightless prison, cut off from the rest of the world and I'm feeling remarkably pissed off right now. That must have made me some kind of surly worm or gopher or some other godforsaken hole-dweller before this. If I had a so-called *previous life*,

I can only hope that a shovel dispatched me quickly. What a load of horse manure."

Mia remained silent, keeping her focus fixed steadily on the road in front of her.

"I'm sorry, did I offend you? Perhaps I appear a little irritable? Frustrated? Angry? You should try being trapped on this side of hell and interrogated by a 'psychic' soccer mom asking you a bunch of pointless questions."

"I am not a soccer mom and I never said I was psychic. And I don't do any of that other 'mumbo-jumbo' as you put it."

"Well if you're not psychic, why am I and the 'alleged' others appearing to you?"

"I wish I knew."

She took a deep breath and worked at unclenching her fingers from their tightened death grip on the steering wheel. She didn't think she would ever feel this miserable again. *Maybe I should just let this one go…*

John's acerbic voice burrowed into her ear like a splinter, "Oh dear. Looks like you're upset again. If you really must know what immediately comes to mind, it's this—let's stop playing detective-shrink already. It's insufferable. I am fed up with being here with no one other than you to depend on for my freedom."

She hit the brake, perhaps a little too hard as the nose of her car dove forward. "Listen, if there is one thing you have correct is that I am most likely the only one you have to depend on. But if I am mistaken and there is a line of other people begging to be insulted and belittled by you that I am unaware of, please, by all means, go plague them instead. Or I know—how about if I stop helping you entirely? I can just ignore you and you'll be stuck rotting there forever, all right? How's that for insufferable?

"Now either you address me civilly or not at all. I am not a soccer mom, nor a crock psychic, nor your whipping boy. We can work to solve this thing together, respectfully, or you can go figure it out all by yourself. All I can say is if you choose the latter, you better get used to the dark." Mia was visibly trembling now but from anger. She hated the fact that he had rattled her.

Silence.

She refused to check the mirror to see if he was still present. A part of her hoped she had angered him enough that he would stop appearing to her altogether. She didn't know how much more of his abuse she was willing to tolerate. A few miles later they were nearing the house.

Her heart immediately warmed the moment she saw home, despite the row she just had with him. She knew people loved and supported her there. And at the sight of the large baby blue sedan that took up the driveway, it looked quite possibly that the count had grown by one more.

"Aunt Lydia?" Mia exclaimed as she open the door.

The two embraced each other with delight.

"Mia Pappas! How are you, darling? You look beautiful," Lydia replied, dabbing tears of happiness from her eyes. "I couldn't wait to see you all. Nathan is gorgeous! Such a big boy already."

"Thank you, Auntie. It's so good to see you! You look fantastic, yourself. How have you been? And what are you doing here on the West Coast? That must've been quite a drive."

"Oh, the drive was nothing. Just some detours here and there. But I'm here to stay with you and catch up. We've got so much to talk about."

"What a great surprise!"

At the sound of his wife's voice, Dan felt it was safe to return to the living room. He carried Nathan who reached out towards his mother. "Do you have groceries? I'll go get them," he said handing her their son and giving her a small peck. He smiled broadly at his wife and arched his eyebrows. Mia knew what his expression meant and winked an apology back.

"Would you please? Thanks, Murph. So Aunt Lydia, have you had lunch yet?" Mia said as they walked into the living room.

"No, I thought I'd wait for you so we could eat together. Dan said you wouldn't be gone long. I can't wait to hear about all that has been going on with you. We must not waste another minute. I want to know all about this new visitor of yours."

"Well that's going to take some explaining. I'm not sure where to begin—"

Placid in Mia's arms, Nathan suddenly let out a screech and immediately started to fuss.

Startled by his extreme reaction, Mia asked, "Oh my goodness. What's the matter, honey?" She checked him over but couldn't find what was troubling him. He buried his face against her and continued to whimper.

"Gracious! What's wrong with him?" Lydia asked with concern. "He seemed fine just a minute ago."

It was then that Mia was compelled to look up into the mirror.

John had indeed returned. His face was painted with pure hostility. "I've made up my mind. If you are the only one who can get me the hell out of here, then so be it," he spat out venomously.

Mia sized him up, but held her tongue. The baby squirmed and threw his head back getting more upset by the minute.

Seeing her niece face the mirror, Lydia asked, "What's going on? Is he here?"

"You've had your say and I'll return if I recall anything. But I will warn you only once—do not ever cross me," John said. "*Ever.*"

He vanished before Mia could reply.

"Is he here?" Lydia repeated, her head toggling back and forth between Mia and the mirror. "Let me get my—"

"He's gone now," Mia said. She held the baby close, kissed his forehead and rocked him to comfort him. But she remained pensive, her eyes fixed on the glass, her heart icy.

"Sweetheart, please. Tell Auntie what is going on, okay?" Lydia said. As she laid her hand upon her niece's rigid back, her touch broke Mia's trance.

"Uh, yes… that would be good," Mia replied.

The only two people that she had ever trusted completely enough to confide her deepest secrets in were her father and her husband. Over time, she had accepted the fact that she never had that kind of bond, if any, with her own mother. And she learned she could never disclose the phenomena she saw or felt with the few friends she had.

Once, when Mia was ten years old, she was invited to a sleep over at a friend's home. When the hour had grown late and the girls became more daring, they started to play rounds of "Bloody Mary" with a candle and a mirror. Thinking it was an opportune time to share, she decided to divulge the things she had unwillingly seen all along to the others. She had only wanted to fit in. However, her descriptions freaked some of them out and horrified the others. She remembered being accused of having a mean streak for scaring the other children, soundly scolded for having a wild imagination, and sent immediately home to a disapproving mother. As a result, she learned to keep any sightings or sensations to herself.

Occasionally, she told her father about particularly disturbing events, but only when they weren't in earshot of Margaret, who had no tolerance for her ability. Stephanos wisely never disbelieved her—he knew she must have been experiencing something to describe it in detail the way she did. She spoke of things she could not know of, never have access to. Yet, he had no explanation or guidance to give her in the matter. He could only reassure her that she could talk to him about it at any time.

So for her to open up and talk candidly with Aunt Lydia now took a leap of faith. She never thought her aunt would shun her or ridicule her, but it took trust to get there.

As for John, Mia knew that she would be dealing with him again in one capacity or another and very soon, unfortunately. She decided that while she would help him, her family's needs were always going to come first.

No matter what.

It was a huge risk. If anyone figured out what she was about to do, she would surely lose her job. She probably wouldn't ever work as a CNA again. But she also knew that the prognosis for recovery grew grimmer with each passing day. The longer Talbot stayed in a persistent vegetative state, the more likely he would suffer irreversible damage or worse—he would never regain consciousness.

He had never given up on her. It was time to repay the favor.

Bailey checked the scrap of paper for the hastily scribbled address one last time comparing it to the house numbers of the dwelling before her. Her mind flashed back to just an hour ago when she had pulled up his personal information in the patient records. She almost gave up then, sweating the fact that anyone could have walked in and caught her copying down his address and home phone number. That alone would have been grounds for her dismissal. Patient privacy was a serious matter that the hospital expected from every employee.

Now, she was actually considering entering his house. She studied the brass key in her hand. She had discovered it tucked in his wallet when she went through the plastic bag marked "Personal Belongings" that stowed his clothes and other things upon admittance to the hospital, looking for anything that would spark some sort of a reaction from him.

Her nerve sputtered and anxiety gnawed at her gut. *It'll be quick. Just got to find a few photographs or mementos. Just a few should do it,* she told herself. *Besides, if there were anyone at all who cares about him, they would have come forward by now to do whatever was necessary to see him through this. Looks like I'm the only one he has.*

Bailey ran through her story in her head. Should she get caught, she decided she would tell whoever saw her entering Talbot's house that she was sent to retrieve some additional clothes and personal items for him. She would act official and calm. She would make sure they noticed her nursing scrubs and work badge.

I must do it…for him.

Counting a silent one, two, three, she took a deep breath and exited her car. A cursory glance up one side of the street in the Boise suburb, then down the other told her that for the time being, she appeared to be alone. She moved quickly to the front of his house, stepped over the uncollected rolls of newspapers strewn about his sidewalk, unlocked the door, slipped in, and closed it behind her. Breathing a huge sigh of relief, Bailey was now hidden from the prying eyes of the outside world.

Inside the foyer she paused to take in the place Tal called home. Nothing like her messy cramped apartment where three kids reigned terror, instead it was modest and tidy, silent and still. The only movement was the steady swing of a pendulum on the antique wall clock keeping time.

Venturing into the living room, the LED on the answering machine sitting on the desk blinked, indicating messages. Next to a stack of hunting magazines on the coffee table, a bouquet of dead flowers shriveled in a dry vase she presumed had been filled with water three weeks ago. In the kitchen, she spied a coffee mug in the sink and a newspaper on the kitchen counter. Picking up the paper, she noted its date was the day he was admitted. *He must've been reading it in the morning with his breakfast. Before his accident…*

Sorrow trickled through her like ice water as she recreated the events in her mind. What if he hadn't survived? Someone would've had to go through his house and look through his things much like she was now. They, too, would've reached this point where luck had apparently run out for Talbot Bradford. *Or had it?*

Bailey refocused and pressed on. The truth was, he was still very much alive and needed her perseverance to help him. Soon she would have to get the kids from her mother's and stop at the store to pick up something for dinner. That didn't leave her much time. She returned to the living room with a singular goal in mind. *Find photographs and mementos.*

She found it curious that there were no photographs in the modest living room or anywhere else in the house, for that matter. She thought about her own home where snapshots of her kids, extended family, neighbors, and friends littered her walls and bookshelves, plastered her refrigerator door, and filled assorted frames. In fact it was very hard *not* to find an image of somebody in Bailey's place. In contrast, Talbot's walls displayed only a few generic art prints so coordinated in color and theme with the furniture that they were purchased most likely with the furnishings as a set. It made her pity him—his house definitely could use a woman's touch in making it homey.

The flashing red three on the answering machine demanded attention. After a moment's hesitation, she hit the playback button deciding there may be an important message from someone in his life—perhaps a parent or best friend out there who wasn't aware of his fate and sick with worry about him. The first call was a man from out of state trying to set up a business meeting concerning student internships with a physical therapy center. The second was a telemarketer pushing a credit card with lower rates. Pretty boring stuff. However, the last message intrigued Bailey to the point in which she had to replay it.

"Tal? It's Cheryl again. I really wish you had joined me for the show. You would have loved it. It's silly how you turned down the tickets and came up with that awful excuse. Can we please stop playing games already? I told you there doesn't have to be anything serious between us anymore if that's what you want. Just don't avoid me. Call me, okay?"

Listening to the smooth feminine voice plead over the small speaker ignited a flame of jealousy within Bailey. She checked through the caller ID list on the phone to find the name and number of one Ms. Cheryl Becker and noted it. If she absolutely had to call her, she would if all else failed. Until then, she would rather not.

The clock read 5:23pm. She really had to get moving. Her mother was only going to keep the kids for so long before she got sore and started demanding for her to hire a sitter instead. In haste, Bailey rummaged through the immediate drawers in sight. Nothing there but typical household items—some bill statements, gloves, rubber bands, matches, a letter opener. Next, the nursing assistant followed the hallway that led to the bedrooms. The first bedroom was hardly furnished, containing only a bed and easy chair on one side of the room and a tall shelf against the wall.

Bailey stopped for a moment to study the taxidermy birds and animals lined on the shelf. A grouse, a dove, several songbirds, two squirrels, and a small brown rabbit occupied the levels, frozen in place as if they were listening intently to the very shot that ended their lives. Personally, she thought that dead stuffed creatures were creepy with their glassy marble eyes and their stiff bodies. *But everybody has to have a hobby*, she contended. The closet held another shelf full of expensive camera equipment and a gun safe that was locked. Other than that, it was empty.

In the equally sparse master bedroom, there weren't many personal mementos or keepsakes among his paperwork and clothes. A dresser drawer yielded a black and white photograph of a well-dressed man and woman. The man looked stern while the woman appeared enervated. Seated between them was an unsmiling little boy. With some imagination, Bailey was able to determine that the boy was a young Talbot. It wasn't the happiest looking family photo and she hoped to find a better one. But another drawer only produced a rusty pocketknife, an old family bible, and a few neckties.

Just when she started to despair in finding anything of significance, the last bedroom revealed the biggest surprise of all. She opened the door to find a young girl's room, complete with a canopy bed made up with a gingham bedspread and throw pillows. Lacey curtains adorned the window, pink shag carpeted the floor while assorted dolls and plush animals lined the room. The discovery shocked her. She had never considered the fact that Talbot may very well be a father. At least he had never alluded to it whenever they had talked.

And then she spied it—a small photo album on the dresser. Bailey flipped the cover open. A little girl of about nine years old, caught in freeze frame, jumped rope on a sidewalk, her long blonde hair fanned out like a net catching the sunlight. In the next photo, this same child stared intently back at her from behind a smattering of freckles. Photo after photo, the child appeared to be the somber sort, hardly ever smiling. *Perhaps she took after Talbot with her serious nature?*

As she thumbed through the book, she came upon another blonde girl, Bailey guessed around seven years of age, the same age as her youngest. There were only two photographs of her—one where she was walking with her brightly colored rain boots between two friends and another of her sitting straight, grim, and alone in one of the high back chairs in the dining room. Bailey assumed that the girls were sisters. She enjoyed noting how similar their facial features were, stamped on each like a family brand.

The last page held what she guessed must be their older sister. This one seemed lively and vivacious while eating pizza with friends at a shopping mall's food court. Bailey guessed her age at about eleven or maybe twelve years old. After that, there weren't any more pictures. *Ah, she's at the age where she doesn't like a lot of pictures taken by Daddy. I've got one of those myself at home,* Bailey smiled to herself, sharing an empathetic feeling of parental woe with Talbot.

She wondered who was caring for the girls while he lay in the hospital bed, which led her to notice how unusual it was that he only had one bed in the room. Given the lack of female domesticity in the house and no other bedrooms dedicated to children, she surmised it must be a divorce situation. She knew she had the tendency to jump to conclusions and make on-the-spot speculations, much to the contempt of her mother who called her an impetuous fool. But Bailey chose to ignore her, believing herself to be exceptionally attuned to others and a people person just like Talbot said she was.

Satisfied with her discovery, the nursing assistant closed the book and clutching it to her bosom, left the house. She hoped an item this precious would be enough to bring Talbot back around. There were even more questions concerning him than before, including the fact that there was potential ex-wife... *or wife?* And three children who didn't know the man who had once been a part of their lives lie in a hospital bed, trapped in a coma vigil.

‡　‡　‡

"What's up, Murph? After dinner you've been walking around like a zombie," Dan asked his wife as they retired to their bedroom. It was a time of day they looked forward to, simply because the opportunity to spend alone time together was growing harder to come by. It was past ten-thirty and the baby had finally fallen asleep and Aunt Lydia had gone to bed.

"I have a headache that just won't give up," she responded, gripping the muscles at the back of her neck. "It's been with me all day."

"Here, come sit down and I'll rub your shoulders. It's probably just a tension headache. It's been quite a day with your aunt showing up and all." He patted the bed beside him. She plunked down readily in front of him, eager to find relief from the pounding in her head. She wasn't one to complain, but the pain was making her weary.

He laid his hands upon her shoulders and started rolling them. She winced and let out a soft groan.

"Yeah, see—you've got a big knot, right here." He knuckled the arch of her shoulder by the base of her neck. "Feels like a good size one, as hard a rock. No wonder you've got a headache."

Mia groaned some more and rolled her head a little, feeling the tension starting to ease under the kneading of his strong hands.

"Unnhhh... that feels good," she murmured. "Even though it's been a long day, it's nice having Auntie over for a visit. It's so good to see her again. How long has it been—what? Since we were engaged? I feel kinda guilty that we haven't been out to see her and she had to drive all this way."

"I'm sure she knows that you've been very busy. We haven't had much down time in the past few years when you think about it."

"Yeah, I suppose so. But it is really sweet of her to come visit us."

"Sweet? The word I was looking for was more like—uh... *unexpected*," he chuckled.

Mia reached behind her to give his leg a playful swat. "Behave," she scolded. "Aunt Lydia has a really big heart and is one of the kindest, most caring people I know."

"I'm not saying she isn't, but you've got to admit that she's 'different.'" He cleared his throat to mimic Lydia's high voice in a croaky falsetto, "'Didn't you know? Microwaves are doing nothing but converting the negative ions in your food to harmful positive ions. It's terribly unhealthy. Here—heat it on the stove instead. It should only take, I dunno, *three hours*'... You know, dinner wouldn't have taken so long to get ready if we could have just used our good ol' positively ionic inducing microwave.

"And then when I saw her bringing in dandelions and crab grass from the yard and tossing them in the salad along with some flowers, I was thinking, 'O-kaaay, I guess I won't have to pay to have yard waste picked up while she's here.' I may be wrong, but I don't think we are supposed to be literally grazing right from our lawn. We're not billy goats. "

"You know she's into natural remedies and herbs," Mia answered drowsily with her eyes half closed, savoring the massage.

"Right. And negative vortices and force fields and charms, and all of that other wacky New Age stuff. I'm surprised she doesn't run around wearing a pyramid hat made from aluminum foil or something like that."

"1987."

"1987? What do you mean...? Wait—you're kidding me, right?"

Mia's eyes remained closed. "Nope."

"And...?"

"And what?"

"Did wearing the pyramid hat made from aluminum foil actually work?"

"Hmmm, depends on what you mean by 'work.' She said it cured the arthritis in her left pinky joint. And she's never had trouble with it again."

Dan laughed. "Sweet. Well maybe if she brought along an extra pyramid in the trunk of her car, you can wear it to get rid of your headache."

"Oh, I think it would take a lot more than a coat hanger wrapped in foil to get rid of this one."

"Really? That bad?" He rolfed her shoulders and massaged alongside of her neck. "What's bugging you, babe? Need me to take Nathan for a few days?"

"No, Nathan's been fine."

"Well what then? C'mon. I know something's up. Things usually don't bug you like this."

She sighed, "It's that guy in the mirror—John."

"He's still coming around? I'm sorry, I guess I must be getting used to these spooks and don't really notice it much anymore. Anyway, what's up?"

"It's just that, well, he's not very likeable."

"But as I recall, Seth wasn't too pleasant in the beginning either."

"Well, no. But it's not the same. Mostly Seth's appearance was frightening at first since so much had happened to him and I wasn't used to having these sorts of visitors. But once we started making a connection, he really improved fast. And Seth was never rude or nasty to me."

"Wait a minute. This guy—John is rude and nasty to you? What's he doing?" Dan asked, growing protective.

Thinking about her antagonist, Mia pursed her lips. "It's just that he's always got some snarky remark to make and says I'm nothing but a phony psychic. Usually I am able to blow it off, but lately, I'm running out of tolerance. And there's something about him that, I don't know, I can't put my finger on... but he just makes me feel uneasy."

Dan stopped massaging and turned her to face him. When she didn't meet his gaze, he lifted her chin with his finger until she looked into his eyes. Her face was lined with worry. "Uneasy? How, Murph? Come on, talk to me," he said gently.

"I don't know why, but he creeps me out. I keep telling myself that I wouldn't be doing so well if I was in his predicament. And it's frustrating because I really don't know what to do for him. With Seth and Samantha, I would ask them questions and they would try their best to remember what they could. We were able to discuss things and eventually figure out where they were from the clues they gave me. With John, he's totally uncooperative and snide. He has trouble remembering pertinent information that would help indentify him, but remembers other insignificant details in his life like a tree he had climbed or going fishing. But that's not what bothers me.

The thing is, he likes to belittle and insult. And when I try to get more information out of him, he gets angry."

"I say forget the asshole, then. No one says that you have to help everyone."

"But what if I'm the only one who can? It would be really horrible if I could help him out of his entrapment and didn't. I've been thinking that although his voice is really distorted, I can still hear him like I heard Samantha. Aunt Lydia was telling me that living sources have much more positive energy than the dead and that might be the reason I was able to hear Samantha. She's alive. So it's quite possible that John is alive somewhere since I can hear him."

"There's that negative/positive energy crap again. Let's suppose for a moment that perhaps it's your skill that is growing more proficient and maybe *that's* why you're hearing them now? Who knows? That guy could be long gone, nothing more than worm food somewhere and maybe that's why he's so pissed off."

Mia hadn't thought about this possibility. What Dan said was plausible. How could she be so sure that John was alive? While Aunt Lydia's theory was provocative, there really was no way of knowing if it were correct.

"Okay, but what should I do in the meantime? There's some reason he keeps appearing to me, but I'm not at all comfortable in dealing with him. Am I just being a wimp? It's not like he can do much more to me than say hurtful things. He's only a reflection in the mirror after all. Maybe I should just toughen up."

"Continue if you want. But if you don't feel like doing it anymore, then don't. Like you said, he's only a reflection. You can't save the world, Murph. And I wonder if some people out there deserve to be saved."

"Yes, but I don't think I should be the judge of that."

"All I know is that you are a wonderful and compassionate person. And I don't take kindly to anyone putting you down, spook or not. If I could only talk to him, I'd tell that son of a bitch where to get off." Seeing her apprehension, he smoothed back her hair away from her cheek. "Nobody better put you down. Listen—why don't we get some sleep? You look tired and probably could use some rest. Does your head feel any better?"

"Yes, it does. Much better. I think the shoulder rub did just the trick. Thanks Murph. I can't tell you how much I love being able to talk with you again, about everything—including this stuff. I missed it so much."

"Don't ever hesitate to talk to me about anything at any time. That's what I'm here for. I'm sorry I was so closed minded before. But I'm really working on it."

"I know you are, and I really appreciate it." She touched her forehead against his and said softly, "And there's another thing I miss."

"Huh? What's that?"

"With everything that has been going on, we haven't had much opportunity for *us* lately." She shared a secret smile with him.

"Are you sure?" he asked. "I mean, you have a headache and it's been a long day."

"I'm not falling back on that old cliché of having a headache. Besides, your hands have miraculous healing powers, what can I say?"

He smiled back. "Well, then. I'm glad that my hands were of good use. I also say that while Nathan is down and you are willing, we better seize the day." He kissed her and laid her back on their bed. "I love you, you know that?" he said tenderly as he stroked the side of her face and let his fingers trace down her neck.

Her body rose to meet his as she returned the kiss. "Yes," she whispered. "I do."

After they had made love and turned down for the night, Mia remained awake. Her headache had been more stubborn than she had let on and hadn't gone away at all, but she was determined not to let it dictate her time with her husband. She needed him. And more so, she needed to make sure their marriage remained strong. It was her anchor. Without it, she would be cut loose, free floating in this world where she could hardly make sense of reality anymore.

At times she wasn't sure, when dealing with these 'entities' that sought her out, whether or not she was making the right choices. From her research on the subject, the paranormal field seemed chockfull of individuals ranging from delusional to hardcore to gifted. It simply took too much time and was vexing to sort through to find credible sources. As a result, she felt there weren't any she could rely on for direction.

However it was becoming evident that she would continue to be visited by apparitions, whether she wanted it or not. Mia didn't feel prepared for the added responsibility of taking care of these lost souls, nor did she welcome it. Life had suddenly become that much more complicated. Motherhood and freelancing each were challenging on their own without the stress of the visitations being added to the mix. It wasn't fair to her or her family.

She wracked her brain wondering why she was chosen and how it came to be that she had this ability. The bigger problem was she had no idea of how to stop it. All of the books and websites she had looked up on psychic phenomenon always focused on enhancing one's ability or enticing spirits to communicate. Short of pursuing exorcism, there wasn't anything mentioned about how to turn off one's ability if it was unwanted. And she certainly did not feel she needed to be exorcised.

Aunt Lydia, while being a very dear person in her life, was not much help beyond emotional support. Although her aunt was more than willing to take on psychic challenges, Mia could see she clearly did not possess the ability to do so. In fact, she wondered what made Lydia willingly choose to get involved in the paranormal at all.

Trying to quiet her thoughts, Mia took comfort in how safe she felt with Dan beside her. She knew he would do anything for her. And the baby was snug in his crib and her Auntie was near. Mia thought back to what her father had said about the blanket of love from people that surrounded her and began to appreciate what he meant.

Thank you again, Daddy. I love you too, she thought peacefully.

The sound of garbled laughter echoed and reverberated moments later in the early hour stillness, bouncing from wall to wall throughout the house. Emanating from its source, it was sinister and threatening, seeking her out.

Mia sat straight up at the sound. *Did I doze off?* Yet, in the darkness, out of the corner of her startled eye, she caught a fleeting shadow—black against the night and wondered how long had he been present in the room.

‡   ‡   ‡

Lydia turned over and snuggled into her pillow. It seemed awfully bright for so early in the morning. *Maybe West Coast sun was different than East Coast sun?* Sleepily, one eye slit to glance at the alarm clock. It read 8:47a.m. Both eyes flew open wide in recognizing the late hour and she hopped out of bed. She hadn't come all this way to sleep late and miss everything. *Oh, how could I have overslept?*

Donning her housecoat and slippers, she grabbed her clothes and headed to the bathroom to take out her curlers and get ready for the day. She did not want to miss another minute. For all she knew, Mia could be talking to him this very instant. She debated whether to retrieve her tarot cards, set of crystals, or candles. There was no telling how this one was going to go. She decided to bring along at least one crystal—her best one—just in case, thinking it was best to size up what was going on first.

When she entered the living room, she found Nathan nestled in his baby jumper seat with assorted toys and Cheerios on his tray. Seeing her, he flexed his chubby knees a few times to hop up and down, then settled on scattering the items around with his hand and babbling, stopping only to feed a piece of cereal to himself. Nearby, her niece was seated on a tall stool in front of the mirror. It appeared at first that she was merely gazing at her own reflection. Within a few seconds, Lydia realized with a start that Mia was currently in the middle of a session. Without saying a thing, she quickly planted herself on the sofa to witness the event. Her heart was beating excitedly. She inwardly kicked herself one last time for not awakening sooner. It would have been extraordinary to catch this from the very beginning.

At lunch the day before, Mia had showed her the notebook and the visitors' writing within it along with the newspaper article on Samantha. She had also cued her in on the exchanges that had transpired since John first appeared.

Lydia studied the mirror and her niece's animated expression as she engaged in dialogue with the visitor. She hated to admit, if to no one but herself, that she could not detect his presence whatsoever. This did not sit well with her since she had no idea how she could help her niece should this situation escalate.

She thought it interesting to see how the baby reacted whenever the specter appeared. Innocents were like that. They always knew pure good and evil when they sensed it. Only time would tell whether Nathan had truly inherited his mother's gift for insight. For now, it was probably better that Mia had him off in the corner and out of sight of the mirror.

Mia caught her aunt's reflection in the mirror and smiled 'Good Morning' to her. Then, redirecting, she replied to the glass, "That's my Aunt Lydia. She is staying with us for a little while."

Lydia saw her niece's sweet smile melt into a serious frown and her brow become furrowed. Something definitely did not feel quite right, although she couldn't be absolutely certain what was amiss. It was more of her intuition nagging instead. From what Mia had told her, this John fellow could be rather difficult and it appeared that he was acting up now.

Mia continued, "No. I don't have a problem with her watching us talk. She knows more about this stuff than I do… No, she is not another 'phony' psychic." She crossed her arms in front of her and set her jaw. "Listen, we can end this discussion right now. I told you I would not put up with… I'm serious. We will continue only if you do it respectfully…What?… Are you certain? You better not be putting me on. All right… Hold on. You recall a building? Wait, let me write it down…" Mia said as she reached for the notebook and pen nearby. "Okay—go on… Red brick, gray tile roof, two story. Uh huh… a hedge up front, tree-lined street. Can you see the house number? 762—19? Okay… Anything else?... All right. Well at least that's something definite we can work with."

The older woman wished that John had written directly in the notebook like the other visiting spirits had done before him. Obviously, her niece could still hear his voice so his writing wasn't necessary. Suddenly remembering, Lydia took her crystal from her housecoat pocket and let it dangle on its gold chain, waiting to see if it swayed, and if so, how, in what direction and at what rate. Instead, the crimson pendant hung stubbornly straight down refusing to cooperate. It frustrated her when these instruments were unreliable. And they always seemed to be the most unreliable when the moment was crucial.

The phone rang in the kitchen.

"That must be my husband. I have to take this call. I will be back in a couple of minutes," said Mia holding up her hand definitively to the mirror as she rose from the stool. "Aunt Lydia, would you mind keeping an eye on Nathan for me, please?"

"Sure, honey," Lydia responded, but her gaze remained glued on the motionless crystal.

While Mia talked to Dan, Lydia refocused her attention to the mirror, carefully studying its surface. He was lurking in there somewhere. The thought of it quickened her pulse and she fought to remain calm. She approached and looked deeply into it, bracing herself for any sudden appearance on his part.

"Hello John. I'm Lydia Castaneda. I hope to meet you face to face very soon," she said slowly and distinctly.

She waited, but nothing materialized. She contemplated scrying but her former attempts with the ancient practice usually didn't yield satisfactory results. Besides, she didn't think she could concentrate with the baby nearby and Mia expected to walk in at any moment when she finished her call.

Spying the notebook, she picked it up instead and browsed through it, studying the ink on the pages. Her hand lightly stroked the handwriting attributed to Seth partly in wonder and partly out of wishing to have witnessed its making. She turned the pages and came across Samantha's heavy child print, and then Mia's notes on everything the little girl had told her. It was thrilling to know that her niece actually saved this one's life.

Just then, the baby started to fuss, tired from sitting in his seat apart from everyone. He arched his back and put his fingers in his mouth as a plaintive expression worried his face.

"What's the matter, darling? Just a little bit more, okay? Mama will be right back," Lydia cooed to him. Nathan stopped for a moment at the sound of her voice, but when action wasn't forthcoming, he started to fret once more.

Lydia placed the open notebook down on the coffee table and went to retrieve him. She looked in dismay at the jumper seat with its array of accessories and safety belts. Baby seats had gotten so complicated since her own were little. It took her a few moments to figure out how to get him out of the seat, but she finally succeeded in freeing him. Cuddling Nathan in her arms, she remained in the corner just in case, until she heard Mia finish her call and return to the living room.

"I think this big boy was getting tired of being in that busy jumper," Lydia told her when she entered. Then she chuckled, "I get tired just looking at it."

"Yeah, I'm sure he's much happier now that he's up in arms. Feel better now that Auntie's got you, mister?" she asked her son. He looked at her and waved his hand. She stroked his head and then faced the mirror. "Well it looks like John left. That's weird—just when he was beginning to recall some things. Must've gotten tired of waiting. Anyway, it's just as well. It takes a lot of energy and patience to deal with him." She picked up the notebook and noticed that the pages had been turned. "Were you looking at this, Aunt Lydia?" she asked, holding it up.

"Why yes, sweetheart. Goodness, was that okay? I didn't mess up anything did I? I'm sorry, I wasn't thinking," Lydia said, concerned.

"No, it's fine. For a moment, I was wondering if John had turned pages or had written in it."

"He can do that?"

"I'm not sure. They seem to have access to whatever is present in any room or area they appear. But I haven't seen where any of them have been able to physically move anything yet. That's why I was curious. If John had actually turned pages, that would've been something new."

"How fascinating."

"In fact, John hasn't seemed to have caught onto tricks the other two demonstrated right away, like appearing on a variety of surfaces and following me about. Yesterday, in my car was the first time I had seen him anywhere else but this mirror. Seth had mastered that one right off the bat. Even little Samantha learned how to do it and she is only seven."

"I wonder why that is? Do you think it's because children learn so quickly?" Lydia asked.

"I don't know. Maybe. John isn't too eager to do much more than complain."

The baby suddenly let out a yowl and threw his head back. He clung to his mother and then shoved a couple of fingers in his mouth to console himself. "Mmumm mumm, mumm, mumm," he repeated disconsolately.

Mia pressed her lips to his forehead. "What's wrong, love?" she asked him, gently. The unhappy infant continued to fuss. "I don't know—he's not been acting himself lately. It's strange because he's usually so good-natured. Maybe it's because we've started weaning. Let me see if he wants something to eat and settle down. I'll be in the nursery if you need anything," Mia told her aunt as she left the living room cradling Nathan in her arms.

While her niece was busy, Lydia decided to head outdoors to have her breakfast in the garden. Sometimes she did her best thinking among living green things with her hands sunk deep in the moist earth, and this morning's event gave her much to ponder. Plants were such lovely spirits and gave off good energy. She missed her greenhouse of herbs that she tended so carefully back home and hoped that Jacqueline was remembering to water all of her babies. She also had her sight set on a nice little selection of dandelions, mint, and foxglove starting to emerge in the corner of the yard by the fence. It appalled her to see Dan throwing away so many beneficial plants into the yard waste.

Shortly after she let the screen door bang behind her and was sipping her coffee, Lydia heard a voice call over the fence.

Mrs. Lopez hailed a greeting, "Hallooo?"

In order to introduce themselves to each other over the backyard fence, the two short women climbed up on their respective perches: Mrs. Lopez on her cinder block and Lydia on the square cut timber that lined the flowerbox.

The neighbor was surprised to see Lydia. "Oh! I thought I heard Mia come out. I always like to talk with her and little Nathan. So are you Mia's family? It is such a pleasure to meet you. I am Adriana"

"I'm Lydia and the pleasure is all mine. Her mother and I are sisters. I thought I'd visit the kids for a while."

"That's good to have a big family. Mia and Dan are wonderful people. I enjoy them so much. And Nathan—qué precioso! You came here to help Mia with the baby?" Mrs. Lopez asked.

"Why, yes, in a way. I definitely came here to lend a hand whichever way I could."

Mrs. Lopez paused, growing somber. "Ay, so you've come to help her fight The Dark One," she said.

"'The Dark One'? Did Mia tell you about him?" The question was completely unexpected, but Lydia could see by the woman's face that she was looking for answers.

"No, she hasn't mentioned anything. But I've seen It before the baby was born. And even though time has past, I have a feeling that It hasn't left them. Something like that doesn't let go so easily. I worry so much about these kids. Dan says everything is okay. But I don't believe it. An infant shouldn't be around all of that. Only bad things can come of it."

"But why did you think that I could help her with it?" Lydia wondered.

"I may sound like I'm crazy and you don't know me yet, but I know what I see. Mi tía practiced Santería. And so did my grandmother. You have the look of one who practices."

"I do?" Lydia got flustered and blushed a little. She never got involved with any of the dark arts and wasn't sure how the neighbor felt about it all. "Well… And do you practice?"

Mrs. Lopez's eyes opened wide at the implication. "Yo? No, no." She held up her hand as if the thought of it was too much to bear and shook her head. "Those things make me very nervous. Some people think it is a joke, all for fun. Like my Adelberto—he thinks it is funny to name the cat Diablo because he says the cat acts like the devil. No. I don't think it is funny. This is not something to laugh at or to fool with." She made the sign of the cross and then kissed her fingertips.

An awkward silence fell between them. In the distance, sounds of children called to each other in play.

Mrs. Lopez continued, "But you let me know how I can assist you. I have tended to mi tía y mi abuela many times. Even though I don't practice, I do know how to help."

"Oh, okay. I will." This pleased Lydia and she smiled with relief. "Well, if you are born with a gift, you shouldn't waste it, I always say."

"That is exactly right," the neighbor affirmed.

The two women beamed at each other with mutual understanding.

"So tell me Adriana, what exactly was it you saw that time before…?"

‡   ‡   ‡

Saturday morning of the Memorial Day Weekend dawned bright and clear. The angle of sunlight grew a little bit longer and the warmth to the air held the promise that summer days weren't far away. Dan thought it the perfect excuse to get away and decompress, and just what Mia needed. She had been so intent on this psychic stuff lately, she hadn't much time for enjoyment like she used to.

"Come on, honey—let's get the stink blown off of us. It looks like it's going to be a beautiful day. How about the three of us go for a drive somewhere? We can get lunch, and then maybe take a hike? I'll load up the jogger stroller and the baby pack. I think it'll do us all some good to get out." Dan suggested.

"Oh, I'm not sure if Aunt Lydia can hike. Her legs have been giving her a lot of trouble lately. So maybe just a walk."

"I said the *three* of us. I've checked with her already. She's says she is happy to stay home. In fact, she said we should get out and enjoy the weather while we can. She's got plans to do something with Mrs. Lopez today anyway. I think it's awesome that those two have hit it off."

"They do seem to have a lot in common, don't they? Well, okay then. I'm up for going. I'll get Nat-a-tat ready," Mia smiled as she gave him a peck. "What a great idea. Now that you mention it, it has been a while and I was beginning to feel housebound."

Dan decided to head to the mountains. The trees along the way were blooming and fields of wildflowers spread like carpets upon the hills. In no particular hurry to get where they were going, they savored their respite away from work and responsibility. In the past, they would have jumped at the chance of a three-day weekend to get away. Lately, they had been so occupied that the dates on the calendar hardly made a difference anymore. The miles rolling on, they sung along to some of their favorite songs on Dan's MP3 player.

As they finished a tune, a classic car pulled up alongside of them at a stoplight in the very next town. For some inexplicable reason, it looked familiar to Mia. As she studied its lines, recognition started to sharpen her focus. A feeling of apprehension mounted, quieting the happy mood she was in.

"Murph, do you know what kind of car that is?" she asked, pointing to it.

Dan turned to look, but just then the light turned green. "It's a Ford Fairlane. '73, I think. Hold on... let me try to get a better look." He let the car pull ahead of them. "Yup, looks like a '73. Man—those cars were brutes. They look so different than the '66. See the way the tail lights are shaped? What a classic."

"Remember that dream I had with Samantha? That's the type of car 'Uncle T.J.' was driving. At least I'm pretty sure that's what it was. It wasn't in as good of a condition as that one, but it was big like that and green with a black top."

"Yeah, that color combination was pretty popular," Dan answered. Apparently, the psychic stuff had surfaced again. He couldn't help but feel miffed. This was their day off and it felt like they were away from all of that bull for a while and beginning to relax. "Anyway, that's all done with now," he said, hoping to switch the topic. "Samantha's probably out somewhere enjoying this day with her family too. We should try and do the same." He kept his gaze fixed on the road before them.

Samantha is that you? Hurry. You don't want to get caught... The disturbing scene of the abduction flashed through her mind. Mia swallowed hard as the terrifying sensations of the event returned once again. *That's all behind us now,* she reminded herself.

"You're right. I've got to start letting stuff go," she conceded. Taking his lead, she said, "I'm getting hungry. How about you? Want to get something to eat?"

"Sounds like a plan to me. You know I'm *always* in the mood to eat," Dan grinned with relief that she had decided not to press the issue. "Point out where you want to stop. I'm not picky."

For the remainder of the day, Dan was greatly satisfied that he had thought of getting them out of the house. He made sure to keep his wife engaged, steering away from references to spirits, dreams, the paranormal, or otherwise. Mia's face relaxed into an easy expression. She hadn't complained of any headache, so it was just the medicine she needed. He made a mental note then and there to make sure they took more opportunities like this away from worries and concerns, just like they used to. Just then maybe, since it looked like the psychic thing was here to stay, they would be able to find a balance in their lives once more.

‡ ‡ ‡

The flame flared brightly as it took hold and started to consume the stick of incense. With a quick puff of air, Lydia blew it out and observed the thin snake of gray smoke serpentine upward. She placed the smoldering stick into a bowl and with both hands, wafted the heady scent towards her in a sweeping motion as she closed her eyes and inhaled.

Adriana Lopez watched her closely from across the round card table they had set up in front of the mirror in the Labont's darkened living room. Upon counting seven sweeps of Lydia's hands, Adriana lit the three candles in the center of the table that surrounded the open notebook and pen as instructed. The only thing that comforted her during these unnerving moments was the weight of her silver crucifix resting upon her bosom.

Lydia's eyes remained closed as she inhaled deeply, raised her chin, and then lowered it to her chest, dropping into deep concentration. Next, she reached out to join hands with Adriana.

"John? Do you hear me? Be guided toward the light of the Living. Make your presence known… Come out and reveal yourself," she commanded in a steady voice.

Although Adriana knew she should be concentrating on John like they had discussed in preparation for this séance, she found it difficult. Instead, she became hyper-vigilant, soaking in the slightest sensory input just in case the Evil One decided to present himself. She didn't tell Lydia, but concealed in one of her pockets was a small vial that she had filled with Holy Water at the church before she came. Her other pocket held a travel bible with a prayer to Michael the Archangel tucked away in its pages. She wanted to make sure she came prepared for just about anything.

"Make your presence known… Reveal yourself… Tell me what it is you are seeking… Tell me," Lydia continued. Her eyes snapped opened and she inhaled sharply. Then she said in a hushed tone, "He is here. I can feel his energy."

Adriana gasped. They both looked up into the mirror. Their faces were reflected back from the depths of the glass, framed by the sunlit borders of the drawn shades on the windows and eerily illuminated. In the dancing candlelight, their eyes appeared hollowed and their wrinkled cheeks deeply creased, making them resemble haunting spirits themselves.

"Write something, John. Tell me what you want. Tell me."

Adriana's eyes went directly to the notebook. She held her breath, afraid to exhale and remembering all too clearly that day when she witnessed the handwriting as it magically appeared on the pages. She fought to control her pounding heart. To her relief, the page remained blank.

"Then speak through me, John. Use my body as your vessel to communicate to the Living. Let me know what you want…Tell me…"

The candle flame flickered sharply as if a breeze had licked it. Adriana let out a stifled cry.

"I know you are with us, John. Make your presence known… Tell us what you want," Lydia repeated, her voice rising.

A thin eerie sound invaded the room and wafted over their heads. Startled, Lydia jumped and opened one eye to look around. Never before had she ever heard a visitor with such clarity. John's presence was very strong here, the strongest she had ever encountered with a subject. Adriana hunkered down and looked about the room with fright. Within moments, the sound started to crescendo until the voice of a young girl screaming clearly emerged. The women looked at each other with alarm and gripped each other's hands. Lydia caught herself and closed her eyes to concentrate, trying to get her wildly beating heart under control.

In the meantime, Adriana fought against fleeing from this house of evil, to her safe abode. But she knew she had to help Lydia and would never forgive herself if something happened to her newfound friend. The prayer to Michael the Archangel reverberated in her head, *Thou, O Prince of the Heavenly Host—by the Divine Power of God—cast into hell, Satan and all the evil spirits, who roam throughout the world seeking the ruin of souls…*

"John, what are you trying to tell us? Who is that calling for help?" Lydia cried out, trying to contain her excitement.

The shrieks continued for a few seconds more. It was followed in chorus by another voice and yet another, until there were several girls screaming in a union of tortured souls. Adriana was gripping hands so tightly with Lydia that their hands started to hurt, but neither of them would let go. A chord of fear ran through Lydia. *What if I can't do this? What if I go too far?* Try as she might, she couldn't let this connection drop. She had to find out what he wanted and why he was here, plaguing the Living.

Summoning up more courage, she continued, "We hear you John, tell us what you want. Write it down. Write it down." A duo of eagerness and fear, the women looked at the notebook with anticipation.

The pen lay still. The page remained blank. The shrieks of the voices intertwined, climbing ever higher, as if they were rising from the dark depths of Hell itself.

"We are waiting, John…" Lydia's voice rose to match them as she commanded him with all of her will.

Abruptly the screams erupted into a round of laughter and giggles, and then all was quiet. The women gaped at each other, puzzled by what just happened. But then, a solo scream started up once more. Again, it was amplified by more screams in unison. Suddenly, a woman's voice could be heard yelling, "Hey! Cut that out! You girls better stop it with all the screaming or you are going to have to come inside. Do you hear me?"

In that instant, Lydia and Adriana realized the voices were not from the Netherworld, but rather from kids playing across the street. The women exhaled in exasperation, released hands, and sat back in their chairs, breathing heavily. Lydia swore under her breath in anger and shook her head in disbelief. Feeling faint, Adriana placed her hand to her forehead.

After taking a moment to compose herself, Lydia rose and went to the window where she pulled up the shade and looked out, searching for the perpetrators. A band of young girls were somersaulting and turning cartwheels on the lawn across the street, gabbing happily with each other and enjoying the sun. Adriana joined her in watching them.

"¡Ay, dios mio! Those children are going to be the death of me," Adriana said, clearly cross.

Lydia grumbled, "Stupid girls! For heaven's sake, I just don't know what gets into them." She loved children, however, she didn't find their antics amusing. What stung even more was the disappointment in what she thought was a genuine psychic encounter in her lifetime of seeking being nothing more than kids goofing off. "This is absolutely intolerable. Their mother should have made them go inside. It's not funny for them to be screaming like that. Somebody could be in serious trouble and no one would know the difference."

"I agree! It's not good for kids to carry on like that," Adriana said as she turned away from the window and headed back to the table. "Sinvergüenzas."

Lydia was additionally perturbed that their séance had been interrupted. How were they ever going to help Mia? "And just when it seemed like we were getting somewhere, too. I don't know if we will be able to pick the thread back up. We really need at least three people to do this properly—" She stopped short when the neighbor laid a trembling hand upon her arm with fingers that were ice cold. "Adriana? What is it?"

Adriana Lopez stood stock-still and stared at what laid on the table. She held her other hand over her mouth agape in horror, a strangled noise emanating from her throat. Lydia turned to look.

Lit by the candlelight, in the notebook where there once was a blank page, now was clearly written:

TAKE HEED.

‡ ‡ ‡

At home by evening's end after their family day out, they had arrived home to find a note from Lydia that said, "Next store at Adriana's. Will be back soon." It seemed a bit mysterious to Mia, but Dan shrugged it off and suggested that they were probably watching a tearjerker movie or out playing Bingo.

As mother settled down child for the night, one of the things Mia held most dear was being able to hold and cuddle Nathan. His warm sweet smell soothed her as she rocked him to sleep in maternal rhythmic sway while humming the song she and Dan had been singing in the car earlier in the day.

Mia longed for her little family to have more times like this, taking part again in a living and normal world with none of the trepidity that had come to dominate their home life. Dan had been relaxed and playful, thoughtful and attentive to both Nathan and her, evidence that he too, had been missing their time together. They reconnected at a level they thought had passed since their engagement days. Mia was relieved John hadn't appeared to her anywhere at all while they were out. It had been too lovely of a day to be marred by his hostile presence.

She placed the sleeping baby in his crib, covered him with a light blanket, and rested her hand upon his stomach. Watching him as his pursed lips continued sucking motions in his sleep, she promised, *Happier times are coming soon, sweetheart.*

A certain disturbance interrupted her thoughts—a low sound of moaning.

Mia tensed, her senses heightened and on alert like prey tracking the nearness of a predator. The sound was sudden and at first she couldn't discern it, but it edged its way past the peaceful stillness of the house. Mia made sure Nathan was secure and then left the nursery to locate the source. A glance at the mirror on her way through the living room indicated that it was clear. Reasoning, she checked outside the front door. *Was Dan all right?*

The moaning filled the house and fluctuated in volume and frequency, like an echo through a cave. Its distorted tones made it hard to pinpoint the source with any accuracy. She opened the garage door to find Dan in the driveway rinsing out some spilled juice from Nathan's car seat. It was obvious that not only was he okay, he wasn't hearing the noise.

The low, grave sound intensified and felt as if it were invading her head. A dark haze forming behind the mirror glass stopped her midstride. The forming swirl was unlike anything she had seen previously with Seth or Samantha, making it difficult to see her likeness or anything else reflected in the room. It grew dense and shifted to resemble things both foul and menacing. She approached it with trepidation, not knowing whether to investigate or flee.

John suddenly sprung forth from its depths, startling her and making her recoil. Clutching the side of his head, he writhed about, appearing to be in excruciating pain. He looked directly at her and screamed, his eyes rolling back to show their yellowed whites. His hoarse voice rose distortedly until it rang shrill and sharp in her ears. Mia cringed, not knowing what to make of the bizarre scene before her.

He winced and fell to his knees, wailing continually. The haze darkened until it morphed into the inky shadow that Mia knew all too well, its reappearance terrifying her. It grew and clung to John's neck, thick tendrils of wickedness draping across his shoulders and down his chest like a shawl.

Alarmed, Mia cried out to him, "What is going on?"

He gripped and shook his head.

"Is It causing the pain?" Her eyes riveted on the shadow.

He shook his head once more and then vanished, leaving the room in a vacuum of silence. The shadow lingered on for a few moments more and seemed to pulse. In the next instant, a searing pain pierced through Mia's own head. Blinded and disoriented, she staggered toward the garage, seeking her husband to help her. Stifled cries could not escape past her clenched teeth. She crashed against the sofa and slid to the floor. The sensation in her head felt nothing less than a heated pick being drilled through her skull. On the verge of tears, she curled up into a ball. The paralyzing pain would not let up. In agony, she grabbed handfuls of her hair and hit the side of her head with her fist.

Just when she thought she was going mad, it ceased, leaving her as quickly as it had come on. Panting, she opened her eyes and blearily looked around her. She was bathed in sweat. Her heart was racing and she felt as if she had just been run over. The room appeared dim, cloaked in a massive cloud, turning down all intensity and contrast.

Drained, Mia lay there, feeling the air chilling her sweat-soaked clothes and thinking of only one thing. Although she didn't have a choice in whether he could appear to her or not, she mentally and morally refused to deal with John anymore. She refused to let him lay claim to her ever again.

It was time to take action. Taking one last look at the others, Dan grasped the doorknob, and slowly turned it to open the door to their darkened living room. The video camera's viewfinder indicated that the night vision was working correctly; through its perspective, the room was bathed in an eerie greenish-gray light

"Are you seeing anything yet, Murph?" he asked. He swung the camera around to record his wife's response. The night vision rendered her face a pale grey with two bright white orbs for eyes glowing in the infrared lighting.

"No, not yet. I'm not sure if he's here." She followed him into the room.

"I'm not picking up anything on the multi-field meters yet—no electromagnetic spikes or frequency fluctuations," said Jenna coming up behind Mia.

Last to file into the room were Ho and Aunt Lydia. Both were turning about and craning their necks on the lookout. Ho operated a second video camera with night vision while Aunt Lydia firmly clutched an amulet in one hand and an unlit candle in the other. Like Mia's, their faces pale and eyes blazing as they fanned out to start their search.

"If you are here in this room, please reach out to us. If you want to say something, say it now. Show us that you are here," Aunt Lydia called out while tracing the candle in a slow arc before her.

"I'm not sure that you want to do that, Aunt Lydia," Mia said quietly.

"What do you mean, Murph?" Dan asked. "Should she put that down?"

"Oh man," Ho said. "I thought I just saw something streak by in the viewfinder."

"I picked up something too. This meter spiked all of a sudden. Wait, I'm going to take a temperature reading," Jenna said as she pulled another instrument off of her belt. "Okay, most of the room is reading about seventy-two degrees Fahrenheit. Except for… was it here, Ho?" She held her hand out in front of her.

"A little more to your right. Okay. Right there. That's where I saw it," Ho directed.

"Holy smokes! The temperature reads forty-three degrees here," she noted. "Are you guys feeling it?"

"Okay, we know that you are here. What do you want? Speak to us. We are listening," Aunt Lydia said solemnly.

"Is she supposed to be doing that?" Dan asked Mia, again. However, she merely looked about without responding. "Are you okay, honey?"

"Huh? Yeah. I'm fine," she answered. But Dan had a feeling she wasn't.

"There it goes again—it's over there now. Are you catching this, Dan?" Ho called out as he swung around and pointed his camera to the opposite corner.

"We got spikes and temp is forty-one degrees there," Jenna added.

"No. I'm not catching anything." Her brother stopped his camera. "Hold on. Everyone cover your eyes. I need to check this thing and I have to turn on my light." Dan removed a small penlight from his shirt pocket. With his finger over the button, he warned, "Okay, is everybody ready? I'm turning it on." He flicked it on and a bright circle of light shone on the side of his camera. He quickly checked the settings and found them in the correct positions where he had set them. He switched the light off. "Okay, clear."

Dan held his camera up to his eye again and trained it on the corner where Ho was seeing something. "Is it still there?" he asked.

"Yeah, man. It's like some kind of wispy cloud thing and it keeps moving slow, like smoke. I don't know how else to describe it," Ho confirmed.

"Then, why am I not seeing it? C'mon spook, where are you…?" Dan muttered as he scanned the corner slowly.

"It's right there, Dan. It's growing bigger. Don't you see it?" Ho asked.

"I see it! The meters are picking it up too!" Jenna said excitedly. "And the temp is still dropping. It's at thirty-six now."

"No, I'm not seeing a thing," Dan answered, frustrated. He swept the room with the camera, trying to pick up any slightest clue.

"You must leave this family alone. They don't want you here," Aunt Lydia commanded.

Dan panned back. His viewfinder spied Mia lying on the ground.

"Hon! What the—?" He pulled the camera away from his eye reflexively but by doing so, he was plunged into darkness unaided by the night vision. To see her, he returned the camera to his eye and then dropped to his knee on the ground beside her. She wasn't moving. "Mia? Mia, honey…?" he asked as he gently turned her face toward him. Her eyes burned like embers and her mouth was slightly agape as if she were in some kind of trance.

"Hey guys, this thing is getting bigger. Look at it!" Hoason exclaimed.

Worried, Jenna asked, "Dan, where is Nat-a-tat? He was right here, just a minute ago."

"Leave this family alone! Your presence is not wanted. This is THEIR house!" Lydia continued. She waved the unlit candle in a large circle and held the amulet out before her like a shield.

"Babe, what is wrong? Why won't you answer?" Dan asked. Her gaze was unseeing. He quickly put down the camera and turned back on his penlight to check her over.

"Dan, where is the baby? Have you seen him?" Jenna persisted.

"I don't know. Something is wrong with Mia. She's not moving," Dan said. He tried lifting Mia off the floor, but she was limp and unresponsive.

"Oh my god. Are you guys seeing this?" Ho asked with alarm.

The rest looked at the wall he was pointing to. Upon it a dark figure, at least twice as big as they, loomed. At first, it appeared to be a mere shadow, but in the next moment, two eyes emerged and shone white like theirs in the night vision. Suddenly they flashed blood red and started tracking, deliberately sizing up each and every one of them in turn.

"Leave this house!! Leave these people!" Lydia commanded.

"Dan, this is getting way beyond us! We've got to get out of here!" Jenna yelled.

"I'm behind that!" Ho agreed.

Dan went to move Mia, but for some inexplicable reason, she grew incredibly heavy. He lifted one arm, but it fell back against the floor. Her expression was blank, frozen in fear. Somewhere lost in the house, he could hear their son crying, but the baby's cries did nothing to rouse Mia from her stupor.

The demonic figure on the wall doubled again in size and then rapidly expanded outwards in a third dimension of space filling the room. Jenna and Ho screamed in unison. Lydia continued her condemnation; her old voice crescendoed to a cackle. Mia was completely gone with no possibility of moving her. Nathan shrieked in terror and pain. It was total bedlam.

"Please Mia, you've got to get up. C'mon, you've got to try!" Dan cried out to his incapacitated wife.

The ominous figure made a deft move and encompassed the entire room. The temperature dropped until it was frigid and frost layered the walls and floor. Ho, Jenna, Lydia, and Nathan's cries rippled and intermingled, like anguished souls burning in Hell. Mia's unseeing eyes and gaping mouth continued to grow larger and larger, until her face was so badly distorted, she no longer looked human.

Dan held his outstretched arms to the dark. Panting wildly, he stared about the room. The greenish-gray cast was fading. *Where was everyone?* He felt about his pockets looking for his penlight. It had to be in there somewhere. *Where did it go?* His eye went to the floor where Mia no longer lay. *Where is she…?* Consciousness engaged as darkness yielded to subdued afternoon light. The TV set chattered with the evening news. He listened to hear the comforting sounds of Mia talking to Nathan in the nursery.

"Oh shit," he muttered to himself as he realized he must have dozed off in his own living room, stretched out on the sofa while watching TV. Feeling deeply unsettled, he rubbed his hand over his head, opened his eyes wide, and repeated, "Oh shit."

He rose and immediately went down the hallway to Nathan's room. There, he affirmed that his wife and son were just as he had heard them—safe and sound. His eyes scanned the room to find everything was in its place. Mia turned a smile in his direction as he stood in the doorway.

"The baby's okay?" he asked, still shaky from the effects of the dream.

"Yeah, I was just changing his outfit. He spat up some peaches on it, that's all. Why?" she asked quizzically. "Wait, are you okay?"

Dan went to her and held her tightly. He kissed her neck and buried his face in her soft warm hair as he tried to come down off the adrenaline that coursed through his veins. Try as he might, he couldn't put the nightmare behind him. This was extremely unusual for him. Typically he hardly ever dreamt at all. On the rare occasions that he did, it was no more than a recap of activities that filled any ordinary day—washing the cars, working at the edit panel, talks with Mia. In contrast, this dream was completely foreign and disconcerting. What's more, he hadn't ever experienced a nightmare while napping.

"It's nothing. I had the weirdest dream just now. Bizarre, like some kind of freak show. I don't know how to explain it. But there were things that were completely surreal. And we were all acting very strange."

"Strange? In what way?"

"I don't know. Everyone was there, even Ho and Jenna. And screaming. And you—" He stopped, realizing that it might not be best to share what had befallen her in his dream. He knew she was sensitive to interpretations.

"And me, what?" She looked concerned.

"Uh, you were screaming alongside of them, but on the floor. I don't know. I told you it was surreal."

"That *is* unusual for you. Do you want to talk some more about it? I'm sorry I didn't wake you sooner, but you looked really comfortable and then Nathan needed a change. I was getting ready to call Aunt Lydia in from the garden, but we could still talk. In fact, she's really good at deciphering dreams."

"No. I'm fine," he lied. "It was just weird. That's all."

The next morning, Dan continued to feel hung over as he picked at his breakfast. *I've got to stop watching that crap*, he told himself. He had logically turned the dream over in his mind all evening long. Eventually, he came to the conclusion that it could be assigned to the influence of the large amounts of reality TV he had been watching lately.

"Is something the matter, Hon?" Mia asked. "You look really out of it today."

"I just didn't sleep well last night. I kept waking up every hour or so. And then it took me a long time to get back to sleep."

"You're not coming down with something are you?" She laid her hand across his forehead and looked into his shadowed eyes. Dan chided himself for complaining when he saw the worn expression on her face. It was obvious that she wasn't feeling well herself.

"Nah, I'm fine. Must be those stupid shows I've been watching or something I ate," he said to her, although deep down he wasn't convinced. "How 'bout you? Did you sleep okay? It seems like last night, you were out."

She sipped her coffee as her fingers ground into her temple. "This headache has come back and hasn't let up any. On Saturday, it felt like my head was going to explode. Yesterday, I was feeling okay, but now the dang thing is back again. And I've taken four aspirin already. I'm hoping once I get some caffeine in me, it'll take the edge off."

"I'm sorry, Murph. Maybe if you get a chance to lie down and put your feet up today, you should do it. Take it easy. You've been going a lot lately. By the way, where's our little buggeroo? He's usually up by now, isn't he?"

"I guess he's doing a little sleeping late himself. Wait…" Mia cocked her ear in the direction of the hallway, "There he is."

As she tended to the infant, Dan looked at the time and downed the rest of his coffee. Just then, he heard Mia call out, "Dan—come here. Something's not right with Nathan."

Hearing the urgency in her voice, Dan immediately came to her side in the nursery. "What's up? What's the matter?"

"He feels hot. Too hot," Mia said, then pressed her lips to the infant's forehead again. "I think he's running a fever."

Dan lay his hand against the back of Nathan's neck "He does feel hot. Where do you keep the thermometer?"

"In the medicine cabinet in our bathroom."

He came back fiddling with the protective cap on the device, pressed the button and inserted the probe into his son's ear. A few beeps turned into a steady tone indicating that it had taken a reading. Dan studied the LCD screen.

"Wait a minute. That can't be right. Hold on, I'm going to take another temperature."

Steady tone.

"What does it say?" Mia asked. She held the listless baby close. Nathan's eyes were glassy and his face was flushed.

"103.2. Same as before. Should I call the doctor?"

"I don't know. It seems awfully high, but I've read where babies can run higher fevers than adults. He might be fighting a bug or an infection. What do you think? Maybe that's what you're fighting too. I'm going to give him some acetaminophen, but if he doesn't cool down within the hour, I'll bring him in to see the pediatrician. Would you please get me a cool wet washcloth?"

"Well, all right," Dan answered returning with the cloth. "But maybe I should stay home. Between him with his fever and your headache—"

"I think we'll be okay Murph. Like I said, he probably has a bug. Who knows? Maybe I'm fighting it too and that's what's causing this headache. I know you're busy with that new project you and Ho have been working on. And Aunt Lydia should be getting up really soon. She might know what this is and will give me a hand too."

"Nah, I don't have to go in. I can do some editing here at home. And I'll call Ho to find out what's up."

"You don't need to miss any more work. Remember last time? Mr. Greenlee wasn't happy that you took off so many days. And you just took your paternity leave not too long ago, so maybe you should go in. Really, we'll be fine."

He hesitated. "Are you sure?"

"Go, hon. I'm sure."

"Yeah, well promise me you won't let your aunt wave some chicken foot over him or feed you tree bark or some weird thing like that, okay?"

Mia smiled and sighed. "I promise."

"Call me and let me know how he's doing? And take care of yourself too. Try and get some rest."

"I will. You better get going or you're going to be late."

"Take care, big guy," Dan said as he kissed the baby on the top of his head and then kissed his wife goodbye. "You're right. Got to go. Remember—call me," he answered and left.

As he backed his Jeep down the driveway, worry over leaving his wife and sick child occupied his thoughts. If it weren't for the documentary they were working on that was behind schedule already, he would have readily stayed home. Still wary from the nightmare's effect, he had a hard time shaking the persistent dread, similar to the kind of memory associated with severe pain or trauma. It was a few blocks later that he finally pinpointed where this familiar feeling of unsettledness was coming from. The last time he had encountered such a feeling was during those dark days of the Occurrence.

It took all of his logic and rationale to keep from whipping a u-turn and heading directly home. *Nothing has necessarily happened. It was just a dream after all*, he told himself. *Mia has things under control this time. And the baby probably has a bug, as kids are prone to catch.* There was nothing tangible to hang this feeling on, only some weird associations that had been ripped directly from images on some crappy reality TV show he had watched one too many times. He'd readily admit to anyone that he was lousy with intuition and 'sensing things.' If he were to give in each time something didn't feel right to him, he would waste a lot of time chasing his own tail over things that wouldn't amount to anything.

Dan drove on.

‡ ‡ ‡

He stared straight ahead. The respirator hissed in and hissed out. Monitors beeped. The air stockings pillowing his legs to prevent blood clots hummed as they ballooned with air and sighed sequentially first one and then the other as they exhaled. It was as if he were more machine than man.

"Your folks are worried about you. They love you and want you back." Bailey presented him the black and white photograph she presumed to be of his parents. She studied his face that was growing more drawn and gaunt every day. Bluish-gray circles framed his eyes. "*I* love you and want you back," she murmured almost inaudibly as she stroked his cheek.

His heart rate monitor continued its monotonous pace. His breathing, even and steady. No other muscle moved. There was absolutely nothing to indicate that her attempts were getting through and her words were being heard.

Dr. Grace Chen, the specialist in comatose victims, however felt that Talbot Bradford was starting to exhibit promising signs of recovery. Continuing EEG recordings displayed good activity with no seizures. The CT and MRI performed within the past week showed a reduction in the swelling of his brain and no detectable tissue damage, so surgery looked unlikely. Talbot also had good pupillary response and registered brain stem activity, and his Glasgow Coma Score had steadily improved from three points up to eight this week.

Reading through his chart, it felt to Bailey as if she were reading about some case study, not Talbot Bradford. The impersonal terminology prevented the attending medical personnel from knowing this was an intelligent and kind man they were dealing with. He was a human being capable of understanding hope, sorrow, and pain even if he didn't appear to perceive anything.

She was relieved that she wasn't present when Chen conducted the battery of painful stimuli tests. Her heart ached when she read the notes that described his strong response when ice water was injected into his ear. She prayed that his recovery would make haste.

Sighing with despair and then catching herself, she straightened up in her chair, her jaw set with determination. It was time to switch tactics with the man before her. "C'mon Talbot. Look. Focus on your darling girls. I'm sure they miss you and are worried about you," Bailey said as she held up the photo album before his catatonic stare and one by one slowly turned the pages. "Cheryl called. She's worried about you too. They all want you to get better really quickly. So try, sweetheart… Now which little girl is this?" She flipped to the next page.

The heart monitor's sleepy red line suddenly grew jagged with rhythmic spikes as his pulse quickened. His breathing rate increased. An alarm went off.

"What is it, Tal? Are you hearing me?" Bailey asked, encouraged by his response. "Are you seeing this? What is it?" She stole a glance at the album. It was open to the photo of the last child at the end.

Ah, of course. She's his oldest, Bailey surmised. *Maybe his favorite, or the one he has the most memories of.*

"You are seeing this! Is she your daughter?" She held the album up to his open eyes. His pulse continued its rapid rate and he drew deep breaths.

"Just what do you think you are doing?"

The sound of the charge nurse's voice sliced through Bailey who quickly shut the album. She did not expect her supervisor to be anywhere on this floor while she worked with Talbot. She must have been summoned by the alarm on his monitor. Usually Meredith was taking her lunch break at this time and cozying up to a resident doc who was twice her age. The way she overtly flirted and carried on with that married man usually turned Bailey's stomach. The CNA didn't know whether to conceal the album or play it cool. She was sure Meredith would make a stink about her overstepping her bounds by taking it upon herself to try to reach Talbot.

"Oh, uh, I don't know if you knew, but Talbot and I know each other. He helped me through school," she fumbled, hoping her forehead didn't start beading with perspiration.

"Is that so? What do you have there?" With a slight tilt of her chin, Meredith indicated to the album in Bailey's hand.

"This? This is an album that was with his personal things. I thought it might help spark something in his memory and provide some stimulation. I was just showing him the photos in it."

Meredith turned a shrewd eye on the scene before her. It was those owl-like pauses that made Bailey dislike the supervisor the most. Usually a criticism, judgment, or penalty was ever present on the tip of her sharp tongue.

"Aren't you supposed to be making your rounds in D-Pod right now?" Meredith asked as she checked the monitor, then crossed around to the other side of the bed and logged into Talbot's chart.

"Oh, I'm headed there right after this," Bailey offered.

"You *do* recall what was discussed at the staff meeting last Monday? *All* of our patients must receive the same level of care, no matter what. They wouldn't be here in intensive care if they didn't need it. There is to be no preferential treatment or extra time given to a patient just because staff may know them personally. We cannot be thought of as practicing nepotism here, is that understood? No exceptions."

Meredith was easily ten years her junior. Bailey never trusted the snarky supervisor who was somewhat of a control freak. In fact she made it a point to never trust anyone who was clawing her way up for power and position. She and the other CNA's had a sneaking suspicion that Joanne hadn't made quite the error that Meredith played it up to be, and it was rumored that the charge nurse may have thrown her under the proverbial bus to cover her own ambitious butt.

"Yes, ma'am. I certainly do understand and I was about to get to the rest of the pod right now. I'm just finishing up with Mr. Bradford."

Bailey placed the album on the service tray table, and then logged in her required notations into Talbot's chart. Before she departed, Meredith reminded her, "And Bailey, make sure you do not make a habit of going through a patient's personal belongings, for *any* reason. Do I make myself clear? Consider this your first and last warning."

"Yes, ma'am. It won't happen again," Bailey said as she quickly exited, preferring to put as much distance between herself and the supervisor as possible.

After the nursing assistant left, Meredith picked up the album and thumbed through it, displeased at the fact that Bailey had been dealing with matters that were off-limits and obviously way over her head. Glancing at the photos, she wondered if the children were Bradford's. One of the little girls looked familiar to her, as if she had seen her somewhere before. Out of curiosity, she decided to hold up the open photo album to the patient once more.

His pulse and respiration rates shot back up again. And then, for the first time since he was admitted, he slowly raised his hand a couple of inches. Meredith went directly to the phone.

"Page Dr. Chen immediately," she said.

"Aunt Lydia, whatever brought my parents together?" Mia posed after ending a brief phone call with her mother. Margaret Pappas had called to let her know that she had extended her time in Medjugorje another two weeks into June with a follow up to see the Vatican. It was clear she was living just fine off of her late husband's pension and company stock plan. The already strained conversation had turned particularly awkward once Margaret found out her sister Lydia was visiting.

After a morning spent in a fretful mood, Nathan had finally fallen asleep out of exhaustion and was resting comfortably with his ear upon his mother's heart as the three of them sat in the kitchen. Mia watched her aunt pour steaming water over a wicker infuser filled with a measured mix of Jamaican dogwood, black willow, and valerian. The fragrant leaves had been carefully selected from the small rosewood chest that rested with its lid open on the kitchen counter, its deep compartments stocked with various dried herbs. Lydia relied on the portable herbal chest any time she traveled.

"What do you mean, sweetheart?" Lydia arched an eyebrow but kept her focus on the task before her.

"I mean they were so different from each other. Dad was so easy-going and happy. And well, you know how Mom is."

Lydia laughed softly and shook her head. "Well, I certainly agree that 'easy-going' is not a term I'd use to describe my sister. Nor happy."

Mia studied her carefully. Under folds of skin sagging from age, Lydia's eyes still sparkled. Remnants of beauty in her face were still evident in her fine nose and proud tilt to her head. Paired with a ready laugh that erupted easily into a merry cackle—Mia imagined she must've been the life of the party.

"Now here, darling, drink this for your headache. And I prepared this aromatic sachet for you to sniff today. It's a little lavender, chamomile, and ginger mix that I think will do just the trick," the older woman said as she approached the table with the steaming aromatic brew in one hand and a small netted bag tied with a string in the other.

Mia gratefully accepted the warm mug and took a sip, and then inhaled the blended scents of the sachet. The combination soothed her. Although it was a difficult subject she was bringing up, she decided to press on with her query. It was a rare opportunity to finally hear answers to some of her lifelong questions and she wasn't going to let it pass.

"But I still don't get it. Mom and Dad were not compatible in any sense; at least none that I ever noticed. They didn't share any hobbies or interests, tastes, beliefs or sense of humor. They didn't even have the same bedtime.

And they never really seemed to talk to each other. She was always reading her bible and involved in her prayer groups and Dad was always alone, unless I was with him. So all through my childhood, a part of me always wondered why they ever married at all."

"You know, people change throughout their lives. The years and experiences build up and they are not the same people they used to be when they were young. It happens to everyone, but some more than others. Your mother was quite different as a girl. She wasn't anything like she is today."

"Dad always said that same thing. He explained that she had changed a lot after losing my siblings that she miscarried." She peered at her aunt from over the edge of her cup before taking a sip. The hot liquid felt as if it was erasing tension and stress on its way down. Savoring the brew, she said, "Oh, this is good."

Lydia finished preparing her own cup of oolong tea and settled down across the table from her niece. Setting down a plate of warm lavender scones she had just baked, she said, "I'm sure the miscarriages had some to do with it. But no, there were things that happened way before that I believe made a bigger difference."

"Really? Like what?" Mia asked, her attention riveted on this newfound information. "Come on, you can't leave it at that."

"Oh Mia, we don't need to go into all of that. Your mother is your mother and that's the way she is and always will be. Me dredging up her past won't change her."

"Auntie, I just need to know. There are times when I have felt and continue to feel that she doesn't want to have much to do with me. It's a feeling I've had since I can remember. And I didn't dare ask my dad about it. He would've only insisted that she cared for me. But there's got to be a reason that things are so difficult between us and why I feel this way. I've been searching for it for a long time. So please. I won't hold it against her if it's something I don't agree with. But maybe, I'll finally understand her."

Lydia hesitated for a moment. The expectant look on her niece's face moved her. *Poor child. All this time she believes her mother doesn't love her. Damn that Margaret...* She reasoned that Mia was a grown woman now with a child of her own. And her beloved father had passed on already. It was about time she knew the truth.

Drawing in a breath, she started, "Okay. But this is strictly between you and me and the doorpost, understand?"

Mia nodded, "Of course, Aunt Lydia."

"Like I said, your mother was quite different before she married your father. *Quite* different, in fact. Given how rigid and humorless she is nowadays, it's very hard to believe that she was pretty wild in her younger years. Drinking, smoking, and going to parties to all hours of the night. Sometimes, she could even be fun."

"*My* mother? Drinking, parties, *and* smoking? And fun? Wow." The thought of her stern, no-nonsense, straight-laced mother with a drink in one hand and a cigarette in another was unfathomable. "You're right. It is hard to believe."

"Oh, she was a crazy one, and frivolous. Your grandmother used to worry about her so. Those two would clash all the time about her behavior. She was always going out and would come home at all hours. Seems that all she wanted to do was play. She wanted nothing to do with responsibilities. Grandma claimed that she took after our father, who had abandoned our family when we were young."

"I still can't imagine my mother like that. It's inconceivable."

"Not to see her now, you wouldn't. But back then it was a completely different story. And then she met the love of her life one day. His name was Randall. Randall Dickson...." Lydia paused for a moment, as if she were lost in memory.

"Go on, Auntie."

"Oh, she fell so hard for that Randall. He was quite the player. 'Dandy Randy,' I used to call him and Margaret would get so angry. Those two were always stepping out. Nightclubs, dancehalls. They were inseparable. And then one day, one thing led to another as they always do and she ended up pregnant."

"Pregnant! She wouldn't let me out of her sight until I was over twenty-one and even then if she could have chaperoned me she would've." For Mia, the idea of an alter ego of her mother was nothing short of astounding. But then another, more sobering idea trumped it. "Wait. The miscarriages she had before I was born—were they with Randall or with my dad?" she asked cautiously.

Lydia explained. "The first baby was Randall's. Early on in the pregnancy while she and Randy were out dancing, Margaret slipped and fell. She lost the child. And then shortly after, Randall was killed in an automobile accident a few months later. He had been drinking heavily and smashed into the back end of a truck. The police reported it as a DUI. Margaret was devastated. She could never understand why those two were taken from her. Worst yet, she couldn't understand why she couldn't communicate with either one of them in the Hereafter."

"Communicate with them in the Hereafter—what do you mean?"

"Your gift, Mia. Where do you think you got it from? Stephanos is your father, there's no denying that. You've got his eyes, intelligence, sensitivity, and his same beautiful nature. But your certain ability-"

"Wait—she can see spirits too? But I remember you telling me that I got my gift from Grandma Vivian."

"It's true—I believe you inherited it from your grandmother, but so did your mother. I have always held back from telling you the truth, sweetheart, out of a promise I made to your mother years ago, especially when your father was still alive. But I can't keep that promise any longer. It's not fair to withhold it from you and keep you in the dark. She never saw as clearly or as strongly as you do, but in our childhood, she was contacted at least a couple of times. Anyhow, they were only minor incidents that happened years and years ago. I doubt they still happen. I never had it quite to the extent that you or your grandmother did, or even your mother, but boy do I wish I ever."

This revelation set Mia back. Hearing that her mother used to engage in irresponsible behavior that she had strictly prohibited her from doing was one thing. Finding out that she was clairvoyant and had not only withheld knowledge of it from her, but punished her over having the same tendencies, was another. Memories of reciting long bible passages, attending church throughout the week, and being grounded to her room for showing any semblance to having the ability resurfaced in her mind.

She grew indignant. "But my mother was always so set against all of that. I remember having to pray on my knees for hours whenever I saw or sensed something she felt I shouldn't have."

"That was because in part, she had no control over it like she wanted to. She just thought she was being punished for being so wicked. But most of all, it frightened her. I used to tell her, as I have told you, 'don't fight it— embrace it.' She never listened and instead wasted her gift."

"But what about my father? Where does he fit in with all of this?"

"Your father was a dear, dear man with a generous heart. But unfortunately, I think he was a bit... Now what is it they call people like that again these days...? Oh, I know, 'co-dependent.' Back then he was just considered a sweetheart. About a year after Randall was killed, when your mother was walking home from the market one day, her bag of groceries tore in the rain and spilled everything out onto the sidewalk. She broke down crying, mostly because she was so blue all the time, and he helped her pick up everything and walked her home."

"I kind of remember a little of that story. Dad told it to me a very long time ago when I was young. I guess even back then I was curious to know how they got together."

"He took pity on your mother and thought that he could bring some happiness to an extremely depressed young woman. I think he may have been attracted to her vulnerability. Now Margaret married him immediately, for what reasons, I'm not entirely sure. Maybe she was worried that she'd turn out to be an old maid. Maybe she didn't want to be alone. Your father was very handsome and charming, so maybe that was some of it too. And once she lost the babies, he couldn't leave her. Fortunately for him, you came along—you were the only light in that dreary marriage. But he never found out about the other side of Margaret—the wild side. And I don't think she ever told him about her first miscarriage either. Nor did he ever know that she, too, could 'see.'"

"Do you know if she still can?"

"I don't think she'd dare. Like I told you, she is terrified and disappointed by it all. And I think that fear is what keeps her nose buried in her bible and denying any of it is happening."

"So then, there is no way she could ever possibly accept me for what I can do or what is happening," Mia said, downcast.

"I wouldn't say never, but unfortunately sweetheart, I think that's the way it might remain. I'm sorry. I knew I should have never brought it up," Lydia consoled, patting her niece's hand.

Mia looked up. "No, Aunt Lydia. Thank you for telling me. I finally have some answers—some reason as to why there has always been an unbridgeable distance between my mother and me. It makes sense now. And I can live with it. I always thought it was something I did that made her not love me."

"Honey, you must believe me when I tell you that your mother does, in fact love you. I know because of the way she has spoken about you to me over the years. Unfortunately, her love for you is not enough to overcome her fears. She was anxious all throughout her pregnancy with you and then once you starting seeing things that were unexplainable, even when you were a little bitty thing, she couldn't take it. She has tried, but she is not a strong person. In fact, I believe your very strength is something that she greatly admires."

"It is?" Mia had always felt that her mother couldn't find any admirable qualities within her. This revelation was perplexing, but comforting. She hugged Nathan closer to her.

"Yes. Somewhere deep inside of her she knows if she had been a stronger person like you, she would have summoned more courage to delight in her only child and survive her losses. Instead, too much of her died long ago with them. In a sense, I think she misses who she was once but she also knows there is no way she'll ever get that back.

"Now you, on the other hand, are a force to be reckoned with," Lydia's eyes sparkled with pride as she studied her niece's face.

"Oh, I really don't think so, Auntie. Truth of the matter is I'm a pretty big chicken myself. I can only hope to live up to your belief in me," Mia answered.

"No doubt you will, child. I have every assurance that you will."

"So, will you teach me how to read tarot cards, conduct séances, and use crystals for divination and all of that?"

"No, dear. Those things are only for old quacks like me. You've got the real deal and that is all you will ever need."

‡   ‡   ‡

Dan examined the unmarked DVD that Ho had just tossed onto his desk that was littered with more DVDs, CDs, flash drives, storyboards, and video logs. "What's this? Please don't tell me it's any more last minute crap detail that producer wants in the doc. If he adds one more thing, we might as well call it a feature length movie," he complained.

"It's something for Mia. I thought she might like it for a memento or something. You know, to start a collection of what she does," Ho said as he plunked himself down in his chair, leaned back, and linked his hands together behind his head, looking quite satisfied.

"What she does? I'm not sure I follow you," Dan said, slipping his finger through the center hole on the DVD. He contemplated the rainbow hologram across its shiny surface.

"Yeah, what she does with being psychic and all. I thought she might like to make up an 'e-scrapbook' of cases solved. When I think about it, that's really not a bad idea… Hmmm, but I wonder if there's any way I can market that with all the other ones out there already?" Ho cocked an eyebrow and looked up at the ceiling in thought.

Dan snapped his fingers at his pensive friend and laughed. "Here, Ho. Stay with me, bud," he teased. "Let's focus now."

"Huh? Oh, right. She's going to make it big with that, so she may as well keep track of all of these events. Who knows? Maybe down the road we can make a documentary or a biopic featuring her. Anyways, that has the news clip about that little girl who was rescued."

"Oh, right, right. Start an archive. We hadn't even thought about looking for the clip of it. Hey thanks, man. She's gonna love it." Dan looked at the DVD on his finger with a new appreciation.

"No prob. Hey, any chance that I can come over again and, you know, bring a friend? This girl I'm seeing really digs that stuff. I thought that maybe, well…"

"What? You can score some points?"

"… maybe."

"On any other day, I'd say maybe too. But sorry, dude. Mia and the baby aren't feeling well. Nathan had a fever this morning and I haven't heard from Mia yet. So I'm trying to finish up some of this B.S. today and possibly get home at least on time tonight."

"They're sick? Uh oh. I hear that there's some kind of bug running around and while I'm not pinning this on Nathan, everyone knows that babies are nothing but little Petri dishes. I hope they feel better. Tell Mia to try some ku ding tea. At least that's what my granny would give me for colds and fever. But watch out—that stuff is so bitter it'll peel the paint off of walls. Anyway, I can cover for you for the last hour if you want to blow out of here."

"Hey sure. Thanks a million, Ho. I owe you."

"No prob. Just let me bring over my friend when Mia and Nathan are better and we'll call it even."

"Deal."

Upon Ho's mention of the herbal tea remedy, Dan's thoughts immediately went to Lydia. He hoped that she wasn't trying any of that New Age hocus pocus on the baby. One thing was her trying to feed that stuff to them, as adults. But he felt there was no room for error when it came to infants.

"Hey Murph. Just calling to see how you two were doing," he said when Mia picked up the phone a few minutes later.

"Oh, all right, I guess. Nathan's fever is down to an elevation now. Still a bit fussy but at least he's sleeping. I'm sorry I haven't called yet. Aunt Lydia and I were talking and I didn't get a chance."

"Speaking of Aunt Lydia—she hasn't given him anything, has she?"

"She gave him a little water in a bottle and a zwieback cookie earlier. But that's about it. Why?"

"Just wondering… How about you? How are you doing? Did your headache ease up any?"

"No. Auntie gave me some tea that seems to have taken the edge off and aromatherapy in a sachet. But I'm still feeling out of it. I think I'm going to lie down after we hang up."

"Yeah, you should definitely do that. I have a chance to get home a little earlier tonight, so I can make something for dinner so you don't have to worry about it."

"That would be great."

"So, anything else from You-Know-Who?"

"No, he hasn't shown up this afternoon. We talked some this morning, but we didn't get anywhere. I can't figure him out. I'll tell you more about it when you get home. Anyway, I'll be relieved when this one is over with."

"Yeah, you and me both."

‡　　‡　　‡

"What is this? Are we going to watch a movie?" Lydia asked as Dan loaded the disc into the DVD player and turned on the TV.

"It's the news footage of when they rescued Samantha from the outbuilding where she was being held. Dan's friend at work made a copy of it for us to keep," Mia explained.

"And this is the missing child you helped the police to locate?" Lydia asked.

"Yup. Mia figured it out all on her own. She saved that girl's life," Dan butted in with pride.

"Oh wonderful! This is so exciting," Lydia exclaimed, putting on her glasses and settling back in her chair as Dan selected the video.

Mia held the baby on her lap and offered him his teething ring to chew on while they watched the screen. "That was really thoughtful of Ho to find this and save it for me," she said. "Please thank him for me."

However, as she sat back to watch, her thoughts were divided. The first time she had seen the story when it aired, Mia was too excited to focus on details. Now as the footage rolled this second time around, she was able to view it with a more sympathetic eye. How lonely and terrifying it must have been for that child to be isolated and so far away from her family. The surrounding area looked rural—mostly woods and fields. Samantha's screams would have been futile if there wasn't anyone near enough to hear her. Mia appreciated even more just how brave she had been.

Nathan squirmed on her lap and fretted. Still fussy from his bout with the fever, he wasn't acting himself. Mia rose to get his bottle of water on the counter.

"Where are you going, Murph? Don't you want to watch this?" Dan asked.

"I can hear it. Nat-a-Tat needs some water. I'll be back."

"I can get it for you, hold on—"

"Don't be silly. I'm already up."

Just as she passed the kitchen doorway, for a second she thought she saw a fleeting shadow across the wall. She froze in place and turned to look back at Dan and Lydia. They were both still in their seats and watching the screen. It couldn't have been either one. Blinking hard, she saw that there was no shadow present and she shook her head in disbelief. Perhaps this persistent headache was making her see things.

While she offered the water bottle to Nathan, she studied every reflective surface in the kitchen. All remained clear although when she returned to the living room, she spied John's telltale silhouette reflected in the pane of glass of a picture frame. The hair on the back of her neck rose. She wondered how many times she thought he wasn't there and hadn't noticed his presence. His features were faint in the glass, however his line of sight went directly across to the TV screen. If she wasn't mistaken, he was watching the footage.

"Do you want me to play it over for you?" Dan asked as the story wrapped up within the next minute.

"No thanks, it's fine, I'm sure we'll watch it again," Mia answered distractedly, not wanting to let on that anything was amiss. She pondered John's attendance, unsure of what he was about to do. It was unusual for him not to demand attention.

Lydia rose from her seat, went to her niece, and hugged her. "I'm so proud of you, darling! You really did a fine job. That child was so fortunate to have found you."

"Huh? Yes, thanks, Aunt Lydia. I'm just glad I was able to make a difference."

"Oh, but you have. You have," the older woman said.

"Well, if everyone is hungry, dinner should be done by now," Dan said. "I followed that recipe in the book to a tee, so hopefully it tastes good." Although he was all thumbs in the kitchen, he couldn't trust Lydia's cooking out of fear of the ingredients she might decide to throw in. Just a few days before, he had caught her stirring an unidentifiable dark green elixir into a soup that Mia was simmering on the stove.

"I'm sure it'll taste great," Mia said, appreciating the extra time and effort it took him to make something halfway edible. Just this simple meatloaf, pot of mashed potatoes, and microwaved peas took him almost an hour and a half to prepare. What's more she was looking for a distraction so she'd stop obsessing about the specter in the glass. *My family comes first,* she thought resolutely as she placed Nathan in his high chair and started to set the table while Lydia poured the drinks. *John's not going to take that from me.*

Dan cracked open the oven door and peeked in. "Time's up. It looks done," he said as he slid out the pan and moved it to the top of the stove to cool. "Hey, wait a minute. What the heck?"

"What's up, Murph?" Mia asked as she peered around him.

"This burnt stuff on top of my meatloaf." He pointed to the blackened leaves scattered across the top of the loaf. "What happened? I know I had the temperature right. Three-fifty, right? What is that?"

"Oh, some of it's marigold, Dan. It has a spicy taste that is similar to saffron, just a bit more citrusy. It's absolutely lovely. And the rest are chive blossoms and bee balm flowers," Lydia explained while setting out the drinks on the table. "You had some coming up in the garden and I thought they would be a wonderful addition to spice things up."

"Spice things up? Well, you thought wrong. Damnit, Lydia, I'd rather not eat yard waste every time I want a meal. Don't you realize that these are toxic?" Dan's patience was starting to run thin with these herbal concoctions.

"I assure you, they're not," Lydia answered with a soft chuckle. "Many flowers are edible. Man has been eating them for as long as they have eaten vegetables and fruits. And I know for a fact that these types are not noxious."

"The hell they're not! I looked it up online the last time you chucked some into our salad. Although the flowers themselves may be all right, I've been using pesticides and herbicides in the yard for years," Dan answered growing more agitated. "And according to numerous sites, they all say they same thing which is you're not supposed to eat it if its been sprayed. But what really chaps my ass is that I had asked you to refrain from doing it and you went against my wishes anyway. What? To prove a point?" His anger was clear now.

"Hon, please watch your language around the baby," Mia interceded. "I'm sure Auntie washed everything thoroughly."

"That doesn't make a bit of difference. According to what the horticultural sites say, the plants absorb the shit up through their vascular systems."

"Oh, how could you?" Lydia exclaimed, "Everyone knows you never ever use chemical insecticides on your plants. That makes them unfit for eating."

"What do you think I'm trying to tell you? I used them because I never expected to be eating directly from my flowerboxes. And if you had respected my wishes and respected *me*, we wouldn't be having this discussion right now. In fact, I don't know how to make it any clearer—I want you to totally can all that herbal crap while you are here. I don't need you getting anyone in my family sick." A look of alarm washed over him as a realization sunk in. "Come to think of it, you didn't feed Nathan anything out of the garden, did you?"

"No! Of course not. Wait—what are you insinuating? You couldn't possibly mean that I made him sick! I would never do that to that precious baby," Lydia cried out in protest.

"Dan, Aunt Lydia—Please, will you both calm down?" Mia pleaded, distressed at the intensity of their argument that seemed to have erupted out of nothing. "It is no big deal. I can make something else for us to eat."

"It would have been fine if he hadn't gone to town with the poison on those perfectly good plants," Lydia argued. "If we had gotten sick from eating them, it would've been because of his ignorance."

Dan's eyes widened and his jaw set. "So it's my fault? We would've been sitting down to dinner already if you hadn't insisted on tossing in half the garden every time we eat! Have you ever once considered that we might not care for that shit, Lydia? This is ruined now and we could've wound up in the hospital having our stomachs pumped all because of your bullshit."

"Dan—watch your language! Nathan can hear you." Mia reminded.

He continued, "And another thing—have you been burning incense around here?"

"Just a few sticks to—"

"Goddamn it! The smell is driving me crazy and you're coating everything with soot."

"You're exaggerating. There is no smell or soot," Lydia answered in defense. "It's all lies."

The rate in which the bickering between her husband and aunt was escalating shocked Mia. Usually, they were considerate of each other's feelings and opinions even when they had differences. It wasn't like either of them. Something wasn't right.

"Stop! We'll just get some take out," she tried again, hoping to diffuse the situation that was spinning out of control.

Lydia faced Dan and pointed her finger up at him. "You know what your problem is? You're a fool. A non-believer with your mind completely closed off. You will never understand anything beyond your own short-sightedness," she said indignantly, her voice growing shrill and cracking with stress.

"Oh I know what my problem is—it's your cockamamie hocus-pocus bullshit and not minding any of your damn business! I wish you'd give it up already, you old bat. You're nothing but delusional."

"Daniel, enough! You don't mean that. Let's just talk about this—" Mia said as she tried in vain to intervene once more.

"I have to make sure that my niece and grand-nephew are safe," Lydia fought back.

"What? That's my job, not yours." He looked the older woman in the eye.

"Ha! Your job? That's a joke."

"And what exactly do you mean by that?"

"Well you didn't do such a good job the last time, did you? If these matters were left entirely up to you, Mia might find herself in a life-threatening situation again like what happened last time, that's what I mean! I still can't believe you had her committed!"

"Oh, you're *way* over the line now, Lydia. You better back off." Dan's jaw clenched and unclenched as his face flushed. His expression was similar to that of a snarling dog backed into a corner. Mia had never seen him so worked up before.

"Both of you need to calm down. Please, something is not right—" she started but Nathan drew her attention when he started to cry from the angry voices and mounting tension in the room.

"Or what? Just what do you intend to do?" the older woman shot back at Dan.

"I have a good mind to walk you the hell right out of here. In fact, now is as good a time as any."

"I'd like to see you try." Lydia set her fists on her hips and jutted out her chin. She was unrecognizable now. Her face was a bright beet red and strands of her grey hair stuck out in all directions from her temples giving her the look of a crazed woman.

"Stop! Please stop!" Mia begged. "You are not yourselves. Listen to me. There is something happening!" Chaos was engulfing the room and closing in with a strangling force. Her loved ones appeared distorted and savage, ready to tear each other to pieces. An intense fear welled up inside of her. At that moment, it appeared as if the light dimmed. Mia looked up and around. "Did you see that?" she asked, but it went unnoticed by the other two still locked in a stare down.

"That's it. You're out of here. We can start with your bags," Dan said to Lydia, with a quick threatening motion. "And your incense, candles, and all that other new-age shit you brought with you."

"Don't you *dare* lay a finger on my things!" Lydia shrieked, her eyes bulging as she started to flail at him.

Suddenly Mia's eye caught it—another shadow. But it wasn't the shape of a man, but that of a large serpent. It snaked its way from corner to corner of the room, running in the angle where the wall and ceiling met.

"Oh my god—look!" she exclaimed as she pointed at it, her finger following the quick movements of the shadow as it shifted. A frightened scream escaped from Nathan as he clung to his mother.

It was enough to halt the others' hostile exchange. Dan's gaze followed her finger upwards. "What? What are you looking at, Mia?"

Lydia glanced around, trying to see what her niece was pointing at. Then she slipped her crystal pendant from her pocket and let it dangle on its chain, holding it before her. It spun crazy circles counter-clockwise and then distinctly shifted direction to a clockwise rotation.

"It's right there! There! Did you see it move?" Mia insisted, watching the phantom image dart about the kitchen.

Nathan howled with anguish and turned red.

"I'm not seeing anything. Do you need me to get a mirror for you?" Dan asked.

"It's a definite energy field. Look at this," Lydia said, holding up the pivoting pendant.

"Will you cut it out with that goddamned thing?" Dan growled and pushed past the old woman. He fetched the mirror and returned, not wasting any time. Then he swapped it for his son who continued to cry inconsolably.

Mia was confronted by John glaring back at her from the mirror, his face twisted almost beyond recognition. He laughed at her startled expression as his mouth contorted to an ugly sneer, his features melting as they writhed and reformed like warm taffy. His unyielding stare from his glowing bloodshot eyes bore into her, threatening to penetrate her very soul. Terrified of the unadulterated evil she held in her hands, Mia reflexively flung the mirror away from her. It hit the tile floor and shattered, sending shards of glass shooting across the kitchen.

Trembling, she could see that John's face was splintered into fragments, pieces of it reflected on each of the fractured slivers. One of his eyes peered up at her from a jagged piece by the island, while his other eye was closer to the dishwasher, about a foot away. She looked down by her feet to see his cruel mouth and tongue running lasciviously over his lips. "Nooo!" she gasped as she jumped back.

Seeing her petrified in place, Dan was perplexed by her reaction to the shattered glass. "Here, take him out of here," he directed Lydia as he handed over Nathan who was sobbing now. "Mia, what is it, honey?" He followed her stare down to the broken mirror on the floor. "Here, I'll clean that up. Watch where you step, there's glass all over the place."

She barely nodded in acknowledgment. Her eyes remained glued on the fragments of the specter's likeness. She knew her husband could not see the gruesome visage that leered at her as he swept up the bits that were scattered throughout the room in corners and crevices around the base of the cabinets. Even the smallest shards showed flesh or hair or part of a facial feature. The fragments reinforced to her how embedded he was in so many facets of their lives.

While the human fragments were unspeakable, what horrified Mia more was the fact that John had succeeded in invading and occupying her family. It was John's sinister spell they were under just moments before when they were at each other's throats. Suddenly it occurred to her—had he made the baby sick as well? His presence was growing stronger, more persistent, and now—corruptive. *What else is he capable of doing?*

Dan swept the last remnants into the dustpan and then deposited them into the trash. Although John was no longer visible, she knew with despair, that it was only a temporary reprieve. How was she going to rid her home and life of him?

At the fast food restaurant, their dinner was a sullen affair. No one had any heart for conversation and even less of an appetite. Usually active and bright, Nathan remained listless, refusing food when offered. To Mia's horror, the black shadow had followed them and John's twisted image leered at her on reflections big and small around her. Of course Dan couldn't see any of it, and Lydia's focus continued to be in a deadlock with him. However, Mia didn't dare mention John's appearance to either one of them in fear that they would start arguing all over again.

Once they finished, they left immediately. Back at home, Lydia retired straight away to her room while Dan retreated to the back porch with a shot glass and a quarter of a bottle of bourbon he hadn't touched since before the baby was born, leaving Mia alone in despair with no one to confide in. He remained aloof for the rest of the evening.

By the time she climbed into bed after rocking the baby to sleep and disposing of the meatloaf, Dan was already asleep. She wished he had been awake to comfort her. Feeling overly anxious, she brought their sleeping child back to their bedroom and secured him in the bed between them.

By 2:46am, she shifted miserably from her right side to her left. Staring with eyes wide open in the dark, the day's disturbing events echoed back at her. *Things are only going to get worse.* With John's treacherous influence pervading her household, what was to become of her family? It frightened her to see two precious people in her life tear into each other like that. *How much further was he going to intrude and for how much longer?* She thought back to her aunt's words, *Now you, on the other hand, are a force to be reckoned with.* Ashamed, she felt that she couldn't be strong at all. She had no control over what John could do and no idea of how to stop him, and the others hadn't the slightest clue as to what was truly going on.

A mix of anger, anxiety, and frustration formed hot tears that rolled down her cheeks and soaked into her pillow. She felt so utterly lost and helpless. More so, she blamed herself for getting them all into this wretched situation.

She knew the visitor continued to lurk nearby, watching her and her loved ones with predatory eyes in the night. In the dead silent room, she could hear the faintest of sounds of the house as it slept—the ticking of hot water pipes cooling down, the brush of a branch against the window… a steady rhythmic scratch-scratch against the fabric of her pillow case. *What is that?*

Feeling on guard she listened very closely as the scratching continued. Only then, did she begin to realize she was simply hearing the pulse of blood through her jugular vein as it beat against the pillowcase. Sighing with relief, she focused on that beat, hoping it would lull her to sleep. Maybe tomorrow, she would find a way to end the madness that was destroying their lives.

"You're next."

Coarse and low, the whisper pierced like a poisonous tip into her ear, making her bolt straight up with alarm. At that very instant, excruciating pain in the form of intense fire radiated through her skull. Crying out, her hands shot up to grip her head as her fingers dug into her flesh in agony.

Blood red flooded across her eyes, bathing the room in blackness. Mia felt her body growing slack and helpless to stop herself from falling back upon the bed. Her vision now gone, the searing pain engulfed her so that she could barely inhale, fighting for breath.

As the enduring torture took over totally and completely, Mia felt her life leaving her. Heart beating wildly in her chest, her body refused to respond to her will and the last thing she heard was Dan's voice calling to her.

It sounded miles away.

It was happening all over again. Dan sat across from the admissions clerk, his hands shaking, face unshaven, and dressed in the tee shirt he had worn to bed.

"Does she have any allergies?" the woman asked him.

All he could manage to perceive of the clerk through the maelstrom of thoughts swirling in his head was that her face consisted of circles. Round nose, round eyes, round cheeks, round head...

"No. Yes. I mean she has seasonal hay fever from time to time," he answered.

"Any allergies to medications that you know of?"

"None."

"Is she currently taking any medications?" the round mouth asked.

"No, ma'am."

"Who's her primary physician?"

"Uh... I don't know."

He tried hard to focus on the questions, but his mind continued to stray, struggling to make sense of what had just happened less than two hours ago. Feeling tired and disgruntled after a lousy evening of conflict with Lydia, he had fallen into a fitful sleep. Next thing he knew, Mia was screaming and writhing about. He woke in time to see her slump over like a limp rag doll. When he turned to assist her, he found their sleeping son lying between them.

"Has she had any surgeries?"

On the clerk's desk, among the framed pictures of her kids, was a bright yellow figurine of a rotund caricature perched before him with its arms outstretched and wearing a sign around its neck that read, "I rUN

On hUGs." *Why is it that these office ladies always go for the corny crap?* he wondered distractedly.

"She had her appendix taken out when she was twenty... and she had a heart valve corrected when she was a teenager. I can't remember the condition right now or exactly how old she was."

"That's all right."

When he fumbled for the light, his wife remained still, sprawled out in an odd angle as if she had been broken and thrown there. Coming around to her side of the bed, he spoke to her and brushed back her hair from her face. She stared beyond him, looking dazed, her eyes half closed as if she had been drugged. When he pressed his ear to her chest, he detected a rapid heartbeat. No matter how he shook her shoulders and called to her, she continued to lie there, unresponsive.

Oh god, Mia. What is wrong?

Frantic, he returned his ear to her chest. Her breathing was shallow. "C'mon, babe, talk to me," he said holding her face and looking into her unblinking eyes.

"Has she had any children?"

Dan snapped to. "Huh? Uh, yes ma'am. One. Our son. He is ten... no, eleven months old."

"That's a nice age," the clerk said as she typed in the information and scanned the screen.

When Mia wouldn't respond, he went for the phone. After reaching the 911 operator, he didn't recognize his own voice saying, "Yes sir, something is wrong with my wife. She is unconscious, but her eyes are open. And she's not moving or responding. Please send someone quick."

He listened to the operator and robotically obeyed all the conveyed instructions given him to revive his wife. Still, no response, Mia's mouth slightly agape. A single tear gathered at the corner of her eye and rolled down her cheek. Nathan whimpered in his sleep, reminding Dan of his presence besides his mother.

"Lydia! Lydia, wake up! Come here!... I need you to come get Nathan," Dan called to her, afraid to leave Mia's side.

"Did she have any symptoms? Any complaints recently?" the admissions clerk sat poised with her fingers above the keyboard, ready for Dan's answer.

"Symptoms?"

How could he explain that she had been seeing things all along? That she had psychic abilities? That she had been locked up in a mental institution before?

"She was complaining of a headache. And tiredness. We just thought that she was coming down with a bug. Our son had a fever and was sick. So we assumed she had caught it too."

"Headache and lethargy…" Type, type, type, scroll, scroll, round eyes rolling around the screen. "Okay, Mr. Labont, if I can just have her insurance card and driver's license. I need to make a copy of them."

After completing the paperwork, Dan stopped at a restroom before heading up to the surgery center's waiting room. He went immediately to the sink and splashed cold water on his face, rubbing hard, trying to rouse himself from this nightmare that he couldn't escape.

Raising his head, he stopped for a moment when he caught his reflection staring back, water running tracks down his cheeks and trickling off his chin. The feeling of déjà vu had returned. There must have been clues that she had been giving off, regardless of what the ER doc told him. *What did I miss this time?*

In retrospect, of course there were symptoms—her headaches. He thought about all the times she had mentioned them and how he chalked them up to one thing or another. And then there he was, arguing with her aunt over some stupid meal. It was clearly upsetting Mia, yet he did not—no—*could not* stop. What was it that made them go off at each other like that? It appeared that Lydia was correct. Perhaps he couldn't protect his family after all.

Out of sheer frustration and anger, he struck himself hard and repeatedly on the forehead with his fist, his knuckles leaving dull red marks from the blows. He couldn't help but feel he kept letting his wife down in one capacity or another. Now her very life was in jeopardy. What if she didn't make it? What would he do without her? What of their son waiting for his mother to come home?

I promise you, Murph, I won't ever let you down again. Just please make it. Please—come back to us…

"With this progress, his recovery is looking promising," Dr. Grace Chen conferred with Dr. Donald Cole, Talbot's attending physician. "His Glascow has progressed to an eleven within this week. I'm feeling confident."

The older doctor nodded his balding head in agreement, looking over the chart with the weary experience of thirty plus years of practice.

Chen turned to Meredith. "Make sure to alert your staff to continue to monitor all of his reactions and to take careful notes." She was tall, calmly confident, and exuded intellect.

"I sure will, Dr. C.," Meredith answered in her best can-do voice hoping to cover her disdain for the painfully obvious directive and her contempt for the woman who gave it. What did Chen expect the nurses to do—look the other way should Bradford get up to do a tap dance?

In contrast, Bailey's heart soared when she heard the doctor's summary. The high-powered staff consulting in the room hardly took notice of her flushing his feeding tube or changing out his Foley bag. The organizational food chain at Bay View Hospital was alive, healthy, and well tended to, and she clearly was a bottom feeder. They never asked her opinion, nor expected her to give one, thus she always felt invisible in their presence.

Bailey lingered, knowing they would wrap up their conference and leave within another minute or so. It was then that she and Talbot could be alone. And it was then that she could elicit more reactions and nurture and encourage him toward recovery.

Anticipating their exit, the CNA busied herself tucking in the sheets around his bed and checking room supplies until the door bumped closed behind the last of them. Their voices grew faint as they moved down the hallway. Alone, at last, she gazed upon Talbot and took up his hand, kissed it, and stroked her cheek gently against it.

"Did you hear what they were saying? Soon, sweetheart, soon. You'll be yourself in no time. And every day you'll get even stronger, I know you will. Just keep trying. I'll be with you every step of the way. You can depend on it."

Talbot's eyes opened and he stared straight ahead. He lifted one arm drowsily and let it settle back down.

"That's right, lover. Keep working it. You're doing great," she said encouragingly.

Just then the door opened again. Bailey quickly released his hand and with a degree of annoyance, turned to see who had interrupted them once more. A strange woman poked her head in and peered about timidly.

"Uh, pardon me. Is this room 410A? I was looking for Talbot Bradford... Oh, there you are."

Bailey did a quick assessment of the stylishly dressed woman in her early forties entering the room. One look told her that this person was used to manicures, boutiques, and spa treatments. She felt self-conscious in her thread worn scrubs displaying various stains that wouldn't wash out.

"I'm sorry, but are you a family member?" Bailey rose and faced her.

"Well, no. Actually, I'm a very close friend of Talbot's."

"It's just that this is the critical care unit and visitation is limited to family members only."

"I don't believe he has any family members to speak of, if I recall correctly. In fact, I think I'm the closest thing to family he's got right now. And the minute I found out where he was, I had to come see him."

"How did you find out?" Bailey swallowed hard. She could only wonder if she had left some kind of trace back at his house. Anxiety sprang up within her as she racked her memory. The last thing she needed was to get caught.

"Oh, it's such a small world. It just so happened that the officer who was working the accident that Tal was involved in is my neighbor. I was talking to him and one thing led to another in our conversation and he mentioned the accident including the car's make and model. It was such a strange accident, with the car being up in a tree and all. He had never seen anything like it. Anyway, I told him that my friend drove a car like that, and he recognized Talbot's name from the report he had filled out. Seems there are not too many people named Talbot in this area, apparently! From there, I did some calling around until I found which hospital he was taken to."

Bailey inwardly sighed with relief. "Well, isn't that something?" she said.

"So, I was hoping to see how he was doing and visit for a little while. I don't have to be to work until three."

The nursing assistant thought hard for a moment. Any stimulus was only going to benefit him now that he was getting so close to coming around. "You know, I don't think that would hurt a bit," she conceded. "In fact, it would be nice for him. We haven't seen any family members come to visit him yet. But just make sure you pay attention to visiting hours. They end at two-thirty p.m. sharp for the patient resting period and resume at four-thirty until nine at night. I can let you stay, but I don't know if the other nurses will be so lenient so they may ask you to leave. Anyway, I'll be back around in a little while. My name's Bailey Hague if you need anything."

"Thank you so much, Bailey. It's so nice to meet you. I'm Cheryl Becker," the woman said graciously as she extended her hand.

"Oh," was all Bailey could manage to say before she left.

‡   ‡   ‡

Defiant eyelids remained closed. Her head felt as if it had been kicked in. It was completely silent about her with not a single sound except for the rasp of her breath as it caught in her throat. When she finally managed to open her eyes, it took a moment to focus on the strange, shifting surroundings. The walls appeared to run and ripple like a dark palette of watercolors in the rain. Mia did not recognize where she was, having no frame of reference or familiar objects about her. It was unnatural and eerie. *Where am I? And... what happened?* Disoriented, she felt like throwing up.

Her arms weighed heavy with the sensation of having fallen asleep. Trying her legs, she found they wouldn't move at all. Pinned down by her body's unresponsiveness, the ground beneath her was as hard and unforgiving as a stone slab. She lay flat upon her back and shivered with an icy frigidness as the unyielding surface rapidly extracted body heat from any curve and bare flesh it made contact with. Although she couldn't be sure, it felt as if she was dressed in nothing more than a short nightgown. Naked beneath the thin fabric, her skin crawled as the cold easily penetrated it.

The dreary watercolors shifted, alternating between a deep crimson red to an abysmal black void that threatened to swallow her up entirely. This cycle pulsed with the steady pace of a heartbeat—too slow to be warm blooded, but like that of something sinister and reptilian instead.

"Dan?" she called out for her husband. "Dan—can you hear me?" Her words folded back upon themselves, mocking her. She strained her ears to catch anything that might give her a clue as to where she was. "Help me! Dan! Aunt Lydia?... Anyone? Please, I need you!" she called again. With the profound silence that ensued, Mia was struck with the absolute certainty that Dan, nor anyone else for that matter, could hear her. She may as well been entombed alive. Her heart was hammering and her instincts registered fear. *How long have I been here?* Something terrible had happened. She knew it. But somehow she couldn't remember exactly what it was.

Her eyes continued their frantic survey of her surroundings, desperate to fall upon any shape that made sense or color other than blood that filled her view. Panic escaped her in the form of short gasps. The overwhelming urge to claw, scramble, and flee welled up within her, but her body wouldn't respond. *What is happening? Where is everybody?* Her mind tumbled with the enormity of her dire situation. She screamed over and over again, her cries swallowed up in the blackness.

"I see you're enjoying your new accommodations." A low voice parted the watercolor and disturbed the deafening silence.

John was with her.

It was then she understood where she was. Mia turned her head but couldn't see him. Her surroundings grew oppressive.

"Lovely shade of deprivation, isn't it? You'll get used to it. And you'll have to get reacquainted with your body to know what works and what doesn't anymore. But don't fret, you might be up and around in no time, like me."

Only able to lift her torso, Mia struggled to turn one way and then the other, trying to see where he was. He seemed to keep just out of view. *If I am here with him, does it mean that I am no longer living?* She choked down the increasing panic rising within her. Had she crossed over to her visitors' imprisoned state of torment?

"Finding it difficult to speak just yet? That's typical. I have no doubt you'll find your tongue eventually. As for here, you simply have to let go of what you used to be. It is then that you will finally be free to be who you truly were meant to be. I know I'm *loving* the new me."

Preceding him, a sinister shadow seeped in and flowed around her like a toxic cloud. Mia fought to rise, but her body stubbornly refused to react. All at once the image of an insect glued down on a web with a deadly spider bearing down it entered her thoughts.

John's face abruptly loomed over hers, only inches away; his eyes bore into hers. "I believe I questioned once before, of all people, why did it have to be you? And now I understand why it had to be you and how we're going to be stuck together for quite a while longer. The one who would so gallantly 'save me' ends up the one who so desperately needs to be saved. It's sheer irony to say the least."

His fetid breath was hot upon her face, as spittle from his mockery clung to her cheek. Terrified, Mia willed herself not to cry out. Instead, she matched stares with him. A cursory glance revealed that John's condition had degraded even more than when she last saw him. The smooth curves of his face had wasted away to severe, hard angles. His pallor was ghastly and pale while his sunken bloodshot eyes were mad with arrogance. His once straight teeth appeared now as jagged spires lining his cruel mouth. The shadow clung and swirled about him like a living cloak. Whereas Seth was tormented by its presence, John seemed to revel in it.

"What's the matter, Soccer Mom? Your incredible psychic abilities don't work here? Or perhaps you finally ran out of inane, pointless questions. If this is indeed the case, then how may *I* help *you*?" His cracked lips twisted into a sardonic sneer. "Better yet, since you're on this side now, how about I give you a look around your new home?"

His hands struck her chest hard with a thump, strong fingers curling up fistfuls of her gown. Roughly, he yanked her from where she was, pulling her into an upright position with seemingly little effort. Mia's useless legs buckled beneath her. She managed to take a feeble hold of his wrists, but he did not ease his powerful grip on her. Instead, he pulled her close enough that their noses touched. It took all of her strength just to hold herself away from him, but she couldn't break loose.

"How about we start in your little neck of the woods?"

Within the watery darkness that flowed about them, John pointed to a small pinhole of light and then dragged her toward it. As they approached, the pinhole rapidly enlarged to the size of a quarter, then a dinner plate, and finally lengthened to a large panel. He approached this rectangle and grabbing her hair, forced her to look at it.

The panel before her displayed the depths of the mirror in reverse. She was staring into her own living room. The scene before Mia so momentarily amazed her, that she released his wrists. This was the perspective of Seth, Samantha… and John. She suddenly felt exposed and vulnerable, realizing how these visitors could observe her and her family—as easily as if they had been viewing her through some kind of surveillance. Just then, a distraught Lydia walked past, holding Nathan. She appeared to be crying and did not stop to look at the mirror, continuing on her way to the kitchen. On impulse, Mia tried to raise her hand and cry out to her, but she could not. Her body refused to respond properly.

"Recognize where you are?" John said as he shoved her roughly toward the glass pane. Bracing herself for impact, she found that she had instead passed into a reversed orientation of her living room where she fell upon the floor. She was surrounded by her own things, and could hear the voices of her family in the kitchen. Mia desperately called out to them, but they couldn't hear her. It was apparent that she had no means of communication.

John pulled her upright and then gripped the back of her head, his fingers digging into her scalp, forcing her to stare down at the notebook her aunt had left open by the glass. Before them were her written notes.

"And this, I see, is your latest success story—little Samantha. You worked so hard at something that should have well been left alone. Why is it that you enabled her to escape her prison, but you won't free me? Which brings to mind a little point that demands justification. Samantha and that boy you 'helped'—you were impressed by their cleverness in getting from surface to surface and yet considered me the imbecile that couldn't figure things out."

Mia's eyes darted toward him.

"That's right, I heard your conversation with your aunt. You look surprised. Do you think that just because you couldn't see me meant that I wasn't aware of you? As you can see, in time, I did indeed figure out how to get around. It was the only form of freedom afforded me in this perpetual hell. In fact, it was liberating to find that I could get to certain places all on my own. I wasn't tied to your apron strings after all."

With a leap, they took off once again. He focused on another pinpoint of light in what seemed like the opposite direction. Mia was nothing more than a helpless mouse, trapped in the talons of a deadly raptor.

The pinhole enlarged and they found themselves viewing a private hospital room. A smartly dressed woman sat beside the bed of an unconscious man. A feeding tube snaked down his nose. A ventilator filled his lungs with air while an IV line dripped life into his arm. The attached monitor echoed a steady, strong heartbeat.

It took Mia a moment to recognize the man in the bed. When she did, her eyes grew wide.

"Oh, so you notice the likeness? Judging by your slow reaction time, I can't say your powers of observation are any keener than your psychic ones. If you will forgive a cheesy cliché from the seventies, it took me some time 'to find myself.' But here I lie—at least my comatose body. However, according to the doctor's prognosis, I should be making a recovery any day now."

The woman in the room picked up the man's hand and held it affectionately. She started speaking to him.

"Talbot, I'm not sure if I'm doing this right, but it's me, Cheryl. I thought I'd stop by and see how you are doing."

"I hate that bloody bitch," John said venomously, witnessing the scene. "Between her and that other stupid whore, I don't know who is worse. One with her paint and wiles or the other with her whimpering and maternal doting—it's the hypocrisy of female dichotomy and completely detestable."

Cheryl continued, "I hope you can hear me. I'm concerned about you. Everyone is wondering what has happened to you. We are all praying that you'll get better soon."

The unconscious man's eyelids began to flutter.

"Are you hearing me, Tal? That's it. Keep trying."

Quite suddenly, John vanished. No longer held in his grip, Mia collapsed upon the ground in a heap. Once again she was plunged into the silent darkness, alone.

‡   ‡   ‡

"Yeah, Ho. They're not quite sure yet… Uh huh. She's in surgery now. It's going to be a while. What?… No, I'm good, but thanks, man. It's probably best if you come over later, when she's in her room… Right. I'll let you know.

I already called in to work—what? You're calling in sick too? Why?… Well all right, but don't feel you have to… Sure, buddy, I really appreciate that. So listen if you are going to do that, there are a couple of favors you can do for me then… Okay, first, remember the news clip you gave to Mia for her 'e-scrapbook'? Will you upload that video to YouTube and then send me the link? There's something I got to do with it… No, I need it ASAP, as a matter of fact. Uh huh… Okay, next, and this is important—do you think you can head on over to my place and just look in on Nathan and Mia's Aunt Lydia for me?… Right. Her aunt was pretty upset when the ambulance came and I know the baby can be a handful sometimes. What?… Okay, great, man. You're friggin' awesome. I really owe you, Ho. Seriously."

Dan hung up. With all the things that were worrying him, at least he could cross *that* off his list. In a time of crisis like this, he appreciated how Hoason had his back and felt relieved in knowing that a sensible person would be there to check in on his son. While his friend had no clue of how to care for an infant, at least Dan was certain that he wasn't going to feed Nathan some weird root or herb nor burn incense over his crib. And, knowing his friend at all, the moment he mentioned uploading the news clip, Ho had probably started working on it as they spoke.

Now all he had to do was wait. He glanced at his watch. It had been close to three hours since they had taken Mia in for surgery. He had contacted his parents and left a message on Jenna's cell. Mia's mother was out of the country with no possible way to reach her. Although Greenlee would be put out that he and now Hoason called in sick today, he knew that his boss was aware that he would resign if he had to.

Dan worked at getting his mind on something else to distract him before the wait drove him crazy. His phone indicated he had an email. Opening it, he saw that it was from Ho and the link to the uploaded video was already awaiting him online. Something had been bugging him since the day he and Mia went on their outing. He couldn't quite put his finger on what it was exactly, but he knew he would recognize it when he saw it. And something told him to start with the news clip.

Dan glanced around the spacious waiting room. Besides him, there were only a few people waiting for others in surgery. Mostly they occupied themselves with watching the non-stop cable news feed on the TV, texting, checking the surgery status update screen, or engaging in quiet conversation with others sitting with them. He settled back in his chair, put his ear buds in, selected the video app on his phone, and started scanning the clip with a discerning eye.

‡   ‡   ‡

"I told Danny that I was coming back after my class trip. He must've forgotten with everything else going on. I was supposed to arrive last night, but the stupid bus broke down by Mt. Shasta and we had to transfer to another one, so it was a three hour delay. But I got his message and I can't believe Mia's in surgery right now!" Jenna spoke in a steady, excited stream. Five minutes ago, she let herself into the house to a find a very surprised Lydia and Ho in the morning hour.

"Yes, we're all very worried about her. Do you need something to eat? Here, why don't you take off your jacket and put your things over there," Lydia said hospitably while guiding her in.

"Hey Jenna, it's been a few years. Wow, look at you—you're all grown up. Remember me from the wedding?" Ho said, as he cast an approving eye over Jenna and smiled charmingly.

"Yes, you're Dan's friend, Howard. Right?" Jenna attempted.

"Hoason. But you can call me Ho."

"All right, Ho." She smiled back.

"Come, let's all sit. The baby was up most of the night and just went to sleep a few minutes ago. I think I need a cup of tea. Does anyone want some tea?" Lydia was pacing.

"Mrs. Castaneda, do you want me to get that for you?" Ho offered.

"Please, it's Lydia. And feel free to call me Aunt Lydia, all right? No, I'm fine, dear. I just need to keep busy, that's all."

When Lydia returned with a steaming pot of tea and a tray of toast and fruit preserves, Jenna beamed at her. "I can't believe Dan's been holding out on me with all of this! It's so freakin' awesome. Ho has been filling me in on what was happening with the mirror, and the little girl Mia saved, and that new guy who is showing up. And he tells me that you are psychic too!"

"Yes, well to a certain extent. Nothing like Mia, but I get by," Lydia answered modestly.

"Well, that is absolutely phenomenal. I wish I would've known what was going on. I would've loved to have asked Mia all about it. And I'm gonna kill Danny for keeping this from me. No wonder he looked all freaked out when I told him that Nat-a-Tat was talking to the mirror. Ha ha. Poor guy," Jenna said, shaking her head.

"Aunt Lydia, do you think it's possible for Mia to be communicating with that dude, John, right now? I mean while she's unconscious and all? Or does that kinda stuff only happen when you're awake?" Ho asked.

"Good Heavens, let's hope not. He's a real menace, not one to be dealt with lightly. And she's in no condition right now to even speak to him," Lydia replied. Although she was reluctant to share it with these two neophytes, inwardly, she was terrified of that very possibility. She and her niece were still unsure of John's true identity, abilities, and motives. He may very well be a dark source reaching out to snare people who were weakened in any capacity to rob them of their life force.

"Well, is there anything you can do to help her if that happens? From what Ho tells me, it sounds like all of these people show up whenever they want, regardless," Jenna asked. "I mean, how would we even know if she is in trouble?"

The expression on Lydia's face was grim as she stared out the rain-streaked window. "I don't know, Jenna. I wish I did. Let's just hope it doesn't happen."

‡　‡　‡

"He's responding, Bailey! He opened his eyes and looked right at me. You should've seen it," Cheryl reported when Bailey returned to Talbot's room.

Although a twinge of jealousy flared within her upon hearing Cheryl's report, Bailey pushed it aside and tried to concentrate on the encouraging outlook. It looked like she might have to call her mother who was babysitting the kids to tell her that she would be home late. Her mother would not be happy about it, but things were getting much closer with Talbot. The last thing Bailey wanted was for Cheryl to be the one there instead of her should he become fully conscious and lucid. She just might have to wait it out until Ms. Becker finally determined it was time to leave.

"Yes, well, he's been responding off and on for the past week or so. Most patients recovering from comas will start to come around like that. It's not an instant waking up process, like you would think. Sometimes it takes a while, but so far, so good. I like showing him his photo album. It seems to get the most reaction from him and it's probably good stimulus."

"Photo album?"

"Yes, watch," Bailey responded confidently as she opened the album and held it up to Talbot. As she paged through the book and gently spoke to him, his eyes focused on the pages before him. Upon seeing the last page, he lifted his hand and blinked.

"Oh my goodness! Will you look at that? That's wonderful!" Cheryl exclaimed. "And do you know who these little girls are?"

Bailey stopped and gaped at the other woman for a moment, puzzled. She was almost certain that Cheryl would know exactly who the girls were.

"You mean, you don't know? Aren't they his daughters?"

Cheryl shrugged as she accepted the album from Bailey. "Not that I know of. I've worked with Tal for the last six years and he's never mentioned any kids or even a wife, for that matter—ex or otherwise. They're cute, though. Especially this little one—she looks so familiar. Where did this album come from?" she asked as she studied the images.

"I'm not sure," Bailey lied. "It showed up when I was off shift. Must've been one of the other nurses who found it."

Although the CNA answered the other woman calmly, her mind churned with questions. *If the girls were not his daughters, why then, would he have these photographs in his house? And who was that girl's room for, then? This Cheryl Becker must be mistaken.* Bailey surmised that Talbot must be private man who wasn't in the habit of divulging his personal life to others, particularly with pushy or nosey people. The girls were relatives of his or… *perhaps he lost his family and didn't like to talk about it.* Bailey's heart swelled at the thought of it. It made perfect sense. Maybe he lost custody of the kids after a divorce or worse yet, perhaps he and his wife lost their children in an accident of some sort. They split up and now he lives alone, keeping the room and his memories intact. Yet, he continues to help people, such as she, as a way of reaching out to others. *Yes, that must be it.* She studied the unconscious man before her and vowed to try even harder to do whatever it took to rescue him from his lingering nightmare.

‡　‡　‡

Desperation and anguish sunk in with the finality of a cold steel blade. Mia could no longer be brave. The ache she felt for her husband and infant son was nothing short of agonizing, as if she had been run through with that blade. She feared she would she never see them again. She wept openly, knowing no one would hear her voice. Her brain could not comprehend this torment that detained her. There was no sense of time or place in this shifting void. It seemed only minutes or hours that she had been here, but what if had been days, months, or… decades? She couldn't be sure. She didn't know if she was still alive

Another hellacious thought was that John would return and then what would become of her? There was no telling when he would be back and how much more threatening he would be. Would she succumb to that shadow like he had? *I have to do something, anything. I can't give up yet!* Paralyzed and struggling to make her body cooperate, she strained to lift her legs and arms. They barely moved. Mia held her panic in check and forced herself to think rationally. There had to be some way to get her bearings.

Grasping at any idea that flashed through her mind in a frantic attempt to survive, she locked on one. If she had the ability to connect with these visitors, could she possibly connect with people she knew?

I must make contact. She concentrated on Dan, uncertain if it would be possible to communicate with him. Thinking it through carefully, she grew discouraged. While she loved him dearly, she knew her husband well. In the remote possibility that her thoughts reached him, he wouldn't know what to do with the message. Instead he wouldn't be likely to share what was going on and more likely to internalize the feelings, reasoning that he was merely going crazy with grief over the loss of his wife.

Aunt Lydia.

Her aunt might be the only one who could sense her *and* believe in any message she was receiving enough to react. But Mia couldn't help but feel doubtful with her as well. While being a believer, the old spiritualist did not seem to possess any true psychic ability, no matter what she claimed. Mia had always looked the other way or waved it off, but deep down, she never took Lydia's claims of clairvoyance seriously.

Seeing where she was however, there was no one else and no other alternative. She would have to take the chance. She recalled their conversation they had in the kitchen only a couple of days ago. If her mother and grandmother had the ability, and now she had it, maybe Aunt Lydia had some of it, after all. Desperation determined her decision.

Mia took a deep breath, trying to allay her fear and dispel her doubts. *This was going to work.* Getting her breathing under control, she started to concentrate. First, on the soft features of Lydia's face, then on the trembling lilt to her voice. *This has to work.* She started to recall memories of her aunt, from the last time she saw her when she said good night to years ago when she was a young child and would crawl into her lap. Focusing on the details, she let the love that she felt for Lydia infuse her memories and thoughts. It was the only way she knew how to attempt this.

The darkness ensued. Mia's heart sunk, but she refocused once again. *I will die trying… there is nothing else left.* Slowly at first, a pinprick of light began to puncture the blackness. Hope surging as she spied it, she poured every ounce of energy into her singular thought of Lydia. The light continued to grow. Just as before, when John showed her, it formed into a panel sized rectangle. Mia could now see her living room. More importantly, she could see Ho, Jenna, and Aunt Lydia. Excitement and relief washed over her as tears ran down her face.

Maybe there was a way, after all.

"So what do we do now?" Jenna asked. "I just checked on the Bugaboo and he's still out. Poor little guy."

It was drizzling outside the window and eight-thirty in the morning fared gloomy and overcast as droplets formed and streaked down the panes of glass. The world seemed dismal.

"We can only wait for Dan to call. She should be getting out of surgery soon," Lydia responded and sighed.

"Yeah, I just texted him, but he says he's still waiting," Ho added as he thumbed through one of Dan's *Stereo Review* magazines.

Each fell into a pensive silence. The house was still except for the increasing tap of falling rain outside as it alternated with the drizzle.

"I'm going to go out of my mind just sitting here. I guess I better make myself useful and clear some of these things," Lydia said as she rose to gather up the breakfast dishes. Suddenly, she inhaled sharply and sat back down heavily in her seat, looking dazed.

"Aunt Lydia, are you all right?" Ho asked, lowering the magazine. He hoped she wasn't showing signs of a heart attack from all of the stress. The last time he took CPR was years ago in high school and he was rusty at best.

The old woman's eyes opened wide and her mouth gaped as if she had seen something shocking. She placed her hand on her bosom and continued to suck air. She blinked and shook her head.

"Lydia, is everything okay?" Jenna questioned as she knelt by her side.

"She's here, you two. Mia is *here*," Lydia said. A look of elation broke over her face. "She's here… ohhh!"

"What do you mean, 'she's here'?" Ho raised an eyebrow and leaned forward, looking on with concern and wondering if she was suffering from some sort of breakdown.

"I can *feel* her. She's with us. Oh! It's like she's hugging me—I can even smell her. Mia, darling! Is it you? Where are you, sweetheart?" Lydia called out, raising her arms.

"Aunt Lydia, Mia's not here," Jenna explained gently as she laid her hand on the older woman's shoulder to calm her. "She's at the hospital. Everything is going to be all right, okay?"

Lydia looked directly into Jenna's eyes and said firmly. "Jenna, you're a sweet girl, but I am *not* losing it. I know what I am feeling. It is my niece and she is contacting me, do you understand? Now I must focus on her. She needs my help."

"But, I can call—"

"I've been at this for close to fifty years already. This is real, Jenna. Mia is *here*."

She said it with such confidence and finality, she realized then that Lydia was not confused or hysterical. All Jenna could answer was, "O- okay…" She then sat back and watched, confounded with wonder.

"But if she's here, what about the hospital? Wait, you don't think that something has happened to her? Oh shit!" Ho said, his dubious expression over what he had just witnessed now turning to one of alarm. He immediately took out his phone and dialed Dan. "Come on, pick up… pick up." He kept the phone to his ear and his eye on Lydia.

"Ohhh… she wants something. I don't know what… we've got to connect with her," Lydia continued, her eyes still searching the room but her face clouded with worry. "We've got to connect with her now. Tell me, what do you need, darling?"

"Damn! He didn't pick up. Voice mail," Ho said with frustration. He looked at his device as if it had betrayed him.

"Here, let me try," Jenna said. She dialed her phone.

"We can't wait for Dan. Mia needs us now! Quick, get the card table from the garage, Hoason. We have to set it up here. I have to call Adriana. She must assist me… Please Mia—hang on, darling. I'm getting help. Stay with me," Lydia called out.

"He's not answering me either. I wonder where he is?" said Jenna. She texted rapidly, her thumbs dancing around the touch screen. "Maybe he'll get this instead."

Lydia phoned the neighbor. "Adriana, come quick. I need you immediately. It's starting," was all she had to say. Then she rushed to her room to retrieve her crystals, candles, photographs, and tarot cards. She threw down these items upon the table that Ho had just placed in the middle of the living room floor. Last, Lydia withdrew a photograph of Stephanos and placed it carefully among the rest of the objects.

A few minutes later, a knock on the door signaled that Mrs. Adriana Lopez had arrived. One look at Lydia and she knew that the spirits were afoot. She entered the house by making the sign of the cross and blessing herself. She nodded in greeting to Ho and Jenna and without a word, started to light the candles at the table and expertly set the other objects in place.

"Ho, Jenna, this is Adriana. Adriana, Mia is trying to contact us. She is trying to say something," Lydia said as she gestured to the table and mirror.

"*Mia*? In the mirror?" Adriana asked, perplexed. "But I don't understand. What is she doing *there*?"

"There's no time to explain. We have to start a séance, immediately. We need to make a stronger connection with her. She is trying to tell me something. Now come and sit. We must begin."

"All of us?" Ho asked.

"Yes. The more people, the better. It will—how should I say…? Oh, I know—it will 'improve signal strength,'" Lydia tried.

"Oh! Gotcha." Ho sat down at the table promptly and eagerly awaited instructions. "This is going to be good," he said, rubbing his hands together in excitement.

Jenna sat next to him and Adriana drew the blinds shut on the windows, darkening the room. The candle flickered from the air movement about her plump figure as she swooped into her seat. One last pat to her sweater pocket assured her that her vial of Holy Water and pocket bible she had snatched up on her way out were securely there. Finally, she was ready to join in.

Lydia drew a deep breath and waved her hands over the candle flame three times. Then she commenced, "Everyone, join hands and focus on Mia. Believe that she is with us. Let her into your minds and hearts."

Ho reached out to Jenna. They hesitated for a moment before touching hands. When Jenna smiled shyly at Ho with a sidelong glance, he gladly took her hand and smiled back.

"Okay, we are ready. Mia, we are all here, sweetheart. Tell us—what do you need us to do?" Lydia asked, her eyes closed and her voice quiet. Upon that, images and sensations of her niece flooded her mind instantaneously. She gasped out loud in wonderment. If her eyes weren't closed, she would have sworn that a living, breathing Mia had materialized right beside her and was holding her hand. The spiritualist was astounded by the clarity of the experience. _This is the real deal. So this is what it is supposed to feel like_ she told herself, mentally noting that she had never come close to anything like this before. Lydia then allowed her mind to clear and receive what Mia was trying to tell her.

Her lips started to form words that filled her head and guided her tongue. "'I… am frightened. In a dark place… no way out. What has happened to me?… Dan? Nathan?'…. OH!" Lydia's eyes suddenly opened wide in amazement. "That's Mia speaking through me! I can actually hear her," The others looked at her eagerly. Embarrassed by her own admission, she cleared her throat, squeezed her eyes shut and concentrated once more. In a few moments, she murmured, "Her messages are coming so fast… Slow down, darling. That's right, we're all here."

With astonishment Jenna exchanged looks of awe with Ho as she mouthed the words, "No way!"

"Am I… dead? Did something happen to me…?' Noo, Mia. No. Everything is all right. You collapsed after you had gone to bed last night. Dan found you. The doctor believes it is an aneurysm. They are performing emergency surgery on you as we speak."

Adriana looked up, shocked at the news the two-sided monologue revealed about her young neighbor. She groaned softly and shook her head in pity.

Lydia continued, toggling between Mia's words and her own. "'Nathan…? Where…?' He's sleeping right now, dear. He was up half the night with everything going on."

"I just checked on him. He's fine. Hi Mia. I love you and am very worried about you," Jenna interjected.

"'Love you too… Jenna. Please don't worry…'" Then, with her brow furrowed in concern, Lydia carefully asked, "Sweetheart, are you there alone?… 'John… was here. Don't know… where he is… now.'"

"What are all of you doing?" Dan said. The entire party jumped, startled at his unexpected arrival. Intent on the séance, they hadn't heard his key in the lock or the door open. "Oh, hello, Mrs. Lopez," he added when he noticed his neighbor among them.

"Dan! We are having a séance. Mia is here! She's talking through Aunt Lydia right now!" Jenna said excitedly.

"No she's not. She's recovering in the ICU right now. All went well with the surgery. The doc said she'll probably be out for another hour or two, so he told me to go home for a bit. I'm just here for a change of clothes and to check on Nathan. What are you doing here, kiddo?" Dan came over to hug his sister. "Was that what you and Ho were calling about? Sorry, I was talking with the doc and couldn't answer."

"I told you I was coming back after my trip, remember? But listen, Mia *is* here. She's been talking to us. Why didn't you tell me about all of this?"

"There wasn't ever a right time. It's not exactly an easy thing to say 'hey, did you know my wife is psychic and dead people visit her in her mirror?' Anyway, not a word of this to Mom and Dad, understand?"

"What, do you think I'm stupid? Mom can barely handle her hair being blown by a fan at a cheesy haunted house for tourists. Could you imagine what she would do with this? We'd never hear the end of it."

"Dan, Mia wants to know if you are okay. She's sorry if she frightened you," Lydia interjected, still holding the train of communication open.

"Yeah, well tell her I'm fine. As well as can be expected," he answered flatly. Then he leaned toward Ho and whispered, "You too? Seriously, man? I sent you here to keep an eye on things."

Ho looked sheepish and shrugged. "Aunt Lydia needed more bandwidth. I was just helping out, like you asked me to."

"But Dan, Mia *is* here! She's talking through Aunt Lydia right now. Don't you want to join in? She is asking for you," Jenna insisted.

"I'm going to look in on Nathan and then I've got to double check on something. In fact, where's the notebook? It was right here. Never mind— got it," Dan answered tersely as he plucked the book from the middle of the table and started paging through it on his way to the nursery.

Confused by his indifference, Jenna said, "What the hey? I thought he would be stoked to hear that Mia is here."

With her eyes still closed, Lydia answered, "Your brother has a hard time believing in all of this, Jenna. He won't unless he sees it with his own eyes, and even then he still doubts it."

"But he saw what happened with the little girl and the last guy that Mia saved, didn't he? I still don't get it. I'm going to have to have a talk with him."

"That won't be necessary. Just wait," was all Lydia answered.

‡　‡　‡

"So far, that's got to be a record for him. He is staying awake for so long. I'm so excited! It's good to give him a break but when we return, we'll get back at it because I think we're on the right track. We'll wait until Joanne is finished in there with him before going in, though. I don't want to raise a lot of questions about why you are there, especially since you are not a family member or spouse," Bailey conspired with Cheryl as they waited together in line at the hospital coffee shop.

"I totally understand. You know, I really appreciate all that you are doing, Bailey. I'm sure that Talbot is grateful as well. So this is how he's been all along, then? Does he ever say anything?"

"Nah uh. This is good. It was much worse before—absolutely no reaction. He just lay there in a classic vegetative state. He's showing some real progress now," Bailey answered. "So, to keep him going, I think we should continue talking to him about memories." Unable to contain her curiosity much longer she asked, "So, do you work with him at the Career Center?"

"I work in the marketing department at Croft. Tal and I used to collaborate together on flyers and brochures for student admissions."

"Well, then, it's good that you are here. I'm sure he has a lot of memories from work."

"And how do you know him? From his stay here at the hospital?"

"Oh, I've known Talbot for a little while. I got my certificate from Croft and he's the one who helped me get through school to become a nursing assistant. I can never forget how kind and encouraging he was with me. I would have never gotten this job without him. This is just a small way I can pay back the favor."

"Is that right? Well, he certainly is a good person."

"And you two are just co-workers?" Bailey tested.

"And friends. Oh, we've been out on a few dates. He was always the perfect gentleman," Cheryl answered with a wry little smile.

"I see," Bailey said, trying to keep the edge out of her voice.

They collected their coffees and walked down the brightly lit corridor to the elevators.

"I've been wanting to ask—if it's all right with you, when we get back to his room, I'd like to hold a prayer vigil for him for at least an hour or so," Cheryl proposed.

"How about we continue talking to him about memories first if he's still conscious. But if he lapses, the vigil would be nice. In fact, it would be great to pray together," Bailey agreed. If it weren't for the fact that Cheryl was direct competition for the man she loved, Bailey would've liked her. She seemed pleasant enough.

When they had reached the pod, Joanne was just exiting the room. Bailey nodded to her discreetly, hoping to keep things mum from Meredith. Joanne received the nod and returned it, using the buddy system the CNAs relied on to cover each other. No words were necessary.

Bailey was relieved to see that Talbot's eyes remained open when they approached his bedside.

"There you are. We're back. It's just us, Tal—Bailey and Cheryl. How about we talk some more about the good old days? I'm just going to check your chart while Cheryl gets started. Sound good?" Bailey spoke in a cheery voice to the man lying in the bed while she went to the computer, swiped her ID card and logged in. Cheryl pulled up a chair and took his hand.

"Go ahead Cheryl. Let him know who you are," Bailey said.

Talbot was staring at the ceiling. Cheryl cleared her throat timidly as she faced him and tried to think of what to say. Finally her face lit up as she struck upon something.

"Hi Talbot. It's me, Cheryl. I'm back, just like Bailey said. Hey, remember last year's Christmas office party? Now wasn't that fun?" she said brightly.

His head rotated suddenly towards her and his dead gaze bore into hers. For a split second, the expression on his face was so demonic, that it made Cheryl's blood turn to ice. She thought she saw him bare teeth that were sharp as spikes and his nostrils flared. Her mind was filled with thoughts of wriggling white maggots and decaying flesh. Unwillingly, she dropped his hand and recoiled out of fright from one of the most evil sights she had ever witnessed. She blinked and stammered; her open mouth would not form sounds.

Unaware of what had transpired and only hearing the pause in the exchange, Bailey insisted, "Go ahead, Cheryl, you're doing great," while scrolling through the notes on his chart.

Cheryl could not look away from Talbot, held like a terrified mouse in a snake's hypnotic stare. "I—I... don't know what else to say," she barely whispered.

"I'll be with you in just a sec. I know—show him his photo album. He seems to really enjoy that."

Feeling on guard, Cheryl hesitantly reached for the book. When her eye returned to Talbot, his face had resumed to the one she had known and cared about before. She took a deep breath and shook her head slightly as if to clear her vision, doubting what she had witnessed. Her mind formulated several sound reasons for what she had just seen—a long stressful day, or the lighting, or perhaps the way he reacted to some medication he was receiving.

Cheryl shifted in her seat and sat upright. She started again, although more reserved this time.

"Okay, Talbot. How about we look at your album? You have such pretty little girls in here. Are they your nieces?" she asked as she opened the book and held it before him.

"Anything yet?" Bailey asked. "I'm logging out..."

"No. Not yet. Now Talbot, who is this cutie?" Cheryl continued. "What is she—twelve or thirteen years old? And wait—it looks like she likes gummi bears. How sweet... Oh my gracious. Bailey look—he's smiling!"

‡ ‡ ‡

Dan couldn't believe what he had heard. The four people in the living room, including his own sister, were more interested in that séance-incense nonsense than hearing that Mia was out of danger and presently resting after her surgery. It dumbfounded him the extent of their collective delusion to think that Lydia was somehow channeling a completely live and healthy person. *How deep are they going to get into that bullshit?* he wondered. He had watched enough shows on paranormal activity to know that séances, if they even worked, were for communicating with dead people. If anything, it confirmed just how whacked out Mia's aunt was.

What's worse, she had all the others bamboozled into believing too. It was obvious that it was a waste of time to have asked Ho to look in on things. He should have known that his friend would be worse than a kid in a theme park with this stuff. And Dan had always thought Mrs. Lopez a sensible woman. As for Jenna—he didn't know where to start with her. How was he going to mitigate all that she had been told? He could feel his safe and carefully structured childhood swaying and threatening to topple like a stack of dominoes. However, he would have to deal with that later. For now, he questioned their combined judgment and considered taking Nathan back to the hospital with him.

He needed to be there for his wife just as he had promised. She was the only person who showed true psychic ability in his opinion. He felt a twinge in seeing how much effort she put into helping out these lost souls as he flipped through the pages of her notes in the notebook. The visitors' scribbles, her careful longhand, maps, question marks, lists...

There it is. He came upon that missing something that had been incessantly nagging him for the past few weeks, yet wasn't able to put his finger on exactly what it was. In the waiting room, with his mind in search mode, he had a chance to review the video clip multiple times while hunting for this singular clue. Yet on the page before him, it was written in her clear hand:

Remembers riding around in his father's '73 Ford Fairlane

Revealed now, it was the perfect fit. In the clip, beyond the reporter and the mudslide, past the rescue workers milling about, in the background beyond the outbuilding where they had dug Samantha out, he had spied the old classic of a car. Mia hadn't noticed it when they watched the clip the second time—perhaps it came up when she had left the room. However, once she pointed out that make and model while they were on the road, he recalled she had mentioned seeing the same car in her dream. His mind closed around that vague detail and wouldn't surrender it until he spotted and confirmed it in the video footage today. It was the cinch around the loose details regarding John and Samantha that tied them together. It was something that his wife would be able to work with.

Dan's thoughts were jarred by the sound of his son waking up in the nursery. Seeing it was his father who entered his room, the baby happily reached out his hands and cooed. When Dan saw how Nathan peered up at him with that bright expectant smile, he felt a pang deep within his chest. Pausing for a moment, he rested his hand tenderly on his son's head. He knew he had to make things right for his family. They were dependent on him.

"How's it going, big guy?" he said to him. "Mommy's coming home really soon, all right? I know you miss her. I miss her too. But everything's going to be okay. And you know what? Daddy found out something important that might help Mommy in getting everything back to normal around here. I think you are the only one in this house, besides me, who appreciates that information."

He changed Nathan's diaper and clothes and returned with him to the living room. Even though the others were engrossed in their séance, he decided to share his discovery with them before things got too out of hand. It might be the touch of reality they needed to get them grounded again. The four remained holding hands around the table as he placed the open notebook down amongst them.

"You guys are wasting your time. Now here is something Mia can really work with," he said triumphantly.

"Dan, that can wait. Seriously—you've got to talk with her. I'm telling you, she's with us right now and she needs our help. We've been talking with her for the last ten minutes or so," Jenna pleaded. "Her messages are coming in strong and clear now."

Deflated and annoyed at his sister's indifference to his key discovery, with growing impatience he said, "I told you before that she is at the hospital, not here."

Nathan suddenly let out a squeal and almost flung himself out of Dan's arms towards the mirror. He arched his small body urging his father to go in that direction.

"Nathan, buddy! What are you doing?" Dan asked with surprise, as he fumbled to keep the squirming infant in his grasp. He brought his son over to the glass, more so to keep him from climbing out of his arms. "What? Do you want the mirror? Aunt Jenna wasn't really thinking when she taught you about them now, was she."

"Mumm mumm, Mumm mumm," Nathan repeated. When he reached the pane of glass, he patted and then kissed it. "Mumm mumm, Mumm mumm," he said happily and planted another sloppy kiss on the mirror again.

"Now what's with you, Nat-a-tat?" Dan asked. "Do you like yourself? C'mon. We've got to go see Mommy."

"He's seeing his mother in the mirror right now," Lydia replied calmly.

"No, he's seeing himself in the mirror," Dan answered in defiance.

"Bro, Mia *is* there and she needs to talk to you," Ho insisted.

"What a fricken' load of horseshit—"

"Mia tells me to tell you, 'Please listen. I am here. I know you can't see me… Nathan can. I love you both so much,'" Lydia repeated Mia's words to him.

"Will you knock it off already?" Dan said to her. "I don't have time for this. I got to get back to the hospital. She should be waking up any time now."

"Danny, will you quit being such a mule?" Jenna piped up. "Open your mind already. She's there. What's so hard for you to believe?"

"Oh no. Not you too. Now you know why I didn't tell you anything. Just because you taught Nathan this little trick with the mirror, I'm supposed to believe that my wife is in there with all the rest of the spooks? Exactly what is that suppose to imply anyhow?" he questioned his sister. "I wouldn't think you would be so gullible to fall for all of this stuff."

"Mia says, 'Murph, please, you told me that you'd always be there for me, no matter what… I need you now. Don't know how long I'm going to be here,'" Lydia continued.

Dan's eyes narrowed. "You know, that's really low, Lydia. And I've had enough. You can stay until Mia is discharged from the hospital, but after that it's time for you to leave."

"Ouch," Ho exclaimed softly when he heard the remark.

"And you stay out of this," Dan growled at his friend. "I thought you had my back."

"She says, 'Please, don't make me prove I really am here,'" the medium persisted.

Dan grew irate. "That's it! I don't know how you're doing this but—"

"'Daniel! Listen to Lydia… Remember how difficult it was in getting Shayla to believe I was communicating with Seth?…. Don't be like her. And please don't make me feel like I did when Gerry sent me away… you stood there and watched. It's *me*, your wife… You told me you'd always be there for me. I don't have much time left to convince you.'"

At the mention of these private memories, Dan's jaw dropped open. They had never disclosed the details about either event to anyone. He and Mia were the only witnesses to that tenuous time when Seth had desperately tried to give the mother of his child a message. It took several attempts to get Shayla to believe it truly was him and not some trick. And then the memory of Mia's pitiful cries and bewildered look of betrayal mixed with fear as the orderlies dragged her out of the therapist's office pierced him with painful remorse.

"What the…? *Murph?*" He glanced about the room in all directions as if she would materialize at any moment. "Oh my god, is it you?"

"'Yes! Sweetheart, please believe it's me!'"

"What are you doing there? Why aren't you at the hospital…? Mia—are you all right? Nothing happened did it?" he said with alarm as panic flared within him. He didn't know whether to face the mirror or Lydia. Nathan continued to kiss and pat the mirror, so he directed his attention that way. "You were fine when I left you at the hospital. The doc told me everything went well—"

"'I feel okay. I just don't know why I'm here. Maybe it's because I'm unconscious right now.'"

"But what does that mean? You're coming back to us, right? I'm really sorry I doubted it was you just now."

"'I think so… Dan, listen. He is here. I met him face to face. He's not with me right now, but he's going to return.'"

"John? There with you? Can't you just leave or wake up or something?"

"'No. I'm stuck here. Arms and legs are sluggish… I can't get them to work right.'"

"But Murph, you've got to get out of there. I have good reason to believe that John is Samantha's abductor. Your notes say he drove a '73 Ford Fairlane. You saw that same car in your dream with Samantha. And I just re-watched the video clip of when she was rescued—it's parked in the background. Those cars are not that common anymore and I think it's just too much of a coincidence."

"Holy cow!" Jenna exclaimed out loud, listening to the exchange. Then she sheepishly pursed her lips in effort to keep her outbursts to herself.

Adriana added, "Ay Dios mio," in a hushed tone, her face creased with worry.

"'But how could he be the same person? He showed me where he is lying in a hospital room just like me. He's hooked up to feeding tube and ventilator. It looked like he was in a coma. Hold on—,'" she faltered.

"What? Mia? What is it?"

"'The man in the coma—his name is 'Talbot.' The man in the dream called himself 'Uncle T.J.'… Talbot John?… Oh my god Dan, do you think it's possible? And if it is, what do you suppose happened to him?'"

"He probably got injured. Maybe he was in some kind of accident after Samantha was released. And maybe that's why he's stuck in there, like you."

"Whoa. Caught between the living and the dead. Freaky," Ho said quietly to Jenna whose eyes opened wide as she shuddered at the thought.

"But how did you find out his name was Talbot? And did you catch what hospital he was in?" Dan asked while all eyes in the room were fixed intently on him.

"'There were two women in the room talking to him, trying to get him to respond… One looked like a nurse and the other looked like a relative or friend. I didn't get a chance to see anything that identified the hospital. Wait—the nurse's ID badge had the hospital logo on it… Collins? Or Conklin?'"

"Murph, do whatever you can to stay away from him, understand? You don't want him to find out that you were the one who set Samantha free. That will probably antagonize him."

"'He knows. He saw my notes in the notebook.'"

With the exception of Lydia, everyone at the table gasped.

"Oh damn, babe. That can't be good. Can this guy do anything to hurt you? I mean he's some kind of spirit or ghost on that side, isn't he? So he can't do anything *physical* to you, right?"

Mia was silent for a moment, and then continued, "'Yes… yes, in here, he can.'"

"Then he's probably capable of just about anything and I bet he's going to be pissed that you set her free. What can I do? I've got to be able to do something to help you. We have to get you out of there," Dan said in anguish.

"'I don't know yet. Wait… I hear something… Dan! He's back… Leave me alone… No don't!... Nooo!'"

Lydia's face was awash with terror when she abruptly stopped speaking. All waited for her to continue, but nothing was forthcoming. Within a few seconds, she opened her eyes and looked about as if awakening from a dream.

Nathan released a sudden cry and gripped his father's arms.

"Mia? Mia? Are you there? Say something," Dan cried out. He looked at Lydia. The old psychic returned his puzzlement and shook her head, raising her hands in question. Then she firmly shut her eyes and sat up straight.

"Mia, honey—speak to us," she commanded with anxiousness creeping into her voice. "We are still here. Speak to us, darling. Where are you? Please, Mia…"

Try as she might, Lydia received no more messages.

"Must all women be so pathetic? I haven't met one yet that hasn't been sniveling, self-serving, manipulative, or mindless."

The only sound present in their prison was his low voice penetrating her skull. John circled Mia, his words spitting like venom while she lay helpless at his feet. By now, he was completely enshrouded in a swirling veil of black that increased his overall size making him appear to tower over her. Previously, Mia had surmised that the inky shadow vitalized him, its presence a source of strength versus a deterrent to him. But now, there was a melding of the two—he and the darkness were becoming one and his sense of power was corrupting into something much more diabolical.

His discordant voice more a threatening growl than speech, his rant persisted, "Take for example the fat twat and lusty cow plaguing me at my hospital bed as I try to recover. Neither of them is worth the effort to blow them to hell. What do they really feel they are accomplishing by holding my hand and showing me photographs? More importantly, what do they want from me in return? Manipulators—after something. Aren't you all?

"And here's you, helpless and simple, just like my mother—inept at saving anyone or herself for that matter. Do you know how long we were made to suffer at my father's hand? *Years.* All because she was too busy hiding behind her god to do anything about it. 'Pray son,' she would say to me. 'Pray for your father to be saved from his sins.' 'Pray to Jesus to deliver us.' That was laughable. Did she pray for me when he did those things to me? She didn't even pray for herself when her head was being bashed in with the iron. She clung to that bible of hers and did nothing. She was a frightened, meek fool."

"But how could you hurt a child? You were hurt when you were young. You know how it feels."

He reached down and grabbed a fistful of Mia's long hair and with strength beyond human, pulled her vertically straight up to eye level. A cry escaped Mia as she dangled helplessly in his grip, her arms remaining useless.

"Children, if they haven't been ruined by fools like you and others of your kind, are pure. They are strong. They aren't twisted and perverted with cunning, manipulation, and selfishness. They know what they want and what they need." He grimaced sadistically at the sight of her wincing face, reveling in her agony. "Oh, I'm sorry. Is there something else you care to say, you pitiful piece of garbage," he said with contempt.

"What do you… want from me?" Mia managed through clenched teeth.

"Want from you? As if you are capable of giving anything of any value. That's amusing to say the least. How about I show you instead just how little you have to offer? In fact, it will give me the utmost pleasure, so, I suppose in that respect you'll be 'giving' me something if it makes you feel any better."

In the next instant they were back in his hospital room. It was apparent his capabilities were well honed now. He moved rapidly at will to whatever location he desired. They viewed him as he lay in the hospital bed where it appeared as if he were merely sleeping. The nursing assistant checked his lines while the well-dressed woman was busy removing a few photos from the album and placing them on the service table. One by one, the images of three little girls were laid down upon the tabletop side by side. Mia gasped when she recognized Samantha's familiar face in the middle of the group.

"Ah, yes. Your little hero, Samantha. I can see why you two hit it off. Somewhere her mind has been poisoned. She is no longer a child, but another conniving bitch like you and these other two twits as well. I was doing the world a service by removing her from the gene pool, like I had with Chloe before her. But instead, you interfered and she was set free. I will be sure to finish what I started with her once I am free of this imprisonment. She won't entice others with her manipulations and spawn her wickedness again. Are you satisfied?"

Mia's hair was being ripped from her burning scalp. She managed to raise her hands enough to grasp his fists and pry at his fingers. But it was futile—she couldn't break the ironclad grip. Her eyes flicked across the photos and stopped at the oldest girl. Suddenly, he shook her violently. She cried out again in pain.

"Do you have the audacity to look at my Leanne? Cast your eyes away, whore, or I'll gouge them out. I won't have you fouling her image. She is pure. You are not. You are not fit to even look at her."

In the very next moment, they were at a different hospital post-op recovery room. It took her a few seconds to orientate herself to where she was. Five patients were resting, hooked to monitors and IVs. Two nurses, a surgery tech, and a doctor in scrubs moved about the beds, checking charts, lines, vitals, and medications. Mia's eyes widened in terror when she identified herself among the unconscious patients.

John erupted into mocking laughter when he saw the reality of her plight register on her face. "Ah, this is absolutely priceless. Finally you get to experience the very hell I've been subjected to. It should be dawning upon you by now that you are in a most precarious position. I am only growing stronger and should regain complete consciousness shortly. Quite the paradox, isn't it? Oh, it's been a tedious recovery to say the least, but with the care I've been receiving I should be regaining consciousness very, very soon. And when I do, I can finally resume my life.

"Your doctor expects you to make a full recovery as well. 'What?' you ask, 'how could John possibly know that?' Well let's just say I was but a stray reflection in your room when he was discussing it. However, I digress. I now have a troubling dilemma on my hands. If your doctor is correct about your situation and you do, indeed, make a full recovery and return to your insipid life, you are now privy to some very sensitive information about me—what I look like, my connection with Samantha, what Leanne looks like. In fact, you are shaping up to be quite a liability for me. I find this most unsatisfactory. So weighing these matters at hand, I decided that you are better off here and I intend to make sure that you stay that way. You weren't much of a service to the world anyway. A psychic? What a joke."

"What! Please—no!" Mia pleaded in a ragged whisper of fright and desperation.

Affirmation sharpened his smile to a thin scythe. "Ah. Sniveling and groveling. You didn't disappoint me after all. I knew you were like all the rest."

‡　‡　‡

"It doesn't look like he's waking back up. So may we start the vigil now? I can only stay for about another hour," Cheryl said checking her watch.

Bailey observed the still man before them and sighed. It seemed that he was so close to coming around only to relapse again. It was a frustrating tug of war. Maybe Cheryl was right. Perhaps it was time for the power of prayer.

"Okay. That may be the best thing right now. He's gonna need all the prayers he can get," she answered while pulling up a chair next to her. She picked up one of the photos and studied it. "I think we ought to add these little ones to our vigil. They must be worried sick about him."

"That's a good idea," Cheryl said. "I only wish I knew how to get in contact with them to let them know where he is."

"Oh, I'm sure he won't waste any time reuniting with them once he regains consciousness," Bailey responded confidently.

‡　‡　‡

"But it's absolutely imperative for us to continue the séance," Lydia insisted. "You have to understand for her to communicate with us, we need to keep the channel open and we need to work together. It takes a unified focus from everybody."

It was going on twelve minutes since they had last heard from Mia. As they scrambled to figure out how to proceed, each of them was frightened beyond the implications.

"If you ask me, I think we should pray. God is all-powerful and protects those who believe," said Adriana. "I even brought the prayer of Michael the Archangel along just in case any of you don't know the words. He's a good one in times like these."

"My granny has always invoked the ancestors whenever there was a crisis. Especially any hairy problems with spirits and stuff," Ho said as he conducted an Internet search on his smartphone based on the details Mia had given Dan. "Maybe we should try that."

Jenna added, "I'm sure if we combine all of our positive thoughts on Mia, I think the good mental vibes will give her the strength to fight him off. He sounds so negative."

Lydia shook her head. "This isn't a matter of mental attitude. This is as real and as physical of a battle as if he were right here among us."

While Dan hunted frantically for his phone charger and car keys, Ho called him over and pointed to the screen on his phone.

"Dan, check this out. There's a Walter P. Collins Hospital in Boise." he said. "And it looks like they have a critical care unit for coma victims there. That's the closest hospital in our region that starts with a 'c' and has a coma unit. I think this may be our boy."

"Thanks, man, for looking that up." Dan took the phone and gave his friend a pat on the shoulder. He skimmed over the info. "I wonder what he's doing in Idaho when he had abducted Samantha here? Something doesn't seem right… Unless… unless that son of a bitch has been crossing state lines to prey on kids!"

"Maybe you're on to something there," said Ho. "Flying under the radar. When you think about it, it probably helps him in going undetected."

Dan's jaw grew rigid. "It's good that he's over five hundred miles away or I'd personally go over there and unplug him myself," he said tersely.

Meanwhile, the group was far from reaching a consensus. "But we were able to get her once before with the séance," Lydia pleaded, "I think that's the best way to help her again."

"She is dealing with the Evil One. We must rely on God," Adriana countered.

Jenna argued, "I agree we need to settle on something, but will she even be able to talk to us if we do contact her? I think we need to join minds—"

Hearing the course of the discussion Dan interjected, "Hey, whatever you all decide to do, you better do it quick. There's no time to waste. I'm heading back to the hospital. Maybe if I can get her to wake up or get the docs to bring her around, she'll be able to return to the real world and escape John."

Upon his prompt, the clamor rose when the four began talking in earnest at once, trying to get one another to accept their preferred strategy.

Dan had found his keys and was about to exit. "Whoa! Whoa!" he said. "Listen, why doesn't everyone just do what they want? I don't think any specific approach to this is really going to matter much, more so that you keep trying. And call me if you get anything. I'll call you if she wakes up." With that, he was out the door.

Horrified at the thought of John being anywhere near Mia, he sped recklessly to the hospital, leaving behind a wake of confused and angry motorists. Just knowing that the apparition was no spook, but instead a living, breathing person *still out there* in the world was enough to evoke a sickening mix of rage and disgust within him. Thinking of little Samantha and how the slime ball had abducted her and did god knows what, churned in his throat. *And now that twisted bastard has my wife.* The realization made him grip the steering wheel so hard, he felt he could have snapped it in two.

If only I could get my hands on that son of a bitch, I'd dismantle him. He recalled how uncomfortable Mia was in dealing with John and wished to God that she would've taken his advice and ditched him early on.

He sprinted through the hospital corridors to the waiting area of the recovery room to find that Mia had been transferred already to a private room. He found her alone, resting in bed, still unconscious. All was quiet except for the steady beep of the pulse rate monitor.

Touching her hair, he studied her face closely. She had been through so much. He was greatly relieved when the surgeon had told him that they were able to take the less invasive approach to clip the aneurysm by going through her nasal cavity rather than having to cut through her skull. The doctor had explained if she had to have an aneurysm at all, she lucked out with it being small and located close to the base of her skull where they could access it more easily. Dan shuddered to think that only twenty years ago, she might have been dead. But she was still far from being out of harm's way.

"Murph, can you hear me? You've got to wake up. Come on… Wake up, honey," he said. He stroked her face and then rubbed her arm. "Come on, Mia, wake up."

She remained still. He gripped her by her shoulder and shook it a little, afraid to jar her after surgery. She was unresponsive. He wasn't sure how much of it was the anesthesia that was still affecting her or perhaps the pain medication.

Suddenly, her pulse rate picked up. Her breathing followed suit. Dan watched as she gasped out loud and trembled. Within the next minute, tears gathered beneath her closed eyelids, escaped and rolled down her cheeks. He grew fearful. *What just happened?* His gut feeling told him that John had something to do with it. Dan immediately dialed his phone. Jenna picked up.

"Have you reached her yet?"

"No. There still hasn't been a thing. We're trying everything over here."

"I'm going to leave my phone on speaker while I keep trying to wake her. Let me know the minute you hear from her."

"All right. We'll keep you posted."

He located the call button and pressed it for a nurse. When no one answered right away, he grew impatient and picked up her hand and rubbed it briskly. "Murph! Come on, babe. Wake up. Please. You've got to get out of there. Do you hear me? Wake up!"

Mia was still but then suddenly jerked violently, gasped out loud again, and moaned. This time, a small spot of blood appeared at the corner of her mouth.

"What the hell?" Dan said as he spied it. He was sorry he had ever doubted her, ever questioned her. "Mia! Wake up," he said desperately. "You've got to *wake up*."

"Okay, Dan's on the line. He wants us to tell him the second Mia contacts us," Jenna spoke over the din around the table as the group concentrated before the mirror.

Lydia loudly repeated Mia's name while holding her mother's amulet over a candle. Adriana recited her archangel prayer over and over. Ho couldn't remember the exact way his granny invoked the spirits, so he meditated while focusing on Mia and chanting a Korean mantra out loud. Sitting in Jenna's lap, Nathan was entertained by the various actions of the adults around him. He chewed on his teething ring and happily screeched along.

‡　‡　‡

Her world was collapsing into nothing but darkness and pain as John took special delight in torturing her. That last hard slap to her face made her head ring. Mia wondered when he would finally tire of her and deliver a fatal blow. But she knew that he would most likely take his time in making her suffer.

Her dream of the man digging out in the woods and the child's hand falling out of the open sack came to her. She now realized that the youngest girl in the photos must have been that child. What did he call her? *Chloe*. If he was vile enough to mercilessly kill an innocent child, she stood a slim chance in escaping this sadistic killer. She would end up another victim like Chloe, left behind in this world between worlds, and no one would ever know. And when he awakened completely from his coma, how many other victims would he claim? How many more lives would he destroy and young girls would he torture?

A kick to her ribs made her coil in agony. She knew she wouldn't be able to withstand his beating much longer. Hopelessness overcame her. Mia could only think about her son and her husband. She wished she could have held them both one last time. The pain from the blows was excruciating, but the ache in her heart for them was worse.

However, when she managed to open her eyes, a horrifying sight momentarily displaced the pain she was feeling. The shadow was flowing around her now. She gasped out loud and pulled away from it as much as possible.

John chortled, "That won't do you any good. It feeds off of desperation and misery. There's no use trying to get away from It, because It will eventually claim you anyway."

"No… No!" Mia shrieked as the shadow climbed her legs.

She had to make one last attempt to contact her family again before she perished. Mia forced herself to focus on Aunt Lydia. She was the only bridge between this hell and the people she loved. Every time another blow landed, she used the intensity of the pain to sharpen that focus. It helped block out the sight of John's demonic face as he grinned with perverse pleasure in delivering her punishment slowly and steadily.

Another kick, this time aimed at her back, and she screamed out loud. *Aunt Lydia! I need you. Oh god! How I need you. Please, Aunt Lydia! Hear me,* she pleaded with her mind as she wept. Maniacally, John roared at her plight. *He can try to kill me, but I'm not going to give in,* she thought willfully. But to her horror, she could not connect with her aunt as she had before. Had it all been in her mind—torture induced delusions of what she so desperately wanted?

‡　‡　‡

"Bailey? What are you still doing here? Weren't you off shift a few hours ago?" Meredith asked as she entered the room to find the two women praying.

Bailey startled at the sound of her supervisor's voice and her eyes opened. How was she going to explain this?

"Mr. Bradford was doing extremely well. He's come around several times this afternoon already with very strong lucid responses. I thought it might be good for him to have some additional stimulus," she fumbled.

"You are not authorized to make those decisions. You should have contacted someone immediately. What were you thinking?" Meredith went directly to Talbot. She opened his eyelid and shone a penlight in his eye looking for pupil responsiveness. Meredith knew that Dr. Chen was going to have a fit if she found out that this progress had not been reported. She dreaded getting her ass in a sling over the incompetence of her staff. With an air of annoyance, she went to the computer and logged in. Clearly, she was not pleased with either of this patient's visitors. "And who are you? Are you family?" she asked the other woman seated beside the CNA.

"I'm Cheryl Becker and I'm a friend of Mr. Bradford. I came to see if there was anything I could do for him. I didn't think a prayer vigil would hurt," Cheryl answered defensively.

"I am sorry, but the ICU is for family members only and there are no other approved visitors listed for him. You are going to have to leave."

"But how can I visit him then? I think I'm the closest thing to family he's got," Cheryl said.

"You're going to have to take that up with Administration. They are located on the fourth floor. In the meantime, I'm going to have to ask you again to leave, now," Meredith said firmly.

"Oh all right, if you say so… Bailey, I'm sorry. It was so nice meeting you. I hope to see you again, and hopefully under better circumstances," Cheryl said as she rose and clasped Bailey's hand in friendship. "I have to head to work now anyway. But I am going to speak with someone in Administration about this tomorrow, so maybe I'll get to see you then."

"Yes, Cheryl. Thanks. It was nice meeting you too," Bailey replied, but she was more preoccupied with what was going to transpire between her supervisor and her once Ms. Becker left the room.

‡ ‡ ‡

"Mia! Please speak to us. Where are you, darling?… Oh my word!" Lydia's face was strained with worry. "I can hardly hear you. What is happening?" She turned to the others and with an urgent whisper, announced, "I can hear her!"

The others around the table looked up with expectation.

"Dan? Are you there? Mia's back! Aunt Lydia can hear her," Jenna spoke low into her phone while her eyes remained glued on the older woman next to her.

"She is? What's happening?" Dan's voice called over the phone's tiny speaker. Jenna set the device on speakerphone and placed it on the table so he could hear what was going on.

"Ohhh!" Lydia moaned, "Mia's in pain. John is hurting her. He's… he's trying to kill her. Darling, wake up, do you hear me? Return to us now!"

Hearing Lydia over the phone, Dan grew frantic. "Tell her to get away from him, Lydia! Tell her to get away from him!"

"She can't move. He's got her pinned on the floor… Please Mia, try to get away. Try to move—anything! Oh! He struck her again!" Lydia described with terror.

Nathan abruptly let out a wail on Jenna's lap. He stretched his hands towards the mirror. "Mama Mama Mama!" he called clearly, saying his mother's name for the first time.

"We all need to concentrate! Everyone focus on Mia. We've got to help her fight him off. Daniel, can you still hear me?" Lydia called towards Jenna's cell phone.

"Yes, Lydia—what is it? What do you need me to do?" Dan answered.

"Think of her. Put your every thought on her and concentrate. Speak to her with your mind. Let her know that you are there and that you love her. She hears you and needs your strength. You and the baby are what matters most to her. She's got to know that you are there."

‡ ‡ ‡

John hauled off and kicked her hard again, but this time it seemed to have hardly any effect on her. She was fading. She could feel it. An icy sensation washed over her and she knew that the shadow had encompassed her. When she opened her eyes, she could see now what had appeared as wisps of black smoke before were actually millions of tendrils wrapping themselves about her and sinking their tips into her flesh with firm holds. Memories of Seth being consumed and taken away by this same insidious entity ignited terror within her, but she was helpless to fight it off.

A fleeting thought crossed her mind. *How was John able to withstand it…? He grew stronger instead of weaker from it…* The answer came to her with stunning clarity. *He was stronger from it… by giving it what it wants.* In order to survive a few precious moments more, she would have to surrender herself to the dark entity.

In that instant, Mia knew what she had to do before she perished under her tormentor's hand. Summoning up her last reserve of energy, she set about turning her anguish first into anger. She concentrated on the fact that her attacker was also her jailer. He had murdered a child. He had abducted Samantha and had intended on killing her too. He had turned himself loose on her family so that her dear husband and aunt turned viciously against each other. *He had touched my baby and made him sick.* She let the pain kindle an intense rage that burned in her gut. With her instincts now locked on revenge, the feeling quickly forged into pure hot hatred.

At once, a vitalizing pulse of strength flowed through her as she permitted the shadow to infect her. As it did so, she felt a raw power surging into her useless limbs. Her arms started to regain feeling. She was able to move her fingertips.

It was true.

As the shadow's energy filled her, she felt confident and sure; an insane ecstasy that made her feel she could do anything she desired. She sharpened the acrimonious thoughts further into a singular one. *I must kill him or be killed.*

Mia decided to stay low, all the while vigor and warmth continued to flow to her cold, dead legs. As the fury pulsed through her, her senses sharpened, honing a predatory awareness. She determined her best strategy would be to use the element of surprise. The only chance at overcoming John was to make sure he didn't know that her strength was returning. As long as she appeared weak, he would think that he had the upper hand. She needed him to believe it long enough to assess her capabilities and formulate a counter offense. *Maybe there was a chance to get away from John after all…*

Now all she had to do was lie still and wait for the right moment.

‡ ‡ ‡

The door opened and Anthony Marcose wheeled in a portable vitals monitor and blood pressure cuff. It was getting close to the end of his shift after what had been a long day with impossible patients. Without saying anything, he simply nodded to the man in the room holding the patient's hand and went about his routine checking her chart, then pressure and temperature. *Hello Ms. Labont. And how are we today?* He had seen her name on his new admits list. This looked like a rough case. Having an aneurysm at any age was bad enough, but the woman lying unconscious before him was no older than he. It made him shudder to think of how unexpected some conditions could be, striking out of nowhere. When he completed his tasks, he left the room and returned shortly with a syringe filled with a clear fluid. He took up the IV line, flicked the syringe a couple of times to get the liquid to settle, and prepared to insert it into the port on the IV.

"Hold on. What is that for?" the man asked. Anthony presumed he was her significant other.

The nurse paused with the needle in mid-air and a question outlining his expression. "It's only a painkiller to help her rest more easily. I noticed that her pulse rate was up and her blood pressure has dropped. It's best to keep up with her pain management so her body can heal quickly and with less stress and complications. It's what her surgeon ordered," he explained.

"You said it would help her rest more easily? Will it make her sleep any longer?"

The man appeared agitated. *Most likely anxious about having to visit his wife in the hospital,* Anthony surmised. *They all seem to get that way.*

"Yes, it has that effect on some patients." The nurse started to feel uneasy. *This guy seems to be wound a little too tight. And why does he keep shaking and rubbing the patient's arms like that?* Although he was small in stature, in the past Anthony had held his own with disruptive family members. And this guy who was grilling him looked like he had the potential to get out of hand. It was just what he needed after the day he had had. *One more crazy.*

"Then no. Don't give it to her. She needs to wake up immediately," the man answered as he continued to rub her arm and hands briskly.

At the unusual request, the nurse eyed his behavior with a raised eyebrow. Typically, the family was asking *for* painkillers for the patient. "Sir, these things take time. If we can stay ahead of her pain before it spikes, it will be more easily managed. If we don't, her pain might get to a point where, once it is elevated, it is much harder to control and the medication might not be as effective," Anthony tried.

"I'm telling you, she needs to become conscious right now. Is there anything you can give her to bring her around instead?"

"She's just been through surgery and her body or her physician will decide how much rest she's going to need. We just can't go around waking her up if she's not ready." *This guy was really unbelievable.*

"Where's the physician then? I need to speak with him pronto," the man demanded, and then turned back to Mia and persisted, "Come on babe. Listen to me—you've got to wake up. You can do it."

"Her surgeon's already left for the day. Dr. Zakaria is on rotation today. He may be busy with other patients right now. I can let him know you want him to stop in. In the meantime, I'm going to give your wife… that is your wife, right?"

"Yes, of course she is."

"Listen, I'm going to give your wife this first dose of painkillers as prescribed by her surgeon to keep her stable. It's just a little morphine to make sure her pain doesn't spike. You can take up the continued dosaging with Dr. Zakaria when he gets here." Anthony reached once again for the IV line.

"You touch that and I'll break your hand. I've already told you, my wife needs to regain consciousness. Call Zakaria in *now*."

The nurse, shocked by the threat, grew indignant and struggled to remain professional with this hostile spouse. He seriously contemplated whether he should call a Code Purple to security. In his experience, these things could turn ugly in a matter of minutes. Summoning his patient-caregiver communication training, he asked, "And exactly why do you feel that way, sir?"

"I don't have time to explain. I just know that if she continues to sleep, it's going to be worse for her," he answered plainly. Then he redirected to his wife, "Mia, come on, you can do it. You have to do it."

Anthony sized Dan up and down carefully, trying to determine if he was an insensitive bastard or just plain psycho. In his seven years in health services, he had had plenty of experience with unsympathetic spouses and this guy with his military buzz cut and no nonsense demeanor looked like just the type. He probably wanted his poor wife up and on her feet as fast as possible to cook and clean for him. This would be the third time this month the nurse had encountered an abusive family member. He was going to be sure to fill Zakaria in about this before sending him in.

"So are you going to get the doc or what?" the husband insisted.

"Yes sir. And I'll be sure to let him know your request," Anthony answered tersely, holding his ground. "But understand that you are jeopardizing your wife's health and recovery by delaying her pain medication."

"*Your* health is going to be in jeopardy if you don't get Zakaria NOW!"

The nurse exited, more than willing to let the doctor explain. When he stepped outside, he could overhear the husband talking into a phone, "Lydia— what's going on? When the nurse came in, it broke my concentration. Did I mess anything up? What is happening with Mia now?"

This guy was really something else.

‡　‡　‡

John's onslaught was lessening. Mia wasn't sure if it was because he was growing bored or she simply wasn't dying fast enough for him. He paused for minutes at a time, as if his attention was being redirected to something else. When he turned his back to her, it was in that brief moment that she took the opportunity to assess her ableness. The shadow had transformed her loathing of him into strength and sinew. She was ready. But before she acted, she inhaled deeply and centered herself. What she was about to attempt was suicidal and she didn't know how she would pull it off.

Mia slowly rose to her feet. She steadied, then tensed, ready to tackle, and trying to determine the best angle of attack. John was clearly a head taller and outweighed her by about sixty pounds. For a second, Mia had doubts. She was no fighter and had never been in a physical altercation, recalling how easily the nurses pinned her down in the mental institution. She had no skills, quickness, or agility. Maybe this wasn't going to work after all.

Just then John turned back around. The black shadow that had cloaked him all along now extended to envelope her completely, inextricably linking them. When he saw her, a look of amusement washed over his face as if he were audience to nothing more than the antics of a clever pet. He laughed out loud.

"Bravo! I see that you finally are starting to understand what I was telling you. Once you set yourself free from who and what you used to be, you can do almost anything here. It's the only thing I'll miss from my incarceration. It has made me finally recognize my true—"

Mia sprung at him with all of her force.

The unexpected impact bowled him off his feet and both of them went crashing down. The wind was knocked out of John as they made contact and his head slammed hard against the ground, stunning him. Mia landed on top of him. Before he could react, in a deft move she jammed the heel of her hand upwards against his nose as hard as she could, remembering a move from a basic self-defense class she took at the community center. There was a discernible crack as his bridge yielded. In blinded agony, John growled fiercely as his hands flew to his bruised face. Blood from his broken nose squirted past his fingers.

Mia drew her legs up quickly when he attempted to grab her by her throat. He grappled to gain hold, but she used her bent legs to leverage herself away from his straining fingers. When he pitched to topple her, she was amazed at her newfound strength. Using a scissor lock with her legs, she kept him pinned down as the two pitted tactics against each other, although she was uncertain whether she could continue holding him off. As he thrashed savagely beneath her, the shadow's dark influence infused her completely with fresh thoughts of revenge, bloodlust, and ultimate power. Her stomach churned with rage and bile filled her mouth. John's words continued to echo in her head, *Set yourself free. You can do anything here.*

Drawing upon a surge of super strength from the shadow's urging for murder, she quickly maneuvered around so one knee and shin slid into place across his neck and applied pressure, kneeling hard into his throat. Her kneecap bore directly down upon his Adam's apple which flexed beneath her.

John's hands loosened their grip. As the tables were turned, his eyes widened with the realization of what she was attempting to do. He fought to gain another hold on her, when she started to crush his windpipe. The shadow swirled like a tornado about them, frenzied with the violence. He grimaced as his fingers flew to her knee, digging into her flesh. He pushed upwards with all of his strength, trying to throw her off of him, but she leaned into him. Panting heavily, Mia focused on hate and murder as she continued to push her knee down hard, employing the full force the shadow provided her. His face turned from deep red to violet and his eyes started to bulge. Her only desire was to see him suffer. She wanted to crush his very life out of him. The perverse and depraved act consumed her.

"Mama Mama!" Nathan cried for her from beyond that desolate place.

In that moment, for the first time Mia clearly heard her son. Shaken, she suddenly questioned what she was attempting. A man was dying by her hand and she only wanted him to suffer more. Afraid and suddenly ashamed, Mia wavered in the pressure she applied to his throat. She had let the shadow control her and would go mad if she surrendered to it completely.

John inhaled sharply and coughed violently. "Argh!! You bitch!" he snarled with fury, when he caught his breath. "I'll kill you! You hear me? And when I wake, I'll kill your family too! I know where you live and will bury you all." His eyes, stained with blood, blazed maniacally.

Nathan broke into a shriek, his voice crescendoed through the blackness in a plaintive pitch, "Maaammaaa!" He called for her over and over again. Her heart hammered at the sound of his voice. Every fiber of her being was filled with the overwhelming instinct to protect her child. When she considered the possibility of this monster escaping to inflict his evil once again, it determined what she had to do to see this through to the end. This time, Mia took control and resolutely understood her course of action.

She would turn herself completely over to the shadow and all of its intent.

‡ ‡ ‡

The alarm sounded on the monitor. Its shrill wail filled the room. At its call, Bailey and Meredith stopped arguing and looked at Talbot who had started to gasp and shake violently in his bed. Bailey rushed to his side, while Meredith quickly checked his feeding tube, his ventilator, and then the monitor.

"What's wrong with him?" Bailey cried.

"I don't know... it sounds like he's choking," Meredith responded as she examined the system of hoses and leads trying to assess the trouble. Everything appeared to be in proper working order. She silenced the alarm, only for it to go off again.

Talbot continued to thrash about gagging and coughing. His eyes opened wide in panic as his hands went to his throat.

"Take it out! Take it out!" Bailey screamed as she reached for the feeding tube that snaked up his nose.

Meredith called in a Code Blue to alert additional staff and then pushed past Bailey to withdraw first the feeding and then the ventilation tubes. Talbot's body forcibly arched upward and he stopped coughing. Instead, only deep grunting and growling noises emanated from his writhing mass as his face turned a violet blue. The RN tilted his head back to open his air passage, feeling for a breath of air against her cheek. None was forthcoming. Just then, a response team comprised of a young emergency resident and three other staff members burst into the room with a crash cart answering the code put in by Meredith.

"He's not breathing!" she informed them.

They took up their positions and worked frantically on the patient who continued to wildly thrash about. Aside the commotion, Bailey stood in a corner and wrung her hands, crying and praying. She had never been so scared before. Although the room was filled with medical professionals attending a myriad of tasks, no one seemed to know exactly what was happening with Talbot as his heart monitor skipped wildly with his outbursts. Calling out statuses and alerts, they drew upon all of their training and skills, but their actions were futile against the unknown force that was driving the life out of him. The team rallied with a defibrillator. However, three attempts later, his body persistently refused to respond.

After what seemed like an eternity to Bailey, Talbot's thrashing body slowed in its struggles. Finally it came to rest and grew still. Within another minute, the line on the heart monitor bumped once, twice, and then flat-lined, its monotonous alarm signaling finality. The staff frenetically commenced CPR and bagged him, following up with epinephrine injected into his line.

Despite their efforts, he lay unmoving on the table, his face cyanotic with broken vessels branching across his cheeks. Bloodied, his eyes protruded from their sockets, giving his skull the appearance of being shrunken. Fixed upon his face for eternity was a sneering grimace with dripping saliva, and a swollen purple tongue hanging partway from his gaping mouth.

"I think that's it, people. We've done all that we can. I'm going to call it… time of death… 16:27," the resident announced looking at the clock on the wall and lowering his mask. The front of his scrub shirt was dark from sweat from the intensity of the workout. "Who's his attending?"

The nurse on the rapid response team logged onto Talbot's chart and started to enter notes. "Time of death for Talbot John Bradford, at sixteen twenty-seven hours. And let me see—it looks like Drs. Grace Chen and Donald Cole are his attendings," she answered.

"All right then, if you would let them know."

Bailey sobbed openly and pushed past them to his side. Tenderly, she clutched and kissed the dead man's cooling hand, her eyes fixed on him. The others in the room exchanged curious looks at her unusual display of affection for this patient.

"But what happened?" she asked. "He was doing fine and Dr. Chen said he was making excellent progress."

"Don't know. Wish I could tell you right off. Chen will probably want to examine him. Maybe she could give you a better idea, but I've seen these things go south before for no apparent reason. It could have been some residual complications from his extensive brain injury, a clot that wasn't detected, or maybe his heart gave out. Who knows? It's hard to tell, but we'll find out. Or then again, maybe we won't," the resident answered with a shrug of indifference while heading for the door.

"Hey, Mer—does he have any family members to contact?" the team nurse asked Meredith as she finished up her notes.

"No Kathy. We haven't seen one yet. He had this photo album here in his belongings with pictures of these little girls in it. They could be family, but I'm not sure. It's the strangest thing though. Listen to this—I thought one of them looked familiar and it turns out I was right. Remember that child that was on an Amber Alert a little while back? The alert pretty much covered the whole Pacific Northwest. She had been abducted and then later found in a shed that was buried in a mudslide somewhere in Washington. A psychic helped find her. It made the news," Meredith said.

"Oh yeah. I remember hearing about that. She survived the slide and was returned to her parents, wasn't she? Why do you ask?"

"I'm pretty sure she's one of the kids. Here—look. This was in his album." Meredith picked up one of the photos that had been knocked from the service table to the floor during all the commotion. She held it up to her colleague.

"Oh yeah, I recall her now. They featured her and her family on a news magazine show shortly after she was rescued. She's a cute little thing. But what was she doing in his photo album? Eww. That's kinda creepy when you think about it," said Kathy.

"I don't know, unless he knew her. But it still seems kinda weird." Meredith put the photo back down on the service table. Then she surveyed Bailey who was still despondent. There was no use in reprimanding the CNA anymore. She looked like she had been through enough. "I'll contact the morgue. Why don't you go home and get some rest?" she told her.

Bailey answered in a tired voice, "I'm okay. I think I'll just wait here until they come to get him."

"Well, suit yourself then. Maybe you can start packing up his things in his personal bag while you wait. We'll talk more about this tomorrow," Meredith said. "Hey Kath, you want to get some coffee? I'm about to go on break."

"Sure," Kathy agreed as she left with Meredith, the door shutting behind them.

Bailey clutched the now cold hand of Talbot John Bradford one last time as fresh tears sprung anew. She would never know what it would feel like to be touched by him.

"We would have been so happy together, Tal," she whispered when the others had left and all was quiet. "I just know we would have…"

‡ ‡ ‡

His body lay unmoving beneath her.

Mia rose to her feet. Adrenaline coursed through her veins making her shake uncontrollably. As she pinned him down in his death throes, the shadow's frigid feel had transformed into a fire-like heat, its malevolent influence ordering her to eviscerate and then rip him to shreds. It whispered and infiltrated every recess of her mind that the grisly actions would not only be just, they would be so very easy to do. All she had to do was continue. Utilizing all of her will power, she instead shut her mind to the shadow's urgings and forced herself to stop.

Unable to influence her with its dark lure, the shadow seized the opportunity to blanket the body in a seething mass of black snakes as it had with Seth. It tumbled wildly, pulsed, and swelled for a few moments. Then it gradually receded, the mass shrinking in bounds until finally it vanished. John was no longer.

Mia looked to where he had lain. Any trace of him was gone. She thought she would feel victorious, but she felt hollow and spent instead. The adrenaline ebbed within her, replaced by a dismal feeling of hopelessness and shame at the horrific deed she had committed. Indeed her tormentor was a child killer, an abductor, a rapist. A creature bent on suffering and torture. But she hadn't shared his intent. Until now. *Am I any better than him?*

Her surroundings fell silent. The walls of ever-changing watercolor hues had returned. She was imprisoned here with no chance of ever leaving this alternate world. She would never see her family again.

Mia's legs folded and she collapsed to the ground. A shiver came over her as the lingering heat that had raged within her just moments before extinguished, leaving her cold and numb. She held up her hands to see they were crawling now with the tendrils of the shadow. *I'm next. There is no escaping it, only through death…*

Her only comfort was in knowing that Nathan would be safe and other children would never fall victim to the horror and pain John would inflict upon them. Overcome by exhaustion, Mia curled up on her side, trying to keep out the chill. *It will be over soon.* The tendrils were sinking deeper into her; their movement upon her like the sensation of millions of crawling insect legs.

Frightened at the thought of where she would be soon, she fixated instead on those most dear to her. She imagined Nathan in her arms, and Dan, her father, Jenna, Aunt Lydia, and Ho, as if they were by her side. She clung to thoughts of them to see her through to the end.

Her tears fell freely as she struggled to remain calm. *I don't want to go. I don't want to leave them. Oh god, please! If there is any way…* It was as still as a tomb except for the teeming frenzy now upon her. She envisioned her husband and son wanting to hold them one last time. *Oh, how I love you both.* She hoped they would feel her thoughts and keep the memory of her love for them forever. *My precious, precious ones. I will always love you.*

The tendrils covered her face, their frenetic motions filling her ears and mouth. She made herself think instead the blanket of love her father had described to her was covering her now. She closed her eyes, took a deep breath, and waited.

As she felt herself teetering upon the edge of an endless black void, her attention was drawn to a small sound that made its way to that place of death. It was not much more than the slightest of murmurs. Uncertain if it was merely her mind grasping at anything it could, she concentrated on it, letting it bid her farewell.

It was the sound of Nathan crying.

Upon recognizing her son, her heart felt as if it were being torn from her chest. *Shhh, shhh don't cry, love. I'm sorry. So sorry.*

But in the next instant, she heard Lydia's voice too. At first, it sounded miles away, but the sound sharpened and amplified until finally she heard succinctly, "Mia! Please! Come back to us…"

Could it be true? Am I just imagining them? she questioned herself. She was held motionless on the precipice. Then, one by one—Jenna, Ho, and Adriana joined in and then… Dan! She heard him loud and clear. *He is here with me!* They were all concentrating on her and she could feel each and every one of them. Her spirits soared.

It was then she knew she wasn't alone anymore.

‡　‡　‡

"I'm telling you, doc. I need you to see my wife immediately! It's critical—a matter of life or death," Dan urged as he briskly led Dr. Zakaria back to Mia's room. Nurse Marcose followed, still flabbergasted by how the persistent husband of this patient managed to track them down. Dan continued as they entered the room, "I don't know how to make you understand, but—"

He stopped mid-sentence when he saw Mia staring up at them from her bed. She managed a weak smile.

"Oh god, Murph. I thought I had lost you," he said as his eyes filled with tears. He grabbed her up and hugged her, fiercely at first but remembering her fragility, worked at letting her go. "You're okay," he said gently. "You're here." Mia reached for him, her trembling fingers lightly grazing his cheek.

"Mr. Labont, exactly what was it that you wanted?" Dr. Zakaria asked.

"Are you safe? Is it over?" Dan asked Mia.

She tilted her head in a slight nod. In that moment, they both understood and knew—the nightmare had ended. He broke into a grin and hugged her again.

"Mr. Labont?"

"Nothing, doc. It's okay now. It's okay," Dan said as he locked eyes with his wife.

Mia's lips formed, 'Nathan,' barely above a whisper.

"He's fine, just missing you! He even called for you. I heard him clearly over the phone—he actually said 'Mama'. Oh—everyone's waiting. Hold on." Dan took out his phone and reported to Jenna who still held an open line with him. She excitedly shared the news with the others at home.

"How are you feeling, Mrs. Labont?" Zakaria asked as he looked over her chart. Then he took up her wrist to check her pulse rate.

Mia softly said, "Okay." She closed her eyes, leaned her head back against her pillow and swallowed.

"Can you feel this?" Zakaria said while touching the end of his pen against her palms, first on one then the next. She nodded. "And this?" he continued, as he tried the soles of her feet. More confirmation.

"Are you feeling any pain?" Anthony asked.

"Not anymore."

The nurse looked puzzled for a moment at her response and then continued, "Okay, well let us know the minute you start feeling anything. We'll give you something to keep the edge off." He cast a furtive glance at Dan and then returned his attention back to Mia. "Here is the button for you to press so you can summon us yourself. Remember—the minute you feel anything. We want to stay ahead of the pain."

She nodded again.

"If you are doing okay and don't have any questions, I'll leave you now. Your doctor will be in this afternoon to follow up. Take care." Zakaria said. With that, he left abruptly followed by the nurse who didn't want to spend any more time than was necessary in the company of the unpredictable and volatile husband.

"Your surgeon came out to the waiting room right after the surgery and said that everything went really, really well. He said that you'd probably feel weak at first, but that's to be expected. It's just going to take some time and we'll have to be patient. Everybody wants to come to see you, but I was told they'd have to wait until you're out of ICU. I wasn't able to reach your mother. And Mom and Dad cut their trip short as soon as they heard what happened. They are heading back right now and should be here by the end of the week."

"Murph...I'm... so sorry," she whispered with effort.

"Hey—what? Sorry? What are you talking about?"

"Putting you and Nathan... through...this."

He took up her hand in his. "You did what you had to, babe. I understand that. I just don't ever want anything to happen to you. But how about we talk about this later, all right?" He watched her closely for a moment as she fought against dozing off. "Maybe I should let you rest. Do you want to sleep?"

Mia's eyes opened wide as she clearly mouthed the word, "NO."

‡   ‡   ‡

She listened carefully. Her ears caught the chatter of staff members in the hallway, the purr and beep of her monitors, and the soft snore of Dan as he slumbered. Mia blinked for a few moments to make sure she really was where she thought she was. When she found her husband asleep in the chair pulled up alongside of her in the softly lit hospital room, she wept with happiness and relief. It was only then that she trusted reality enough to permit a brief return to sleep.

By that afternoon, a good prognosis and check up transferred her from ICU to a regular room, although she wouldn't let on about the remaining soreness her body felt from the blows she had endured from John. She put it all aside when she was reunited with her beloved son. When Nathan said 'Mama' as he reached for her, Mia thought her heart would overflow. Her life began anew as they clung to each other, not wanting to let each other go. It was he who had ultimately saved her.

Reassured by the presence of her family, she concentrated on her physical and speech therapies. A slight slur when she spoke was evidence that she still had further to go. The pressure exerted on her brain from the rupture and hemorrhage resulted in weakness in her left arm and leg, forcing her to rely on a walker to get around. Her condition had been caught in time so that the damage was minimal. However, fatigue and weakness were expected to linger for months to come and Dan was instructed to be on alert for any mood or behavioral changes. Eventually as she healed, the symptoms were expected to diminish.

Once they knew of her recovery, the others started to show up as soon as they could. It surprised Mia when Ho and Jenna arrived hand in hand apparently after enjoying a lunch date. Mrs. Lopez stopped in with flowers and a silver crucifix for Mia to put around her neck immediately. Last, Aunt Lydia came looking a bit frazzled but bubbling with happiness.

Mia noticed that they all were behaving differently as they clamored around her bedside. Observing their interactions as they teased, talked, and joked with each other, it was evident that a newfound cameraderie had been forged between them. It made her wonder what all had transpired among them during her showdown with John.

She tried to lose herself in the midst of the attention, love, and affection they showed her. But it wasn't enough to offset the overwhelming sense of guilt that hung over her like a cloud. Remaining thoughts of her harrowing experience continued to play in her head, reminders that while she was indeed alive, it was in exchange for someone else's life in return. In her family and friends' excitement and triumph, they had no way of knowing exactly what had unfolded in that dark hell during those long hours and how she had given in to what evilness and despair had forced from her.

To them, John was nothing more than a name embroiled in bizarre circumstances. He was not a man of tangible flesh and blood they had met or even knew to exist. They merely believed in him because they believed her. But for Mia, the depravity of his glare, the chilling sound of his voice, and the terrifying power he used to exact his torturous physical punishment would remain with her for the rest of her days. Yet, was she any better than he? Although she could argue that she did what she had to do for the safety and wellbeing of everyone she loved, despite all of his horridness—*she had killed him.*

Her mind simply would not let go of feeling John's movements cease beneath her, his body slumping and releasing a slow sad sigh, nor the image of a fine red web of broken capillaries lacing his cheeks, his bloodshot eyes glazing over as they stared off into nothingness, the stream of saliva dripping from his gaping lips blue from lack of oxygen. And when all was final and still, how the demonic shadow had completely devoured his body until it was gone, leaving behind no trace. Mia knew most likely where it was headed with John and she was the vehicle that had sent him there.

Worst yet, she had given up and surrendered herself to the shadow and all it demanded. The knowledge of what she did would remain with her forever like a stain on her soul. As she paged through her notebook that she had asked for during her hospital stay, she came across a note in John's hand. Only now she understood the truth behind his prophetic warning:

TAKE HEED LEST YE FALL

It was a quiet afternoon and Mia longed to go home, to be surrounded by her things and to take time to process all that had happened. Two weeks had come and gone since her surgery and to her frustration, the medical staff had not yet determined her release date. There was much for her to do in preparation for Nathan's first birthday that was fast approaching. What's more, although Dan and Lydia seemed to be on the way to mending their differences, the relationship between them remained strained. It hurt her to see them this way. Most of all, she wanted to get things back to normal for everyone involved.

In her hospital room, while she read to Nathan who was settling down for a nap, Dan researched online articles on his tablet. Suddenly struck with a bright 'a-ha' look on his face, he sat up straight in the recliner, eager to share what he had found with her.

"Hey, Murph, remember how you had those dreams—the one about Samantha's abduction and the other one with John digging in the woods at night? I'm beginning to wonder—do you suppose in some way that maybe they were coincidental?"

She stopped reading. "Coincidental in what way? What do you mean?"

"Hear this. Remember when I fell asleep on the sofa and I had that really bizarre dream? You know, the day before Nat had the fever? Well that dream basically foretold of everything that has since happened—your collapse, John's presence, everyone pitching in to help—like some sort of premonition. In fact, I was even beginning to wonder if this psychic stuff was spreading, you know—to Lydia and Nathan, and to me, even."

"Like some kind of contagion?"

"Well, yes… er, no. Not that I think I'm even remotely psychic. I'm just tossing around ideas, that's all. I figured I must've internalized the events and setting from all of those paranormal activity shows I had watched on TV. But anyway—"

Mia contemplated him with a raised eyebrow, unsure of where he was going with this.

"—I just associated them into my dream. I don't know… Or maybe I made up some kind of scenario in my head that I thought was plausible. You got to admit, things were getting pretty intense at that time."

"Okay, maybe that's how your brain works. But I don't think that's necessarily the same as what I've been experiencing, so I'm not sure I follow you."

"With you, I'm thinking that Samantha was already on your mind so in your dream you simply assigned a scenario you speculated most likely *could* have happened. For example, you probably saw her in an Amber Alert on the news sometime and didn't recall it. Then you filled in all the blanks on who the abductor was and how it happened."

"So what you are trying to tell me is that I cooked this all up in my imagination."

"Not necessarily, but get this—this online article I'm reading on aneurysms says that in some cases, because of the pressure they exert on the brain, aneurysms have been known to induce hallucinations in some people to the point where they are not only seeing, but *hearing things too*. Like you know how you were seeing and hearing Samantha and John? And the doc told me that some aneurysms take time to develop and some even go undetected for years. Who knows how long you had that thing? It might explain a lot of what's been happening."

"All right, but how about when I called 911? They knew where to find Samantha because she had given me clues. Otherwise, how would I have known where to send them to search? And what about Chloe Schuster, John's first victim? Once I knew that monster was responsible for her murder, the police didn't have any problems finding her body in the woods behind his parents' old home out in Orting with the anonymous tip I called in last week. It was the same place he imprisoned Samantha—all his victims, in fact."

"Lucky guesses? Okay, I'll give you that. I'm still stumped myself. Even so, there's got to be a reasonable explanation and I think it lies somehow in the way you process information. You could be very astute on picking up the most subtle clues and details and aren't even aware that you are doing it."

"Okay, well how about when you and I communicated through the séance? You experienced that yourself, first hand!"

"Mass hysteria? I was so jacked at that point I would've believed anything. And the others readily buy into all of that stuff without batting an eye."

"Murph, I know what I saw. I know what I've been through." She crossed her arms. "I can't believe that you still have such a hard time with all of this."

"I'm really trying. You've got to admit that. But see? That's the thing—everything and anything we perceive is filtered and interpreted through our brains as well as everything we believe. Who knows? Mine might not pick up or register these things because I have trouble believing in them. But your brain could easily register it as having experienced it since you do *in fact* believe it. Or maybe it's a little of all three—you have some psychic intuitiveness paired with a hallucination-inducing aneurysm, *and* good powers of deductive reasoning. All I'm saying is just to consider alternative possibilities, that's all."

She lowered her voice. "But I know what I experienced. Although it was bizarre, it was reality—as real as you and I are right now at this moment. And I know I killed John. I know it for a fact."

"Maybe, but that is only if he ever was real. We don't know *that* for a fact. While Samantha and Chloe are actual people, John might have been someone you hallucinated or conjured up, given the circumstances surrounding the abductions. Get it? You never even knew where he was exactly."

"But he was the murderer and abductor of those girls."

"*Someone* was, that's true. But whether *John* was is a different story."

"Okay, but why did I see him in the hospital, lying there in a coma?"

"Or at least you believed you saw him. Your brain can make up anything, or get inspired from a movie you watched or a story you read. Who knows? Your reality is only as good as how your brain perceives that reality. Can you see what I'm getting at?"

"But why a hospital, of all places?"

"Since you were in a hospital yourself, albeit unconscious, maybe you picked up on your environment through your senses. Let's face it—there aren't many places that smell or sound like hospitals. Hey, I got caught up in it myself with all the excitement. I could actually visualize the bastard lying in a bed somewhere in Idaho and I was ready to make the five hundred mile drive to do some unplugging."

Although Dan's logical explanation did little to improve Mia's spirits, for a brief moment she tried to understand his rational. When he got like this, it took quite a bit of effort to convince him otherwise. "I guess. I'll have to think about it some more," she shrugged with a sigh, although a part of her was hesitant to drop her vigilance completely.

"You really should, honey. Saving a child or helping one out? Yes, I can see you doing that totally. That's the kind of person you are. But there is no way you're a killer. Not you. And choking a six-foot-two grown man to death with super-human strength? You got to admit, it sounds pretty farfetched. You might be beating yourself up over nothing." Dan rose and kissed her on the forehead. "But most of all, I don't like to see you so down. It's not going to help you heal any faster. In the meantime, how about I move Mr. Tat to the sofa?" He indicated to the now sleeping infant cuddled up next to her.

"Okay. His blanket is at the foot of the bed. Will you spread it out and place him on it, please?"

"I was just thinking that," Dan said knowingly as he gently lifted his son. "Hey, isn't it time for you to take your walk? I can go with you, but we'll have to wait for Lydia to get here to watch Nathan."

"No, hon. Why don't you stay here with Nathan? Geoff says that I'm doing well enough to get around on my own with no worries. In fact, I think I'm going to take a longer route and go the other direction today."

"Are you sure?"

"Uh huh. I'll be fine."

"Okay, but promise me you won't be doing any sprints?" Dan said as he positioned her walker next to her.

With effort, she swung her legs off the side of the bed and then slowly rose and grasped the aid. Leaning towards him for a kiss, she answered, "I promise. The other patients will be safe for now."

Dan's theory echoed in her head as she worked her way down the corridor and forced her legs to cooperate as her physical therapist had shown her. *Perhaps Murph is right*, she permitted herself to entertain. *Maybe John was only a hallucinogenic effect caused by my condition, or surgery, or involvement with Samantha. Or maybe all three. It could be possible that he never was real.* It was all too confusing to sort through. How could she be sure that she knew the difference between reality and fantasy at this point?

When it came down to it, all she desired was a normal life again. And if it meant conceding that this was simply a delusion from an aneurysm, and her aneurysm was now repaired, she was willing to accept logic. At least she knew one thing to be certain—after the surgery, John never appeared to her in mirrors or other reflective surfaces again.

She turned the corner and as she continued on her way, she noticed an elderly man sitting in one of the armchairs situated by a large window at the far end of the walkway. Staring out the window, he was obviously distraught, and silently weeping and swabbing his eyes with the handkerchief he had pulled from the pocket of his plaid sport coat. Just then, Mia heard a voice call to her from the open doorway she had paused in front of.

"Miss? Miss? Can you help me?"

Inside the room, Mia could see a thin old woman lying flat on her hospital bed. She waved her shriveled arm, beckoning for her to enter. Mia glanced around to see there was no one else present in the area. She looked back at the woman, pointed to herself and queried, "Excuse me, do you mean me?"

"Yes. Please, can you help me?"

"Uh, sure. Do you need me to call the nurse?"

"No. I need you."

Mia entered the dim room and maneuvered her way past the drawn back curtains, and a disconnected IV pole and silent heart monitor that had been set aside. The elderly woman smiled warmly as Mia approached. Her eyes were bright embers against her dark brown face, her hair a billowy white halo encircling her head.

"There you are," she said pleased. "Thank you for coming in."

"Hello," Mia replied, "What can I do for you, ma'am?"

"Did you notice a mature gentleman somewhere out in the hallway? He's quite good looking in my book, although he might be upset."

"Yes. He's seated in an armchair by the window."

"Do you suppose you can give him a message for me? I can't leave this room and I don't have much time."

"Do you want me to call him over for you?"

"No, I've tried, but he won't listen to me."

"Uh, okay," Mia answered, confused.

"Please tell him that he can't keep moping around here all day. He's got to go home and get the guest room ready. Our baby girl Lenora and our grandbaby are flying in tonight. He needs to be there to tell them the news. I don't want them to have to hear it over the phone."

"All right," Mia replied, even more perplexed. "Are you sure you don't want me to bring him here for you?"

"No. It'll just confuse him. But you can also tell him that Gwendolyn says it's been a wonderful seventy-three years and she'll be seeing him soon. That's it. Go ahead now. His name is Robert."

"Okay, I will." Mia turned her walker around and started heading for the door. "I'll be right back."

"Thank you so much, miss," the woman said.

When Mia reached the end of the hall and gave Robert the messages, the startled man could only look at her through a mix of bewilderment and wonder. Then, nodding his head, he rose and without a word, walked past her to the elevator and left.

She thought it unusual and could only attribute the reaction to the man's emotional state. Pondering whether or not she should relay what had transpired to the woman when she returned to see her, she caught sight of Aunt Lydia coming down the hallway searching for her.

"Look at you! You're doing wonderful, sweetheart. You're looking so much stronger," Lydia said as the two of them circled back to Mia's room. "I stopped at your room and Dan said you were taking a walk. What were you doing way over here?"

"Thanks, Auntie. I decided on a longer route today and then I had to deliver a message for someone."

"Really? For whom, dear?"

"A lady in this room right here." Mia said when they arrived at the doorway. "In fact, it was pretty strange. Here, hold on a moment. I told her I'd come back to let her know that I delivered her message."

As she entered the room, she exclaimed, "What? That's the oddest thing… Wait a minute…"

"What's the oddest thing?" Lydia asked, unsure of what she was referring to. She joined her niece in the vacant room.

Dumbfounded, Mia replied, "The lady who gave me the message. I swear she was right here less than ten minutes ago. In fact, she said she couldn't leave this room. That's why she wanted me to go in her place. Wait—" She steadied herself on her walker and backed up a couple of steps to check the room number, then glanced up and down the hallway. "Yes. I'm sure it was this room, 423A. And there is no way the staff could have taken her out of here without me noticing. I had a clear view from over there by those chairs where you found me."

"And you're sure this is the room?"

"I'm positive. She's this sweet old lady who wanted me to relay her message to a man I think was her husband. She said he wouldn't listen to her, so she asked if I could do it for her. He was very upset when I saw him, but after I gave him the message, he left straight away without saying a thing to me. It was all very strange… I don't get it. She was *right here*. I know she was."

Lydia smiled, a knowing tugging at the corners of her mouth. "She most likely was, dear and I believe you did indeed see her."

It took a moment for Mia to understand her aunt's implication. "What? But I saw her in person! You couldn't mean that I… that I…" Mia stammered in shock, at a loss for words until she felt Lydia place something in her hands. Looking down, she saw it was the amulet from around her aunt's neck and a photograph of her father in his twenties that she had never seen before.

"It just means that you are evolving, my dear. Your gifts are getting stronger. You are getting stronger. Why, you fought and triumphed over the corruptive powers of pure evil! You didn't succumb and you didn't knuckle under either. I want you to have your grandmother's amulet. It's more rightfully yours than mine, given your talent, and will serve you well. I also brought this picture of your father for you. He would have been so very proud of what a remarkable woman you've become."

"But Aunt Lydia, I can't do this. I barely survived this last ordeal. And I took a life in the process. What about Dan and Nathan? I can't continue doing this to them. And now—this? What am I going to do? I can't do this. I just can't."

Her aunt gently grasped her niece's chin and looked directly into her bewildered eyes. "I know you, Mia Pappas. And I know you have the ability, not only to get through what has already happened, but what is yet to come.

"You'll find a way, child. You'll find your way."

More Stories from Tess Marset

With My Little Eye
(Book One of The Mia Series)

978-1-7333609-0-6

Gothic Suspense, Thriller

Shelf Unbound Award Winner – Best Indie Book 2016 Runner Up
I spy with my little eye…

Mia Labont is going insane. Or is she? After enduring the loss of her beloved father and a devastating miscarriage, she cannot surface from the depths of her depression, so much so that her husband, Dan, arrives home to find her suffering a breakdown with a gun in her hand. They are launched into a perilous journey of madness when Mia starts to see grisly images in mirrors and other reflective surfaces. The terrifying events become vivid, manifestations of a teen—but is he real or delusion? Mia must untangle a web of clues that will determine destinies and Dan is the only one who can save her. Will he reach her in time?

On Frogs and Princes

978-1-7333609-3-7

Contemporary Romance

When Stazie Royale sets her sights on something, she usually gets it. The pampered daughter of a successful defense attorney for celebrities is used to having her way. However, life begins to change for her one rainy night once she runs over Rey Natal while he is riding his bicycle during a blackout. Trying to come to terms with guilt and depression over a tragedy in his past, independent Rey is more than a challenge for Stazie's willful wiles. Encountering more mishaps, this unlikely pair must get beyond misperceptions to gain awareness for what they each had all along: love and appreciation for what they didn't think was possible. On Frogs and Princes is a story of abandonment, forgiveness, acceptance, and discovering that while all frogs aren't princes, even princesses can have warts.

X-Mas Tree

978-1-7333609-2-0

Novella

In this coming-of-age tale, 15-year-old Peter gets his first glimpse at the responsibility and commitment it takes in being a provider. X-Mas Tree is about a father and son's love for each other that is tested by the challenges of progress overshadowing tradition and the transformation of a boy to a man.

Like Us, The Polar Bears

978-1-7333609-4-4

Young Adult Novel

Seventeen-year-old Molly needs to figure out how to get her brilliant plan to save polar bears into action while dealing with a few … challenges:

☑ Phobias + self-doubt

☑ Anxiety + more anxiety

☑ Loss of BFF

Hope arrives in the form of Sig, the last-available lab partner, who has an audacious idea for saving the polar bears and—a secret. He accepts Molly as she is, problems and all, and challenges her to follow through on her polar bear rescue plan. She accepts his challenge, putting her well outside her comfort zone. But as Molly and Sig set off to raise funds for the cause, complications threaten to melt the thin ice that keeps Molly from drowning in her own problems.

Just like the polar bears she is trying to save, her world is rapidly changing. Can Molly hold on long enough to survive?

Tess Marset lives in Edmonds, Washington with her husband, two sons, and a cheeky parrot. She encourages readers to visit her website at *www.tessmarset.com*.